THE
TICKET
THAT
EXPLODED

THE TICKET THAT EXPLODED

The Restored Text

William S. Burroughs

EDITED AND WITH AN INTRODUCTION BY
Oliver Harris

Grove Press
New York

Second revised edition published by Grove Press in 2014.

Published simultaneously in Canada
Printed in the United States of America

ISBN: 978-0-8021-2209-4
eBook ISBN: 978-0-8021-9720-7

Grove Press
an imprint of Grove/Atlantic, Inc.
154 West 14th Street
New York, NY 10011

Distributed by Publishers Group West

www.groveatlantic.com

14 15 16 17   10 9 8 7 6 5 4 3 2 1

Contents

Acknowledgments

It is a privilege to edit works by William Burroughs, and a pleasure to thank James Grauerholz for making it possible and for all the support he has given. It is also a pleasure to thank the following for their expert help: Jed Birmingham for assistance with little magazines; Keith Seward for razor-sharp feedback; and above all, Véronique Lane, for working with me from start to finish, being by my side in the archival vaults, sharing ideas, reading every word I wrote, and for living with the Fish Boys and the Vegetable People for two years.

For the great archival assistance they have provided, I also want to thank John Bennett of the Rare Books and Manuscript Library at Ohio State University, Columbus;

Rob Spindler of the Archives and Special Collections at Arizona State University, Tempe; Isaac Gewirtz, curator of the Berg Collection at the New York Public Library, and his staff; and Michael Ryan and all his staff at the Rare Books and Manuscript Library, Columbia University. I would also like to acknowledge the support of the Research Institute for the Humanities at Keele University. Thanks finally to Jeff Posternak of the Wylie Agency, a great guy to have on your side, and to Peter Blackstock at Grove Press.

Introduction

"A SERIES OF OBLIQUE REFERENCES"

"OF COURSE, I'VE HAD IT IN THE EAR BEFORE"

A million people who've never heard of William Burroughs, let alone made it as far as the "operation rewrite" section of *The Ticket That Exploded*, can *sing* lines from the book. That's because Burroughs' book is where Iggy Pop found the raw materials of "Lust for Life"—it's where Johnny Yen comes from along with those hypnotizing chickens and the flesh gimmick, the striptease and the torture film. The name is a typically

Burroughsian composite, idiomatically mixing sex and drugs—a "Johnny" being both a condom and what goes inside; "to yen" meaning to yearn for it—which is why Johnny Yen comes *again* and is gonna do *another* strip-tease, and *another*. The repetitious lyrics recycle *The Ticket* to make Johnny a singing telegram for the endless bad kicks and insatiable lusts of consumer capitalism. Since Burroughs' words have an indelible originality it's no coincidence they've inspired an A to Z of musicians, writers and artists from Kathy Acker to Frank Zappa, but the art of recycling words was also the method of "operation rewrite," Burroughs' mission to kick the habit of language itself by cutting it up.

An outrageous hybrid of pulp science fiction, obscene experimental poetry and manifesto for revolution, *The Ticket* was part of Burroughs' 1960s Cut-Up Trilogy, along with *The Soft Machine* and *Nova Express*. A lazy mythology has either damned or praised the books as crazy word collages thrown together at random, with the result that little is known about them—from the meaning of their titles to how they were written or how they're supposed to be read—and their novelty remains simply shocking. The difficulty is that the urgency of Burroughs' message goes together with the radicalism of his method, and *The Ticket* calls itself "a novel presented in a series of oblique references" because that's the only way to get it: *obliquely*. In which case, before giving the backstory to its creation and clarifying how this new edition revises the text and its position in the trilogy, it makes sense to start with the musical history of a minor character—or in Burroughs' own words, "with one average, stupid, representative case: Johnny Yen."

Traces of *The Ticket* return in the lyrics of "Lust for Life" not just because Burroughs' cultural influence has reached far and wide but more precisely because the book has produced a reception made in its own image. *The Ticket* is by far the most musically-minded of all Burroughs' books, referencing the Beatles and the Rolling Stones and mixing fantasies of drum-playing Sex Musicians with a World Music sound-track that ranges from Moroccan flutes to the call of Irish bagpipes. Whole pages consist of nothing but song titles and sampled lyrics, collages of nursery rhymes and jazz standards, torch songs and blues ballads, cowboy tunes, Negro spirituals and Tin Pan Alley sentimental melodies. Iggy Pop knew this when he and David Bowie worked together on "Lust for Life" in West Berlin in 1977, so there's nothing coincidental about Burroughs' most musical cut-up book itself being cut up for the lyrics of a song: this was a case of "operation rewrite" in action.

Pop and Bowie probably knew the heavily revised 1967 edition of *The Ticket*, but had they seen the 1962 original they would have read the jacket blurb describing it as "an incantation sung by a crazy muezzin," which turned book into song and writer into singer. In any case, they couldn't have known that Burroughs actually planned to name his book either after a song—one with a Johnny in the title: "Johnny's So Long at the Fair"—or after the act of singing itself—"If You Can't Say It Sing It." Far from being a sweet song of innocence, the title "Johnny's So Long at the Fair" symbolized Burroughs' acute distrust of "the gimmick" referred to in Iggy Pop's lyrics as "something called love." *The Ticket* not only proposes that love lyrics communicate love sickness but that the essential human activities of communication and love *are* both a sickness. The other title, "If You Can't Say It Sing It," also spelled out the extremism of Burroughs' book, privileging singing over speaking to point beyond verbal expression and exchange altogether. As the text bluntly says: "There are no good relationships—There are no good words—I wrote silences." The "ticket" in the title he finally chose is an image of hidden determinism that invokes the insides of music machines, like the punch cards in an old fairground organ or the perforated rolls of a player piano. *The Ticket That Exploded* also sums up the other titles in Burroughs' trilogy, *The Soft Machine* and *Nova Express*: as a figure for cultural and genetic programming, the "ticket" is written into us on the "soft typewriter" of the body, and it is "exploded" after a countdown to nova that is for Burroughs our only hope of rewriting the scripts that dictate our lives.

Burroughs is relentless to the point of tedium, but eventually we get the point: words don't just describe something, through repetition they make it happen, so that the future is in effect prerecorded by the past. The "do you love me?" section which precedes "operation rewrite" accordingly slices and dices romantic songs to diagnose desire as an infectious disease, a communicable fever kept going by the repetitious lyrics of mass culture like a fairground ride going round and around, drumming and humming away in our heads. Cutting up old song lyrics, Burroughs sadistically mocks the sentimental longings they evoke and the result is a paradoxical composite typical of *The Ticket* and one reason this was the book that hooked me as a reader of Burroughs: the viciousness in its treatment of words somehow produces moments of a yet more haunting lyricism. It's "the old junk gimmick" that identifies Burroughs' text as both research into and a performance of the self-replicating virus of cultural communication that the evolutionary biologist Richard Dawkins called a "meme." From memorable tunes to seductive ideas, memes spread themselves about, influencing and infecting, copying and mutating, and exhibiting their own autonomous and insatiable *lust for life*. As Burroughs reminded his cut-up collaborator Brion Gysin in loud block capitals in summer 1960, two years before starting his book, "YOU KNOW HOW CATCHING TUNES ARE."[1]

Burroughs certainly had an ear for what was catching, and despite its often disorientating difficulty, his work is seductively quotable. This quality went together with a politically sharp sense of his own inescapable complicity in what he opposed: cut-up methods were a way to bring the verbal virus out into the open and to fight fire with fire. Burroughs noted that he and the poet John Giorno once "considered forming a pop group called 'The Mind Parasites,'" on the basis that "all poets worthy of the name are mind parasites, and their words ought to get into your head and live there, repeating and repeating and repeating."[2] While he probably took the band's name from the title of Colin Wilson's novel, there's also an echo in it of what Burroughs had found back in October 1959, when he first began to work with cut-up methods at the Beat Hotel in Paris. In a typescript explaining how "WORD LINES" dictate our "LIFE SLOTS," he described how cutting up audiotape revealed noise in the cybernetic system that had a life of its own: "LIKE INTERFERENCE ON THE RADIO. 'PARASITES' THE FRENCH CALL THAT SOUND. GOT IT? IT GETS YOU."[3] It is in this sense, of the word as an alien organism, that *The Ticket* cuts words up and splices them back in together, treating text like audiotape in order to hear how the language virus works at the molecular level: "biologists talk about creating life in a test tube . . all they need is a few tape recorders."

The Ticket also explores how the meme migrates from one medium to another, modeling the kind of media-crossing, collage-based cultural practices that Iggy Pop and David Bowie experimented with in the late 1970s

and that in the digital age we take for granted. Framing
The Ticket in terms of not one medium but four, Burroughs starts with an Acknowledgment that credits four
collaborators, thanking Michael Portman, Ian Sommerville, Antony Balch, and Brion Gysin respectively for
contributions in writing, audiotape, film, and artwork.
It's an astonishing opening note for what looks like a
novel. But since *The Ticket* abjures the development
of plot, character, or the texture of daily human life,
it is no more a "novel" in any conventional sense than
Burroughs is a "writer." We have to bear in mind that
it was part of not only a Cut-Up Trilogy but of a much
larger, decade-long experiment—the Cut-Up Project—
that crossed media and treated the book as one technology among others. *The Ticket* was both prescient and
productive, inviting the cut-up lyrics of "Lust for Life"
and mapping out the multi-media career trajectory of
the Pop-Bowie collaboration from the moment the two
musicians found inspiration watching TV one day. What
prompted them was the U.S. Armed Forces station ID,
whose signal ironically echoed the refrain of guerrilla
resistance that runs throughout Burroughs' book ("From
the radio poured a metallic staccato voice [...] 'Towers,
open fire'"): "At four o'clock in the afternoon," Pop
recalled, "the channel came on with this black-and-
white image of a radio tower, going beep-beep-beep
beep-beep-ba-beep," and Bowie reportedly turned to
him and said, "Get your tape recorder."[4]

Just as television, radio, and audiotape segued naturally into one another in the process of musical composition, so too the song's success mirrors back the collage aesthetics and cultural appropriations of Burroughs' *Ticket*. It's only natural that "Lust for Life" didn't become a major hit simply because of its stomping drum reverb and ferociously sung yet witty lyrics but because it was borrowed for the film adaptation of the novel *Trainspotting*, whose subject matter (heroin addiction) owed a debt to Burroughs that went without saying. What does need to be said is that the success of the song via the film of the novel acts out the viral logic that is the subject of the book by Burroughs that inspired the song in the first place. And if it was inevitable that Pop would quickly cash in and franchise "Lust for Life" for crass commercial use, Burroughs could see that one coming too. In *The Ticket* he shows his scorn for how lustfully capitalism sucks the life out of everything and everyone by proposing what he calls *"creative advertising,"* so that his book's revolutionary hero can sell out to the Nova Mob, the 1% who are screwing our planet, by promoting the deadly top brand of commodity addiction in "advertisements that tell a story and create characters Inspector J. Lee of the Nova Police smokes Players."

In the context of this Madison Avenue parody, it may seem like a joke about product placement that at this point in *The Ticket* Burroughs makes numerous references to "the Philips Carry Corder." In fact, the references establish a point of intersection between his book, 1960s music and the counterculture more broadly—a nexus that in turn predicts possibilities fulfilled by the digital environment of the twenty-first century. Tape recorders played a part in *Nova Express* through "The Subliminal Kid," and in the original 1962 edition of *The Ticket*, but for the 1967 book Burroughs expanded their role through new narrative episodes and, most importantly, in sections advocating their practical use. Burroughs' invitation to readers to follow his example by conducting experiments in cutting and mixing tape on their own equipment ("Go out and buy three fine machines") went back to the launching manual of cut-up methods, *Minutes to Go* (1960), and technically updated it. Giving away a tool for active individual production rather than advertising a product for passive mass consumption, the manifesto had opened with Gysin's announcement that "the writing machine is for everybody do it yourself."[5] Introduced in Europe in 1963, the compact audio cassette was a major breakthrough in portable technology at affordable prices, and in fall 1965 Burroughs bought a Carry-Corder 150, the model used by Ian Sommerville, his close friend and a technical adviser who Burroughs shared at this time with Paul McCartney. "Guess you've all seen the Philips Carry Corder," he comments, directly addressing a youth audience defined by their interest in both the latest technology and

popular music: "suppose you are a singer. Well splice
your singing in with the Beatles, the Rolling Stones, the
Animals." This was, Burroughs optimistically hoped,
a potentially new revolutionary class that could be
mobilized to take over the means of reality-production,
as indicated in his play on Marx's rallying cry: "Carry
Corders of the world unite. You have nothing to lose
but your prerecordings."

Immediately after completing his revised manuscript of *The Ticket* in October 1966, Burroughs told
Gysin that his aim was "to get the children exchanging
tapes."[6] That was also why he wrote a further expansion of this material as "the invisible generation," an
essay appended to *The Ticket* that was first published in
The International Times, the major British underground
newspaper. Confirming the media-crossing circularity
of influence, *IT* was launched that same October with
a gig in London featuring Pink Floyd and a recently
formed band named after another book in the Cut-Up
Trilogy, *Soft Machine.* Although now in his early fifties,
Burroughs was being ironic in stressing the generation gap, aware as he was of his rising cult status in
the 1960s youth counterculture. The revised edition
of *The Ticket* was published in June 1967, the same
month the Beatles released *Sgt. Pepper's Lonely Hearts
Club Band*—with Burroughs' now iconic face on Peter
Blake's Pop Art album cover.

"AT THE FAIR"

The Ticket That Exploded is a pastiche and bricolage of materials including fragments from "the Shakespeare squadron," especially Joyce and Eliot, whose own major works were pastiches and bricolages of materials. But since *The Ticket* was part of a larger experimental project whose means were multi-medial and whose research goals were as scientific or political as they were artistic, the literary frame of reference is in some ways misleading. This is one of the genuine peculiarities of a Burroughs book; that it can seem both literary and viciously anti-literary at the same time, and the same goes for his cut-up methods. On the one hand, they were scandalous chance operations that seemed to reduce artistic creativity to the "writing machine" described in *The Ticket*, which "shifts one half one text and half the other through a page frame on conveyor belts." On the other hand, while the results were still uneven, the many hundreds of archival draft pages prove how hard Burroughs worked to make the cut-up machine serve his writing.

In a 1960s context his methods resemble those of Pop Art, and *The Ticket* references James Dean and the recently dead Marilyn Monroe, while for *Nova Express* Burroughs felt a "pop art cover is definitely indicated."[7] But the cut-up text both parallels the mechanical genius of Andy Warhol's silkscreen factory and exceeds it. Whether using fragments of Rimbaud or old song lyrics, *The Ticket* demonstrates a manipulation of material whose precision has never been recognized. The book's original title, "Johnny's So Long at the Fair," is a representative case, the nursery rhyme ballad condensing a complex intertextual network that shows how signs get around on what Burroughs called "association lines." It takes a while to realize it, but in training us how to read his text—which all experimental writing has to do—Burroughs is training us how to read the culture around us, or rather the culture *inside* us.

Just two words of "Johnny's So Long at the Fair" occur a single time in *The Ticket*: "the fair." Is this really an allusion? It's ambiguous since what fascinated Burroughs and in turn makes his own work so fascinating is the subliminal or contingent message, communication that slips beneath consciousness or seems to arise by chance from the material itself. In broad cultural terms, he promoted cut-up methods as strategies of *détournement*, as the Situationists called their contemporaneous response to the emerging "Society of the Spectacle," the all-pervasive sign systems of the news media and consumer capitalism. Burroughs' didactic political writing often made explicit calls to action, as in one early 1960 typescript: "TEAR THEIR ADVERTISEMENTS FROM WALLS AND SUBWAYS OF THE WORLD."[8] Such direct statements were necessary

because his creative counter-measures were, by definition, experimentally indeterminate: the results of writing
with scissors were impossible to predict and exemplary
in function, opening up new possibilities rather than
serving fixed outcomes. Burroughs therefore identified
his methods with asymmetrical warfare rather than political programs—*The Ticket* cites part of Mao's formula
for guerrilla tactics ("Enemy advance we retreat")—and
he categorically differentiated his methods from those of
commercial advertising: "I'm concerned with the precise
manipulation of word and image to create an action,"
he told an interviewer in 1965, "not to go out and buy
a Coca-Cola, but to create an alteration in the reader's
consciousness."[9]

In this context, "the fair" is a necessarily ambiguous
sign. In fact, even if it is recognized as a subliminal
trace of lyrics, a molecule of music, the ambiguity of
the allusion remains: since there are two mentions of the
city's name in the same paragraph, the "fair" must also
reference the St. Louis World's Fair of 1904. That fair
inspired another song, "Meet Me in St. Louis, Louis,"
and forty years later the Hollywood film directed by Vin-
cente Minnelli. Located in the city of Burroughs' birth—
which is named over twenty times in *The Ticket*—the
St. Louis World's Fair was famous for its 265-foot-high
Ferris wheel, and such wheels return repeatedly in *The
Ticket*, their rotary motion coinciding with the circularity
of the songs' lyrics. Because "Johnny's So Long at the

Fair" and "Meet Me in St. Louis, Louis" share the same
theme—the broken promises of desire—as well as the
same seductive sign of "the fair"—the merry carousel
of capitalism—it perhaps doesn't matter whether Burroughs was referring to Johnny or Louis, but a cut-up
source typescript confirms it was actually both: "Oh
oh what can the matter be, John?—Our revels now are
ended—These our actors at St Louie Louie meet me
at spirits and are melted into air."[10] Mixing in the two
song titles with Prospero's great speech from *The Tempest*, Burroughs turns Shakespeare's valediction to stage
magic into a farewell to the fair.

   These unused lines from the manuscript also confirm
Burroughs' working methods in *The Ticket*, specifically
his editorial process of redaction, as he cut and re-cut
his source materials to make the external referential
function of words ever more cryptic. However, once
we've learned to read on lines of association and juxtaposition, the accumulation of allusions makes his larger
theme clear enough. Whichever way we identify "the
fair," as a musical or historical reference, the cut-up
method makes the words operate in a chain of internal
cross-referencing that recycles the genetic code of the
Burroughs oeuvre from text to text.

   At the end of *Naked Lunch* there's a passing, enig-
matic allusion to one person watching another while
"humming over and over 'Johnny's So Long at the Fair,'"
and in 1960 Irving Rosenthal asked Burroughs about it

as he helped edit the book for its American publication: "Come now Irving," Burroughs replied. "You have heard that tune a thousand times. We all have."[11] Rosenthal seemed to have forgotten not only the song from childhood but also that the opening of *Naked Lunch* had set it up and implied its significance. Early on Burroughs introduces a drug pusher who "walks around humming a tune and everybody he passes takes it up," peddling such songs as "Smiles" or "I'm in the Mood for Love" (both of which appear in *The Ticket*). A drug in itself, the music of love is used to sell other drugs, and this nexus of addiction, contagion, subliminal advertising and brainwashing through popular culture is captured in the seemingly mundane act of humming a tune. As the original title of what became *The Ticket That Exploded*, "Johnny's So Long at the Fair" signifies both the enduring pain of personal loss—nostalgically for childhood innocence, melancholically for love—and its manipulation according to the false promises and addictive kicks of consumer capitalism. "O dear, what can the matter be?" Johnny's so long at the fair because, like a hypnotized chicken, he's been *hooked*.

The intertextual thread of the fair leads back from *The Ticket* via *Naked Lunch* to Burroughs' early novel, *Queer*, a vital point of origin for both biographical and aesthetic reasons. Here, it's the sinister Skip Tracer, a psychic Repo Man dreamed up by William Lee to track down Eugene Allerton, the lover that has abandoned him, who "begins humming 'Johnny's So Long at the Fair' over and over."[12] Again, it's "over and over," implying that the desire and the pain will *never* be over. His first novel, *Junky*, describes Burroughs on drugs, but the writing of *Queer* shows him hooked by desire, which makes it more essential to the oeuvre that followed. Indeed, despite the gulf between early autobiographical novella and radical experimental text, *Queer* predicts *The Ticket* at a precise formal level. It does so by embedding the menacing song in passages of recurrent images and phrases, including the sound of humming, which create uncanny effects of déjà vu. This eerily repetitious textuality becomes the very hallmark of Burroughs' writing from *Queer* onward, and it's no coincidence that for the 1967 edition of *The Ticket* Burroughs created a new opening section that recycled the narrative of *Queer*.

The narrative Burroughs added to *The Ticket* re-played the "possession" of Lee by Allerton and is crucial because it retrospectively grounds the cut-up text in Burroughs' experience of traumatic desire. The link confirms that his research into the virus of language was less "experimental writing" than scientific self-experimentation. The reduction of "Johnny's So Long at the Fair" in *Queer* to "the fair" in *The Ticket* cuts up the song's refrain to separate Johnny from the fair, as if surgically removing a tumor of lovesickness. Since late 1959, when his discovery of cut-up methods coincided with a dramatic break from psychoanalysis and his adoption of Scientology techniques for erasing traumas, Burroughs' logic had been that our consciousness and sense of reality are verbally programmed from without, so reversing the mechanistic process should lead to deconditioning: "Get it out of your head and into the machines." Making trauma into a text, the cut-up method was one such machine and the tape recorder its obvious technological extension. But on the evidence of *The Ticket*, the actual results were mixed or, as Alan Ansen suggested, quite paradoxical: "Are not cut-up and fold-in the music of obsession, fragments that evoke rather than destroy?"[13]

On the one hand, the text achieves its own self-ruination and the result is page after page of mechanically atomized prose: a "disastrous success," to borrow Burroughs' own ironic warning. More interestingly, the text that explodes gives rise to "tentative beings," "flicker ghosts," and cybernetic aliens that spin "free of human coordinates" to reveal hybrid creatures with bodies "of a hard green substance like flexible jade—back brain and spine burned with blue sparks as messages crackled in and out." Applying a similarly post-human aesthetic to music lyrics, *The Ticket* produces monstrous human-machine composites out of the charming "Daisy Bell" ("love skin on a bicycle built for two," "i'm half crazy all for the love of color circuits"). Burroughs was writing this in 1962, the same year that a physicist at Bell Labs synthesized the very same song on the vocoder of an IBM

704 to demonstrate the first singing computer. When HAL sings "Daisy Bell" while being disconnected in Kubrick's *2001: A Space Odyssey* (released in 1968, a year after the revised *Ticket*), the pathos of the dying machine seems to mock our belief in human subjectivity, memory and emotion. For as capitalist technology makes our machines smarter and softer, so we come to appear more stupid and automated. Individual identity is reduced to the effects of a mechanical device, repeating like the roll of music in a player piano or vinyl going round on a turntable—as Burroughs suggests in a mid-1960s text courtesy of lyrics from Irving Berlin's "The Song Is Ended": "but the melody lingers on . . . but the melody lingers on . . . but the melody lingers on . . ."[14]

On the other hand, a ghost remains in the Burroughs machine, a poetic lyricism and a humanity that is all the more deeply felt and mourned for being so surprising: "sad shadow whistles cross a distant sky . . . *adiós* marks this long ago address . . ." *The Ticket* succeeds above all in such elegiac gestures of farewell, its paradoxically memorable enactments of forgetting, especially in the last pages: "I lost him long ago . . . dying there . . . light went out . . . my film ends." With a shocking pathos worthy of this flawed but fascinating book, when Burroughs died in August 1997, Patti Smith attended the funeral at Bellefontaine cemetery in St. Louis and did a graveside rendition of . . . "Johnny's So Long at the Fair."

This valedictory quality is particularly fitting because, contrary to the standard history, *The Ticket That Exploded* was not the middle volume of Burroughs' Cut-Up Trilogy, following *The Soft Machine* and preceding *Nova Express*; it was the final one.

THE TICKET MACHINE

The Soft Machine, Nova Express and *The Ticket That Exploded* have been grouped together for fifty years. This is partly because they are so unlike anything else and partly because the identity of each book is blurred by Burroughs' recycling of material across and between them. And yet, although the term is impossible to avoid, "the Cut-Up Trilogy" was always a misnomer. This is because Burroughs never planned to write a series of three books and didn't himself use the term, and because calling them "the trilogy" has the effect of domesticating these wildly experimental texts and glossing over the differences between them. But equally, it's because over a seven-year period this "trilogy" materialized itself as no fewer than six quite different books: three versions of *The Soft Machine* (1961, 1966, 1968); two of *The Ticket That Exploded* (1962, 1967); and one of *Nova Express* (1964). Given the publication dates, it's possible to generate half a dozen sequences that would form "trilogies." Burroughs made a joke out of the resulting confusion, referring in the 1966 edition of *The Soft Machine* to "a novel I hadn't written called *The Soft Ticket*," and the gag itself could be permutated from *The Nova Machine* to *The Express That Exploded*. The consequences for interpretation have been serious, however, since critics need to map the development of his work using a beginning, middle and end to "the trilogy," and, lacking the chronology or muddling up the editions, misread the texts accordingly.

In practice, this multiplicity has been conveniently concealed by being reduced to simply "the trilogy" in a single order: first *The Soft Machine*, then *The Ticket That Exploded*, finally *Nova Express*. Since this order follows the sequence of first publications of each title, it appears logical, but it's false at both a material and philosophical level: materially, because the differences between editions of the same title are significant; and philosophically, because "the trilogy" represents exactly the false essentializing linguistic usage against which Burroughs deployed cut-up methods in the first place— put most succinctly in his attack on the definite article in *Nova Express*: "Alien Word '*the*.' '*The*' *word* of Alien Enemy imprisons '*thee*' in Time." Burroughs' revisions of "the trilogy" over time were contingent and materially motivated, arising from a tension between his creative methods and the nature of book publication, but they certainly served the philosophical goal of scrambling traditional notions of fixed identity and linear chronology.

The standard sequence is also misleading in entirely practical terms of available editions. In June 1961 Maurice Girodias's Olympia Press in Paris published *The Soft Machine*, followed eighteen months later by *The Ticket That Exploded*. Like the original Olympia edition of *Naked Lunch*, which appeared in July 1959,[15] these were physically small softback books wrapped in distinctive olive green papers and artwork dust jackets (with designs by Burroughs himself, then Gysin, and finally Sommerville). In addition to having a very special look and feel as physical objects, the Olympia trilogy has become eminently collectible, and the two cut-up volumes are especially rare because, after the initial print run of 5,000, they were never republished. For almost all their history as titles, therefore, the available editions of both *The Soft Machine* and *The Ticket That Exploded* have not been the original books but the later revised versions—each of which were published after *Nova Express*, the supposedly final title of the trilogy. Leaving aside the Calder 1968 British edition of *The Soft Machine*, the Grove Press *Ticket* was therefore the final text of "the trilogy," since it appeared after both the Grove *Nova Express* (1964) and *Soft Machine* (1966). But this deals only with histories of publication, whereas the most revealing history affecting how we read *The Ticket That Exploded* is that of composition.

Since *The Ticket* was first published in 1962 and *Nova Express* in 1964, the general assumption has always been that Burroughs wrote *The Ticket* long before *Nova Express*, but this is not the case. Following the appearance of *The Soft Machine* in summer 1961, Burroughs began work on *Nova Express* that August, and by the end of March 1962 had mailed a full manuscript to Barney Rosset at Grove Press. Although he would submit a revised manuscript in October 1962 and continue to make changes up until July 1964, nevertheless the great majority of the book published as *Nova Express* in November 1964 had been written by March 1962. Burroughs' first reference to what would become *The Ticket That Exploded*—informing Rosset, "I am currently working on a new novel" (*ROW*, 106)[16]—does not appear until late June 1962, and although he must have started it the previous month, this still confirms that *The Ticket* was not even begun until at least a month after the first draft of *Nova Express* was finished. And so while the history of publication invites us to think of *The Ticket* as preceding *Nova Express* by two full years, the history of composition tells us to see it as following straight after.

Then again, since almost all readers of *The Ticket* only know the revised edition of 1967, to understand how the parts of Burroughs' trilogy relate to one another we need to know the writing history of not one but two versions of the text—even as one of the results of the trilogy is to call into question our very concept of "version" or "original."

"WHAT AM I AN OCTOPUS?"

While he refers to it as a "short piece" rather than as part of his new novel, Burroughs first mentions material destined for *The Ticket* in a letter to Paul Bowles sent from the Beat Hotel in mid-May 1962.[17] Titled "East Clinic Information," it formed the start of the "vaudeville voices" section, although what's most revealing is not the material Burroughs began with but the method: "Using the fold in technique more and more, results usually interesting if sometimes cryptic." As Burroughs implies, he had already been folding rather than cutting his material for some time, and had in fact hung up his scissors almost three months earlier. The significance of this change in method is to separate *The Ticket* from *The Soft Machine* and *Nova Express*, both of which were begun (although not in the latter case completed) using his original cut-up technique. In contrast, *The Ticket* was a fold-in from the start.

As for the method itself, Burroughs gave the fullest descriptions in his talk "The Future of the Novel" at the Edinburgh International Writers' Conference in August 1962, an event that was a turning point for his reputation, and as a Note published with a longer version of "vaudeville voices": "In writing this chapter," he begins, "I have used what I call 'the fold in' method that is I place a page of one text folded down the middle on a page of another text (my own or someone else's)—The composite text is read across half from one text and half from the other—The resulting material is edited, rearranged, and deleted as in any other form of composition."[18] In private letters and in published statements such as this, Burroughs would repeatedly stress not the radical difference of his compositional methods but their similarity to others in respect of editing. This was a strategic counter to those who accused him of lazily producing haphazard nonsense, like the famous "UGH" reviewer for the *Times Literary Supplement* who in 1963 derisively compared his work to "the unplanned dribbling and splashing of the action painter."[19] Likewise, the review in *Time* magazine in November 1962 dismissed the fold-in method for taking pages of "newspaper, Shakespeare, or whatnot" and sticking them together "at random," so that *The Ticket* "came daringly close to utter babble."[20] Burroughs' counterattack included cutting up both hostile reviews, a ritualistic act of revenge that produced new material for the 1967 edition of the book in which he mocked *Time*'s own mocking phrases. But just as importantly, his insistence on exercising artistic control through careful editing responded to those who *praised* him for his techniques, including his own publishers.

In particular, Burroughs must surely have been frustrated by John Calder—as staunch a supporter of his work in London as Girodias in Paris or Rosset in New

York—for the jacket blurb on *Dead Fingers Talk*. Published in Britain in 1963, this composite trilogy, made from selections of *Naked Lunch, The Soft Machine* and a good deal of *The Ticket That Exploded*,[21] hailed Burroughs' style as having "much in common with American action painting." Around this time Burroughs drafted a defense of his methods, insisting "I am not an action writer whatever that may mean."[22] "The procedure," he explained, "is not arbitrary but rather directed toward obtaining comprehensible and useable material—There is careful selection of the material used and even more careful selection of the material finally used in the narrative." On the other hand, the comment he made in September 1962 when submitting his manuscript of *The Ticket*—"Find myself returning to straight narrative style of *Naked Lunch*" (*ROW*, 114)—suggests the problem he had lost sight of, since *Naked Lunch* is nobody else's idea of a straight narrative.

The other problem with Burroughs' experimental methods, and one of the difficulties they pose for anyone discussing them, is that there is no typical cut-up text or, within a book like *The Ticket*, even a typical cut-up section: he used multiple methods with multiple results and made multiple claims for their function—creative, political, therapeutic, scientific, even mystical ("Table tapping? Perhaps").[23] Burroughs used cut-ups for "poetic bridge work" and as a "fact assessing instrument" (*ROW*, 45), and the only common denominator was that his methods were neither random nor indiscriminate but driven by an empiricist's sense of curiosity. Burroughs prized cut-up and fold-in techniques as ways to make discoveries that exceeded the predictable reach of the rational mind, so that the material itself led him to discover meanings and make connections. *The Ticket* illustrates Burroughs' creative procedures through its blurring of distinctions between poetic fantasy and scientific fact and its equation of textual body with human body—pointing to the book's origins as a testing of limits in terms of publishable form and content.

When Burroughs informed Barney Rosset that he was working on a "new novel" in June 1962, he specified that he was pushing the limits precisely in terms of the text's most recurrent word, the body: "I am elaborating some far out areas with scenes and concepts more 'obscene' than anything in *Naked Lunch* or *The Soft Machine*," he explained; "I was interested to carry certain concepts to the furthest possible limits as an experiment in writing technique" (*ROW*, 106). A thesis regarding sexual repression was essential to his analysis of power in his new book—"Now do you understand who Johnny Yen is? The Boy-Girl Other Half striptease God of sexual frustration"—and was implicit in *The Ticket*'s alternative working titles "Johnny's So Long at the Fair" and "If You Can't Say It Sing It" (108). Openly homosexual, Burroughs in the early 1960s was at the forefront of enlarging the scope of what could be said, and Grove

Press's publication of *Naked Lunch* in 1962 duly became a legal and cultural landmark in that history.

The Ticket has more orgasms and penises than *The Soft Machine* and *Nova Express* put together and its descriptions of alien sex are perversely poetic, but Burroughs seems to have emphasized how sexually far out his new book was in order to deter Grove Press. Although he asked Rosset in June if he wanted to see the "thirty or forty pages" he had already written, and although the editor's autograph note on the received copy states "yes very much," Burroughs was already in negotiations with Maurice Girodias.[24] And unlike Rosset, who was still anxiously holding back *Naked Lunch* (keeping copies locked in the warehouse until November 1962), Girodias had no fear of obscenity trials in Paris for publishing an English language book. Whereas Burroughs worked on *Nova Express* throughout 1962 expecting it to help pave the way for Grove to publish *Naked Lunch*, he wrote *The Ticket* for Olympia without worrying about its sexual, censorable content.

Burroughs composed *The Ticket* at almost twice the pace of *Nova Express*, which had taken eight months. At the start of July 1962 he announced he had already "half finished" the novel, which he "wrote at the rate of ten pages a day while writing a film scenario with the other hands, making recordings."[25] The rapid progress of *The Ticket* reflected Burroughs' shift from cutting to folding, a quicker, far less messy procedure. Connecting

the speed of writing to his experimental work in audio
and visual media, Burroughs also echoed comments he
had made eighteen months earlier that *The Soft Machine* "writes itself" and was "more like taking a film"
than writing; "But why draw lines and categories?"
(*ROW*, 65). Like the Dadaists and Surrealists before
him, Burroughs found that collage-based methods ef-
faced traditional distinctions between media, and what
started with paper and scissors ended up turning the
writer into a poly-practitioner—working a typewriter
with one hand, a tape recorder with the other, and a
movie camera . . . "What am I an octopus?" Burroughs
liked to ask.

The verbal-visual relationship was especially important for *The Ticket*, and as soon as he had finished writing
the final section in mid-August 1962, Burroughs mailed
the 3-page typescript to Brion Gysin and invited him to
complete the text as a physical object: "I would like to
end it with a page of calligraphs to follow after the last
lines—'Silence to say good bye'—Could you do like
some terminal writing and send along so i can finish the
novel like that?"[26] For all his notorious shortcomings as
a businessman, Girodias always let Burroughs define the
artwork for his Olympia titles, and he agreed that Gysin's
art "would be the best ending" for *The Ticket*—although
at this point the title was still not fixed (*ROW*, 112).
Indeed, Burroughs seems to have dropped "Johnny's So
Long at the Fair" and taken up "Word Falling—Photo

Falling" before, in late September 1962, for the very first time he refers to it as *The Ticket That Exploded*.[27] That same month he submitted a 132-page typescript and the book was launched in the English Bookshop at the start of December. Shortly after, Burroughs left Paris and the famous Beat Hotel—which on and off for three years had been Cut-Up Headquarters—closed down. It was the end of an era, but the end of only the first of two *Tickets*.

"A COMMENTARY AND EXTENSION"

When Burroughs informed Paul Bowles that *The Ticket* was about to be published, he mused: "Perhaps I have said what I had to say—Hope so at any rate."[28] Despite the air of optimism and finality, just two months later the seeds of a new edition were already being planted. In January 1963 he asked Alan Ansen for his opinion while making clear his own: "I am not altogether satisfied with it."[29] This was how Burroughs reacted to every version of his cut-up books, and for the same reason: there was always a kernel of contradiction between his methods and book publication. Even before *Naked Lunch* was finished in 1959, Burroughs had come to "wonder if any writing now has much *raison d'être*," and the impact of Gysin's painting and calligraphy led him further to query the codex form.[30] His subsequent experiments with drawing, scrapbooks, tape recorders, film, photography and photomontage fed into his writing but also confirmed the limitations of texts. At least the little magazines of the 1960s mimeograph revolution allowed variety in typography and layout—such as newspaper-style three-column pieces—while the rougher aesthetic of some magazines well represented the provisional, process-based nature of his mass of short experimental work. In contrast, the book was an old technology that depended on publishing houses with limited formal options and fixed procedures for copyediting and printing. Burroughs was *bound* to be dissatisfied.

In his January 1963 letter to Ansen, Burroughs explained that the need for revision had come to him when assembling *Dead Fingers Talk*: "While doing this job of selecting and rearranging I became so dissatisfied with *The Soft Machine* that I have completely rewritten it."[31] Two years later, he confirmed that *The Ticket* would be next for Operation Rewrite: "It's not a book I'm satisfied with in its present form. If it's published in the United States, I would have to rewrite it."[32] Burroughs made no move to revise *The Ticket* until summer 1966, when Richard Seaver at Grove Press reminded him that they would need to publish any new version "by early 1967 in order to keep the copyright."[33] As a determining factor in revising the book, this was a nice irony, given *The Ticket*'s recycling of cultural materials and therefore assault on concepts of originality and ownership. The timing for Burroughs was difficult, however, and in mid-October he appealed to Seaver for patience on delivering the manuscript. In a decade of being constantly on the move, living out of suitcases between London, Paris, New York and Tangier, this was the first time he struggled to meet a deadline. Although Burroughs demonstrated a remarkably consistent responsibility toward his publishers, he also did not want to be rushed by Grove on *The Ticket*; he surely hadn't forgotten his intense frustration over their editing of *The Soft Machine* a year earlier, when Seaver (not unreasonably) had called a halt to his making revisions. Equally, the economic realities of his writing career were not his strong suit. "I hope that you feel as I do," he wrote on October 26, 1966, the day after finally mailing the manuscript, "that it is now a much more readable and saleable book."[34] The fact that the print run of the revised *Ticket*, published in June 1967, was barely half that of the revised *Soft Machine*, published by Grove in March 1966, suggests they knew it was not going to be a bestseller.

There are four main areas of difference between the Olympia edition of 1962 and the Grove revised version of 1967: without altering the sequence of material in any way, Burroughs made cuts, additions, changes to presentation and to the ending of the text. First, he made some forty-three separate cuts—many as small as a single phrase—so that in total the revised edition lost just over 400 words of the Olympia text. Why these particular cuts were made is not at all clear, and in several cases the loss is certainly meaningful, so they have been restored for this new edition. Second, there was the addition of new material written over the previous three years, parts of which had appeared in little magazines in 1964 and 1965. There were nineteen separate insertions, ranging in length from ten to 4,500 words, so that, including "the invisible generation" appendix, in total the 1967 edition was 50 percent longer than the original (rising from just over 40,000 to 60,000 words). The addition of "the invisible generation" reflected Burroughs' sense that his tape recorder experiments were being enthusiastically taken up, and yet his pitch of the essay to Seaver was tentative—"If the book is not yet set up, this piece could be used to advantage as an appendix"—and the editor probably didn't realize that a quarter of the 3,500-word article had already been added to *The Ticket*.[35]

Burroughs' plan to make the new book more "readable" did not, therefore, entail deleting cut-up material to any meaningful extent, and indeed a fifth of what he added was also cut-up, so that the overall change was modest: just over half the 1962 text consists of cut-up, just under half of the 1967 text, although the impossibility of defining what is and isn't "cut-up" (or "fold-in") makes more precise calculations meaningless. Of the book's twenty sections, only the first ("see the action, B.J.?") was entirely added for the 1967 edition, eleven sections remained exactly the same, and eight were expanded. Of those eight, the first and last sections of the original book ("winds of time" and "silence to say good bye") were expanded by far the most, so that the impact of Burroughs' revisions was heavily concentrated on the beginning and ending. Although they include some of the funniest passages in the book, the additions he made to the final section created a structural problem, since *The Ticket* was already long enough and it was surely a mistake to introduce so much new material so late on. Burroughs needed novel-length books in order for his methods to produce uncanny flashes of déjà vu in the reading experience—a unique and beautifully disorientating sensation—but there was a point of diminishing returns and in *The Ticket* he probably reached it.

All Burroughs' cuts and insertions are documented in the Notes section, which also gives details of editorial changes involving about a hundred minor corrections and includes significant selections from the major archival variants. The aim is not only to show exactly how Burroughs updated *The Ticket* and to carry out some necessary restorations but to make visible for the first time the bigger picture of the manuscript sequences from which the published text was cut.

The 1967 Grove jacket blurb rightly observed that "the new material serves both as an expansion of and as a commentary on the original," and this is clear from the very first insert, in the "winds of time" section. The new writing declares its status by looking back at the original edition, commenting on the opening two pages: "That was in 1962." The material was explicitly self-reflexive ("I am reading a science fiction book called *The Ticket That Exploded*," says the narrator of the opening section)—but not only in terms of *content*. What's striking about Grove's jacket blurb is that it precisely echoed how Burroughs himself had described the *formal* appearance he wanted for his text: "The new material added to *The Ticket That Exploded* has been spliced into the original text," he explained to Marilyn Meeker at the publishing house; "In this new material I have as you notice used slightly different punctuation and I think that this altered punctuation should remain so that the splice ins will be apparent forming as it were a commentary and extension of the text."[36] Recognizing the tendency of editors to regularize, Burroughs sounds cautious, but he took very seriously the visual impact of orthography on the page, which is the third major difference between Olympia and Grove editions.

To begin with, the biggest change was not actually made by newly added material but by alterations to the original text. In particular, Burroughs revised to lower case many hundreds of upper-case letters, removing capitals from the first person ("I" became "i") and from words at the start of sentences or in specific phrases ("Nova Police" became "nova police," "Board Books" became "board books," and so on). The result is a lack of consistency that at first strikes the reader as a series of errors, then as a challenge to discover a principle, and finally as an indeterminable system that can only be accepted for what it is. Since it's part of Burroughs' critique of literary and linguistic conventions, from an editorial point of view the whole concept of error and intentionality is put into question and the only certainty is that it would be a mistake to impose consistency. On the other hand, nor should the past errors of copyeditors, printers, or Burroughs himself be fetishized as if there were a degree zero of editing. It's not just that "Harly St" should become "Harley St" or "Gothenberg" "Gothenburg," but that *"hassan i sabbah"* should be *"Hassan i Sabbah"* since the name was only put in all lower case when Grove misinterpreted Burroughs' request to change block capitals from the first edition (including at one point "HASSAN I SABBAH") into lower-case italics. Burroughs was a poor proofreader but the archival evidence shows he neither passively accepted nor actively embraced mistakes at the editorial stage.

More coherently, Burroughs extended his experimentation with punctuation, which went back to the use of parentheses and ellipses in *Naked Lunch*. Like *Nova Express*, but unlike *The Soft Machine*, the 1962 text of *The Ticket* had used the em dash (—) as radically as one of Burroughs' major influences, Louis-Ferdinand Céline, had used the ellipsis (. . .). The Olympia edition of *The Ticket* had just a single three-dot ellipsis but some *four thousand* em dashes which function, as the French novelist said in the mid-1950s of his own punctuation, like the rail tracks on which the metro of the writing depends. But just as Céline surprisingly made the ellipsis, normally a sign of suggestion and enigma, the electric dynamo of prose that "charges right into the nervous system," so the surprise of *The Ticket* is to find the dash used for more than a sense of urgency.[37] Burroughs never explicitly theorized punctuation as Céline did, but he was well aware that the material he added in 1967, containing some four hundred two-dot ellipses, a dozen three-dot ellipses, and about a hundred more em dashes, transformed the page. All these dots and dashes make the entire text of *The Ticket* an encrypted signal, a code or "system," as one draft typescript puts it, "like Morse with scales of intensity and speed."[38] Because they cannot be spoken aloud or put into words, the em dashes and ellipses are crucial to the physical sensation of the reading experience, but Burroughs' practice was more than a generalized aesthetic. On the contrary, on close inspection *The Ticket* shows how subtle and precise his use of a dash was in literary terms. Take the example of the section "combat troops in the area."

The first half of "combat troops" appeared in the 1962 edition, shown in its use of the em dash some 250 times, an average of every ten words. The second half of the section, added in 1967, has only a single em dash and the main punctuation is the two-dot ellipsis, of which there are more than seventy. The placement of the one em dash—so visibly out of place in a paragraph sprayed with a dozen ellipses—is carefully contrived in lines that refer to the experimental poet e.e. cummings: "his gentle precise fingers on Bill's shoulder fold sweet etcetera to bed — EE Cummings if my memory serves and what have I my friend to give you? Monkey bones of eddie and bill?" The obvious anomaly is that Burroughs puts the poet's name in upper case, rather than using the lower-case letters that exemplified cummings' famously nonstandard orthography. This is the tip-off to three more subtle manipulations. First, there's the title of cummings' poem "my sweet old etcetera," which Burroughs alters by inverting the word order and turning "old" into "fold" to make a self-reflexive pun on his fold-in method. Second, the phrase "eddie and bill" has also been subject to a precise restructuring, since Burroughs has separated the run-together names "eddieandbill" from another cummings poem. Finally, and not by chance, this other poem has an em dash in its very title: "in Just—" Although it's easily missed, Burroughs has named the second poem *just* through his use of the dash, and encoded his work in a tradition of typographic poetic experiment.

Such precision at the microscopic level demonstrates an attention to detail for which Burroughs is almost never given credit. It also suggests why it is necessary to edit

The Ticket with rigor, and the Notes section provides textual and archival evidence in support of changes made or, in the case of certain apparent errors, not made. However, the text was also determined by more contingent circumstances at the formal level, by chance factors that pose a different challenge to the editor, as they do to the reader and literary critic. Out of all Olympia and Grove Press editions of the trilogy, *The Ticket* is actually the odd one out in its use of the em dash, for here the dash is printed with a space on either side; a small difference, but one that makes a definite impact on the look of the page and therefore the experience of reading. Since the question of agency is central to the text and the method of its production, we have to ask: was this *intentional*? The answer is in the typesetting manuscript Burroughs submitted to Olympia Press in September 1962. The first forty-four pages have the spaced em dash, which seems to have invited the typesetters to follow suit. The remaining two thirds of the manuscript, however, uses Burroughs' standard dash without spacing, and comparison of the two parts establishes that the first third was typed not *by* Burroughs but *for* him. On its own, such evidence is inconclusive, but Burroughs' intentions are confirmed in the Olympia page proofs—the final stage before printing—which include his last-minute addition of a typed insert, a paragraph using more than a dozen of his standard em dashes, without spacing.[39] Letting the spaced em dashes stand for the 1967 Grove edition, Burroughs in effect granted the material its own agency, tacitly recognizing that texts are collaborative and that the work has a life of its own independent of the supposed author. The most important collaboration between design and contingency in the production of the two *Tickets*, and the final major difference between editions, concerns the very end of the text.

"SILENCE TO SAY GOOD-BYE —

In 1962, Burroughs asked Gysin to produce some "terminal writing" in order to solve the problem of ending a book that subverted the linearity of traditional narrative. Gysin's calligraphy terminates the text physically by permutating in pen the section title—"silence to say good bye"—turning typed words into graphic forms and changing words that can be spoken into silent shapes. By canceling the referential function of the sign, the calligraphic line puts an end to the voice and the illusionism of realist language. In this way Gysin's terminal writing is a perfect complement to the final section's invocation of *The Tempest*: "These our actors bid you a long last good bye." As the text's characters line up to bid adieu like performers on a stage, they now appear as just *characters*—merely typographic signs on sheets of paper, their voices only words inside speech marks. Theme and form coincide in terms of simultaneously inscribing and unraveling identity. Thematically, it was all a masque, and we are such stuff as dreams are made on. Formally, in making the transition from anonymous print to artist's pen—and we notice that Gysin signs with his initials— the calligraphy echoes the unexpected switching of type and script on the Olympia Press jacket cover. There, beneath Sommerville's photo-collage, the book title is written in large red ink in Burroughs' own distinctive script above his name, while his name is not signed by hand but perversely typed in black block capitals. The cover by Kuhlman Associates for Grove in 1967 was also typographically striking, producing various letters out of a hat that seems to belong to Charlie Chaplin, but neither the comic tone nor the Dada-esque design has anything to do with the artwork inside the book or with questions of authorship and identity.[40]

The final feature that makes the ending of the Olympia edition so intriguing is the precise transition between Burroughs' text and Gysin's drawing. The transition not only silences language but spatializes time, as the temporal march of words from left to right gives way to a spatial arrangement. This farewell to Time draws attention to what lies beyond words literally on the page, as the 1962 *Ticket* ends with the word "good-bye —" hyphenated and split at the end of the line, so that all six lines of text on the final page end with either an em dash or a hyphen:

tain wind of Saturn in the morning sky —
From the death trauma weary good-bye then" —
    Hassan i Sabbah: "Last round over —
Remember i was the ship gives no flesh identity — Lips fading — Silence to say good-
bye —

The effect of these solid lines one above the other is to
resemble the first hexagram of the *I Ching*—Ch'ien (The
Creative), made up of repeated trigrams for "Heaven."
Burroughs and Gysin were familiar with how the ancient
Chinese system of divination had been used as a method
of chance composition—most famously in music by John
Cage since the 1950s—and because nowhere else in *The
Ticket* are so many horizontal lines stacked like this,
the ending seems to simultaneously identify the creative
principle of the text and abandon it in a single gesture.
Significantly, the text's one-word final line ends without
any closing speech marks, so that the last em dash points
with a straight line into empty space. Immediately below
this final line, Gysin's script and calligraphy begin, the
right side of which ends with a series of horizontal lines
paralleling the printed em dashes and hyphens of the
typed text above it, so creating a second potential hexagram. However, the most important element is simply
that Gysin's calligraphy is reproduced beneath the last
typed words on the same page, which is also the final leaf
in the book. The closer you analyze it, the more perfect

the fusion of type and script seems to become. But again, was any of this *intentional*?

On the last page of his 1962 typesetting manuscript Burroughs signaled his attention to visual detail by typing, rather than his usual two dashes, five dashes after the final word "good-bye," indicating his aim to end with an especially elongated line. The archival record also shows that the key feature of the Olympia Press design—the printing of Gysin's artwork immediately after his text to form a single and complete last page— was not some happy accident. On the contrary, an editor at Olympia put a note on the penultimate sheet of the page proofs requesting that lines of text be moved precisely in order to make this happen: "*faire passer au moins 4 ou 5 lignes à la p. 183.*"[41] As regards the actual layout of text on the last page of the Olympia edition, with its striking line-up of dashes and hyphens, there's no evidence to suggest that this was determined by anything more than the number of words and the narrow line width. In which case, the hexagram of lines for Heaven was the product of a material accident, which is entirely fitting given the role of chance in the philosophy and practice of both the *I Ching* and cut-up methods. We are left not with a choice between meaningful creativity or meaningless mysticism but with a way of reading beyond the binary of belief and skepticism.

The 1967 Grove Press edition dramatically changed the book's ending. The addition of new material made the last section five times longer, while the final paragraph shifted the tone and created a sense of circularity by echoing lines of speech from the book's opening section. The last paragraph also ended with a new final phrase, closed by speech marks: "Are you listening B.J.?"' The typed words were now separated off from Gysin's script, which, in the most radical change, was reproduced on the facing leaf. And finally, this was no longer the final leaf in the book, since it was followed by "the invisible generation" Appendix, a text without punctuation that concluded with words from *The Tempest* ("into air into thin air") followed by empty silent space.

In different ways, the Olympia and Grove editions of *The Ticket* created complex open endings, and given the book's project to transcend time, it would be ironic to fetishize the past and deny change by repeating the products of particular historical circumstances. This edition ends by making choices that point in contrary directions—cutting "the invisible generation" essay as an appendix of historical interest (key passages are referenced in the Notes; the full text is available elsewhere)[42] and restoring the integration of Gysin's calligraphy as the book's great transcendent gesture. After all the lyrics and melodies in *The Ticket*, all the "vaudeville voices," "riot noises," "sounds of lovemaking," "City sounds," "jungle sounds," "crackling static," and "sound of feedback," the composite formed by print and script ends the most musical book of the

Cut-Up Trilogy on a soundless note. The book silences the noisy lusts of life, stops the fairground circus that stupidly spins us round and around, and takes its leave with an open-ended vision of an elsewhere. A book of paradoxes—cynical yet elegiac, polemical but poetic, obscene and spiritual—*The Ticket* ends by visualizing silence, a vital space of possibility beyond words, "where the unknown past and the emergent future meet in a vibrating soundless hum."[43]

Oliver Harris
July 1, 2013

1. Burroughs to Gysin, July 26, 1960 (William S. Burroughs Papers, 1951–1972, The Henry W. and Albert A. Berg Collection of English and American Literature, New York Public Library, 85.2; after, abbreviated to Berg).

2. Burroughs "Voices in Your Head," introduction to *You Got to Burn to Shine*, by John Giorno (London: Serpent's Tail, 1994), 6.

3. Undated typescript, circa 1960, Bancroft Library, University of California, Berkeley.

4. Iggy Pop interviewed by David Fricke in *Rolling Stone* (April 19, 2007), 59.

5. Brion Gysin in *Minutes to Go*, by Sinclair Beiles, William Burroughs, Gregory Corso, Brion Gysin (Paris: Two Cities Editions, 1960), 5.

6. Burroughs to Gysin, October 25, 1966 (Berg 86.9).

7. Burroughs to Seaver, July 21, 1964 (Berg 75.1).

8. Undated typescript, circa 1960 (Berg 48.22).

9. *Burroughs Live: The Collected Interviews of William S. Burroughs, 1960–1996*, edited by Sylvère Lotringer (New York: Semiotext(e): 2000), 80.

10. Undated typescript, circa 1962 (Berg 20.50).

11. Burroughs, *Naked Lunch: the Restored Text*, edited by James Grauerholz and Barry Miles (New York: Grove, 2003), 194, 251. For the definitive study of musical references in the text, see Ian MacFadyen's "A Little Night Music" in *Naked Lunch@50: Anniversary Essays* (Carbondale: Southern Illinois UP, 2009).

12. Burroughs, *Queer: 25th Anniversary Edition* (New York: Penguin, 2010), 118.

13. Alan Ansen, *William Burroughs* (Sudbury: Water Row Press, 1986), 22.

14. Burroughs, "The Dead Star," *My Own Mag* 13 (August 1965), 12.

15. The Olympia edition was published as *The Naked Lunch*, with the definite article, as were British editions.

16. *Rub Out the Words: The Letters of William S. Burroughs, 1959–1974*, edited by Bill Morgan (New York: Ecco, 2012), 106. After, abbreviated to *ROW*.

17. Burroughs to Bowles, May 20, 1962 (Paul Bowles Collection, Harry Ransom Humanities Research Center, University of Texas, Austin; 8.10). After, abbreviated to HRC.

18. Burroughs, "Note on Vaudeville Voices" in *The Moderns: An Anthology of New Writing in America*, edited by LeRoi Jones (New York: Citadel, 1963), 345.

19. John Willett, "UGH," reprinted in *Burroughs at the Front: Critical Reception, 1959–1989* (Carbondale: Southern Illinois UP, 1991), edited by Jennie Skerl and Robin Lydenberg, 43.

20. "King of the YADS," *Time* (November 30, 1962), 96–97.

21. Since its purpose was to head off censorship of *Naked Lunch* in Britain, *Dead Fingers Talk* unsurprisingly cut down explicit sexual content. Almost all *The Ticket* material is in the second half of the book and, unlike the *Soft Machine*, which is often mixed with passages from *Naked Lunch*, appears mainly on its own, so that seven of the last ten sections derive exclusively from *The Ticket*.

22. Undated half-page typescript, circa 1963 (Berg 37.2).

23. Burroughs, "The Cut-up Method of Brion Gysin," in *The Third Mind* (New York: Viking, 1978), 32.

24. Rosset's autograph comment appears on the archival original of the letter published in *Rub Out the Words* (Grove Press Records, Special Collections, Syracuse University; after, abbreviated to SU).

25. Burroughs to Ansen, July 2, 1962 (Ted Morgan Papers, Arizona State University; Box 1). After, abbreviated to ASU.

26. Burroughs to Gysin, August 15, 1962 (Berg 85.6). Gysin's contribution to Burroughs' book had a precedent: in 1960 four pages of his calligraphs had completed their coauthored cut-up pamphlet, *The Exterminator*. That same year Burroughs tried to incorporate drawings in Grove's edition of *Naked Lunch*, having already included some with episodes published in *Big Table* magazine the year before.

27. The phrase "the ticket that exploded" first appeared in "Twilight's Last Gleamings" in *Evergreen Review* 6.22 (January

1962), as an episode of *Novia Express* (sic). Grant Roman offered $150 for "your original manuscript and/or typescript, together with final version and galley sheets, of your new novel entitled Words—Falling—Photo Falling" (Roman to Burroughs, September 6, 1962; Berg 80.16).

28. Burroughs to Bowles, November 21, 1962 (HRC).

29. Burroughs to Ansen, January 23, 1963 (Ted Morgan Papers, ASU).

30. *The Letters of William S. Burroughs, 1945–1959* (New York: Viking, 1993), 414.

31. Burroughs to Ansen, January 23, 1963 (Ted Morgan Papers, ASU).

32. Lotringer, 77.

33. Burroughs to Seaver, July 14, 1966 (SU).

34. Burroughs to Seaver, October 25, 1966 (SU).

35. Burroughs to Seaver, November 29, 1966 (SU).

36. Burroughs to Meeker, November 10, 1966 (SU).

37. For his ironic eulogy to the ellipsis ("the gimmick of the 'metro-all-nerve-magic-rails-with-three-dot-ties' is more important than the atom!"), see Louis-Ferdinand Céline, *Conversations with Professor Y*, translated by Stanford Luce (Champaign, Ill: Dalkey Archive, 2006) 107.

38. The phrase appears on an archival typescript following "the liquid medium of his body" in the "black fruit" section of *The Ticket* (Berg 10.3).

39. Olympia Press page proofs (William S. Burroughs Papers, Ohio State University SPEC.CMS.85; after, abbreviated to OSU).

40. Burroughs' own verdict on the design was lukewarm: "Received the covers everything O.K." (Burroughs to Seaver, April 3, 1967; SU).

41. Olympia page proofs (OSU 3.8).

42. The essay is printed in full in *Word Virus: The William S. Burroughs Reader* (New York: Grove, 2000), edited by James Grauerholz and Ira Silverberg.

43. Burroughs, *The Yage Letters Redux* (San Francisco: City Lights, 2006), 53. Burroughs repeats the phrase in *Naked Lunch* (91).

THE
TICKET
THAT
EXPLODED

posed little time
so I'll say
"good night"

Foreword Note

The sections entitled *in a strange bed* and *the black fruit* were written in collaboration with Mr. Michael Portman of London. Mr. Ian Sommerville of London pointed out the use and significance of spliced tape and all the other tape recorder experiments suggested in this book. The film experiments suggested I owe to Mr. Anthony Balch of Balch Films, London. The closing message is by Brion Gysin.

It is a long trip. We are the only riders. So that is
how we have come to know each other so well that the
sound of his voice and his image flickering over the
tape recorder are as familiar to me as the movement of
my intestines the sound of my breathing the beating of
my heart. Not that we love or even like each other. In
fact murder is never out of my eyes when I look at him.
And murder is never out of his eyes when he looks at
me. Murder under a carbide lamp in Puyo rain outside
it's a mighty wet place drinking *aguardiente* with tea
and canella to cut that kerosene taste he called me
a drunken son of a bitch and there it was across the
table raw and bloody as a fresh used knife . . sitting
torpid and quiescent in a canvas chair after reading last
month's Sunday comics "the jokes" he called them and
read every word it sometimes took him a full hour by

a tidal river in Mexico slow murder in his eyes maybe
ten fifteen years later I see the move he made then he
was a good amateur chess player it took up most of his
time actually but he had plenty of that. I offered to play
him once he looked at me and smiled and said: "You
wouldn't stand a chance with me."

His smile was the most unattractive thing about
him or at least it was one of the unattractive things
about him it split his face open and something quite
alien like a predatory mollusk looked out different
well I took his queen in the first few minutes of play
by making completely random moves. He won the
game without his queen. I had made my point and
lost interest. Panama under the ceiling fans, on the
cold winds of Chimborazo, across the rubble of Lima,
steaming up from the mud streets of Esmeraldas that
flat synthetic vulgar CIA voice of his . . basically he
was completely hard and self-seeking and thought
entirely in terms of position and advantage an effec-
tive but severely limited intelligence. Thinking on
any other level simply did not interest him. He was
by the way very cruel but not addicted to the practice
of cruelty. He was cruel if the opportunity presented
itself. Then he smiled his eyes narrowed and his sharp
little ferret teeth showed between his thin lips which
were a blue purple color in a smooth yellow face. But
then who am I to be critical few things in my own past
I'd just as soon forget . .

What I am getting at is we do not like each other we simply find ourselves on the same ship sharing the same cabin and often the same bed welded together by a million shared meals and belches by the movement of intestines and the sound of breathing (he snored abominably. I turn him on his side or stomach to shut him up. He wakes and smiles in the dark room muttering "Don't get ideas") by the beating of our hearts. In fact his voice has been spliced in 24 times per second with the sound of my breathing and the beating of my heart so that my body is convinced that my breathing and heart will stop if his voice stops.

"Well," he would say with his winsome smile, "it does give a certain position of advantage."

My attempts to murder him were usually direct . . knife . . gun . . in some one elses hand of course I had no intention of getting into social difficulties . . car accident . . drowning . . once a shark surfaced in my mind as he plunged from a boat into the tidal river . . I will go to his aid and clutch his torn dying body in my arms like a vise he will be too weak from loss of blood· to fight me off and my face will be his last picture. He always planned that *his* face should be my last picture and his plan called for Cinerama film sequences featuring the Garden of Delights shows all kinds masturbation and self-abuse young boys need it special its all electric and very technical you sit down anywhere some sex wheel sidles up your ass or clamps onto your spine

centers and the electronic gallows will just kill you on
a conveyor belt the Director there bellowing orders:

"I want you to shit and piss all over yourself when
you see the gallows. Synchronize your castor oil will
you? And give the pitiless hang boy an imploring look
for Chrisakes he's your ass hole buddy about to hang
you and that's the *drama* of it . . ."

"It's a sick picture B.J."

Well it seems this rotten young prince gives off whiffs
of decay when he moves but he doesn't move much as
a rule has eyes for one of the prisoners wants him for
his very own fish boy but the younger generators are on
the way. Partisans have seized a wing of the studio and
called in the Red Guards . . . "Now what do you boys
feel about a situation like this? Well go on express your-
selves . . This is a *progressive* school . . These youths
of image and association now at entrance to the garden
carrying banners of interlanguage . . Her fourth-grade
class screamed in terror when I looked at the 'dogs'
and I looked at the pavement decided the pavement
was safer . . Attack enemy over instrument like pinball . . Shift tilt STOP the GOD film. Frame by frame
take a good look boys . ."

"They got this awful mollusk eats the hanged boys
body and soul in the orgasm and they love being eaten
because of this liquefying gook it secretes and rubs
all over them but maybe I'm talking too much about
private things."

"You boys going to stand still for this? Being slob-
bered down and shit out by an alien mollusk? Join the
army and see the world I remember this one patrol had
been liberating a river town and picked up the Sex Skin
habit. This Sex Skin is a critter found in the rivers here
wraps all around you like a second skin eats you slow
and good . . Well these boys had the Sex Skin burned off
by the sun crossing the plain they could just crawl when
they reached the post quivering sores they was half eaten
mostly shit and pieces of them falling off so I called the
captain and he said best thing was bash their skulls in
and bury them in the privy where he hoped the smell
might pass unnoticed but there was stink in congress
about 'unsung heroes' and the President himself nailed
a purple heart to that privy you can still see where the
old privy used to be other side of those thistles there . .

"Now that should show you fellows something of
the situation out here and the problems we have to
face . . take the case of a young soldier who tried to
rescue his buddy from a Sex Skin and it grew onto him
and now his buddy turns from him in disgust . . anyone would you understand and that's not the worst of
it it's knowing at any second your buddy may be took
by the alien virus it's happened cruel idiot smile over
the corn flakes . . You gasp and reach for a side arm
looking after your own soul like a good Catholic . . too
late . . your nerve centers are paralyzed by the dreaded
Bor-Bor he has slipped into your Nescafé . . He's going

to eat you slow and nasty . . This situation here has given rise to what the head shrinkers call 'ideas of persecution' among our personnel and a marked slump in morale . . As I write this I have barricaded myself in the ward room against the 2nd Lieutenant who claims he is 'God's little hang boy sent special to me' that fucking shave tail I can hear him out there whimpering and slobbering and the Colonel is jacking off in front of the window pointing to a Gemini Sex Skin. The Captain's corpse hangs naked at the flagpole. I am the only sane man left on the post. I know now when it is too late what we are up against: a biologic weapon that reduces healthy clean-minded men to abject slobbering inhuman things undoubtedly of virus origins. I have decided to kill myself rather than fall into their hands. I am sure the padre would approve if he knew how things are out here. Don't know how much longer I can hold out. oxygen reserves almost exhausted. I am reading a science fiction book called *The Ticket That Exploded*. The story is close enough to what is going on here so now and again I make myself believe this ward room is just a scene in an old book far away and long ago might as well be that for all the support I'm getting from Base Headquarters."

"You see the action, B.J.? All these patrols cut off light-years behind enemy lines trying to get through some fat-assed gum-chewing comic-reading Technical

Sergeant to Base Headquarters and there is no Base Headquarters everything is coming apart like a rotten undervest . . but the show goes on . . love . . romance . . stories that rip your heart out and eat it . . Now how's this for an angle? Are you listening B.J.? This clean-living decent heavy metal kid and a cold glamorous agent from the Green Galaxy has been sent out to destroy him with a Sex Skin but she falls for the kid and she can't do it and she can't go back to her own people because of the unspeakable tortures meted out to those who fail on a Mission so they take off together in a Gemini space capsule perhaps to wander forever in trackless space or perhaps?"

winds
of time

The room was on the roof of a ruined warehouse swept by winds of time through the open window trailing grey veils of curtain sounds and ectoplasmic flakes of old newspapers and newsreels swirling over the smooth concrete floor and under the bare iron frame of the dusty bed — the mattress twisted and molded by absent tenants — ghost rectums, spectral masturbating afternoons reflected in the tarnished mirror — The boy who owned this room stood naked, remote mineral silence like a blue mist in his eyes — sound and image flakes swirled round him and dusted his metal skin with grey powder — The other green boy dropped his pants and moved in swirls of poisonous color vapor, breathing the alien medium through sensitive purple gills lined with erectile hairs pulsing telepathic communications — The head was smaller than the neck and tapered to a point — A silver globe floated in front of him — The two beings approached each other wary and tentative — The green boy's penis, which was the same purple color as his gills, rose and vibrated into the heavy metal substance of the other — The two beings twisted free of human coordinates rectums merging in a rusty swamp smell — spurts of semen fell through the blue twilight of the room like opal chips — The air was full of flicker ghosts who move with the speed of light through orgasms of the world — tentative beings taking form for a few seconds in copulations of light — Mineral silence through the two bodies stuck together in a smell of KY and rectal mucus fell apart in time currents swept back into human form — At first he could not remember — winds of time through curtain sounds — blue eyes blurred and twisted absent bodies — The blue metal boy naked now flooded back into his memory as the green boy-girl dropped spaceship controls in swirls of poisonous color — The blue boy reached out like an icy draught through the other apparatus — They twisted together paralyzed — He and Bradly grinding against each other in pressure seats, while heavy metal substance guided their ship through the sickening twist of human cloud belts — galaxy X chartering a rusty swamp smell — Their calculations went out in a smell of ozone — opal chip neighborhood of the flicker ghosts who travel the far flung edge of Galaxy X hover and land through orgasm — flickering form of his companion naked in copulation space suit that clung to his muscular blue silence — smell of KY and rectal mucus in eddies of translucent green light — his body flushed with spectral presences like fish of brilliant colors flashing through clear water — tentative beings that took form and color from the creatures skin membrane of light — pulsing veins crisscrossed the two bodies stuck together in slow motion time currents — lips of tentative faces, rectums merging structure one body in translucent green flesh —

Bradly's left arm went numb and the tingling paralysis spread down his left side — He felt crushing weight of the Green Octopus who was there to block any composite being and maintain her flesh monopoly of birth and death — Her idiot camp followers drew him into the Garden of Delights — back into human flesh — The Garden of Delights is a vast tingling numbness surrounded by ovens of white-hot metal lattice with sloped funnels like a fish trap — Outside the oven funnels is a ruined area of sex booths, Turkish baths and transient hotels — orgasm addicts stacked in rubbish heaps like muttering burlap — phantom sex guides flashing dirty movies — sound of fear — dark street life of a place forgotten — "It might take a little while." The Garden of Delights . . GOD . . Remember my old C.O. standing there with a hangman's noose in his hands . . "You see this noose, Lee? This is a *weapon* . . an enemy *weapon*."

That was in 1962. In the years that followed I contacted a number of undergrounds with various aims methods and organizational setups among which was an equivocal group of assassins called the "White Hunters." Were they white supremacists or an anti-white movement far ahead of the Black Muslims? The extreme right or far left of the Chinese? Representatives of Hassan i Sabbah or the White Goddess? No one knew and in this uncertainty lay the particular terror they inspired. The District Supervisor received me in a paneled room with fireplace, a country house it would seem rain outside a misty landscape. After motioning me to a deep leather armchair the D.S. walked around behind me talking in a voice without accent or inflection, a voice that no one could connect to the speaker or recognize on hearing it again. The man who used that voice had no native language. He had learned the use of an alien tool. The words floated in the air behind him as he walked.

"In this organization, Mr Lee, we do not encourage togetherness, *esprit de corps*. We do not give our agents the impression of belonging. As you know most existing organizations stress such primitive reactions as unquestioning obedience. Their agents become addicted to orders. You will receive orders of course and in some cases you will be well-advised not to carry out the orders you receive. On the other hand your failure to obey certain orders could expose you to dangers of which you can have at this point in your training no conception. There are worse things than death Mr Lee for example to live under the conditions your enemies will endeavor to impose. And the members of all existing organizations are at some point your enemy. You will learn to know where this point is if you survive. You will receive your instructions in many ways. From books, street signs, films, in some cases from agents who purport to be and may actually be members of the organization. There is no certainty. Those who need certainty are of no interest to this department. This is in point of fact a *non-organization* the aim of which is to immunize our agents against fear despair and death. We intend to break the birth-death cycle. As you know inoculation is the weapon of choice against virus and inoculation can only be effected through exposure . . . exposure to the pleasures offered under enemy conditions: a computerized Garden of Delights: exposure to the pain posed as an alternative . . you remember the ovens I think . . exposure to despair: 'The end is the beginning born knowing' the unforgivable sin of despair. You attempted to be God that is to *intervene* and failed utterly . . . Exposure to death: sad shrinking face . . he had come a long way for something not exchanged born for something knowing not exchanged. He died during the night."

A series of oblique references: "Zurich Saturday morning meet the so convenient Webber family at the B.P. Auto Stop. Hear realize that B.P. is not only and you'll find them buying everything from organization Shannon believe they can tape recorded at 23 Mount St it is that's what I thought and there's a little boy that's been reproduced in a lot of books hasn't it? He has a plate camera is it going to be published in *Vogue*? Part of the city's Friday child loving Tuesday for that matter oh really St. Louis Encephalitis of birth and nickname that's the only time 19 have died but the disease quickly spread. What in Germany? He had been meaning Sexexcellency Sally Rand cunning Navy pilot Alan B. Weld two acts for three saints in outer space proudly registered in Phoenix was it are you sure that's right infectious night biter Mo. 18 I'm going to answer the doorbell definitely definitely the first time in thirty years Houston's outbreak the first time in who said Atlantic City? I was supposed to have done the sets for it and B. was supposed to acquire the virus from birds yeah then I think they paid a dollar for infectious disease processing the actual film but the disease quietly spread to all West Texas beauty unscheduled in outer space . . 'You mean you did it yourself you didn't have your assistant do it?' . . 'Nope just spreading epidemic of St Vacine maybe we should' . . 'How long did it take you to process this photo to squirt at anything that flew dyeing and all that it's all part of the city's sudden healthy people infectious beauty disease spreading epidemic of immune humans . . Half an hour? St. Louis Mo. giving hope you mean it's not finished yet? This photo the stripper exuberance its going to fade away? You should have that have a page fading away Time September—(a number not clear)—It is a musical family . . parachute just in case . . I can now drink reservoirs of the disease is that a new play to get at the source spray everything? I heard Friday's child loving a registered stripper nicknamed Conny oh are you going to remember this later that last of the last ditches like you came through the door in his moon suit maybe he's there? Oh no . . It's getting too spooky I'm getting the spinal cord and brain a male with female laughter they have this script he just dropped it like that they always start hissing it's all part of the game of war infants pay the price female laughter just came out of Time Starlet Weld Tuesday what? That's beautiful that is fogged out in distance there should be somebody so called actually this is how the old saw "I think sex is healthy" just two stoned Germans naturally did the same long shuffle . . That's the clock if you set it two hours in advance the last of the last like we are in London a sentence words together in and out you know Manic Goddess 18 of 19 was done the painting was done never look at a model uninhibited disease by us astonishing we had done it without ever having a model starlet trapped in the sentence with full stop young painter are models myself look have you been there already?'"

Leafing through the GOD files . . Ref. The Big Survey
page 71: "Monday May 9" chills light fever . . my brain
feels like all the connections are burnt out . . electric
sex prickles . . The Garden of Delights kinda run down
now charred wooden beams blue and pink tinsel dirty
pictures flapping in the wind smell of coal gas . . heavy
darkness of underexposed film has settled in that gloomy
valley . . The body of a hanged man the rope around his
neck is laying across the trap of a wooden gallows . . Carl
standing there . .

"You led me into this ambush?"

He laughed and threw himself back on a bunk tossing
his legs in the air, "What and me so young and genial?"
a male with female laughter.

I walked away from him in disgust. Two guards were
there one named "Rose." "Rose" was the more commu-
nicative and friendly and I asked him about the hanged
man I had seen. He shrugged . . "Thought he would
learn something . . his pants . . the plague."

I had walked up a slight incline. The garden was
built in a valley quite bare except for scrub and vines.
The whole place presented the sordid and run-down
appearance of an abandoned carnival.

"Who planned all this?" I asked.

The other guard answered: "Maybe it was him," pointing to Carl. "He will show you his country card in the
end and the end is you hang on Tuesday."

Furniture stacked up for storage or removal and I find an old Webley .455 revolver in a dusty desk drawer. Standing there with the gun in my hand and Carl laughed again. The first bullet smashed into a beam a quarter-inch from his neck. Wood splinters spattered the young cheek with red dots. He rubbed a hand across his face and looked at the blood. He stopped laughing and looked at me his mouth a little open. At the second shot a jet of black liquid from the gun hit him in the mouth. His face turned black and old and he sagged against the beam muttering: "sleeping pills."

"genial"? hummm an odd word to use . . Ah here we are . . ref. East Beach File page 156: "This is a novel presented in a series of oblique references . . shave? . . did he? . . an amputation . . three young burglars one wearing a black overcoat stopped on the stairs by two English detectives . . *One of the thieves is nicknamed Genial* . ."

I put through a call to Scotland Yard . . "Inspector Murdock please."

"Who shall I say is calling sir?"

"Klinker."

"Just 'Klinker' sir?"

"That's all."

"Oh hello Lee what can I do for you?"

"Anybody in your files nicknamed 'Genial'?"

"Hold on I'll check . . . ." I put in another six pence waiting. "Yes here we are . . name Terrence Weld . . age

20 . . 5 feet 11 inches . . ten stone . . hair sandy . . eyes green . . known M.P. . . arrested three times suspected of breaking and entering . . no convictions . . ."

"How did he get that nickname?"

"smooth talker . . cool . . laughs a lot . . well genial on the surface at least."

"I see . . anything else?"

"Well yes . . about two years ago a chap named Harrison John Harrison hanged himself in the barn of his country place near Sandhill . . Harrison was living with young Weld at the time . . Weld was picked up in Harrison's car . . That's how it came to our attention . . needless to say no charges . ."

"Needless to say . . Was Weld staying with Harrison in his country place at the time of Harrison's death?"

"No he was in London."

"Nothing to connect him with Harrison's death?"

"Nothing whatever."

"Anything unusual about Harrison's suicide?"

"Well yes . . He'd rigged up a gallows with a drop . . must have taken half an hour to build."

"Anything else?"

pause . . cough . . "The body was completely naked."

"You're sure he was alone at the time?"

"Quite sure . . It's a small town . . easy to check."

"And his clothes . . all in a heap?"

"Neatly folded."

"And the tools he used?"

"Each tool returned to its place . . the barn was used as a workshop . . Carpentry was one of Harrison's hobbies."

"Did Harrison own a tape recorder?"

"How should I know? If you're all that interested I can give you a number to call in the S.B."

"Seems odd they should be interested in a routine suicide."

"A lot of the things they do seem odd to the rest of us. I do know they spent some time on the case . . Ask for Extension 12 . . Mr Taylor."

I could tell by the way he repeated the name Mr Taylor knew who I was.

"Yes Mr Lee?"

"I'd like some information about a man named Harrison who killed himself two years ago . . country place near Sandhill . ."

"I remember the case . . rather not talk over the phone . . Can you meet me this evening in the Chandos Bar? around six?"

Mr Taylor was dressed in a light-blue suit the shoulders so broad as to give an impression of deformity . . little scar where a harelip had been corrected . . red face . . light-blue eyes. We found a quiet corner. Mr Taylor ordered a Scotch Old Fashioned.

"John Harrison was 28 at the time of his death . . He was fairly well off . . flat in Paddington . . country place . . interested in the occult . . wrote bad poetry . . painted bad pictures . . good at carpentry though . . made his own furniture."

"Did he own a tape recorder?"

"Yes he owned three tape recorders arranged with extension leads so he could play or record from one to the other. They were in the Paddington flat."

"You heard his tapes?"

He drank half his drink. "Yes I heard his tapes and read his diary. He seems to have been obsessed with hanging . . the sexual aspects you understand."

"That is not so unusual . . when you consider the extensions . . "

He finished his drink. "No it's not so unusual and that is precisely what concerns this department."

"Did you interview a young man named Terrence Weld in this connection?"

"Young 'Genial'? Yes I interviewed that specimen."

"He was genial?"

"Impeccably so. I considered him directly responsible for Harrison's death. When I told him so he said

"'What and me so young?'

"Exactly. And then he laughed."

"Interesting sound."

"Very."

"You recorded it?"

"Of course."

"Rather stupid on his part wouldn't you say so?"

"Not stupid exactly. He simply doesn't think the way we do. Perhaps he can't help laughing like that even when it would seem to be very much to his disadvantage to do so."

"I would suggest that 'Genial' is that laugh . . only existence 'Genial' has."

"Infectious laughter what? Yes he's a disease . . a virus. There have been other cases. We try to keep it out of the papers."

"And cases that no one hears about? Perhaps the operation has been brought to the point where actual hanging is no longer necessary . . death attributed to natural causes . . or the victim is taken over by the virus . . 'Genial' himself may well have been 'hanged.'"

"I'd thought of that of course. What we are dealing with here is a biologic weapon used by what powers and for what precise purpose we don't know yet."

"Also an ideal weapon for individual assassinations. Any reason why anyone might have wanted Harrison out of the way?"

"None whatever. He simply was not important. I concluded that his death was purely experimental."

"Was 'Genial' paid off?"

"It would seem so. He went to America shortly after I talked with him."

"Still there?"

"No he's back in London."

"You've seen him?"

"Yes. He didn't recognize me . . on junk and barbiturates . . looks ten years older . . down for the count I'd say . . But any one 'Genial' isn't important plenty more where he came from: out of a tape recorder."

"You made copies of Harrison's tapes?"

"Yes. Play them for you if you like."

Taylor's flat was compact carpeted . . a desk a typewriter two filing cabinets a long table by the window with four tape recorders connected by extension leads. He pointed to the recorders . . "I got the idea from Harrison's setup."

"Did Harrison install the recorders himself?"

"No he was good at carpentry but had a blind spot so far as machinery goes especially electrical equipment. 'Genial' wired the machines for him."

He put on a tape. "The voices of Harrison and 'Genial' alternated. They both recorded a short text then the two tapes were cut into short sections and spliced in together. This produces a strong erotic reaction. Curiously enough the content of the tape doesn't seem to affect the result. In fact the same sexual effect can be produced by splicing in street recordings recorded by two subjects separately."

two voices reading one cruel mocking the other muffled and broken by comparison alternated at short intervals conveyed a sensation of charged electric intimacy easy vulgar and therefore disgusting.

"Now listen to this." The words were smudged together. They snarled and whined and barked. It was as if
the words themselves were called in question and forced
to give up their hidden meanings. "Inched tape . . the
same recording you just heard pulled back and forth
across the head . . You can get the same effect by switching a recording on and off at very short intervals. Listen
carefully and you will hear words that were not in the
original text: 'do it-do it-do it . . yes I will will will do it
do it do it . . really really really do it do it do it . . neck
neck neck . . oh yes oh yes oh yes . .'

"You heard?"

"Oh yes oh yes oh yes." (I reflected it would be interesting to inch a speech in the U.N., Congress, Parlia-
ment, or wherever and play back a few seconds later. You
can run a government without police if your conditioning
program is tight enough but you can't run a government
without bull shit.) "Yes I heard."

"Here's another one from the same original tape alternating Harrison and 'Genial' 24 times per second. I
suspect this was the tape that dropped Harrison."

A familiar sound I had heard it for years barely au-
dible . . loud and clear now a muttering hypnotic cadence. He shut the machine off.

"The sound track *illuminates* the image . . 'Genial's' image in this case . . almost tactile . . Well
there it is . . biologists talk about creating life in a test

tube . . all they need is a few tape recorders: 'Genial 23' at your service sir . . a virus of course . . The sound track is the only existence it has no one hears him he is not there except as a potential like the spheres and crystals that show up under an electron microscope: Cold Sore . . Rabies . . Yellow Fever . . St. Louis Encephalitis . . just spheres and crystals until they find another host . . just an arrangement of iron molecules on a tape until 'Genial 23' takes another queen . . . of course parasitic life is the easiest form to create . . . I wonder if . . ."

"If one could make a good 'Genial'? I don't know. Experiments along this line are indicated . . ."

("You see the angle, B.J.? a *nice* virus . . beautiful symptoms . . a long trip combining the best features of junk hash LSD yage . . those who return have gained a radiant superhuman beauty . . !")

"Was 'Genial' staying in the Paddington flat at the time of Harrison's suicide?"

"No. He left Harrison a month before Harrison's death. Apparently Harrison offered him all the money he could raise to come back and live with him but 'Genial' refused. He was living with a young man, name was Cunningham . . Robert Cunningham . . splicing themselves in together . . so long as the spliced tape finds an outlet in actual sex contact it acts as an aphrodisiac . . nothing more . . But when a susceptible subject is spliced in with someone *who is not there* then it acts as a destructive virus . . the perfect murder weapon with a built-in alibi. 'Genial' was not there at the time. He never is."

"'Genial' didn't work this out for himself."

"Hardly . . This is obviously one aspect of a big picture . . what looks like a carefully worked out blueprint for invasion of the planet . . Anyone who keeps his bloody eyes open doesn't need a Harley St psychiatrist to tell him that destructive elements enter into so-called normal sex relations: the desire to dominate, to kill, to take over and eat the partner . . these impulses are normally held in check by counter impulses . . what the virus puts out of action is the *regulatory centers in the nervous system* . . We know now how it is done at least this particular operation . . We don't know who is doing it or how to stop them. Every time we catch up with someone like 'Genial' we capture a tape recorder . . usually with the tapes already wiped off . . ."

"You must have some idea."

"We do . . You know about the Logos group?? . . claim to have reduced human behavior to a predictable science controlled by the appropriate word combos. They have a system of therapy they call 'clearing.' You 'run' traumatic material which they call 'engrams' until it loses emotional connotation through repetition and is then refiled as neutral memory. When all the 'engrams' have been run and deactivated the subject becomes a 'clear' . . It would seem that a technique a tool is good or bad according to who

uses it and for what purposes. This tool is especially liable
to abuse. In many cases they become 'clear' by unloading
their 'engram' tapes on somebody else. These 'engram'
tapes are living organisms viruses in fact . . This does
give a certain position of advantage . . any opposition
crippled by 'engram' tapes . . the 'clears' burning with
a pure cold flame of self-interest a glittering image that
lights up clearer and clearer as it fragments other image
and ingests the dismembered fragments . . Yes we know
the front men and women in this organization but they
are no more than that . . a façade . . tape recorders . . the
operators are *not there* . ."

"Program empty body what?" I got up to leave.
"Where can I find 'Genial'?"

"Boots any midnight. You won't get anything out of
him. He doesn't remember."

The guard was wearing a white life jacket — He led
Bradly to a conical room with bare plaster walls — On
the green mattress cover lay a human skin half inflated
like a rubber toy with erect penis — There was a metal
valve at base of the spine —

"First we must write the ticket," said the guard (Sound
of liquid typewriters plopping into gelatine) —

The guard was helping him into skin pants that burned
like erogenous acid — His skin hairs slipped into the
skin hairs of the sheath with little tingling shocks —
The guard molded the skin in place shaping thighs and
back, tucking the skin along the divide line below his

nose — He clicked the metal valve into Bradly's spine
— Exquisite toothache pain shot through nerves and
bones — His body burned as if lashed with stinging
sex nettles — The guard moved around him with little
chirps and giggles — He goosed the rectum trailing like
an empty condom deep into Bradly's ass — The penis
spurted again and again as the guard tucked the burning
sex skin into the divide line and smoothed it down along
the perineum, hairs crackling through erogenous purple
flesh — His body glowed a translucent pink steaming
off a musty smell —

"Skin like that very hot for three weeks and then —" the
guard snickered — "wearing the Happy Cloak . . Happy
Cloak addicts lasted about two years on the average. The
thing was a biological adaptation of an organism found in
the Venusian seas. It had been illegally developed after
its potentialities were first realized. In its native state
it got its prey by touching it. After that neuro-contact
had been established the prey was quite satisfied to be
ingested you remember they make happy cloaks from a
submarine thing that subdues its prey through a neuro-
contact and eats it alive — only the victim doesn't want
to get away once it has sampled the pleasures of the
cloak. It was a beautiful garment a living white like the
white of a pearl, shivering softly with rippling lights,
stirring with a terrible ecstatic movement of its own as
the lethal symbiosis was established" . . quoted from
Fury by Henry Kuttner Mayflower Dell paperbacks,

Kingsbourne House, 229231 High Holborn, London
WC1 . .

Bradly was in a delirium where any sex thought immediately took three-dimensional form through a maze
of Turkish baths and sex cubicles fitted with hammocks
and swings and mattresses vibrating to a shrill insect
frequency that danced in nerves and teeth and bones
— "a thin singing shrillness that touched the nerves
as well as the ears and made them vibrate ecstatically
to the same beat" . . quote from *Fury* by Henry Kuttner
page 143. The sex phantoms of all his wet dreams and
masturbating afternoons surrounded him licking kissing
feeling — From time to time he drank a heavy sweet
translucent fluid brought by the guard — The liquid
left a burning metal taste in his mouth — His lips and
tongue swelled perforated by erogenous silver sores —
The skin glowed phosphorescent pink purple suffused
by a cold menthol burn so sensitive he went into orgasm
at a current of air while uncontrolled diarrhea exploded
down his thighs — The guard collected all his sperm in
a pulsing neon cylinder — Through transparent walls
he could see hundreds of other prisoners in cubicles
of a vast hive milked for semen by the white-coated
guards — The sperm collected was passed to central
bank — Sometimes the prisoners were allowed contact
and stuck together melting and welding in sex positions
of soft rubber — At the center of this pulsing translucent
hive was a gallows where the prisoners were hanged

after being milked for three weeks — He could see the terminal cases carried to the gallows, bodies wasted to transparent mummy flesh over soft phosphorescent bones — Necks broken by the weight of suspension and the soft bones spurted out in orgasm leaving a deflated skin collected by the guards to be used on the next shift of prisoners — Mind and body blurred with pleasure some part of his being was still talking to the switchblade concealed under his mattress, feeling for it with numb erogenous fingers — One night he slipped into a forgotten nightmare of his childhood — A large black poodle was standing by his bed — The dog dissolved in smoke and out of the smoke arose a dummy being five feet tall — The dummy had a thin delicate face of green wax and long yellow fingernails —

"Poo Poo," he screamed in terror trying desperately to reach his knife — but his motor centers were paralyzed — This had happened before — "i told you i would come back" — Poo Poo put a long yellow corpse fingernail on his forehead vaulted over his body and lay down beside him — He could move now and began clawing at the dummy — Poo Poo snickered and traced three long scratches on Bradly's neck —

"You're dead, Poo Poo! dead! dead! dead!" Bradly screamed trying to pull the dummy head off —

"Perhaps i am — And you are too unless you get out of here — i've come to warn you — Out of present time past the crab guards on dirty pictures? — There's a Chinese boy in the next cubicle and Iam is just down the hall — He's very technical you know — And use this — i'm going now" —

He faded out leaving a faint impression on the green mattress cover — The room was full of milky light — (Departed have left mixture of dawn and dream) — There was a little bamboo flute on the bed beside Bradly — He put it to his lips and heard Poo Poo speak from an old rag in one corner — "Not now — Later" —

He contacted the Chinese boy who had smuggled in a transistor radio — They made plans quickly and when the guard came with the heavy liquid turned on the metal static and stabbed the switchblade deep into insect nerve centers — The guard fell twisting and flipping white juice from his ruptured abdomen — Bradly picked up the guard's gun and released the other prisoners — Most of them were too far gone to move but others they revived with static and formed a division of combat troops — Bradly showed the guard's weapon to Iam —

"How do you work this fucker?" —

Iam examined the mechanism with long fingers precise as tooled metal — explained it was a camera gun with telescopic lens equipped to take and project a moving picture vibrating the image at supersonic speed — He attached the radio to the camera gun so that the static synchronized with the vibrations — Bradly had the gun ready in his hand as they zigzagged out of the hive rushing the metal points of the ovens — Guard towers opened up with magnetic spirals and Bradly lost half his men before he could hit the central control tower and deactivate the mechanical gun turrets — (His troops had one advantage — All the guards and weapons of the enemy were operated by machine control and they had no actual fighters on the location) — Zigzagging he opened up with camera gun and static — Towers and ovens went up in a nitrous blast of burning film — A great rent tore the whole structure of the garden to the blue sky beyond — He put the flute to his lips and blue notes of Pan trickled down from the remote mountain village of his childhood — The prisoners heard the pipes and streamed out of the garden — The sperm tanks drained into streets of image forming thunderbolts of plasma that exploded The Garden of Delights in a flash of silver light — The Green Pine Inn is on a bluff over the river . . a lawn with chairs and tables stretches down to the edge of the bluff. The family is sitting on a screened porch fried chicken hot biscuits iced tea on the table. At one end of the table opposite his father is a boy about 18 dressed in a blue suit . . a slash of red on each cheekbone. He is looking across the valley.

The Demolition Squad has arrived. The G.O.D. is being pulled down and stacked into piles for burning. A lean leather-faced man with pale grey eyes looks sourly at a broken gallows covered with pink tinsel. A tape recorder gasps, shits, pisses, strangles and ejaculates at his feet. He listens his face impassive. He swings his heavy metal tipped boot. The noise stops. He leans forward and picks up a piece of twisted film streaked with excrement and holds it up to the late afternoon sun. He lets his arm drop and the film twists from his fingers. He glances around. "All set I guess."

Men step forward sloshing pails of gasoline. The foreman throws a match and steps back. Other fires are starting here and there across the valley the smoke hanging black and motionless in the still September air. The Demolition Squad is walking up the hill to their truck . . a clank of tools. The two garden guards, who have been waiting there for a lift to town, get in . . a grinding of gears . . sound of a distant motor. Behind them in a darkening valley the Garden of Delights is scattered piles of smoldering rubbish . . . scrub and vines grow through blackened tape recorders where goats graze and lizards bask in the afternoon sun. G.O.D. is the smell of burning leaves in cobblestone streets a rustle of darkness and wires frayed sounds of a distant city.

The Guard named Rose sitting on a bench in the back of a swaying truck with the silent demolition men. He does not know where he is going or what he will do when he gets there . . . "getting old . . watchman in a warehouse . . museum guard maybe . ."

I stopped at a newsstand on Shaftesbury Avenue and bought a copy of *Encounter* contemplating under Eros the feat of prose abstracted to a point where no image track occurs.

(The concomitance or rather juxtaposition with this relentlessly successful though diagrammatic schemata by sexualizing syntactically delinquent analogous metaphor)

It was 11:50 PM when I stepped into the entrance of Boots and there was "Genial" standing outside blue neon on his face you thought of diseased metal when you looked at him a face burning in slow cold fires.

(desperately effete negation of societal values fecundate with orifices perspective and the ambivalent smugness of unavowed totalitarianism.)

I knew why he was standing there. He didn't have the ready to fill his script. He was waiting for somebody he could touch.

(foundering in disproportionate exasperation he doesn't even achieve the irrelevant honesty of hysteria but rather an uneasy somnolence counterpointed by the infantile exposure of fragmentary suburban genitalia.)

"Need bread for your script, man?"

He turned and looked at me decided I wasn't the heat and nodded. I passed him a quid. "That should buy six jacks. I'll see you outside."

He nodded again went in and sat down in the script line.

(ironically the format is banal to its heart of pulp ambivalently flailing noneffectual tentacles of verbal diarrhea)

I waited half an hour of word sludge.

(confirming the existence of their creator their peri-
odically jolted lives starved of direction or vector by the
recognizable official negative analogues banal "priva-
tisation" being the most reliable)

"You can fix at my place if you like."

I could tell he had no place of his own. He just nodded and we got in a cab. I had to wake him up when we
got there and help him up the stairs. He'd been hitting
the goof balls waiting on his script. I deposited him in
a chair. He slumped forward and his tongue lolled out.
He opened one eye and looked at me.

"Don't I know you from some place?"

"Right back where we started from born knowing."

His eyes touched me inside. He smiled twisting a
Sammy scarf in his dirty fingers.

"You should have let me finish the job instead of
leaving it half done."

(species spawning for such a purpose to ask reputably
informed complacent "What is it for?" Accessibility is
I feel to beg the question.)

"I'm immune now remember."

"Yes thanks to me."

"Thanks 'Genial.'"

"So what did it get you?" He pointed to the mirror.
"Look at you . . burnt out used up . . ."

(to traduce or transfigure and reduce a man's pulsating
multiplicity to untranslatable inchoate word for latent
consensus of "otherness")

"And look at you 'Genial' . . . sex scar tissue on anyone I ever asked alive or dead I should know."

(Mr S. who latterly became something the point is simply the contradictions of an inherent territory prophet
stridently inclined to gritty acceptances depending on
banal illiterate process of perceptive engagement)

I found "Genial" in the police shed on top of the
hill. He was sitting on a bench his face blank as an
empty screen. A police sergeant behind a desk squinted
through cigarette smoke. "Much trouble this one," he
pointed to "Genial," "papers *muy malo no en ordenes . .*"

"He has a passport?"

"Oh yes but the date here and the date here *no corre-
sponde . . muy malo . .* perhaps the passport is false . . it
will have to be sent to the Capitol of course . ."

He watched my hand and checked the denomination
of the note I was slipping under the frayed green blotter.

He picked up the passport and leafed through it. "Oh
yes . . here is the date of entry . . Yes everything quite
in order . . your passport *señor . .*"

"Genial" stood there with the passport in his
hand . . "Come along 'Genial.'" I put a hand under his
arm and led him out onto the road.

"*Adiós señores.*"

"*Adiós.*"

I guided "Genial" with one hand under an elbow. He
weighed no more than his clothes. We sat down under
a tree worn smooth by others who sat there before or

after time switched the tracks through a field of little
white flowers by the ruined signal tower. We remember
the days as long procession of the secret police always
everywhere in different form. Outside Guayaquil sat on
a river bank and saw a big lizard cross the mud flats
dotted with melon rind thrown from passing canoes. It
was the end of the line. My death across his face faded
through the soccer scores the urinal and the bicycle
races . . faded into Iam's face at the Green Inn looking
across the valley.

He was standing on a Moroccan hillside with his
troops and around them the Pan pipes calm and impersonal as the blue sky — From his pocket he heard
Poo Poo say "Take me with you" — He felt a little
plastic bag and drew it out — There was a flat grey
membrane inside it — He moved away on Pan pipes
to the remote mountain village of his childhood where
blue mist swirled through the streets and time stopped
in the slate houses — Words fell from his mind —
He drifted through wind chimes of subway dawns and
turnstiles — Boys on roller skates turned slow circles
in a shower of ruined suburbs — grey luminous flakes
falling softly on Ewyork, Aris, Ome, Oston — crumpled
cloth bodies through the glass and metal streets swept
by time winds — from siren towers the twanging tones of
fear — positive feedback Pan God of Panic piping blue
notes through empty streets as the berserk time machine
twisted a tornado of centuries — wind through dusty

offices and archives — board books scattered to rubbish heaps of the earth — symbol books of the all powerful board that had controlled thought feeling and movement of a planet with iron claws of pain and pleasure from birth to death — control symbols pounded to word and image dust; crumpled cloth bodies of the vast control machine — The whole structure of reality went up in silent explosions under the whining sirens — Pipers from his remote mountain village loosed Pan God of Panic through streets of image — dead nitrous streets of an old film set — paper moon and muslin trees and in the black silver sky great rents as the cover of the world rained down in luminous film flakes — The 1920's careened through darkening cities in black Cadillacs spitting film bullets of accelerated time —

through the open window trailing swamp smells and old newspapers — orgasm addicts stacked in the attic like muttering burlap — the mattress molded on all sides masturbating afternoons reflected; "Difficult to get out" — word and image skin like a rubber toy dusted with grey spine powder — The boy who owned this room stood naked to his mountain village and swirled the vampire guards out of his path — Blue notes of Pan trickled down silver train whistles — calling the imprisoned Jinn from copulation space suits that clung to his muscle lust and burning sex skin — The green fish boys dropped their torture of spectral presence and like fish left the garden through clear water — Tentative

beings followed the music membrane of light and color
— Pipes of Pan trickled down sleeping comrade of
his childhood — pure blue jabs through the Garden of Delights — Alien beauty cutting the black
insect — He slipped out of time in a flash of absent
bodies — His camera gun blasted memory — The blue
boy reached from the remote mountain village other
apparatus — They twisted cool and impersonal as
the sky against each other in pressure seats — stuck
together in slow-motion faces — crisscrossed with
tentative whistles of other lips and slipped suddenly
out of other apparatus twisted the guards in a flash
of speed — Masturbating afternoon of spectral presence went out in clear water — The Board that had
controlled sperm bank of a planet with sex prisoners
broken now from birth to death — control skin melted
leaving crumpled cloth bodies of muttering burlap —
Explosion swept through empty sex thoughts as the
sperm tanks drained into streets of image — the cover
of the world rained down — all from an old movie will
give at his touch.

in a
strange bed

Lykin was the first to awake — He could not remember where he was — Slowly his blue eyes blurred with
exhaustion registered glowing red rocks and metallic

shrubs with silver leaves that surrounded the little pool where he lay — The ghastly night flooded back into his memory — Controls of their space craft had suddenly blanked out by the intervention of an invisible alien force like an icy draught through the cabin — Not only the mechanical controls had been put out of action but their nerve centers had been paralyzed — He and Bradly the Co-pilot had sat helpless in their pressure seats for two hours while the invading force guided their ship in a sickening spiral through the poisonous cloud belts of an unknown planet — Lykin and Bradly had blacked out when they landed — How had they gotten out of the ship? — He stood up and tripped over the sleeping form of his companion naked except for the skin-tight transparent space suit that clung to his muscular body — He decided to have a quick look at the terrain before waking Bradly — He was at the bottom of a gully surrounded by red rocks of some translucent substance — He climbed out of the gully and found himself on a plateau — A fantastic landscape of multicolored rock carved like statues of molten blue lava interspaced with stalagmites of a pearly white intensity he had never experienced in his previous explorations — The sky was like a green ocean — There were four suns on the horizon around the plateau, each sun of a different color — Blue, green, red, and one (much larger than the others) a brilliant silver — The air was of a tingling clarity that seemed to support his body so that movements were incredibly precise and

easily performed — He turned and started back down the
gully toward the pool — He felt a click in his brain like
a crystal flare and heard a silver voice: "Come stranger"
— Bradly was accustomed to telepathic phenomena but
this voice was unusually clear and immediate — He
climbed over a large rock and saw the pool — His friend
was still asleep — Beside him sat an amphibious green
fish boy shimmering with water from the pool — The
creature pulsed with translucent green light that flooded
through the flesh in eddies — The head was a pointed
dome that sprang from a slender neck on either side
of which protruded gills like sensitive spongy wings —
The creature was covered by a membranous substance
with a network of transparent veins — The body surface
was in constant motion like slow water dripping down a
statue — The face was almost flat but with lips and nose
sharply and beautifully delineated and huge liquid eyes
above the high ridged cheekbones the delicate structure
of which shone through transparent skin — The being
was sitting in a cross-legged position and from its thighs
jutted small silver fins of fine gauze — The slender
sinuous legs ended in webbed flippers — Between the
legs Lykin could see the genitals half aroused in curiosity as the fish boy stroked the head of his sleeping
companion and touched the space suit with tentative jabs
of its long green fingers — Lykin moved cautiously so
as not to frighten the creature back into the pool — The
fish boy turned and looked at him with a shy dreamy

smile — An electric shiver ran up his spine and burst in crystal fish syllables: "Approach stranger — Have no fear" — The creature's mouth had not moved — Lykin moved forward with excitement tingling through his body and knelt beside the water boy who extended a dripping hand and lightly clasped his shoulder — A thrill ran through him from the contact — Underwater memory bubbles burst in his brain — He was in the alien medium, squirming in crystal rock pools and basking on edges of limestone fanned by giant ferns in the sound of dripping water — Swimming through ruined cities with the water creatures twisting in slow swirls of orgasm, shooting out explosions of colored bubbles to the surface, trailing blue streamers —

Ali woke in a strange bed to find the proprietor standing over him, "Who the fuck are you and what are you doing in my apartment?" Ali flashed back to the suburban cocktail party — music from the '20s — old women doing the Charleston — and the Irishman with iron-grey hair who looked like a con cop from vaudeville —

"Easy way and a tough way to do things, kid — i can put you up for the night in this apartment — The owner is out of town and i don't *think* he'll be back before tomorrow night —"

"But Mr O'Brien said —"

"Tell O'Brien he can stay in his own precinct — This happens to be my apartment — Put on your dry goods and cut —"

Ali dressed hastily — Tucking his shirt he slipped
out into the American suburb — The streets were empty
and clean like after a heavy rain — At an intersection
of cracked concrete boys turned slow circles on roller
skates under a half-moon in the morning sky, swept
by storms of color as the sun rose — Ali felt his steps
lighter and lighter — He floated away on eddies of
blue and green — He alighted in the clear atmosphere
of a green land where every blade of grass shone as if
framed in crystal — The gravity pull was light so his feet
barely touched the ground as he ran along clear streams
of water under dripping trees — came to a city of worn
marble streets and copper domes — In the lobby of a
luxury hotel page boys in elaborate uniforms assessed
his financial status with experienced eyes — On the
wall was a little sign:

The Nature of Begging
Need ? —— Lack -
Want? —— Need -
Life? —— Death -

Ali walked out into the main square — fish smells and
dead eyes in doorways — obscene gestures of proposition
— In a dark side street off the square Ali found what looked
like an old chemist's shop with jars of colored liquid in the
window — A little black man, body bent by a fibrous tumor
came forward to meet him with a chirp of interrogation —
He was wearing double lens glasses that slid down on his

nose — Ali drew out the plastic bag he carried with the flattened grey membrane inside — The shopkeeper took it in smooth black fingers and held it up to the light — He gave a little chirping call and his assistant came in from shadow recesses of the shop — It was some creature like a large grasshopper with a body that changed color as he walked past the jars — The eyes were crystal lens — His penis, which was held in upright position by a long silver cord extending into the abdomen, moved in flash erections to currents of color — He held the membrane in adzes and grafting tools that fitted into his fibrous finger stumps — As he looked his body pulsed a brilliant green — The shopkeeper nodded and brought out a jar about two feet high full of a heavy white fluid — The assistant opened the envelope with a little curved knife and dropped the membrane into the jar — As Ali watched the membrane stirred like a Japanese flower and blossomed into a tiny green newt with human head — The creature opened black liquid eyes for a few seconds then curled into foetal sleep and sank to the bottom of the jar — The shopkeeper covered the jar with a cloth and put it on a dark shelf — He smiled and drew a map on the counter — Starting from the shop a dotted line led to a system of canals, a pump, two penises in orgasm, closed eyes of sleep five times — Then the dotted line led back to the shop — He looked at Ali to be sure he understood — Ali nodded and walked on the dotted line — The marble streets ended in mud — He could see a system of canals with thatched huts and

gardens and tanks tended by little black men with fibrous
tumors and moles from which sprouted green hairs — They
looked up from their work and flashed quick smiles — A
heavy smell of compost heaps and rotten ponds filled the
air — As he passed over a bridge a green newt boy surfaced
in a canal smiled and masturbated quickly ejaculating an
iridescent fluid that glinted in the clear light — He twisted
with a mocking laugh and dove out of sight in the black
water — Ali walked along the canal and found himself in
a maze of pumps and locks and could not find how he got
there or the way out — At the bottom of this maze a man
in a green tattered uniform motioned him to come down
pointing to an iron stairway that led out on a wooden ramp
— The man stood waiting at the end of the ramp — Ali
walked toward him smiling like a dog — "i am a stranger
here — i am sorry if — i do not know your laws" — The
guard was smiling too — a slow familiar smile like: "Perhaps you don't go into the prison if" — flashed back to
customs shed in South America — Ali bent over a chair
feeling quick pants of the young policeman on his naked
back — The carbine leaning against one wall sharp and
clear in the flash bulb of orgasm — "So" — he thought
"things are not different here" —

The man led him to a shed — Inside was a pallet
on the floor — Clothing hung from wooden pegs — In
another room he could see levers and wheels obviously
controlling the pumps and locks — The man flicked
Ali's clothes — He undressed slowly dropping his pants

with a wriggling motion as his cock flipped out and up
— The man stood naked in green light that filtered into
the shed from overhanging vines and fruit trees — He
picked Ali up in his arms and kissed him — His breath
had a vegetable smell slightly rotten like tropical fruit
— He carried Ali to the pallet and shoved his knees up
to his ears — From a shelf he took a little jar of what
looked like frogs' eggs and gave off an odor of moldy
proteins — He rubbed the eggs into Ali's ass — Ali
could feel something coming alive in his rectum and
wriggling down into his testicles — The man slid his
cock in — Ali squirmed teeth bared wriggling feelers
caressing his penis rubbing around nerves at the tip
— The man caught his ejaculation in the jar — Tiny
green frogs with sucker paws stirred in the sperm —

He stayed for five nights with the man sleeping on
the pallet and eating meals of fruit from the garden and
helping with the wheels and levers — At the end of five
days the man gave him the jar of eggs and he went back
to the shop and gave the eggs to the shopkeeper —

The shopkeeper smiled and took the other jar down
from the shelf — The green newt boy, still curled in
sleep, had grown until it filled the jar — The shopkeeper
drew a map on the counter dotted line to a hut in the
canal system — And Ali walked out carrying the jar
along the line to a hut where an old man greeted him
— Ali uncovered the jar — The man clapped his hands
softly and made a little clucking noise — He showed

Ali a series of tanks behind his hut like an elaborate cesspool, one tank draining into another — In the tanks were green newt boys in various stages and the last tank opened out into black water of the canal — The man emptied the jar into the first tank — Ali turned to walk away and felt the man's hand on his shoulder, led him back into the hut — He measured Ali's neck like a tailor and selected from a shelf two dried gills which he fitted carefully and gave to Ali in a plastic envelope — He motioned to the sky — He made a choking sound and pointed to the bag —

Ali began hustling around the square where the nobles cruised in the evening — dark street life of a place forgotten — The city was swept by waves of giant carnivorous land crabs and Ali learned to hide himself when he heard their snapping claws like radio static — Explosions of time film was another danger in the city — One evening in the square he heard a rumble like muffled thunder — Everyone running for the canals and shouting "The Studio went up" — A cloud of red nitrous fumes settled on the city — Ali, gasping and choking, remembered and reached for his plastic bag — He put the gills around his neck and dove into a wellhead carved to resemble a stone rectum — As he fell deep into the green water he could feel the gills cut into his neck — A sudden sharp taste of blood and he was breathing and swimming along an underground passage — He could see light ahead and came out into one of the open canals —

*   *   *

Ali woke in a strange bed — As you listen fill in with him "Who the fuck are you and what are you doing in my image track?" Ali was wide awake now and clicked "out of here," female impersonators, music back to the '20s, suburban pool halls and vaudeville voice of a grey-haired Irishman who turned over a steady stream of "easy way and a tough way to do time" — Meanwhile i had forgotten the owner in this apartment — scent of memory pictures — people gone — back tomorrow night —

"But Mr O'Brien said" —

"Tell O'Brien to stay in his own precinct — This happens to be my dawn wind in other flesh" —

Ali dressed hastily and slipped out — Board members, look, the streets are empty — Young faces melted the law, turned slow circles on roller skates — Nova Police look at the wired color sunrise — Errand boy floating on eddies of red and green alighted in slow-motion flashes of clear atmosphere — The gravity pull was lighter — does not know the frequency of junk — marble streets and copper domes — Darkened eyes of page boys in elaborate physical skin put his financial status out in the streets — East St. Louis music on chirping call — His genitals were voices out into other dressing rooms — long silver thread that extended in flash erections back and forth — switch to office of a garage — sharp desire held the membrane —

"Yes you have grafting tools — Without you i on pavement" —

The shopkeeper nodded good bye — translucent white fade-out — Sticky office spattered light on naked knives — from his face newsreels of riots moving in fast — Ali round the Board —

"What's this Japanese flower blossomed into sinking ship? You trying source of human head on screen?"

Boneless mummy curled into foetal tank — The shopkeeper covered — fade-out at dawn — Hurry up — Hands put it on a dark shelf — He smile and twist brain — starting with the shop a dotted corpse last round — the gate from two cocks in orgasm — men smoking on the end of the line — sleep five times — then the dotted line —

"We been subliminated in doorways," looked at Ali to be sure he understood, "Beside you wind voices on dotted line trailed system of canals — not think the Doctor on stage" —

They looked up from their work — empty all hate faces — vapor trails writing the sky — Some boy surfaced in the canal — Iridescent harbor glinted in the stellar light — mocking laugh of absent tenants — ghost riots along the canal and found himself in a garage — Stood naked — good bye of hydraulic pumps spattered on his face — out at the bottom interrogate substance of green uniform was motioning "want it" — tentative empty flesh of KY and rectal mucus? — End of the ramp man stood waiting — gate from human form — "We been subliminated like a dog — stranger face sucked in other apparatus" — "sorry if" —

The man was smiling, flapping vapor like rusty swamp smell — flicker back to a custom shed in South America — ("First we must write the ticket") — Feeling the quick pants of mummy — goosed his ass — carbine leaning against one wall — burning orgasm — wind voices beside masturbating pallet on the floor —

"Out of here, female impersonators" —

Wooden pegs in another room forgotten memory controlling the structure of his Scandinavian outhouse skin — The man flicked Ali's clothes — Prisoner pants with wriggling movement stood naked now in green mummy flesh, hanging vines and deflated skin — Death kissed him — His breath talked to the switchblade — He dropped Ali on the last parasite from the shelf before newsreels shut off — Looked like frog eggs — He was shoving the eggs — Poo Poo snickered, coming alive in his rectum like green neon — Into the prostate his slow fingers — Ali squirmed his teeth bared — The man caught his spurts like a pack of cards — He stayed for five nights in the tarnished office eating meals of fruit from color vapor — At the end of five days newsreels of riot move in fast — The eggs went back to boneless mummy — Ghost keeper smiled and fade-out at dawn — Hands of light fell apart in corpse — last jar — The shopkeeper drew a map in absent bodies — empty the

canal area — Ali twisted through open shirt — He found
his way to their ship in the harbor — The man travel on
newsreels — Exquisite screen penis spurted again —
corpse tanks — end of the line and last jar — led the
Doctor on stage — Sex phantoms emptied the jars into
afternoon image track — He turned to walk away and
suffused the hut — people gone — Diarrhea exploded
down from a shelf —

"Ali hanged after being milked, see?" made a choking noise and pointed — orgasm of a place forgotten
— Corpses hang from gallows — "Land crabs" — He
dissolved in smoke and crumpled cloth —

"All right, Doctor — Indications enough — i told you
i would come — healed scars — The Studio went up — a
cloud of nitrous Big Fix" — Ali gasped and choked and
reached courage to pass without doing pictures around
his neck — He could feel suddenly shut-off taste of
blood and all the Garden of Delights — He could see
sex scenes in the open canals of time —

do you
love me?

The young monk led Bradly to a cubicle — On a
stone table was a tape recorder — The monk switched
on the recorder and sounds of lovemaking filled the
room — The monk took off his robe and stood naked
with an erection — He danced around the table

caressing a shadowy figure out of the air above the recorder — A tentative shape flickering in and out of focus to the sound track — The figure floated free of the recorder and followed the monk to a pallet on the floor — He went through a pantomime of pleading with the phantom who sat on the bed with legs crossed and arms folded — Finally the phantom nodded reluctant consent and the monk twisted through a parody of love-making as the tape speeded up: "Oh darling i love you oh oh deeper oh oh fuck the shit out of me oh darling do it again" — Bradly rolled on the floor, a vibrating air hammer of laughter shaking flesh from the bones — Scalding urine spurted from his penis — The Other Half swirled in the air above him screaming, face contorted in suffocation as he laughed the sex words from throat gristle in bloody crystal blobs — His bones were shaking, vibrated to neon — Waves of laughter through his rectum and prostate and testicles giggling out spurts of semen as he rolled with his knees up to his chin —

All the tunes and sound effects of *"Love"* spit from the recorder permutating sex whine of a sick picture planet:: Do you love me? — But i exploded in cosmic laughter — Old acquaintance be forgot? — Oh darling, just a photograph? — Mary i love you i do do you know i love you through? — On my knees i hoped you'd love me too — I would run till i feel the thrill of long ago — Now my inspiration but it won't last and we'll be just a photograph — i've forgotten you then? i can't sleep,

Blue Eyes, if i don't have you — Do i love her? i love
you i love you many splendored thing — Can't even eat
— Jelly on my mind back home — 'Twas good bye deep
in the true love — We'll never meet again, darling, in
my fashion — Yes eyes ever shining that made me my
way — Always it's a long trip to Tipperary — Tell Laura
i love my blue heaven — Get up woman up off your big
fat earth out into cosmic space with all your diamond
rings — Do you do you do you love me? — Lovey lovey
dovey brought to mind? What? Do you love me with a
banjo? — Please don't be angry — i wonder who — If
i had learned to love you every time i felt blue — But
someone took you out of the stardust of the skies — Your
charms travel to remind me of you — together again —
forgotten you eat — Don't know how i'll make it baby —
blue eyes the color of — Do you love me? Love is *para
olvidar* — Tell Laura oh jelly love you — i can't — Got
you under my skin on my mind — But i'll always be
true to my blue heaven — Love Mary? — Fuck the shit
out of me — Get up off your big fat rusty-dusty — It's
a long way to go, St. Louis woman — prospect of red
mesas out to space — Do you love me? — Do you love
void and scenic railways back home?? And do you love
me with a banjo permutated through do you love me?
— i wonder who permutated the structure every time i
felt blue — But that was ferris wheels clicking in the
stardust of the sky — on perilous tracks — i had a dog
his name was Bill aworking clouds of *Me* — Tearing his

insides apart — Need a helping hand? — understanding
out of date — Find someone else at this time of day?
Torch cutting through the eats? —

Don't know how i'll make it, baby — Electric fingers removed *"Love"* — Do you love me? — Love is
red sheets of pain hung oh oh baby oh jelly — The
guide slipped off his jelly — I've got you under my
skin pulsing red light — Clouds of *Me* always be true
to you — Hula hoops of color formed always be true to
you darling in my Bradly — Weak and torn i'll hurry to
my blue heaven as i sank in suffocation panic of rusty
St. Louis woman — With just a photograph, Mary, you
know i love you through sperm — Contraction turnstile
hoped you'd love me too — Orgasm floated arms still i
feel the thrill of slow movement but it won't last — i've
forgotten you then? — i love you i love you and bones
tearing his insides apart for the ants to eat — Jelly jelly
jelly shifting color orgasm back home — Scratching
shower of sperm that made cover of the board books —
It's a long way to Tipperary — soft luminous spurts to
my blue heaven — Pieces of cloud drifted through all
the tunes from blue — Exploded in cosmic laughter of
cable cars . . . Me? — Oh, darling, i love you in constant motion — i love you i do — You led Bradly into a
cubicle on my knees — love floating in a slow vertigo
of you — perilous tracks where wind whistled long ago
— i can't sleep, baby, skin pulling loose if i don't have
you — a peg like many splendored thing — i've got you

deep in the guides body enclosed darling in *my* fashion
— yes cool hands on his naked flesh my way — evening
intestines of the other — Tell Laura i love her sucked
through pearly genital woman off your big fat shower of
sperm — Diamond rings spurt out of you — Should be
brought to mind — Ejaculated bodies without a cover —

I learned to love you, pale adolescents — Someone
took you out of the creature charms — We'll travel weak
and torn by pain together — Silver films in the blood
para olvidar — Tell Laura black fish movement of food
love you — i can't sleep reflected in obsidian penis —
Follow the swallow and released dream flesh in Isle of
Capri — The truth in sunlight, Mary — memory riding
the wind — It's a long way to go — someone walking
— mountain wind —

Do i love you? — Crumpled cloth body ahoy — But
remember the red open shirt flapping wind from you so
true — Do you love me? — Vapor trails writing all the
things you are — The great wind revolving what you could
have — Indications in the harbor muttering blackbird
— bye bye — Who's sorry now? — This time of day
vultures in the street — 'Twas good bye on vacant lots —
weeds growing through broken road — smell of healed
and half-healed scars — all the little things you used
to do on a bicycle built for little time so i'll say: "You
on sidewalk" — if you were the only girl in green neon,
your voices muttering in the dog rotation — Dollar baby,
how cute can you be in desolate underbrush? You were

meant for me? battered phonograph talk-face — I'm just
a vagabond pass without — Can play the game as well as
you, darling — train whistle open shirt flapping the cat
and the fiddle — i am biologic from a long way to go —
Nights are long with the St. Louis suburb — Music seems
to whisper Louise Mary on the pissoirs — i had a dog his
name was Bill — (In other flesh open shirt flapping) on
the railroad — He went away — Many names murmur
— Someone walking — won't be two — i'm half crazy all
for the love of *"Good Night"* — Shadow voices belong to
me — Found a million acoustic qualities couldn't reach
in a five-and-ten-cent store — Naked boy on association
line but you'll find someone else this time of day —

The levanto dances who's sorry now? — Hey diddle
diddle the cat and the fiddle — Long way to Tipperary
— fading khaki pants — Since you went away i see
that moon hit the road into space — Do you love me
Waltzing Matilda rock around railroad back home? lovey
lovey dovey St. Louis Woman after hours — Do you love
me with a banjo permutated Dead Man Blues? — If
you don't i wonder who permutated the structure —
Everybody love my baby — Lover man, that was ferris
wheels clicking in a loverly bunch — solitude through
the cables — turkey in the straw —

"BAR MAID WATCH THE EATS!!" —

Don't Know how i'll make it — one meat ball —
Pull my daisy ding-dong love — Do you love me, love
sheets? — Everybody's gonna have religion oh baby oh

jelly — The guide slipped Paul under my skin pulsing
red light — pallet on the floor darling Bradly — weak
and torn sank in bones and shit of rusty St. Louis woman
— when the saints go marching through all the popular
tunes waiting for the sunrise in cosmic laughter of cable
cars — the Sheik of Araby in constant motion — Blue
moon — Margie — ice cream on my knees — Love
floating in perilous tracks —

Do you love me, Nancy of the laughing sex words? —
Still i feel the thrill of your charms vibrated to neon —
giggling out all the little things you used to do — 'Twas
good bye on the line of Bradly's naked body — love skin
on a bicycle built for two — like a deflated balloon —
Your cool hands on his naked dollars, baby — You were
meant for me sucked through pearly genital face — Still
i feel the thrill of you spurting out through the orgasm
seems to whisper:: "Louise, Mary, swamp mud" — In the
blood little things you used to do — recorder jack-off
— Substitute mine — Bye Bye body halves — i'm half
crazy all for the love of color circuits — Do i love you
in throat gristle? Ship ahoy but remember the red river
body explode sex words to color — Do you love me?
— Take a simple tape from all the things you are —
Moanin' low my sweet 8276 all the time — Who's sorry
now in the underwater street? 'Twas good bye on color
bicycle built for response in the other nervous system —

I'm just a vagabond of the board books — written in
can play the game as well as you — (That is color written

the two compete) — Do i love you? i wonder — loose?
if i don't have to? a peg like every time i felt blue? It's
a long way through channels — Who's sorry now?
chartered that memory street — Bye Bye — bodies
empty — ash from falling tracks — Sweet man is going
to go — Keep raining the throat designed to water —
Remember every little thing you used to do — fish
smell and dead — Know the answer? vacant lot the
world and i were the only boy — jelly jelly in the
stardust of the sky — i've got you deep inside of me
enclosed darling in my fashion — Yes, baby, electric
fingers removed flesh my way — Sheets of pain hung oh
baby oh i love her sucked through pearly jelly — i've
got you under big fat scratching clouds of me — Always
be true to your diamond rings — Tell Laura black slow
movement but it won't last — i've forgotten you then?
Decay breathing? Black lust tearing his insides apart
for ants? Love Mary? — The rose of memory shifting
color orgasms back home — Good bye — It's a long
way to go — Someone walking — Won't be two —

operation
rewrite

The "Other Half" is the word. The "Other Half" is
an organism. Word is an organism. The presence of the
"Other Half" a separate organism attached to your nervous
system on an air line of words can now be demonstrated

experimentally. One of the most common "hallucinations" of subjects during sense withdrawal is the feeling of another body sprawled through the subject's body at an angle . . yes quite an angle it is the "Other Half" worked quite some years on a symbiotic basis. From symbiosis to parasitism is a short step. The word is now a virus. The flu virus may once have been a healthy lung cell. It is now a parasitic organism that invades and damages the lungs. The word may once have been a healthy neural cell. It is now a parasitic organism that invades and damages the central nervous system. Modern man has lost the option of silence. Try halting your sub-vocal speech. Try to achieve even ten seconds of inner silence. You will encounter a resisting organism that *forces you to talk*. That organism is the word. In the beginning was the word. In the beginning of what exactly? The earliest artifacts date back about ten thousand years give a little take a little and "recorded" — (or prerecorded) history about seven thousand years. The human race is said to have been on set for 500,000 years. That leaves 490,000 years unaccounted for. Modern man has advanced from the stone ax to nuclear weapons in ten thousand years. This may well have happened before. Mr Brion Gysin suggests that a nuclear disaster in what is now the Gobi desert wiped out all traces of a civilization that made such a disaster possible. Perhaps their nuclear weapons did not operate on the same principle as the ones we have now. Perhaps they had no contact with the word organism. Perhaps the word itself is recent about ten thousand years old. What we call history is the history of the word. In the beginning of *that* history was the word.

The realization that something as familiar to you as the movement of your intestines the sound of your breathing the beating of your heart is also alien and hostile does make one feel a bit insecure at first. Remember that you can separate yourself from the "Other Half" from the word. The word is spliced in with the sound of your intestines and breathing with the beating of your heart. The first step is to record the sounds of your body and start splicing them in yourself. Splice in your body sounds with the body sounds of your best friend and see how familiar he gets. Splice your body sounds in with air hammers. Blast jolt vibrate the "Other Half" right out into the street. Splice your body sounds in with anybody or anything. Start a tapeworm club and exchange body sound tapes. Feel right out into your nabor's intestines and help him digest his food. *Communication must become total and conscious before we can stop it.*

"The Venusian invasion was known as 'Operation Other Half,' that is, a parasitic invasion of the sexual area taking advantage, as all invasion plans must, of an already existing fucked-up situation ('My God what a mess.' The District Supervisor reminded himself that it was forbidden not only to express contempt for the natives but even to entertain such feelings. Bulletin 2323 is quite explicit on this point. Still he was unable to

expunge a residual distaste for protoplasmic life deriv-
ing no doubt from his mineral origins. His mission was
educational . . . the natives were to be scanned out of
patterns laid down by the infamous 5th Colonists. Soon
after his arrival he decided that he was confronting not
only an outrageous case of colonial mismanagement but
attempted nova as well. Reluctantly he called in the
Nova Police. The Mission still functioned in a state of
siege. Armed with nuclear weapons the 5th Colonists
were determined to resist alterations. It had been necessary to issue weapons to his personnel. There were
of course incidents . . casualties . . . A young clerk in
the Cultural Department declared himself the Angel of
Death and had to be removed to a rest home. The D.S.
was contemplating the risky expedient of a 'miracle' and
the miracle he contemplated was *silence*. Few things
are worse than a 'miracle' that doesn't come off. He
had of course put in an application to the Home Office
underlining the urgency of his case contingent on the
lengths to which the desperate 5th Colonists might rea-
sonably be expected to go. Higher command had been
vague and distant. He had no definite assurance that
the necessary equipment would arrive in time. Would he
have 3D in time?) — The human organism is literally
consisting of two halves from the beginning word and all
human sex is this unsanitary arrangement whereby two
entities attempt to occupy the same three-dimensional
coordinate points giving rise to the sordid latrine brawls

which have characterized a planet based on 'the Word,' that is, on separate flesh engaged in endless sexual conflict — The Venusian Boy-Girls under Johnny Yen took over the Other Half, imposing a sexual blockade on the planet — (It will be readily understandable that a program of systematic frustration was necessary in order to sell this crock of sewage as Immortality, the Garden of Delights, and *love*) —

"When the Board of Health intervened with inflexible authority, 'Operation Other Half' was referred to the Rewrite Department where the original engineering flaw of course came to light and the Venusian invasion was seen to be an inevitable correlate of the separation flesh gimmick — At this point a tremendous scream went up from the Venusians agitating to retain the flesh gimmick in some form — They were all terminal flesh addicts of course, motivated by pornographic torture films, and the entire Rewrite and Blueprint Departments were that disgusted ready to pull the switch out of hand to 'It Never Happened' — 'Unless these jokers stay out of the Rewrite room' —

"The Other Half was only one aspect of Operation Rewrite — Heavy metal addicts picketed the Rewrite Office, exploding in protest — Control addicts prowled the streets trying to influence waiters, lavatory attendants, *clochards*, and were to be seen on every corner of the city hypnotizing chickens — A few rich control addicts were able to surround themselves with latahs and sat on the terraces of expensive cafés with remote cruel smiles unaware i wrote last cigarette —

"My God what a mess — Just keep all these jokers out of the Rewrite Room is all" —

So let us start with one average, stupid, representative case: Johnny Yen the Other Half, errand boy from the death trauma — Now look i'm going to say it and i'm going to say it slow — Death *is* orgasm *is* rebirth *is* death in orgasm *is* their unsanitary Venusian gimmick *is* the whole birth death cycle of action — You got it? — Now do you understand who Johnny Yen is? The Boy-Girl Other Half strip tease God of sexual frustration — Errand boy from the death trauma — His immortality depends on the mortality of others — The same is true of *all* addicts — Mr Martin, for example, is a heavy metal addict — His life line is the human junky — The life line of control addicts is the control word — Control word *"the"* — That is these so-called Gods can only live without three-dimensional coordinate points by forcing three-dimensional bodies on others — Their existence is pure vampirism — They are utterly unfit to be officers — Either they accept a rewrite job or they are all broken down to lavatory attendants, irrevocably committed to the toilet —

All right, back to the case of Johnny Yen — one of many such errand boys — Green Boy-Girls from the terminal sewers of Venus — So write back to the streets, Johnny, back to Ali God of Street Boys and

Hustlers — Write out of the sewers of Venus to neon streets of Saturn — Alternatively Johnny Yen can be written back to a green fish boy — There are always alternative solutions — Nothing is true — Everything is permitted —

"No Hassan i Sabbah — we want flesh — we want junk — we want power —"

"That did it — Dial *police*" —

*the
nova police*

Bulletin from Rewrite: We had to call in the nova police to keep all these jokers out of the Rewrite Room — Can't be expected to work under such conditions — Introducing Inspector J. Lee of the nova police — "i doubt if any of you on this copy planet have ever seen a nova criminal — (they take considerable pains to mask their operations) and i am sure none of you have ever seen a nova police officer — When disorder on any planet reaches a certain point the regulating instance scans *police* — otherwise — Sput — Another planet bites the cosmic dust — i will now explain something of the mechanisms and techniques of nova which are always deliberately manipulated — i am quite well aware that no one on any planet likes to see a police officer so let me emphasize in passing that the nova police have no intention of remaining after their work is done — That is, when the danger of nova is removed from

this planet we will move on to other assignments — We
do our work and go —

"The basic nova technique is very simple: Always create as many insoluble conflicts as possible and always
aggravate existing conflicts — This is done by dumping
on the same planet life forms with incompatible conditions of existence — There is of course nothing 'wrong'
about any given life form since 'wrong' only has reference
to conflicts with other life forms — The point is these
life forms should not be on the same planet — Their
conditions of life are basically incompatible in present
time form and it is precisely the work of the nova mob
to see that they remain in present time form, to create
and aggravate the conflicts that lead to the explosion of
a planet, that is to nova — At any given time recorders
fix the nature of absolute need and dictate the use of total
weapons — Like this: Take two opposed pressure groups
— Record the most violent and threatening statements
of group one with regard to group two and play back to
group two — Record the answer and take it back to group
one — back and forth between opposed pressure groups
— This process is known as 'feedback' — You can see it
operating in any bar room quarrel — In any quarrel for
that matter — Manipulated on a global scale feeds back
nuclear war and nova — These conflicts are deliberately
created and aggravated by nova criminals — The Nova
Mob: 'Sammy the Butcher,' 'Green Tony,' 'the Brown Artist,' 'Jacky Blue Note,' 'Limestone John,' 'Izzy the Push,'

'Hamburger Mary,' 'Paddy the Sting,' 'the Subliminal Kid,' 'the Blue Dinosaur,' 'Willy the Rat' (who informed on his associates) and Mr and Mrs D also known as 'Mr Bradly Mr Martin' also known as 'the Ugly Spirit,' thought to be the leader of the mob — the nova mob — In all my experience as a police officer i have never seen such total fear and degradation on any planet — We intend to arrest these criminals and turn them over to the Biological Department for the indicated alterations —

"Now you may well ask whether we can straighten out this mess to the satisfaction of any life forms involved and my answer is this — Your earth case must be processed by the Biological Courts — (admittedly in a deplorable condition at this time) — No sooner set up than immediately corrupted so that they convene every day in a different location like floating dice games, constantly swept away by stampeding forms all idiotically glorifying their stupid ways of life — (most of them quite unworkable of course) — attempting to seduce the judges into Venusian sex practices, drug the court officials, and intimidate the entire audience chamber with the threat of nova — In all my experience as a police officer I have never seen such total fear of the indicated alterations on any planet — a thankless job you see and we only do it so it won't have to be done some place else under even more difficult circumstances —

"The success of the nova mob depended on a blockade of the planet that allowed them to operate with impunity

— This blockade was broken by partisan activity directed from the planet Saturn that cut the control lines of word and image laid down by the nova mob — So we moved in our agents and started to work keeping always in close touch with partisans — The selection of local personnel posed a most difficult problem — Frankly we found that most existing police agencies were hopelessly corrupt — The nova mob had seen to that — Paradoxically some of our best agents were recruited from the ranks of those who are called criminals on this planet — In many instances we had to use agents inexperienced in police work — These were of course casualties and fuck-ups — You must understand that an undercover agent witnesses the most execrable cruelties while he waits helpless to intervene, sometimes for many years, before he can make a definitive arrest — So it is no wonder that green officers occasionally slip control when they finally do move in for the arrest — This condition, known as 'arrest fever,' can upset an entire operation — In one recent case, our man in Tangier suffered an attack of 'arrest fever' and detained everyone on his view screen including some of our undercover men — He was transferred to paper work in another area — Let me explain *how* we make an arrest — nova criminals are not three-dimensional organisms — (though they are quite definite organisms as we shall see) — but they need three-dimensional human agents to operate — The point at which the criminal controller intersects a three-dimensional human agent

is known as 'a coordinate point' — And if there is one
thing that carries over from one human host to another
and established identity of the controller it is habit:: idiosyncrasies, vices, food preferences — (we were able to
trace Hamburger Mary through her fondness for peanut
butter) — a gesture, a special look, that is to say the *style*
of the controller — A chain smoker will always operate
through chain smokers, an addict through addicts —
Now a single controller can operate through thousands
of human agents, but he must have a line of coordinate
points — Some move on junk lines through addicts of
the earth, others move on lines of certain sexual practices and so forth — It is only when we can block the
controller out of all coordinate points available to him
and flush him out from host cover that we can make a
definitive arrest — Otherwise the criminal escapes to
other coordinate" —

Question: "Inspector Lee, i don't quite understand
what is meant by a 'coordinate point' — Could you make
that a little clearer? —"

Answer: "Certainly — You see these criminal controllers occupy human bodies — ghosts? phantoms? Not at
all — very definite organisms indeed — True you can't
see them — Can you see a virus? — Well, the criminal
controllers operate in very much the same manner as
a virus — Now a virus in order to invade, damage and
occupy the human organism must have a gimmick to get
in — Once in the virus invades damages and occupies

a certain area or organ in the body — known as the tissue of predilection — Hepatitis, for example, attacks the liver — Influenza the respiratory tract — Polio and rabies the central nervous system — In the same way a controller invades, damages and occupies some pattern or configuration of the human organism" —

Question: "How do these controllers gain access to the human organism?"

Answer: "I will give an example: the controllers who operate through addiction to opiates — that is who occupy and control addicts of the earth — Their point of entry is of course the drug itself — And they maintain this coordinate point through addiction" —

Question: "What determines the choice of coordinate points? Why does one controller operate through addiction in preference to other channels?" —

Answer: "He operates through addicts because he himself is an addict — A heavy metal addict from Uranus — What we call opium or junk is a very much diluted form of heavy metal addiction — Venusians usually operate through sexual practices — In short these controllers brought their vices and diseases from their planet of origin and infected the human hosts very much in the same way that the early colonizers infected so-called primitive populations" —

Question: "Inspector Lee, how can one be sure that someone purporting to be a nova police officer is not an impostor?" —

Answer: "It is not always easy, especially during this transitional period. There are imposters, 'shake men,' who haunt atomic installations and victimize atomic scientists in much the same way as spurious police officers extort money from sexual deviants in public lavatories — In one recent case a well-organized shake mob, purporting to represent the nova police, confiscated cyclotrons and other atomic equipment which they subsequently sold on the Uranian black market to support their heavy metal habits — They were arrested and sent away for the thousand year cure — Since then we have encountered a few sporadic cases — cranks, lunatics for the most part" —

Question: "Inspector Lee, do you think that the nova mob can be defeated?" —

Answer: "Yes — Their control machine has been disconnected by partisan activity —

"Now we can move in for some definitive arrests —

"'Sammy the Butcher' dissolved his dummy cover — His burning metal eyes stabbed at the officer from the molten core of a hot blue planet — The officer moved back dissolving all connections with the Blue Planet, connections formed by the parasite dummy which had entered his body at birth, carefully prepared molds and association locks closed on empty space — Sammy's eyes burned and sputtered incandescent blue and went out in a smell of metal — His last white-hot blast exploded in empty space — The officer picked up the microphone:: 'Sammy the Butcher,' arrested — 'Paddy the Sting,' arrested — 'Hamburger Mary' has defected — 'Green Tony' has surrendered — move in for the definitive arrest of 'Mr Bradly Mr Martin' also known as 'Mr and Mrs D' also known as 'the Ugly Spirit' —

" 'Sammy the Butcher' dissolved his ranks of self-righteous millions and stabbed at the officer dripping Marilyn Monroe Planet — Locks closed on empty space lettering 'My Fair Lady' — In three-dimensional terms 'The Ugly Spirit' and 'Mrs D' screamed through female blighted continent — So we turn over the Board Books and all the ugliness i had forgotten — criminal street — punitive legislation screaming for more association locks in electric chair and gas chamber — technical death over the land — white no-smell of death dripping nova — 'the Ugly Spirit' was flushed out of one host cover after the other — blanked out by our static and silence waves — Call the Old Doctor twice 'Mr and Mrs D' — He quiets you remember? — finished — no shelter — a handful of dust — Screaming, clawing for the nova switch 'the Ugly Spirit' was dragged from the planet — from all the pictures and words of ugliness that have been his place of residence since he moved in on the New World — The officer with silent inflexible authority closed one coordinate point after another — Only this to say:: Would you rather talk to the partisans 'Mr and Mrs D' — Well? — No terms — This is definitive arrest — 'Sammy the Butcher' has been taken — There

are no guards capable protect you — Millions of voices
in your dogs won't do you a bit of good — voices fading
— crumpled cloth bodies — Your name fading across
newspapers of the earth — Madison Avenue machine is
disconnected — Errand boy closing their errand boys —
Won't be much left — definitive arrest of the board as
you listen, as the officer closes track — Self-righteous
ugliness of their space program a joke — Written in
symbols blighted America::: $$$ — american scent of
memory pictures — the idiot honky-tonks of Panhandle
— humiliation outhouse and snarling ugliness of dying
peoples — bourbon soaked legislators from 'marijuana
is deadlier than cocaine' — board book symbol chains
lynch mobs — the White Smoke pressure group rely-
ing on rectum suburbs and the no-smell of death —
Control Avenue and Hollywood, look at the bread line
— The Ugly Spirit retreated back to the '20s in ser-
vants and police and the dogs of H.J. Anslinger — into
one battered host after another — Blanked out board
instructions — Silence — Silence — Silence — Call
the old money equipment information files of memory
— Finished — No shelter — A hand falls across news-
papers of the earth for the nova switch — Won't do you
a bit of good, collaborators with ugliness and degraded
flesh — Traitors to all souls everywhere moved in on the
New World — The Old Doctor cleaving a heavy silent
authority closed one coordinate point after another —
The board is near right now — This is to say: 'Would

you rather talk up relying on money? — Fading voice
terms? — This is definitive arrest through dying air
— There are no guards now capable guide humiliations — Poisonous cloud, millions of dogs won't do
you a bit of good — parasites, crumpled cloth bodies
— Your control books fading cross newspaper of the
earth couldn't form nova — Operation completed —
planet out of danger — Proceed with the indicated
alterations'" —

writing
machine

The Exhibition extended through many rooms and
corridors — Booths spilled out into a composite garden formal sunken and terraced — Pools and canals
reflected flower floats — (arrangements inextricably
mixed with flower and garden pictures) —
In a room with metal walls magnetic mobiles under
flickering blue light and smell of ozone — jointed metal
youths danced in a shower of blue sparks, erections
twisted together shivering metal orgasms — Sheets of
magnetized calligraphs drew colored iron filings that fell
in clouds of color from patterns pulsing to metal music,
off on, on off — (The spectators clicked through a maze
of turnstiles) — Great sheets of magnetized print held
color and disintegrated in cold mineral silence as word
dust falls from demagnetized patterns — Photomontage

fragments backed with iron stuck to patterns and fell
in swirls mixing with color dust to form new patterns,
shimmering, falling, magnetized, demagnetized to the
flicker of blue cylinders pulsing neon tubes and globes
— In metal booths brain waves wrote the flickering message passed back and forth, over and through shifting
grills — The magnetic pencil caught in calligraphs of
Brion Gysin wrote back into the brain metal patterns
of silence and space — orgone accumulators flickering
blue over swimming tanks where naked youths bathed
in blue — sound and image flakes falling like luminous
grey snow — falling softly from demagnetized patterns
into blue silence — Metal heads reversed eyes felt tingling blue spark erections — Metal orgasms flickering
rainbow colors — came in wet scenic railways of dream
— Electrodes from the brain wrote out boys on roller
skates in a shower of ruined suburbs — Naked youths
bathed in blue against the pinball machine danced and
clicked — Old fashion plates falling like luminous snow
falling softly dark-haired light-haired clicked deeper
and deeper into the blue silence — The light travel
machine is a revolving park turns around the traveler
spilling metal music and nitrous fumes — Pinball acute-
ness twisted shivering in metal — Metal birds buzzed
off in blue light — Jissom cartwheels in glass and mirrors reflected masturbating afternoons — (Naked youths
bathed in blue distance now) — Flicker cylinders spill
sandwich booths music and laughter across the water

— Roller skates twisted in metal arcades — Pools
and canals reflected grey suits carrying umbrellas —
flickering over swimming boys as the magnetic silver
light popped sound and image flakes — color writing
a composite garden — layers peel off red yellow blue
pools reflecting translucent tentative beings with flower
hula hoops naked in blue twilight — metal youths shivering in stars and pool halls — In rooms flooded with
sunlight panels of painting moved past each other on
conveyor belts to music all the masters of the world
past through each other in juxtapositions of light and
color — Painting projected on screens mixed color and
image — The Exhibition shaded into a vast amusement
park with orchestras and rides and movie screens, stages
and outdoor restaurants — All music and talk and sound
recorded by a battery of tape recorders recording and
playing back moving on conveyor belts and tracks and
cable cars spilling the talk and metal music fountains
and speech as the recorders moved from one exhibit
to another — Vast mobile sculptures of music boxes
and recorders wind chimes and movies of the exhibit
reflected from ponds and canals and islands where restaurants enclosed in flicker cylinders spilled light and
talk and music across the water — Plays on stage with
permutating sections moved through each other Shakespeare, ancient Greek, ballet — Movies mix on screen
half one half the other — plays in front of movie screen
synchronized so that horses charge in and out of old

Westerns — Characters walk in and out of the screen flickering different films on and off — Conversations recorded in movies taken during the exhibit appear on the screen until all the spectators are involved situations permutating and moving — (Since the recorders and movies of the exhibition are in constant operation it will be readily seen that any spectator appears on the screen sooner or later if not today then yesterday or tomorrow as the case may be in some connection — and repeat visitors of course —)

A writing machine that shifts one half one text and half the other through a page frame on conveyor belts — (The proportion of half one text half the other is important corresponding as it does to the two halves of the human organism) Shakespeare, Rimbaud, etc. permutating through page frames in constantly changing juxtaposition the machine spits out books and plays and poems — The spectators are invited to feed into the machine any pages of their own text in fifty-fifty juxtaposition with any author of their choice any pages of their choice and provided with the result in a few minutes.

You can say could give no information — Rinse my mouth of a few words: "What have i my friend to give? — dominion dwindling — We intersect on empty kingdom read to by a boy — Five times i made this dream — Consumed brandy neat, muttering in the last terrace of the garden — Light and shade departed have left no address — For i have known the body of a

God bending his knees — Isn't time is there left? —
The bitter foliage my friend to give you? — an odor
of deluge and courage to let go — In the open air a
boy waiting — Smiles overtake someone walking —
The questions drift down slowly out of an old dream
— mountain wind caught in the door — the odor of
drowned suns trailing her linen sweat in the final ape of
history — Like i'd ask alterations but blue sky on our
ticket that exploded — any case a great leisure in the
stern circumstances — Remember i was the ship and
we drown — window rotting at the far end of creeks —
The door couldn't reach flesh — naked dream beside
you and the dreamer gone at dawn whisper — Put on
a clean shirt and takes his way toward the sea —

"Written on the door pure information — Vast thing
police speak of a high condition, give you identity fading out — revolving lights is all — bread knife in the
heart falling in the dark mutinous body without a shadow
— Five times of dust we made it all — Relics give no
shelter — dust trade — And those dogs knew nothing
— Circumstances in the rawness of evening to give
you? — smoke up the path — with such hair a colorless dreamer — brandy neat streaked with violence the
door — solitude of morning washed to neon — Departed
have left mixture of dawn and dream — leaning say good
night under surges of silence, ebbing carbon dioxide" —

"Truly at this point many a one has failed — Mr
Bradly Mr Martin is like pulp beside you — A man

walks through dream shirt in another — Stopped suddenly to crown a God bending great sheets of magnetized U turn back to cool mineral silence — grey snow
like bites of sunlight falling softly from noon — the
naked good bye then silence — hints as we shifted masturbating afternoons through Ali's body — Magnetic silver
flakes closed your account — nitrous screens crackling,
genitals spilling scenic railways in sleep — Recorders
of the city rotting — vast music in the throat of God —
Movie screens went out from darkened restaurants —
Dream and dreamer took their way flapping dead sections
through each other — Juxtapositions of light made this
dream — It has consumed image between the mirrors
— Spectators are noon and the naked good bye since
the recorders' 1920 movie — (It will readily be seen
nitrous flesh) — dust from demagnetized brain waves
— The dreamer with dirty cheeks passes over streaked
with violence — Pinball machines clicked wind chimes
of subway dawns and turnstiles — roller skates, camp fire
and red fuck lights reflected over swimming boys — old
Westerns rotting at the far end of creeks — Blue notes
drift through slate houses and nitrous fumes — jissom
cartwheels in a sweetness of aging roots — Light layers
peel off red yellow blue to crown tentative beings with
flowers — spectral smell of naked ghost people — A
maze of penny arcades and mirrors reflect masturbating
afternoons — Color and image bloom out of an old dream
in the odor of outdoor restaurants — Outside East St.

Louis in the dominion of aging roots, ten-year-old keeping watch — Cracked pool hall and vaudeville voices
made this dream — distant coffin between the mirrors
of time that meanwhile i had forgotten — in a deserted
cemetery the body of a God bending his knees — Yes
you have his bitter skin" —

"Put it on — Without you i on pavement — Good bye
in the open air — Someone walking trails my Summer
dawn flesh" —

"Panama night pictures explode odor of naked
rectums — sweat flipped from his face — milk in his
crotch — Young faces melted dead nitrous streets —
Naked brain splintered on empty flesh — bleeding
dream and the dreamer is lying there — last round —
the body without a shadow, without relics — breath of
the trade winds on his face healed and half-healed, in
the rawness of evening" —

"Like, man, good bye then — Silver film took it —"

The dreamer with dirty flesh strung together on scar
impressions exploded in the kerosene lamp — open
shirt flapping in the cool path — now calm his face —
The street blew rain from solitude of morning, mixture of
dawn and dream in doorways — surges of silence ebbing
from the death trauma — Urine in the gutter weaves
window people and sky picture through eyes of wine —

Evening blue over swimming tanks reflected ten-year-
old keeping watch — in the kerosene lamp open shirt,
erections — shivering knees twisted together — surges

of silence ebbing from ruined suburbs — Naked youths
came in wet sleep — windows people and sky like luminous flakes falling —

"Remember i was a battery of tape recorders at the
door — Departed have left spectators involved — Good
night under surges of silence since the recorders and
movies in this point have failed — It will readily be seen
beside you a man walks through screen — The exhibition reflected dominion dwindling — Photo flakes fell in
swirls on our ticket — sound identity fading out — light
travel — In this point many a one has failed — courage
to go deeper and deeper into the blue — ebbing carbon
dioxide — A writing machine shifts last terrace of the
garden — Isn't time is there left? halves of the human
organism to give you? — An odor of deluge through page
frames — Shakespeare and Rimbaud permutating last
round — The spectators are invited to evening of their
own text in fifty-fifty" —

substitute
flesh

The sex area of the amusement park can only be
reached through channels — Anybody applying for
entry must submit to naked photographic processing
for ten days during which the applicant is photographed
in all stages of erection, orgasm, defecation, urinating,
eating — The pictures are cut down the divide line

of the body and fitted to other pictures of prospective
partners — The photos vibrated and welded together in
orgone accumulators* — sex lines crossed and chartered so that memory tracks merge and the area is already seen when the applicant comes in — All sex acts
that take place in the cubicles, Turkish baths, scenic
railways, ferris wheels and pools where the subjects
circulate in aqualungs are photographed and screens
permutate partners divided down the middle line until
there is no way to distinguish film from flesh and the
flesh melts — For example two boys fucking in front of
a cubicle screen can see their pictures developed after

* Reference to the orgone accumulators of Doctor Wilhelm Reich
— Doctor Reich claims that the basic charge of life is this blue orgone-
like electrical charge — Orgones form a sphere around the earth and
charge the human machine — He discovered that orgones pass readily
through iron but are stopped and absorbed by organic matter — So he
constructed metal-lined cubicles with layers of organic material behind
the metal — Subjects sit in the cubicles lined with iron and accumulate
orgones according to the law of increased returns on which life functions
— The orgones produce a prickling sensation frequently associated
with erotic stimulation and spontaneous orgasm — Reich insists that
orgasm is an electrical discharge — He has attached electrodes to the
appropriate connections and charted the orgasm — In consequence of
these experiments he was of course expelled from various countries before
he took refuge in America and died in a federal penitentiary for suggesting
the orgone accumulator be used in treating cancer — It has occurred to this
investigator that orgone energy can be concentrated to disperse the miasma
of idiotic prurience and anxiety that blocks any scientific investigation
of sexual phenomenon — Preliminary experiments indicate that certain
paintings — like Brion Gysin's — when projected on a subject produced
some of the effects observed in orgone accumulators —

a few seconds and permutated with other sex acts in other cubicles half one half the other shifting back and forth speed-up slow-down line cutting the two halves apart to neon — through the open window trailing other pictures — Prospective ectoplasmic flakes welded together with a blue torch chartered the mattress twisted and molded by absent memory tracks merged the masturbating afternoons — Reflected applicant enters and he is already boy who owned that room stood naked with erection permutations in his eyes — The sound and image baths dusted his skin in sense withdrawal swirls where the subject circulates through sensitized photos pulsing telepathic communication — permutating the neck taped on a silver line until the two being flesh melts body in electric waves — rectums merging a few seconds after blue movies and other sex acts with flicker ghosts shifting back and forth orgasms of the world — tentative copulations of light down the dividing line — sound tracks merged in a smell of KY and rectal mucus — A maze of mirrors and screens reflected sex acts in slow motion to a thousand sound tracks shifted and permutated — slow waves of orgasm in a muttering sea of nitrous film flesh — slow knees up to the chin now — prostates quivering in pearly spasms — limestone flesh over silver pools — encrusted music releasing picture flares in moonlight — slow smooth bodies to sound track of phallic statues — pulsing human skin stuck to faces and pictures in scalpel flashes — Adolescent ejaculated

in a thousand cots — First spurts he could feel the tip
process together — Tentative being struck drums of
memory on his back vibrating focus flesh — shifting
erect penis and half-remembered skin instructions to
accent of the attendant — thoughts and memories of
melting ice — the prostate quivering pearly spasms
to his penis in London hotel room — Adolescent lust
ejaculated in stale underwear of penny arcades — The
canals reflected excitement slipping through legs —
Cock flipped out and up — Pearly spasms received
and transmitted, nitrous flesh molded amber afternoons
— Laughing suburb odors spatter out sound track —
ejaculated in stale underwear filtered through encrusted
odors of the world — Returning Mexican adolescent took
my hand in room with a thousand cots — left muttering
skin instructions to answer other thoughts and memories
— Cock flipped out quivering in kerosene light — Old
dead sound track shifting over you conceived in worn
memory of first sex experience — Tingling implications
try once more magnetic drums — Red nitrous odors
spatter out sound track dummy to circumstance brown
ankles — Ejaculated in stale underwear during execution, shirt flapping, pants slide — substitute excrement
slipping through legs Almighty God with two coordinates
immediately appropriate — We beg thy greased amber
memory for the process — Pubic District Court vibrating focus flesh — half-remembered rectum on volun-
tary fertilizer tanks — youth grouped along the borders

of melting ice — pearly spasms stirring skin instruc-
tion applicant — Dream flesh unexpectedly received
and transmitted on smell of sewage denominationally
molded to million dollar sale — at the earliest possible
moment ejaculate in stale underwear almighty encrusted
odor of three penises — Rapid calculations in room with
a thousand cots warning combat troops — ejaculated
with adequate military protection — First spurts touch
intestine drums of memory — toothache punch cards
muttering skin instructions written before explosion —
Other thoughts and memories referred from quivering
press statement — Adolescent lust broadcast over a
thousand cots — What awaits you on substitute flesh? —

Bradly was met by a white-coated Cockney attendant
he had known some years before in a London hotel room
by Earl's Court —

"How are we? — Leave your gear here" —

He led Bradly to a room with metal walls that smelled of
ozone and flash bulbs — Bradly stood naked under flood-
lights while the attendant took pictures — Full-length,
close-ups, following the divide line down under his nose
along his penis down to the rectum — The attendant
made measurements chartering his body and wrote the
numbers down in a note book —

"Full length now — That's right — Turn around —
Bend over — Lie down — Knees up to the chin now" —

Bradly sat in a booth and electrodes were attached to
his skull and penis and lips — He watched the wavering

lines on a view screen jump and dance as the attendant touched him adjusting the electrodes — Small microphones were attached to the two sides of his body the sounds recorded on two tape recorders — He heard the beating of his heart, the gurgle of shifting secretions and food, the rattle of breath and scratches of throat gristle — crystal bubbles in the sinus chambers magnified from the recorders — The attendant ran the tape from one recorder onto the other to produce the sound of feedback between the two body halves — a rhythmic twang — soft hammer of heartbeats pounding along the divide line of his body — He ejaculated in a wet dream of scenic railways —

The attendant led him to a cubicle with cot, washstand, toilet and shower — He sat down on the cot with the attendant and the pictures just taken were flashed on a view screen that formed one wall of the cubicle —

"And now how are *we*?" —

Flashed a series of composites made by cutting Bradly's image down the middle and fitting to half-images of the attendant — Discrepancies smoothed out by vibrating focus scalpel of the projector until one body was picture in a series of positions —

"Full length now — That's right — Turn around — Bend over — Lie down — Knees up to the chin now" —

Lines of brain wave and electric discharge from erogenous zones appeared on screen shifted back and forth across each other in permutating grills welding two brains and bodies together with vibrating feedback

— The screen shifted into a movie — Bradly was lying naked with the attendant on the cot — The divide line of his body burned with silver flash fire shifting in and out of the other body — rectal and pubic hairs slipping through composite flesh — penis and rectums merged on screen and bed as Bradly ejaculated — He woke up with other thoughts and memories in Cockney accent of that attendant standing there with a plate of food — saw himself eating on screen composite picture tasting food in the other mouth intestines moving and excrement squirming down to the divide line of another body —

Next day a Chinese attendant put Bradly through gymnastic positions on rings and hand-bars — the pictures repeated and cut in with composites of the attendant — tasting Chinese food the characters like neon in his throat — Other attendants: American, German, Spanish, Italian, Arab, Negro — composites of all the attendants cut in together shifted and permutated through his body —

Now for the story of Bradly's clothes — painted human skin half-inflated — worn amber rectum valve at base of the spine — Attendant took pictures — Close-ups wrote the ticket to yellow and blue dawn trailing Pan pipes — Slow discrepancies smooth unknown bodies out the projector until one body of sex position to the sound track melted — Now turn around and bend over for the story of absent legs up to your chin — Mirror line of his body burned with second halves shifting erect

penis and rectums — pulsing human skin stuck to faces
half-remembered — vibrating focus scalpel flashes broken glaciers and skin instructions — He woke up with
other thoughts i have touched in accent of the attendant
— Pools and canals reflected excrement mixed with
flowers — story of absent legs up the tarnished mirror
— In a rusty privy youth bends over — faint drums of
memory on his back — green boy of broken glaciers and
skin instructions — encrusted music woke in jungle
sounds of pools and canals cross the drenched lands
— clouds of color under orange gas flares — worn
amber memory of rectal swamps — Place exploded
in muscles — First spurts he could feel the other body
slipping all process together — Tentative being stuck to
his penis half-remembered — Hyphenated line of his
body shifting the applicant awoke — erect penis and
rectum different — the story of penny arcades and dirty
pictures — Unknown body slipped out of sex position
to grow on us — Hairs rub the halves — Electric waves
loosen you up a bit — other thoughts like luminous snow
falling through London hotel room accent::
   "How are we?" —
Timeless in flash bulbs here — Electrodes were
attached in bath cubicles and locker rooms — Body
burned with silver flash fire ejaculated in a few seconds
— Flash bulbs along the penis popped sound and image
flakes — The Other Half fades in mirror of beating
heart — feedback sound of wind through the trees —

The sexual acrobats balance a chair on high wires and ejaculate from the tension — They masturbate from bicycles on the wire from tumbler pyramids and in the air of trapeze acts — (In the penny arcade he got a hard-on looking at the pictures and Hans laughed pointing to his fly — "Let's make the roller coaster" he said — We were the only riders and as soon as the car started we slipped off our shorts — We came together in the first dip as train roared up the other side throwing blood back into our drained genitals shirts flapping over the midway — boys swinging from rings and bars jissom falling through dusty air of gymnasiums — slide down into the pool of moldy jockstraps and chlorine ejaculating from the shock of water — ferris wheels falling silently through tumescent flesh) —

Bulletin from Rewrite:: "The point of these exercises is to maintain a state of total alertness during sexual excitement — Try simple exercises first like jacking-off while balancing a chair — Driving full-speed on dangerous road — Flying plane — Performing precision operations at the same time like target shooting — So you can maintain alertness in the sex act and not be taken by the sex agents of the enemy who move to soften you up with sentimentality and sexual frustration to buy ersatz goo of their copy planet" —

The two boys got in the cub naked and took off climbing to an altitude of two thousand feet with dual controls — Hans put the plane into a spin while the other boy jacked him off — slipping, looping, ejaculated from the shift of blood came in with a hard-on for a spot landing — shooting coins flipped into the air cock pulsing in the afternoon sun —

Bradly moved into a maze of orgone accumulators — circular rooms lined with magnetic iron — He entered the maze with three other boys — In the first chamber they found iron frames on which they stretched their bodies in different positions of exposure — A vibrating silence hummed through the magnetized air — Tingling blue light touched his rectum and genitals playing along the divide line left a taste of metal in the mouth — Smaller accumulators with hose attachments turned directly on erogenous zones the message of orgasm received and transmitted — He passed now to other rooms with magnetized sex symbols on revolving walls — The three other boys were not there now — They had been replaced by precise copies in a substance like flexible amber molded from their bodies, the two halves welded together — Odors spattered out as electric vibrators sidled the dummies toward him — smell of rectal mucus, sweat, carbolic soap, jissom, and stale underwear over clean young flesh — From transistor radios in the throat drifted all the sex words of his wet dreams and masturbating afternoons — The penis canal was a jointed iron tube covered by sponge rubber — Pubic hairs of fine wire crackled with blue sparks — The dummy cocks rose in response to magnetic attraction of the wall symbols

— "Bend over" Bradly stretched himself over an iron frame — The dummy that was precisely *me* penetrated him with a slow magnetic movement — Tingling blue fire shot through his genitals transfixed by the magnetic revolving wall symbols — The vibrator switched on as the others watched — idiot lust drinking his jissom from screen eyes — Sucking cones of color that dissolved his penis in orgasms of light —

"Better than 'the real thing'? — There is no real thing — Maya — Maya — It's all show business" —

Picture flesh — felt the penny arcade in his crotch — fly full of dust, pulled up his pants — back into drained genitals — Intersection of these exercises spattered light on total alertness during sexual flight — naked for physical riders as stomach muscles exploded in altered pressure — "Wheee" the sex act soften you up to buy death in orgasm of copy planet — Other side throwing the orgone accumulators — take over all sexual apparatus — smell of moldy jockstraps and chlorine ejaculating —

Bulletin from Rewrite: "Sex is electric output of the organism in message received and transmitted — Sex words evoke a dangerous that is to say *other* half of the body — Precise attraction — So what is ejaculation? Shooting at target — The orgasm is a flash bulb that takes your picture — Charge of course is electrical hose attachments they turned on — Rusty image of a separate being — feed-back noise of accumulators — You

see the caustic layers of organic material? That is what
they need from earth::: Three other boys to make more
marble flesh, ass and genitals vibrated by the iridescent
attendant — Orgasm death is to other half of the body
— So what is ejaculation? substitute patterns twisting
through electrical pubic hairs, feed-back throat hum,
recorder jack-off — Hose attachment substitutes all
cocks — They turned off nervous system to the metal
ray — switch on off body sound magnetic patterns —
Where 'the passengers' came together recorders jack-off
in flash coordinates — back into your drained genitals
all junk and cool circuits — Virus punch cards waiting
before organism — 8276 runs out in iridescent road
naked with a hard-on shooting torture films — Maintain
your alertness in eyes glinting with slow fish lust — sex
agents of the enemy who color sex words with ersatz
goo — pass along the orgone in throat gristle alternating body — take a simple tape from one hum between
the hose attachments — Orgones through iron repetition setting off word tape response in the other nervous
system — image of a separate being touched lungs penis
and electric body hairs — now passes along orgone in
throat gristle alternating sex words to color:: 'Bradly'
entered the controlled prisoner body — tingling blue
light in a simple tape from one drifting hum for the
act between hose attachments — layers of organic material rubbing off the encrusted odors of three other
boys and so a 'conversation' that has ass and genitals

spelt out in his mouth — ejaculation output of control
system received and transmitted — Sex words evoke
the other half of the body open shirt flapping viscera
— So what is ejaculation in the throat? torture films
of course — that is electric eyes glinting with insect
lust — alternating amber beads and little tunes taken
centuries to accrete — hum and taste of metal in the
beads — Stroking music from hose attachments they
turn virus punch cards to magnetic patterns — past
time energy units — That is to say a *dead land* — 8276
whispered through iron from pale word dust stirring tape
— marble parasite image of a separate being — dream
flesh held together by sex words" —

The Sex Musicians drift through streets of music trailing melodious propositions — In bath cubicles of a rotting
pier over tide flats a boy played the jade flute while Bradly screwed him following the notes out of his body into
birdcalls lapping water and distant music on the trade
winds — In a cool blue room sucked off a clarinet player
to a climax of wind chimes, subway dawns, and clicking
turnstiles — Under red fuck lights bent over a black hotel
chair beating a drum as a Mexican boy with street dust
in his hair fucked him to the drumbeats — these sounds
recorded and carried through streets of music — The
Sex Musicians drift in and out of combos as colored light
pulses to their instruments — on a rotting pier: "Here
goes" — Bradly bent over a chair and spread ass cheeks
— Smoke finger fucked him to drumbeats — as colored

light pulsed through old photos turning sex words and singing dust — ghost rectums drum and pipe to silence from satellite rings — The units turn faster and faster through streets of music trailing word dust over the tide flats — Faster played the flute — Here goes word dust planet — his body into birdcalls and distant music on the wind — "I wanta screw you" in a cool room with rose wallpaper — faces naked of word dust in a shower of ruined suburbs — rings of Saturn in the morning sky as a Mexican boy stirred slow rectum gate — "Want screw you — Over" — "Here goes" — Spin the walls and orbit sex words back to color — Played the flute in flash bulb of orgasm — tarnished mirror of subway dawns in the bath cubicle — "Bend over" — sex words back to slow movement of rivers — young faces lapping water — wind chimes from Attic frieze — drumbeats of ghost people — "You is coming?" into birdcalls and jungle sounds — In red light felt his pants slide — Cock flipped out and up — Beat a drum on knees like *como perros* — "Slow, deep, Johnny" — The notes twisting Johnny's thighs — candle shadow bent over a chair — Fucked to music from the casino — flicker faces and bodies fade-out in old photos — toilet smell of subway dawns — Greek vases give out slow crystal music of phallic statues and limestone centuries — Played the flute with fingers light and cold over my naked body — City sounds drift through a blue room under the slate roof — penny arcades on the rotting pier — "Here goes" — flesh sparks to drumbeats — Played the flute faster and faster — limestone flesh stirring in old movies — Hairs rub the rose wallpaper — "You wanta screw me?" trailing flash bulb of orgasm in other flesh — "You is coming?" — pale smell of dawn rectums over a chair — Questions pulse to their instruments — rings of Saturn in the morning sky — Fucked to ebbing carbon dioxide — "Mr Bradly Mr Martin" is smell of subway dawns — Played the flute with fingers light and cold in the door — City sounds drift through the final ape of history —

"Remember i was the movies, the door flash bulb of orgasm — sex words in the cold Spring air — pale smell of dawn shirt — distant proposition in bath cubicles, there the boy played a flute, ten-year-old keeping watch — cracked out of his body into birdcalls and vaudeville voices — distant music to crown a God with street dust — in the gutter urine sounds — naked brain stranded in the tide flats — Fade-out overtakes a rotting pier — Young faces turn faster and faster through dead nitrous streets — open shirt in the bath cubicle — The street blew rain — You is coming in the death trauma?" —

Distant coffin pulses to their instruments — odor of naked rectums on the rotting pier — "Here goes" in his crotch — Here goes word dust planet — faces naked of old dream — Rings of Saturn in the morning sky melted sex words back to color — Tarnished mirror of subway dawns lying there — Last round over — sex words back to the trade winds — rose wallpaper bleeding dream — Clicking turnstiles left no address — For i have known street dust in his hair — "Isn't time is there left to give you" — A boy waits on the rotting pier — Departed have left distant music from the casino — over the water "good night" in old photo — sleep breath under the slate roof — solitude of morning stirring old limestone flesh — Leaning say: "You is coming? — ebbing carbon dioxide — Man, like good bye then — Remember i was movies — Played the flute in last terrace of the garden — City sounds drift through a blue room — Left no address — For i have known arcades on the rotting pier — Isn't time is there left? — Played the flute faster and faster to you — Sex words drifted slowly out into the cold Spring air — pale smell of dawn in the door — Played the flute with fingers fading" —

hands of light in the morning sky — rotting mummy moved out at dawn — The doctor on stage — end of the line —

"All right, doctor, before stranded in the tide flats indications enough — i told you i would heal scars — i am the big fix talking of orbit on scar impressions — Suddenly shut off in the gutter urine sounds, all the Garden of Delights — God of Panic piping blue notes — invisible intervention — last round over — last parasite muttering there:: 'Man, like good bye then'" —

Memory pictures and singing dust went up in slow motion — Scandinavia outhouse skin forgotten — rings

of Saturn in the morning sky — errand boy of subway
dawns remitted back to the trade winds — slow silence
ebbing from centuries — rose wallpaper bleeding youth
body without a shadow — smell of dawn flesh in a privy
— precise identity fading out — And these boys circumstance the orgasm leaving — beat a drum twisting
Johnny's healed scars — over the pass without doing
pictures — all toilet smell at this point — tarnished
mirror through dying peoples — words back to the trade
winds — errand boy remitted — leaning say "Good bye
— fading my name — silence in tarnished offices — last
rotting pier — Isn't time — the Doctor on stage — end
of the line — Played the flute in empty room, fingers
fading — Doctor on stage — Played the flute in last
errand boy — Closing — Left no address" —

"All right, doctor, before silence indications enough
— i told you i would come — Silence healed scars" —

Bradly stood naked with ten subjects in a room
lined with metal mirrors — They helped each other
into loose fitting cellophane envelopes — A trap door
opened in the floor of the cubicle — and the subjects lowered themselves into the sense withdrawal
tank and floated a few feet apart in darkness with
no sound but* feedback from the two halves of ten

---

*The most successful method of sense withdrawal is the immersion
tank where the subject floats in water at blood temperature, sound and
light withdrawn — Loss of body outline, awareness and location of the
limbs occurs quickly, giving rise to panic in many American subjects —

bodies permutated to heartbeat body music vibrating through the tank — Body outlines extend and break here — The stretching membrane of skin dissolves — Sudden taste of blood in his throat as gristle vaporizes and the words wash away and the halves of his body separated like a mold — Fish sperm drifted through the tank in silent explosions — Skeletons floated and crab parasites of the nervous system and the grey cerebral dwarf made their last attempt to hold prisoners in spine and brain coordinates — screaming "You can't — You can't — You can't" — Screaming without a throat without speech centers as the brain split down the middle and the feed-back sound shut off in a blast of silence.

His body extend and break here — He watched the wavering stretching membrane of skin jump and dance to rhythmic feed-back noise from the electrodes — Magnified sperm drifted through water tape in silent explosions — flash fire shifting hairs through composite outline — a sudden taste of blood on screen as Bradly vaporized the words — Other thoughts and memories

---

Subjects frequently report feeling that another body is floating half-in and half-out of the body in the first part — Experiments in sense withdrawal using the immersion tanks have been performed by Doctor Lily in Florida — There is another experimental station in Oklahoma — So after fifteen minutes in the tank these marines scream they are losing outlines and have to be removed — I say put two marines in the tank and see who comes out — Science — Pure science — So put a marine and his girl friend in the tank and see who or what emerges —

separated like a mold — Mirror line feed-back from erect penis to heart beat rhythms half-remembered dissolving skin instructions — Cellophane membrane over absent legs outline his body with second halves — Encrusted music separated like a mold — First spurts he could feel outline together — hyphenated line of amoebic process — Hairs rub the skin membrane jump "I wanta screw you" from the electrodes —

"Here goes Johnny — His body extend and break here — One track out" — Clear erection stretching membrane of skin — Film track feed-back noise of rectal mucus and carbolic soap — Pale heartbeats through his body — all process in the throat — Sick dawn smell of sperm drifting through water on all cocks in silent explosion — genital night of black fruit that grows dream flesh — Heartbeats wrote the numbers through his body: blood in throat gristle "That's right — His body extend and break here — Knees up to the chin now" —

Bulletin from the Rewrite Department:: "Now look, you jokers — We are not here to rewrite G.O.D. (Garden Of Delights) you got it? Watch those fuckers — Still on the old evacuation plan" —

Blind crab parasites of the nervous system attempt to hold prisoners in idiot green boys — throat gristle sex words on two halves of the body — Sucker paws vibrating the spinal column — Now screaming without fingers shared meals as the brain split down the middle contract of rectum flight — metal hairs falling like dry leaves — crystal body music vibrating the two recorders — A Chinese attendant put the crab parasites through rings of Saturn — "You can't" — Now screaming with composite attendant like neon in the throat — worn amber body music — They fade out in old photos here — Neon fingers magnified present time tape in silent explosions — past time units whirl evening faces into drifting smoke and dead land of black lagoons — a slow whisper in his brain — The units turn faster and faster — Full length now — Washed green light from penis and lips — His body attendant break here — Here goes Word Dust Planet and crab parasites —

("Now for me — The story of two halves — other parasite possessing every possible out for this painting — first it's Symbiosis Door Con — There are no good relationships — There are no good words — I wrote silences — a storm leaving his brain centers — evening faces into the ponds — I wept in a land of black lagoons and skies — crumbling stone villas — green-black fruit that grows in jars — lonely lemur calls in ruined courtyards — ghost hands at paneless windows — ancient beauty in stone shapes") —

Hospital smells and the wooden numbness of anesthesia — He saw his body on an operating table split down the middle — A doctor with forceps was extracting crab parasites from his brain and spine — and squeezing green fish parasites from the separated flesh —

"My God what a mess — The difficulty is with two halves — other parasites will invade sooner or later — First it's symbiosis, then parasitism — The old symbiosis con — Sew him up nurse" —

the
black fruit

Lykin lay gasping in the embrace of the fishboy who was gently tugging at the space suit, running delicious cold fingers down his spine — Finally it found a hold and ripped the tough material in one violent tear right up the back — Lykin, who had so far not been exposed to the atmosphere of the planet, found himself choking as though ice claws were tearing his insides apart — A great smothering blackness descended on him and he fell back in the boy's arms, unconscious —

He was drifting through space, wafted by currents of glowing gases — Myriads of floating forms passed in front of him some familiar and others alien — For a moment he was back in the brown canals of Mars in the grip of a giant clam, which takes a week to satisfy its consuming sex habit and spits out its unfortunate victim covered with its discharge like a gelatinous pearl on the dry red sands —

Thousands of voices muttered out of the darkness, twittering creatures pulling and tugging at him and dancing on their way leaping from soaring black heights into deep blue chasms trailing the neon ghost writing of Saturn through vast wells of empty space — From an enormous distance he heard the golden hunting horns of the Aeons and he was free of a body traveling in the echoing shell of sound as herds of mystic animals galloped through dripping primeval forests, pursued by the silver hunters in chariots of bone and vine —

Lonely lemur calls whispered in the walls of silent obsidian temples in a land of black lagoons, the ancient rotting kingdom of Jupiter — smelling the black berry smoke drifting through huge spider webs in ruined courtyards under eternal moonlight — ghost hands at the paneless windows weaving memories of blood and war in stone shapes — A host of dead warriors stand as petrified statues in vast charred black plains — Silent ebony eyes turned toward a horizon of always, waiting with a patience born of a million years, for the dawn that never rises — Thousands of voices muttered the beating of his heart — gurgling sounds from soaring lungs trailing the neon ghost writing — Lykin lay gasping in the embrace can only be reached through channels running to naked photographic process — molded by absent memory, by vibrating focus scalpel of the fishboy gently in a series of positions running delicious cold fingers "Stand here — Turn around — Bend" — Ripped the tough material in brain waves — Lykin who had not so far been on screen of the planet found himself choking,

the two brains tearing his insides apart — Smothering
from the four halves and he fell back in the boy's arms
naked on the space bed wafted by currents glowing in
and out shifting forms passed in front of him — Body
burned with silver flash for a moment he was back in the
brown rectal hairs of a giant clam — halves shifting and
permutating out of the darkness — He drifted off into
deep blue chasms and memories of Saturn — vast faces
and pieces of distance — He heard the golden medium
and was free of his body — Touched hunting horns of the
Aeons silver hunters in chariots with flowers — picture
temples in a land of black food — ghost hands twisted
together in stone shapes —

Found himself choking as unknown bodies tear his
insides apart — Wafted by currents of glowing halves
shifting mist in electric waves — He was back in a
giant clam which spits out its memory skin discharge
like gelatinous rectal swamps fermenting darkness —

He drew the black berry smoke deep into his lungs
and symbol language of an ancient rotting kingdom
bloomed in his brain like Chinese flowers — myriads
of floating sex symbols and the bronze flesh familiar —
Now thousands of voices muttered and pulsed through
him pulling tearing — His body trailed the neon ghost
writing as the two halves separated and sex words exploded to empty space — Lonely lemur calls whispered
his knees up to the chin — smelling black movement
of the other in ruined courtyards — slow color orgasm

under ghost hands reflected on silent obsidian walls —
The ancient rotting kingdom softened and glowed with
black berry smoke drifting through pubic hairs under
eternal moonlight to dust and shredded memories —
pale word dust stirring spider webs from penis and lips
— weaving memories of blood in his throat — rectum
naked to color focus of the fish language running delicious cold fingers rubbing off encrusted odors in slow
turns of amber — glowing torture films in a land of black
food — Ghost apes tear his insides apart — He was in
a ruined garden under two moons — one red the other
a pale clear green — He could see pulsing black fruit
growing in crystal jars — In front of him stood a young
man molded in polished black bronze with streaks of
green patina on the high cheekbones — From the lips,
half-open in a dreamy cruel smile, drifted a faint smell
of decay as if he were rotting inside the bronze mold
— With a slow gesture he led Bradly along a path of
cracked flagstones — Bradly saw that he had webbed
feet leaving prints of silver slime that glittered in the
moonlight — They came to a summerhouse of circular
shape overgrown with vines from which dangled the
black fruit in crystal jars — The summerhouse was lined
with a glistening black substance traced with phosphorescent writing in blue metal that filled the room with
a pulsing blue twilight — The guide focused projector
pupils talking in color blasts to some other being Bradly
could feel stirring response in the liquid medium of his

body — Color flashed through his body in chirps and giggles shifting to slow visceral pulses — Still talking to the other inside, the bronze boy put slow cold hands on Bradly's shoulders — As the metal hands drew him forward his clothes shredded to dust — He caught a faint whiff of decay like tropical fruit on the wind — His body melted from within — The bronze mold sank into his flesh like a black seal — The other moved back seeking some precise coordinate point with the blue wall symbols — The room hummed and vibrated — Pubic hairs of black wire crackled in blue sparks and a quivering blue line divided his body — Bradly felt his own body split down the middle like a cracked egg the two halves rubbing against each other, held together by some sticky gelatinous substance that leaked out the crack and dripped into the obsidian platform where he stood — From the open bronze mold emerged a transparent green shape crisscrossed with pulsing red veins, liquid screen eyes swept by color flashes — a smell of sewage and decay breathing from years of torture films, orgasm death in his black eyes glinting with slow fish lust of the swamp mud — Long tendril hands penetrated Bradly's broken body caressing the other being inside through the soft intestines into the pearly genitals rubbing centers of orgasm along his spine up to the neck — Exquisite toothache pain shot through his nerves and his body split down the middle — Sex words exploded to a poisonous color vapor that cut off his breath — The floor dropped away beneath his feet and he fell into black water with the green creature twisted deep into his flesh, vine tendrils twisted round the throat — Green flares exploded his brain — He ejaculated in twisting fish spasms knees up to the chin — a taste of blood as fish syllables tore gills in his throat — He was breathing now in a silent medium — slow color orgasms deep in the iridescent lagoon — long tendril pubic hairs caressing other memory, vibrated dead genitals — weaving orgasm deep in his testicles — twisting in slow marble ghost hands — gathering stone shape —

He moved through shadow alleys and canals of the lagoon city — fish smells and dead eyes in doorways — sound of fear — dark street life of a place forgotten — slow memory bubbles bursting in his brain — broken picture warnings — grey foetal lampreys along the canal walls, crab police with magnetic claws, dungeons where the prisoners are broken to insect forms under cruel idiot fingers of the Green Guards, slim elegant men with smooth brown flesh the color of an eel's side hand ending in a crystal bulb and a dripping stinger: the Orgasm Sting that twists a victim to quivering pulp eaten by cruising Mugwumps with beaks of black bone and purple penis flesh — The Mugwumps milked for the orgasm meal by vampire women embalmed in predigested sperm, faces of smooth green alabaster giving off a smell of phosphorus as they sip spinal fluid through straws — He felt now the weakness of death in his fading larval flesh — He needed "The Slow Boat To China" — He found his way to "The Flower Market" where the nobles cruise languidly in gondolas of paper-thin black wood watching slow color bubbles of the fishboys climb to the surface and burst in flares of iridescent propositions — An answer vibrated down through the water:: "Two Black Fruit" — Thin and no conditions to bargain he bubbled back: "It's a deal" surfaced and slid into a gondola where a young man lay naked on a bed of flowers — His legs were amputated at the hip and the stumps glowed with slow metal fires — The fishboy lay down beside the young man — His translucent green penis rose pulsing in the moonlight — Negro boys the color of glistening black tar beat little drums from a dais in the center of the lagoon — Lonely lemur calls drifted from islands of swamp cypress — Slow rocket burst over the water — They rolled on the flower bed crushing out clouds of odor — color fingers through his larval flesh feeling along his fish spine — Spasms shook his body and green erogenous slime poured from glands under his gills covering the two bodies with a viscous bubble — softening flesh and bones to jelly — He sank into the client — Spines rubbed and merged in little shocks of electric pleasure — He was sucked into other testicles — A soft pearly grotto closed round him pulsing tighter and tighter — He melted to sperm fingers caressing the penis inside — Quivering contractions as he squirmed through pink tumescent flesh to a crescendo of drumbeats shot out in a green flare falling into slow convolutions of underwater sleep —

Shifting dominion of the other inside — bronze mold blooms slowly from old dream odors trailing sweat of genitals before daybreak — slow orgasm in green roses — What you have loved remains stirring response in the fading body — naked pubic hairs caressing dream and the dreamer weaving orgasm in his ghost hands —

Coffin put slow cold hands on Bradly — body split down the middle like sunlight and shadow — (Have you lost your dog?) — leaked out the crack of dead nitrous flesh — Sex words exploded to a poisonous sky — raw testicles twisting in slow marble — the evening you hear shredded to dust — last terrace of the garden in rotting fruit — dawn whisper knees up to the chin — Who is speaking? — Memory vibrated dead genitals without names — crackling paper shredded to dust —

"For i have known fires — Isn't time is there left, cool finger running on our ticket that exploded, larval circumstances at far end of the creek? And these dogs knew nothing shifting the dominion of circumstances — What bronze mold blooms in aging roots? — response in the fading body beside you?" —

Could give no response in words — Like wind his body melted from within — crumpled cloth flapping wind —

Could have indications enough man lay on a bed of flowers — The stumps glowed with slow metal good bye on vacant lots — smell of healed and half-healed genitals — penis pulsing in the dog rotation — the bronze sweetness of khaki pants — feeling cool fingers on his naked dollars — larval erogenous face spurting out through orgasm —

"Talk, Face" —

"I'm just a vagabond along his spine and feeling well as you, darling — a biologic from viscous bubble with the St. Louis suburb" — I had a dog rubbed and merged to drumbeats open shirt flapping — shadow eggs through the other penis slowly reformed in delicious naked boy — (See that the client is satisfied this time?) —

'Twas good bye on the line — since you went slowly out of old dream odors into space —

Bradly's canoe of paper-thin black wood grounded on an island of swamp cypress — He strapped on his camera gun and walked along ancient paths and stone bridges over canals where the fish people swirled sending up color bubbles of orgasm that broke on the iridescent surfaces — He caught the twittering chirping sound of the tree-frog people like wind chimes in the trees and one of them leaped down from an overhanging branch and attached itself to his chest with sucker paws — It was about two feet in length of a translucent green color — The obsidian eyes were all pupil and mirrored a pulsing blood suction to rhythms of a heart clearly visible in the transparent flesh — A network of veins filtered through the green substance like red neon tubes suffusing the frog boy with a phosphorescent pink light — The mouth above a small pointed chin was of glistening black gristle that dripped a pale yellow saliva — Others leaped down from the dark cypress chirping and giggling — Sucker fingers unstrapped his gun and pulled down his shorts — Naked he lay down in warm swamp mud that gave slowly under him stirring a black smell of decay — He felt the soft mouth close over his penis and hang there pulsing, sucking his body to a vacuum — Earth and water stones and trees poured into him and spurted out broken pictures — The creature dropped off and rolled itself into a foetal ball of sleep — Bradly picked up another and held it in his hands — The creature vibrated like a radio — Little shocks ran up Bradly's arms — The frog boy kicked in spasms ejaculating spurts of black liquid that gave off a musty smell of damp roots, jasmine and sewage — Now he hung limp in sleep eyes veiled by green lids like a black pond covered with delicate algae — And Bradly fell slowly into the deep uterine sleep, frog boys curled between his legs and under his arms and on his chest streaked with iridescent slime from their sucker paws —

He woke to drifting golden notes of distant hunting horns — He sat up — The frog people were gone — The horns were louder and clearer now — Into the clearing where he sat burst a pack of dogs with human skin and faces — The animals were the size and shape of small greyhounds — They surrounded him snarling and yapping — A young man appeared standing in a weightless medium so that his feet made no impression in the swamp mud — Naked except for a quiver of silver arrows and a bow, he radiated a calm disdainful authority — He lifted a slow hand and the dogs were silent — He looked at Bradly with something too neutral to be called contempt and spoke in English: "I see that the blockade is broken and we expect such visitors — Street boys fed on scraps and garbage" —

The dogs were smiling and whimpering now rubbing against Bradly, squirming and ejaculating under his fingers — The young man looked at the dogs and he looked at Bradly — He smiled a slow smile old as the rotting kingdom — "Well, Mr Bradly, we shall see" — He picked up Bradly's camera gun — Looked at it from a vast distance and dropped it into the mud — Several bearded naked huntsmen had entered the clearing carrying long golden horns —

"Come, Mr Bradly — There is much for you to learn and quickly — Otherwise you must assume some form acceptable to the Old Controller — Your present form is quite intolerable, of course — No, you won't need your clothes" —

They came to a palace of crumbling stone covered by trailing vines from which dangled the glistening black fruit in jars — a ruined garden decorated with phallic statues — The Prince stopped before two marble youths kneeling in the act of sodomy their faces turned up to the

eternal moonlight remote and dreamy with slow pleasure of
limestone centuries — As Bradly watched they shifted in
a slow movement and a pearl stood out on the boy's erect
penis, glittered in the moonlight — The bronze statue of a
masturbating boy yielded a drop of phosphorescent black
ichor — "That is where the Black Fruit comes from —
Then it is grafted into the vines and it must ripen in the
jars until it is ready" — There were other statues of silver
and gold and porcelain all yielding the slow fruit of time
— They were walking now along ruined porticoes where
youths of translucent amber caressed each other stroking
out encrusted odors and whiffs of music —

all members
are worst
a century

"Ward Island is afflicted by a disease so terrible
that the entire ceremonial life of the natives revolves
around fear of the disease and precautions to avoid it
— The onset is sudden — The victim is seen abusing
himself publicly while addressing some unseen presence with endearing terms — He becomes dirty and
emaciated — In the final stages he is literally eaten
alive by his invisible partner and subsides into the state
of an insect larva paralyzed, slobbering and covered by
a caustic green slime that seeps from the rectum — In
this condition they are carried out into the mud flats by

the superstitious natives and left to the mercy of land crabs — (Note: This practice has been forbidden by the resident governor) — The island is almost level with the water and surrounded by shallow lagoons so that boats must anchor about two miles off shore" —

So writes an early traveler — It was evening when the boat anchored and i could see nothing of the island — i had my equipment for the expedition packed and my boy Jimmy helped me to load it into a gondola of thin black wood — The boatman was a young man with the lithe frame of a Malay and bright red lips — He kept his eyes cast down with the closed beaten expression of dying peoples — He propelled us through iridescent oily water that gave off a rank odor under his strokes — We tied up at a rotting pier that extended out into the shallow water — Sting rays and crabs stirred clouds of black mud — We were met at the pier by a middle-aged Dutchman who was proprietor of the only hotel — He led the way along a wooden catwalk to the hotel which was a three story structure of split bamboo on high stilts over the swampy ground — Darkness was falling and after unpacking we descended to the veranda and had a whisky with the proprietor — i asked him about the disease — "It is here in the head — So they are scaring themselves to the death — i am now twenty years here — In other times we used to export much fruit that grow here — So a special fruit black with such a taste — Then these stupid stories come out and the island is now quarantine" —

When i told him of my plan to make an expedition to the interior of the island he said it would be impossible to obtain any native guides or bearers since the disease is supposed to have its origin in the swamps and jungles of the interior —

July 7, 1862 — Saw something of the island and the natives — Surrounding the hotel is a village criss-crossed with catwalks over the mud flats — The entire island seems to consist of swamp delta — The natives are silent and sad conveying the impression of faded photos — As the proprietor predicted we were unable to enlist any native guides or boatmen — With his help we have purchased one of the flat gondolas — with an outrigger attachment and mats of split bamboo we can pitch our tent over the boat — We will start for the interior tomorrow —

July 8, 1862 — We got an early start poling and paddling our canoe up the river — There seems to be little wild life about — nothing but swamp with here and there islands of swampy ground and cypress — At twilight we tied up to a cypress stump and put out our night lines — After a meal of tinned food we spread the mat of split bamboo and lay down under mosquito netting — The night pressed against our naked bodies like a damp mold spread to jungle sounds and lapping water — Am writing this at dawn —

July 9, 1962 — Disease of the image track — The onset is sudden voices screaming a steady stream

— I had forgotten unseen force of memory pictures
— Muttering slobbering outhouse skin seeps from his
rectum — island of dying peoples surrounded by shallow lagoons — The boatman smiles — Wired red lips
entered the '20s in drag from the Ward Island natives —
slow motion through iridescent oily water — Absent tenants stood naked — Ghost disease spattered on victim
— Muttering to himself interrogates substance of the
other invisible presence — He becomes dirty with the
speed of "Want it" — Tentative being eaten alive by
empty flesh of insect larvae — Human form been covered by caustic green slime — Faces sucked into other
land that is almost level with the water — Passengers
are picked up by flicker — It was early morning when
mummy fingers goosed his ass — round gate from burning sex skin — wind voices beside the man with lithe
frame of a Malay — Sullen female impersonators listen
— the faces all forgotten — Orgasm of memory strokes
gave off a rank smell under his law — Prisoners in the
terminal case carried to crabs — mummy flesh over
middle-aged deflated skin — death's own boy — talk
to switchblade of bamboo — Business dissolved in
smoke and errand boy of such a taste — "All right,
Doctor, quarantined" he gestures at indications enough
"i told you i would come naked on our beds — Healed
scars cry from Jimmy saying he had to pass without
doing pictures — i found enemy all right — Suddenly
shut off excitement" —

July 9, 1862 — We pulled in our night lines and found a large fish with a smooth yellow skin — The meat was soft and phosphorescent and had a metallic taste — In the late afternoon we grounded the boat on a sand bar and got out to bathe in a shallow pool that came up to our ankles — As Jimmy was rubbing soap on my back we noticed an orchid covered by brilliant green and red flowers hanging over the water — As we touched the plant long tendrils covered by erectile hairs stung our necks and shoulders — A burning itch ran over my body exploding in rectum and genitals like liquid fire — With an animal cry Jimmy forced his soapy penis into my rectum — We fell rolling and i ejaculated into the soft swamp mud — We lay there panting — Simultaneously we were both attacked by a scalding diarrhea — The burning itch swelled our tongues and lips — Clawing screaming we twisted in water brown with excrement, ejaculating again and again — bone wrenching spasm that popped silver light in our eyes —

July 11? 12? 13? 1862 — Sinking deeper and deeper into sexual deliriums — obsessed by fantasies of hanging and death in orgasm — Once in India i saw a young man hanged — His loin cloth slipped off in the drop and he hung there naked twisting in bone wrenching spasms, ejaculated again and again his feet rustling weeds under the gallows —

We are both emaciated now — The entire pool is brown with our excrement — Is Jimmy really there?

— He is turning into a phantom woman with red hair and green flesh — i woke in the moonlight to find her entwined around my body — She opened her mouth and tendrils covered by stinging red hairs squirmed out penetrating my mouth and throat, feeling into my rectum and penis, twisting around the spine touching electric centers of orgasm in the neck that popped silver light in my eyes — The creature was pointing now to the tie-up rope that trailed from our boat — In a flash i realized that if i followed her obvious suggestion i would be eaten body and soul by the orchid people — i summoned the strength to resist — Tomorrow i will make an attempt to leave the orchid pool —

July 11, 12, 13, 1962 — Present Time leads to an understanding of knowing and open food in the language of life — the entire dia through noose in four letter words — It will be seen that "havingness" muttering in the night — Went back other identities — Remember my medium of false identities? — All that links the murders is Game Hate Box — Opponents are future time 1962 — The donar was released folk singer Logos — Uncontrolled flash bulbs popped — It is a grand feeling — Language of virus (which *is* these experiments) really necessary? Message of life written "We have come to eat"? ? —

i have said the basic time to go — Everyone here:: knowing officers at the delicate lilt — all dia through noose with just the right shade of absolute need — condition empty but process known as "overwhelming"

— Flak holes told him that "havingness" unknown
and hostile land — The Cycle of Action: the Cycle
of Venus — sickness of hunger — flesh naked for the
delicate lilt — clear fingers in stale New Zealand —
Assailant of sleep in the naked Panama night was such
a deal — Shadow passing and transparent lodging is
not done abruptly — *Unknown and hostile land* — *we*
are all parasites of the area — i have said basic time to
go — Wind of morning disintegrates Present Time —
    July 14, 1862 — i woke up in the silent dripping
dawn — i was lying beside the boat and as i watched
little grey men played on the deck hoisting invisible
sails — They formed a chorus line and danced away into
the dawn mist pointing as they faded out to a dangling
vine — i got up and stripped leaves and bark from the
vine and brewed a tea — i drank the tea from a tin cup
— Almost immediately i vomited so violently that my
body seemed to crack open — i leaned against the boat
panting and gasping — Slowly my whole being fused to
incandescent resistance — A young male face of daz-
zling beauty moved in and i was free of my body — The
orchid girl floated over the pool toward me and i rushed
her stuttering back sex words that tore her tentative
substance like bullets — i caught a final glimpse of her
agonized face eaten by caustic slime — A scream faded
out in birdcalls and jungle sounds and lapping water —
    July 14, 1962 — Present Time — "i told you i would
come with tower fire — vomited the ghost food moved

noose — Four letters at dawn fell apart in 'havingness' — muttering absent bodies hanged after being milked of identities — Remember identities swirled through slow motion all that links the green amphibious creature as they rolled future time 1962 — I told you the skin underneath flash bulbs was healed scars — male spirits trapped in dead nitrous flesh — aroused courage to pass without doing picture — i saw now forgotten memory controlling Game Hate Box — Opponents in green mummy get out here — Donar popped — It is a grand feeling — Half-healed scars peeling off these experiments between mutual erections — other flesh flapping through noose" —

"Just remember i was fish smells and absolute need — condition empty but know the way to overwhelm — Flak holes told him khaki pants shifted ejaculating hostile land — flash of rectums naked in whiffs suddenly clicked to color — Invisible passenger took my skin off in sheets — burned like ice" —

"i told you i would come — Won't be much screen now — i have said basic time to go — Wind of morning disintegrates Present Time —"

combat
troops in
the area

As the shot of apomorphine cut through poisons of Minraud he felt a tingling burning numbness — his body coming out of deep freeze in the Ovens — Then viscera exploded in vomit — The mold of his body cracked and he stepped free — a slender green creature, his hands ended in black claws covered with fine magnetic wires that extended up the inner arm to the elbow — He was wearing a gas mask to breathe carbon dioxide of enemy planet — antennae ears tuned to all voices of the city, each voice classified on a silent switchboard — green disk eyes with pupils of a pale electric blue — body of a hard green substance like flexible jade — back brain and spine burned with blue sparks as messages crackled in and out —

"Shift body halves — Vibrate flesh — Cut tourists" —

The instructions were filed on transparent sheets waiting sound formation as he slid them into mind screens of the planet — He put on his broken body like an overcoat — Silent and purposeful under regulating center of the back brain, he went into a bar and stood at the pinball machine, his hard green core sinking into the other players writing the resistance message with magnetic wires — The machine clicked and tilted in his hands, electric purpose cutting association lines — Enemy plans exploded in a burst of rapid calculations — Vast insect calculating machine of the enemy flashed the warning —

"Combat troops in the area" —

Combat troops to fight the Insect People of Minraud for control of this planet — Crab guards gathered around the machine, sliding forward to feel with white-hot claws for the human spots of weakness opened up by The Green Boy of the Divide Line — The crab guard was not finding the spots — He pressed closer breathing the dry heat of Minraud, while flying scorpion men sank stingers into empty flesh, injecting the oven poison — Too late the crab guard saw the jade body and the disk eyes pounding deep into his nerve centers — The eyes converged in a single beam forcing the guard back like a fire hose — The pressure suddenly shut off as the eyes vibrated in air hammer synchronization — pounded the guard to writhing fragments —

The Scorpion Electricals buzzed away screaming — His converging eye beams exploded them in the air and they fell in a shower of blue sparks — He was standing over the green boy spitting words into his nervous system —

"Show me your controller — quickly or i kill" —

The green boy nodded — An old woman appeared on screen spitting phosphorescent hate, screaming for her shattered guard — the Lord of Time surrounded by files and calculating machines, word and image bank of a picture planet — It was over in a few stuttering seconds — Under vibrating pounding eyebeams that cut flesh and bone with electric needles her image blurred and exploded in a burst of nitrous film smoke — where she had stood a vast low-pressure area — winds of the earth through archives of Time as film and newspapers shredded to dust in a tornado of years and centuries —

"Word falling — Photo falling — Time falling — Break through in Grey Room" — Combat troops antennae crackling static orders poured inflexible violence along the middle line of body — took the planet in a few seconds cutting virus troops with stuttering light guns — galactic shock troops who never colonize — clicking tilting through pinball machines of the earth — lighting up the Board Books and dictating message of total resistance —

"Shift linguals — Cut word lines — Vibrate tourists — Free doorways — Pinball led streets — Word falling — Photo falling — Break through in Grey Room — Towers, open fire" —

Electric static orders poured through nerve circuits in stuttering seconds —

"Body halves off — appropriate instrument pinball color circuits — Sex words exploded in photo flash — Nitrous fumes drift from pinball machines and penny arcades of the world — Photo falling — Break through in grey room — Click, tilt, vibrate green goo planet — Towers, open fire — Explode word lines of the earth — Combat troops show board books and dictate out symbol language of virus enemy — Fight, controlled body prisoners — Cut all tape — Vibrate board books with precise shared meals — scraps — remains of 'Love' from picture planet — Get up off your rotting combos lit up by a woman — Word falling — Free doorways — Television mind destroyed — Break through in Grey Room — 'Love' is falling — Sex word is falling — Break photograph — Shift body halves — Board books flashed idiot Mambo on 'their dogs' — with pale adolescents of love from Venus — Static orders pour in now — Venus camera writing all the things you are — Planet in 'Love' is a wind U turn back — Isn't time left — Partisans showing board books in Times Square in Piccadilly — Tune and sound effects vibrating sex whine along the middle line of body — Explode substitute planet — Static learned every board book symbol with inflexible violence — color writing you out of star dust — took board books written in prisoner bodies — cutting all tape — Love Mary? — picture planet — Its combos lit up a woman — 'Love' falling permutated through body halves — Static orders clicking — Word falling — Time falling — 'Love' falling — Flesh falling — Photo falling — Image falling" —

Controllers of the Green Troops moved in now — Light-years in eyes that write character of biologic alteration — Vampires fall to dust — crumpled cloth bodies on the glass and metal streets — The Venusians are relegated to terminal sewage deltas — The Uranians back to the heavy cold mist of mineral silence — Dry heat and insect forms close round the people of Mercury — Consequences and alternatives flash on off — Accept Rewrite or return to conditions you intended

to impose on this colony — No appeal from eyes that
see light-years in advance — Explode substitute giving orders — Green metal antennae crackling static in
the transient hotels — cutting virus troops with static
noises — Galactic shock troops break through moving in fast on music poured through nerve circuits —
stuttering distant events — In a few seconds body halves
off from St. Louis — Ghost writing shows board books
— Vibrate dead nitrous film streets — Fight, controlled
body prisoners — Cut flute through board books —
Scraps to go, doctor — cleaving new planet — Get up,
please — Television mind destroyed — Love is falling
from this paper punching holes in photograph — Shift
body halves in the womb — a long way from St. Louis —
total resistance — cobblestone language with inflexible
violence — Combat troops clicked the fair — a Barnum
& Bailey world — Word falling — Time falling — The
fade-out — Good bye parasite invasion with weakness
of dual structure, as the shot of apomorphine exploded
the mold of their claws in vomit — Insect People Of
Minraud preparing exact copy of scorpions crawling over
his face — preparing exact copy of Bradly's body molded
in two halves — Green boy slips the mold on during
sex scene — Remember strange bed? mold heated up
to 10,000 Fahrenheit — His street boy senses clicked
an oven in transient flesh — Call in the Old Doctor —
heavy twilight — A cigarette deal? — Kiki stepped
forward —

"True? I can't feel it" —

"Yes, smiling" —

The man was only a face — Sex tingled in the shadow of street cafés — On the bed felt his cock stiffen — open fly — stroked it with gentle hands — Healed scars still pulsing in empty flesh of KY and rectal mucus — flicker ghost only a few years older than Kiki — Outskirts of the city, masturbated under thin pants — orgasms of memory fingers — Blue twilight fell on his Scandinavian skin — shadow beside him, KY on his slow fingers — As you listen fill in with a pull — teeth ground together the image track — Muscles relax and contract — Kicked his feet in the air — steady stream of drum music in his head — forgotten scent of pubic hairs in other flesh with loud snores —

"Without you i on pavement — Saw a giant crab snapping — Help me — Sinking ship — You trying Ali God of Street Boys on screen? — So we turn over knife wind voices covered — From the radio interstellar sirocco" —

The room was full of white pillow flakes blowing out from a conical insect nest of plaster — Scorpions crawled from the nest snapping their claws — He felt the conical nests attached to his side — white scorpions crawling over his face — He woke up screaming: "Take them off me — Take them off me" —

The dream still shuddered in milky dawn light — Kiki lay naked in a strange bed — His street boy senses clicked back: standing in a doorway his collar turned up against the cold Spring wind that whistled down from the mountains — The man stopped under a blue arc light in the heavy twilight — He put a cigarette to his mouth, tapped his pockets, and turned his hands out — Kiki stepped forward with his lighter extended smiling — The man was only a few years older than Kiki — thin face hidden by the shadow of his hat — They had sandwiches and beer at a booth where a kerosene lamp flickered in the mountain wind — The man called a cab that seemed to leave the ground on a long ride through rubbly outskirts of the city — It was a neighborhood of large houses with gardens — In the apartment Kiki sat down on the bed and felt his cock stiffen under thin pants as the man stroked it with gentle abstract fingers — Blue twilight fell through the room — He could only see a shadow beside him — Kiki took the man's hand and closed the fist and shoved a finger in and out —

"I fuck you?" —

"*Sí*" —

The man put on a tape of Arab drum music — Kiki had been a week in the cold streets dodging the police who were everywhere checking papers after the manner of their species — He dropped his worn pants and stood naked — His cock slid out of the foreskin pulsing — As he sat down again on the bed a drop of lubricant squeezed out and glistened in the faint bluish light — The man sat down beside him and kissed him feeling

his cock — Kiki pushed the man back on the bed — He
found a tube of KY on the night table — On his knees
above the dark shadowy figure he rubbed the KY on his
cock — He put his hands under the man's knees and
shoved them up to the ears and rubbed the KY into the
man's ass with a slow circular pull — Teeth ground together as Kiki slid his cock in feeling the muscle relax
and contract in spasmodic milking movements — The
man kicked his feet in the air — *"Juntos"* said Kiki —
He began to count and at the count of ten they came
together — Kiki fell into a light sleep the drum music
in his head — He woke up to find the man lighting a
candle — "Cigarette?" — The man brought a package
of cigarettes and lay down beside him — Kiki blew the
smoke down through his pubic hairs and said "Abracadabra" as his cock rose out of the smoke — He rolled
the man over, then pulled him up onto his knees and
fucked him to the music — He draped himself over the
man's back with loud snores — He was in fact very tired
after the street, yawned as he crawled under the covers
and snuggled against the man's back —

The man was not in bed beside him but seated at a
table crumpled forward his head sunk into the collar
of a heavy silk dressing gown — A muffled sound like
muttering cloth drifted from the crumpled form — Kiki
got out of bed naked and touched the man's shoulder
— There was nothing there but cloth that fell in a heap
on the floor leaking grey dust — Kiki found the man's

wallet and slipped out the large bills — The man's
clothes were too large so he put on his own clothes and
went out shutting the door softly — He listened for a
moment then stepped quickly down the stairs — In the
doorway he stumbled over a pile of rags that smelled
of urine and pulque — empty streets and from radios
in empty houses a twanging sound of sirens that rose
and fell vibrating the windows — The air was full of
luminous grey flakes falling softly on crumpled cloth
bodies — The street led to an open square — He could
see people running now suddenly collapse to a heap of
clothes — The grey flakes were falling heavier, falling through all the buildings of the city — Cold fear
touched his street boy senses — A vista of phosphorescent slag heaps opened before him —

On the smoldering metal he saw a giant crab claws
snapping — A voice in Kiki's head said "Stand aside"
as Ali God of Street Boys from the neon cities of Saturn
moved in — Dodging from side to side over the snapping
claws his plasma knife tore a great rent in the crab's
body that leaked black rusty oil — Ali doubled back
from above and behind hitting the crab at the base of
its brain — The claws flew off — The eyes went out —
There was nothing but a smear of oil on the pavement —

"This way — To the Towers" — Ali pointed to an office
building that dominated the square — Kiki ran toward the
building covered now by tower fire — Hands pulled him
into a doorway — On the roof of the building was a battery

of radios and movie cameras that vibrated to static — A
green creature with metal claw hands was giving orders to
a group of partisans who manned the gun tower — From
the radio poured a metallic staccato voice —

"Photo falling — Word Falling — Break through in
Grey Room — Towers, open fire" —

Totally green troops in the area, K9 — You are as-
signed to organize combat divisions at the Venusian Front
— appalling conditions — total weapons — Without
inoculation and training your troops will be paralyzed
by enemy virus and drugs — then cut to pieces in the
pain-pleasure signal switch — The enemy uses a vast
mechanical brain to dictate the use and rotation of
weapons — Precise information from virus invasion
marks areas of weakness in the host and automatically
brings into effect the weapons and methods of attack
calculated always of course with alternate moves —
They can turn on total pain of the Ovens — This is
done by film and brain wave recordings mangled down
to a form of concrete music — A twanging sound very
much like positive feedback correlated with the Blazing
Photo from Hiroshima and Nagasaki — They can switch
on electric pleasure leading to death in orgasm — (The
noose is a weapon — The weapon of Kali) — They can
alternate pain and pleasure at supersonic speed like a
speed up tough and con cop routine —

You are to infiltrate, sabotage and cut communications
— Once machine lines are cut the enemy is helpless

— They depend on elaborate installations difficult to move or conceal — encephalographic and calculating machines film and TV studios, batteries of tape recorders — Remember you do not have to organize similar installations but merely to put enemy installations out of action or take them over — A camera and two tape recorders can cut the lines laid down by a fully equipped film studio — The Ovens and the orgasm death tune in can be blocked with large doses of apomorphine which breaks the circuit of positive feedback — But do not rely too heavily on this protection agent — They are moving to block apomorphine by correlation with nausea gas that is by increasing the nausea potential — And always remember that you are operating under conditions of guerrilla war — Never attempt to hold a position under massive counterattack — "Enemy advance we retreat" — Where? — The operation of retreat on this level involves shifting three-dimensional coordinate points that is time travel on association lines — Like this::

sunlight through the dusty window and sat down on the sofa the pearly drops of the basement workshop . . "You're pearling." flaking plaster . . you finish me John's face grey and whispy spurts of semen across off ". . long ago boy a soft blue flame in the dusty floor the static still in image speed of light his eyes as he bent over his ears rose shadows on the ten years the pool hall the crystal radio set young flesh . ." John is it true on Market St. Bill leaned touching dials and "if

we were ten light-years away we across the table and
wires with gentle precise fingers could see ourselves
here John goosed him with "I'm trying to fix it so we
can both ten years from now? a cue and he collapsed
listen at once." "Yes it's true." "Well couldn't we across
the table laughing . . he was opening a headphone on
the bench travel in time?" they had not seen much
with a screwdriver . . "It's more complicated than you
think." of each other in the two heads so close John's
"well time is past ten years . . Bill had been fluffy
blond hair brushed Bill's getting dressed and away at
school and later forehead. undressed eating sleeping
not the Eastern University. John had "Here hold this
phone to your ear" actions but the words became a
legendary figure Do you hear anything?" "What we
say about what we living by gambling . . he used "yes
static." do. Would there be any time if systems for
dice and horses based on "Good" John cupped the
other phone we didn't say a mathematical theories . . to
his ear. anything?" "Maybe not. Maybe that St. Louis
summer night outside smell the two boys at poised
listening coal gas the moon red and out through the
dusty window first step" smoky . . they walked through
empty across back yards and ash pits . . "Yes if you
could learn park frogs croaking" "John the tinkling
metal music of space to listen and not lived in a loft
over a Bill felt a prickle in his lips talk" . . over the
hills and speak-easy reached by that spread to the

groin. far away . . sunlight through outside wooden
stairs . . sunlight through the dusty window of the
basement workshop John's face grey wispy a soft blue
flame in his eyes as he bent over the crystal radio set
touching dials and wires with gentle precise fingers.

"I'm trying to fix it so we can both listen at once."

He was opening a headphone on the bench with a
screwdriver the two heads so close John's fluffy blond
hair brushed Bill's forehead.

"Here hold this phone to your ear. Do you hear
anything?"

"Yes static."

"Good."

John cupped the other phone to his ear. The two boys
sat poised listening out through the dusty window across
back yards and ash pits the tinkling metal music of
space. Bill felt a prickle in his lips that spread to the
groin. He shifted on the wooden stool.

"John what is static exactly?"

"I've told you ten times. What's the use in my talking
when you don't listen?"

"I hear music" . . faint intermittent 'Smiles.' Bill moving in time to the music brushed John's knee . . "Let's
do it shall we?"

"All right"

John put the headphones down on the bench. There
was a storage room next to the work shop. Bill opened
the door with a key. He was the only one who had this

key. smell of musty furniture . . smears of phosphorous
paste on the walls . . Bill turned on a lamp a parchment
shade with painted roses . . chairs upside down on a
desk a leather sofa cracked and shiny. The boys stripped
to their socks and sat down on the sofa.

"You're pearling."
spurts of semen across the dusty floor static still in his
ears rose shadows on young flesh . .

"John is it true if we were ten light-years away we
could see ourselves here ten years from now?"

"Yes it's true."

"Well couldn't we travel in time?"

"It's more complicated than you think."

"Well time is getting dressed and undressed eating
sleeping not the actions but the *words* . . What we *say*
about what we do. Would there be any time if we didn't
say anything?"

"Maybe not. Maybe that would be the first step . . yes
if we could learn to listen and not talk."

Over the hills and far away sunlight through the dusty
window a soft blue flame in his eyes as he bent over . . his
ears rose shadows on the crystal radio set . . He shifted
on the wood the dusty window . . "Come up for a while"
he said . . stool semen on the sofa a soft blue flame in
"All right" Bill felt a tightening "John what is static exactly?" his eyes as he bent over in his stomach . . it was a
room "I've told you ten times what his ears rose shadows
on with rose wallpaper use of my saying anything. the

crystal radio set partitioned off like a stage set when you don't listen?" . . "I'm trying to fix it so we can both . . Bill saw a work 'I hear music' ten years from now listen at once" he was bench tools and radio faint intermittent 'Smiles' . . opening travel in time sets from the light John Bill moving in time to the with a screwdriver" hold this turned on . . the music brushed John's knee. phone to your ear the words do you door he had painted Bill turned to John smiling hear anything? . . we didn't say to his ear a number like "Let's do it shall we?" anything maybe not maybe the two hotel door No. "All right" boys poised listening out through 18 . . "Sit down" John took out a John put down the headphones on the dusty window would cigarette from a box on the bench be the first step across back yards and ash pits the night table there was storage room next to the yes if you could it was rolled in brown workshop. Bill opened learn the tinkling metal music of space paper . . "What is it?" the door with a key . . "That static gave me a hard-on." "Marijuana . . ever try it" "No" he was the only one who had like something touched me he lit the cigarette and the key. The smell and he brought his finger up . . passed to Bill "Take it all musty furniture smears in three jerks sitting with their the way down and hold phosphorous paste on the walls arms around each other's that's right . ." Bill Bill turned on a lamp parchment shoulders looking down at feet a prickling in his shade with painted roses the stiffening flesh flower smell lips . . the wallpaper chairs upside down on a desk of young hard-ons "Let's see who can seemed to glow leather sofa cracked and shiny shoot the farthest" then he was laughing the boys stripped to their socks they stood up Bill hit the wall until he doubled "I'm trying to fix it so we can both ten years from now listen at once." opening travel in time with a screwdriver "Hold this phone to your ear. the words Do you hear anything?" We didn't say to his ear anything maybe not maybe the two boys poised listening out through the dusty window would be the first step across back yards and ash pits yes if you could learn the tinkling metal music of space "That static gave me a hard-on like something touched me" he brought his finger up in three jerks sitting with arms around each other's shoulders looking down at the stiffening flesh flower smell of young hard-ons.

"Let's see who can shoot the farthest."

They stood up. Bill hit the wall . . the pearly drops . . flaking plaster . .

"you finish me off" . . .

long ago boy image . . speed of light . . ten years . . the pool hall on Market St . . Bill leaned across the table for a shot and John goosed him with a cue he collapsed across the table laughing. They had not seen much of each other in the past ten years. Bill had been away at school and later at an Eastern University. John had become a legendary figure around town who lived by gambling he used a system for dice and horses based on a mathematical theory which accounted for the only constant factor in gambling: winning and losing comes in streaks. So double up when you are winning and fold up when you are losing . . St. Louis summer night outside the pool hall smell of coal gas the moon red they walked through an empty park frogs croaking John lived over a speak-easy by the river . . a loft reached by outside wooden stairs.

"Come up for a while," he said.

"All right." Bill felt a tightening in his stomach. A room with rose wallpaper had been partitioned off from the loft like a stage set. As John turned on the light Bill saw a work bench tools and radio sets in the loft. On the door to the bedroom John had painted a number like a hotel door No. 18 . .

"Sit down" . . John took a cigarette from a box on the night table. It was rolled in brown paper.

"What is it?"

"Marijuana. Ever try it?"

"No" . . John lit the cigarette and passed it to Bill. "Take it all the way down and hold it . . That's right . ."

Bill felt a prickling in his lips. The wallpaper seemed to glow. Then he was laughing doubled over on the bed laughing until it hurt his ribs laughing. "My God I've pissed in my pants."

(Recollect in the officers' club Calcutta Mike and me was high on Ganja laughed till we pissed all over ourselves and the steward said "You bloody hash heads get out of here.")

He stood up his grey flannel pants stained down the left leg sharp odor of urine in the hot St. Louis night.

"Take them off I can lend you a pair."

Bill kicked off his moccasins. Hands on his belt he hesitated.

"John I uh . ."

"Well so what?"

"All right." Bill dropped his pants and shorts.

"Your dick is getting hard . . . Sit here." John patted the bed beside him.

Bill tossed his shirt onto a chair. He stretched his legs out and knocked his feet together.

John tossed his shirt onto the floor by the window. He stood up and dropped his pants. He was wearing red shorts. He pulled his shorts down scraping erection and draped the shorts over the lamp testing the heat with his hands. "All right," he decided his gentle precise fingers on Bill's shoulder fold sweet etcetera to bed — EE Cummings if my memory serves and what have I my friend to give you? Monkey bones of eddie and bill? John's shirt in the dawn light? . . dawn sleep . . smell of late morning in the room? Sad old human papers I carry . . empty magic of young nights . . Now listen . . ugh . . the dust the bribe . . (precise finger touching dead old path) . . was a window . . you . . ten-year-old face of laughter . . was a window of laughter shook the valley . . sunlight in his eyes for an instant Johnny's figure shone to your sudden "do it" . . stain on the sheets . . smell of young nights . .

vaudeville
voices

Clinic outside East St. Louis on stilts over the wide brown river took in a steady stream of distant events — That week they could stay on the nod — time there after a rumble in Dallas — Music runs back to the '20s — Ten-year-old keeping watch — cracked pavements — sharp scent of weeds that grow in suburbs — pool hall and vaudeville voices —

So we turn over steady stream of distant events and we flush out traces of a time that meanwhile i had forgotten — wet air thick and dirty on the garage — sharp scent of memory pictures coming in — Looked for him he was gone — I met everybody in deserted cemetery with wooden crosses — There was a mulatto about —

"True? — i can't feel it — Yes you have his face — healed and half-healed skin — Put it on — Without you i on pavement — perhaps if you had helped me — Good bye then — That silver film took it away from me — Well fade-out" —

Trails my Summer dawn wind in other flesh strung together on scar impressions of young Panama night — Pictures exploded in the kerosene lamp spattered light on naked rectum open shirt flapping in the pissoir — Cock flipped out and up — water from his face — The street blew rain from spurts of his crotch — Young

faces melted to musical clock hands and brown ankles
— dead nitrous streets — fish smell in doorways —
Look at the wired electric maze of the city — Stop
— No good — Wait a bit — the long mat — It was an
errand boy from the death trauma — Nobody walks
out on one — In heart or brain spread out they fight on
blocking his time — The boy who entered the '20s had
his own train — Room in the half-light source of second
wind spread the difference between life and death —
Boneless mummy was death in the last round —

So we turn over what he did not know:: Window people
and sky pictures fade out at dawn — Hurry up — Hands
crowd — In the tremendous flash your brain splintered on
empty flesh — bleeding boneless panting death in the last
round — the gate from darkened eyes of wine still loaded
with physical skin — Put it on??:: *End Of The Line* —

Remember i was fish smell and dead eyes in doorway
— errand boy from last stroke of nine — room in the
half-light beside you — Great wind voices of Alamout
it's you? — My duty has been remitted muttering: "Not
think any more of your harsh thoughts" — But who am i
to say more? — Empty is the third in vacant lot — Duty
remitted — Sound of fear and i dance — crumpled cloth
bodies empty — ash from falling tracks — open shirt
flapping wind from the South — the throat designed
to water — I stay near the basin and shadow pools —
Invisible man on webs of silver cut tracks — Vapor

trails writing the sky of Alamout and back i shall go
— indications enough in the harbor — muttering of
dry rivers — fish smell and dead eyes in doorways —
The sirocco dances to sound of the crowds — harsh at
this time of day — vultures in the street — Know the
answer? — Around in vacant lot 1910 — weeds growing
through broken towers — His face screen went dead
— smell of healed and half-healed scars — silver film
at the exits — Won't be much left — Little time so I'll
say: "Good night" — not looking around — talking away
— Now the Spanish fly would not be again steady stream
of distant events in green neon — You touched from
frayed jacket — improvised shacks — mufflers — small
pistols — quick fires from bits of driftwood — Shadow
voices muttering in the dog rotation — Acoustic qualities
couldn't reach flesh — between suns desolate underbrush
— sharp scent of weeds that grow in old Westerns —
battered phonograph talking distant events — Important
thing is always courage to pass without stopping —

Naked boy on association line — i stay near right
now — be shifted harsh at this time of day — The
levanto dances between mutual erections fading in
hand — trails my Summer afternoons — Slow fingers
in dawn sleep tore the flesh from words — fish smell
and dead train whistles — open shirt flapping — wind
of morning in the harbor — My number is K9 — I
am a Biologic from frayed jacket sitting out in lawn
chairs with the St. Louis suburb — not looking around

— talking away — arab drum music in the suburban air — fading khaki pants as we shifted this pubescent banner on the pissoirs the river and the Summer dawn — Semen in other flesh open shirt flapping spurts from beyond the tomb showed a brass bed — Many names murmur of human nights — I am dying cross wine gas far now — I am really dying — Remember hints as we shifted commissions stranger like death in your throat? — breathless flute through Ali's body from beyond the tomb — Slowly fading against the silk of seas — my name — faded through the soccer scores. Tuesday was the last day for signing years . . July 7 St Auberge — (ambiguous sign of an inn) . . stand in for Mr *Who??* My name was called like this before rioters bleed without return . . *We want to hear pay talk dad and we want to hear pay talk now* . . Yes that's me still there waiting in the empty Tangier street . . sunshine and shadow of Mexico . . a night in Madrid . . You let this happen?? (holding the laser gun in his hands) . . wrecked markets half-buried in sand . . smell of blood and excrement in the Tangier streets . . ("We wont be needing you after Friday returning herewith Title Insurance Policy No. 17497.") . . You don't remember me? showing you the papers I carry . . diseased bent over burnt-out inside . . coordinates gangrene . . Hiroshima gangrene . . "Frankly doctor we don't like to hear the word 'nova' here . . bringing you the Voice of American . . This is November 18, 1963 . . This is

Independence Day in Morocco . . The Independence
is in the harbor of Tangier . . The Independence is an
American boat . . The *American* Independence is in Morocco . . This is Independence Day in Morocco . . This is
American Independence Day in Morocco . . This is July
4, 1964 in Morocco . . Brook's Park . . the old swimming
pool kinda run down now . . Mack the Knife over the
loudspeaker . . (He has loosed the fatal lightning of his
terrible swift sword) . . Ghostly looking child burned a
hole in the blanket . . brief flight to Gib . . Our business
now has no future . . know human limitations? Captain
Clark welcomes you aboard . . Remember show price?
— (holding the gun in his hands) . . You don't remember this sad stranger there on the sea wall wishing you
luck from dying lips? And remember the 'Priest' . . They
called him and he stayed . . (boat whistling in the harbor) . . Well that's about the closest way I know to tell
you and papers rustling across city desks . . fresh south-
erly winds a long time ago . . going through the files
like this . . agony to breathe in sad muttering voices . .

"Now how's this for an angle, B.J.? *a real American
stand* . . Everything America ever stood for in any man's
dream America stands for now . . Everything this country could have been and wasn't it will be now . . Every
promise America ever made America will redeem
now . ."

agony to breathe in the Boy's Magazine . . as I have told
you sad guards remote posts . . came to a street half-buried

in sand . . transitory halting place in this mutilated phantom . . smell of strange parks . . shabby quarters of a
forgotten city . . his cold distant umbrella to the harbor
office . . last intersection there smell of ashes . . tin can
flash flare . . wind stirs a lock of hair . . a young man waiting . . hockshop kid like mother used to make . . distant
hand lifted sad as his voice . . "quiet now . . I go . ." (flickering silver smile) . .

"A militant writer's union . . All American writers
recalled to base . . Stand by for orders . . All you jokers
in the Shakespeare Squadron return to base immediately
and stand by for orders . ."

The Frisco Kid he never returns . . in life used address I gave you for that belated morning . . agony to
breathe in this mutilated phantom . . last intersection
dim jerky far away voice . .

"It's the greatest story conference in history,
B.J. . . . All these writers assembled in the warehouse
of the Atlantic Tea Company . . These writers are going
to *write history as it happens in present time* . . And I
don't want to hear any Banshee wails from you sky-
pilots . . Now the way I see it is this: *America stands
for doing the job* and that's what's wrong with America today . . half-assed assassins . . half-assed writers . . half-assed plumbers . . a million actors . . one
corny part . . So we write a darned good part for every
actor on the American set . . You gotta see the whole
scene as a *show* . ."

"Remember show price? Know who I am? . . . 'Good
Bye Mister' is my name . . . 'Wind and Dust' is my
name . . 'Never Happened' is my name . . ."

Soccer scores — The driver shrugged — His sound
i could describe to the open street car passing whiffs of
Spain — long empty face — his eyes the evening breeze
where the awning flapped — Violence roared past the
Café de France cleaving a heavy summons — Mr Bradly
hurry up — Wind Ariel closed your account — Hurry
up please its street — harbor lights gently moving water
smiles dimmer at the edges — arab memory of flesh far
now — Such people made a wide U turn back to the
'20s — Expectancy growing in vaudeville voices —

Totally green troops in the area — We come to shape
the five new combat divisions through clear process
in the United States — slow your brain area trade —
Impressions of present time played electrical music —
Faded guards blew red nitrous fumes over you — khaki
pants fully understood all of idiot Mambo spattered to
control mechanization — hot sex words crackling paper
and punching holes in it —

rectums naked in whiffs of raw meat — Jissom fell
languidly bare feet afternoons — a Mexican about twenty
shifting Johnny's knees — He was in the room on genital
smells finger shared meals and belches — feeling like
scenic railways in sleep — suitcases all open — on
association line electric spasms — burning outskirts
of the city — dark street life of a place forgotten —

Invisible passenger took my hands in dawn sleep of
water music — Broken towers intersect cigarette smoke
memory of each other — healed hands like ice — Won't
be much — Screen went dead — He dressed hastily shirt
flapping — stared out from darkened eyes of wine gas —
    "Good bye then — I thought" — He walked through
dawn mirror of Panama — Memory hit spine outside
1920 movie theater — sat down open shirts flapping
— Many did not listen — silver film at the exits —
Weilest du? — dead nitrous flesh — dirty look through
glass — Who is that naked corpse? — Come along
ladies and gentlemen — screaming on the deal in many
lips? — She didn't get it — Cut the image like back in
the restaurant — Wait a bit — No good — half-healed
electric needs — dead scars — Leave him to me —
Won't be much left — For a room in the shoeshine boy
Swedish river of Gothenburg? — Release without more
ado what? — When i left you hear little tune cut the
image —
    "i am surrounded through cafés and restaurants —
Rabble rousers fade in coffee cup reflections — Blood?
— There is no Jewish blood flash scarlet invitations to
young anti-Semites — Tourist as all the Jewish people
i see myself impoverished tired hustler — Anti-Semite
is buried forever in my deferential nods — Today i am
as old in years as flapping human genitals in Mexico
— i am surrounded — bodies and water everywhere —
Blood runs in the pale door — My early rabble rousers

give off a stench of rotten lips departed — nothing here
— wind voices" —

terminal
street

"Bradly passed through the twisting intestinal streets
— terminal streets of Minraud — A boy of dead nitrous
flesh wafted from a doorway of tarnished silver —

"Me good sewage and frozen jissom — beautiful
peoples" —

They talk in clouds of scent from glands in the groin
— A whiff of KY and rectal mucus drifted out in propositions of memory orgasm — scent talk of dead film
people — terminal guide here, Mister — He made of
1920 movie — In a vacant lot a scorpion boy was eating
a pile of metal excrement — He peered up at Bradly
from phosphorescent glittering eyes —

"Me good guide, Meester — Here very bad peoples"
— The boy vibrated his stinger — "Very bad peoples
— So you fucked, Johnny" —

They moved through paths in a vast rubbish heap
— Came to a cliff city that towered out of sight in the
hot blue sky — cubicles connected by catwalks and
ladders and platforms — The guide moved on music
currents waiting for the beats and chords that lifted
them up ladders and ramps, swept them along perilous
platforms over voids of billowing heat —

"You learn quick, Meester — Music talk — In
here" —

They clicked through melodious turnstiles — The
walls glowed with slow metal fires — Music currents
swirled through the room — The guide twisted out of his
scorpion shell — a being two feet tall covered by fine
red hairs that vibrated in puffs of nitrous smoke — His
head converged to a sharp beak — The penis of black
gristle was covered with the fine red hairs except for the
naked tip which came to a quivering point —

"We fuck now — Then i taking you to the Elder —
Very old — Very wise — You see" — Bradly took off
his space suit and lay down on a pallet that pulsed to
sex music — The fine red hairs penetrated his pores
— His body dissolved in a choking erogenous mist of
burning sex films — The pointed penis penetrated his
rectum — He ejaculated spurts of red smoke —

"Now we going to the Elder — He *inside* — Never
come out" —

Came to a round metal chamber lined with switch-
boards and view screens — Embedded in a limestone
dais was a grey foetal dwarf, his brain clearly visible
under a thin membrane pulsed with colored lights as
he controlled the switchboard —

"He make all music," said the guide —

The dwarf turned his eyeless face to Bradly — Bradly
could feel radar beams map his outlines — Words passed
through his mind on silver ticker tape —

"No one of your race has ever been here before — As a visitor you are disastrous — That is why i attempted to block you — When i did not succeed i knew of course that our blockade was broken by intervention from the Saturn Galaxy — Now it seems we must submit to basic alterations — We do not have 'emotion's oxygen' in our atmosphere — The heat here kills what you call 'emotion' — That is where centipedes and scorpions come from — a heat that kills emotion and animates a bundle of nerve wires — Very few were able to survive here and those few paid the price of specialization" —

Last controls fade out at dawn — young faces moving absent bodies — empty source of second suit — open shirt in the dim light — Ejaculated skin back into dying forms — the face a picture — people gone —

"Me good guide, Meester" — (suffused a time that i had street boy head) —

"i take you see all Garden Delights" —

Boys hang from gallows, turn flapping against each other — dissolved in smoke and crumpled cloth — guided by metal music the doctor on stage —

"i told you i would cover being of healed scars — The doctor still am the Big Fix" —

The whole being suddenly shut off in puffs of nitrous smoke — music cure last parasite — The face was broken — Do not have slow-motion flashes — Dying forms overtake "Mr Bradly Mr Martin" — moving slowly out of the sick lies — No trying source of second rectum

tape — smell of empty condoms in the dim light —
brain of Gothenburg moved on at dawn — bread knife
currents — the cold *adiós* without a shadow — here
caught in the door — no shelter — A street boy's head
questions board room breath trade — Glittering eyes
peered up and: "Man, like good bye" — Ding dong
bell — Silence — Solitude — Bradly leaning say:
"Good bye then in currents waiting for the carbon
dioxide — Truly *adiós*" — Bitter price — Martin is
like pulp behind —

A prospect of red mesas rising from blue depths
— Suspended over the void a precarious iron city of
cable cars, elevators, ferris wheels, scenic railways and
plane rides all in constant motion — "Here" said the
guide and clicked Bradly into a cubicle that permutated
through the structure, floating in slow vertigo of ferris wheels, clicking along perilous tracks where wind
whistled through the cables — The guide turned up his
eyes like a blue torch cutting along the divide line of
Bradly's naked body — Electric needle fingers removed
his skin, pulling it loose in red sheets of pain hung it
on a peg — The guide slipped off his own skin like a
garment, peeled penis pulsing red light, clouds drifting
through his remote blue eyes — Hula hoops of color
formed around the guide's body and enclosed Bradly
weak and torn with pain cool hands on his naked flesh
as he sank in blood and bones and intestines of the other
suffocation panic of spermatozoa sucked through pearly

genital passages and spurted out in a scratching shower
of sperm — sunlight through bodies without cover —
soft luminous spurts drifting in the cold blue wind —

Body tension in genital rings and he fell into the
explosion of sperm — Contraction turnstiles ejaculated
bodies without cover — Iridescent orgasm floated from
pale adolescents — Slow movement of body hairs ejaculated the creature who talks in color blast — iridescent
weak and torn by pain, decay breathing from years spurting out through the orgasm death in black lust of the
swamp mud — black fish movement of food, intestines
shifting color orgasm reflected in the obsidian penis
— Silver films in the blood and bones tear his insides
apart — He was sucked from penis suffocation and
released dream flesh in a scratching shower of sperm
— sunlight through pubic hairs — soft luminous spurts
of memory riding the wind — Pieces of cloud drifted
through someone walking — Mountain wind around his
body trailing sweat drew him into other body alterations,
sky blue through viscera of the other — solitude of
morning cool on his skinned flesh —

last
round over

Now for me — the story of one White — That's why
darkies were born — way human skin inflated "Master"
— a long good night in metal valve at base of the spine

— now for the story of one absent today far from the old
folks — softly singing Old Black Joe to "music" (i made
an ambiguous gesture) of cold crystal grave — ghost
rectums of cotton — Semen fell like opal cane — Weep
no more — absent tenants — silence to say good bye
adiós — controllers from the ancient white planet of
frozen gasses — a vast mineral consciousness near absolute zero thinking in slow formations of crystal — silent
female navigators blank space eyes swept by Northern
Lights — yeti men with burning metal eyes and long
claws covered with purple hair shock troops carried by
the navigators — controllers of the White Smoke and the
utilities, monopolized and froze the earth — The White
Smoke and the White Light keeps the Djoun forces away
and in darkness they assume malignant forms — So you
need the White Light to keep them away —

"It's the old junk gimmick — Freeze the mark —
Thawing hurts you got it? — Sex and pain forms hatching out in paralyzed flesh — and hatching out hungry
— so you need more and more of the white stuff to keep
your ass in deep freeze — Junk is not blue and it is not
green — Junk is *White White White* — like the colorless
no-smell of death from kicking addicts — That's where
they get the White Smoke, from sick addicts — bottled
in precinct cells of America — in Lexington, Kentucky
— You got it? — Sex and pain *form* flesh identity" —

At far end pale flesh blooms slowly out of a life cannot exist in pictures — bleeding formations of crystal

— that body without a shadow without relics — blank face, healed and half-healed dream flesh hatching from the death trauma — outside East St. Louis a cold *adiós* — silence — weary — They tell you of distant coffin — Won't be much left on Panama night — empty condom ticket — erogenous cotton flesh lying there streaked with phosphorous — someone walking —

"Man, like good bye then" —

(In the lunar caves black newt boys, eyes lips and genitals glowing with slow metal fires — penis rose in a smell of phosphorus — blue radium symbols on the wall) —

Now explosions of Colored South from mixture — surges of silence from long metal night weaves people and sky story of one absent today — on a slow boat to China, Master, a long good night — the cold *adiós* — Got no home? — So we'll sing one song: a big bank roll and Cousin Miranda making a Monday line — So we'll sing one song in your dreams — And that heart grows weary — They'll tell you of money in the cold cold grave? — on a slow boat to China, *adiós* — keeps on rolling a big word line — sugar line — secondhand erogenous corn — softly singing Old Black Joe to: "i'm tired of you and i'm checking out" — Just to raise the price of a ticket angle voices calling Old Black Joe — orgasm death in the cold empty condom — Look, Master, God's wind blew icicles in black slow-motion faces — singing phosphorus in flash darkies weeping — broken glaciers

and skin of cotton — Weep no more — absent tenants
— ghost voices calling false human hosts — (i made
an ambiguous gesture) — Cold crystal semen fell like
opal cane — slow motion sky swept by Northern lights
— Thawing hurts — White form hatching in painted
human skin inflated "Master" — long hunger of the
spine — Story of your ass in deep freeze? — Semen fell
like opal canes from phallic statues of ice under Northern Lights — the cold of interstellar space in his spine
— sex and pain explosions of colored flesh hatching
out — That's why darkies were born — way the White
Stuff keep "Master" — Colorless Utilities monopolized
land of the free — Keeps the Djoun forces in secondhand erogenous corn — So you need more and more of
death because your ass is in deep freeze — White White
White spurted again and again from death of kicking
addicts — need the White Light to check out — It's
the old gimmick — Darkies are the pipes you got it?
— sex and pain price of a ticket — flesh hatching out
in cotton-covered orgasm cocoons —

(The ship came apart here like a rotten undervest —
The yeti thawed to stings of white-hot scorpion people in
the Ovens — Blasted his way out white sheets dripping
purple fire — metal eyes burning in nova) —

Earthquakes and hurricanes exploded setup of mineral dreamer — space eyes blank as polar moon of
morning — The question caught our ticket that exploded
— need the White Smoke to circumstance — Remember

i was the door — It's the old naked dream beside you —
You got sex and pain information? — mouth of hair? —

(An orchid with brilliant red and green flowers hanging over the swamp mud — As i touched the plant
long tendrils covered with fine erectile hairs stung my
naked body, liquid fires feeling into mouth and penis
and rectum) —

ancient evil odors on the trade winds — bottled female smells in corridors of silence —

"We intersect on empty kingdom where picture cannot exist — Bleeding i made this dream five times without a shadow without relics in the last terrace of the
garden — Sex dawn and dream flesh left no address
— For i have known East St. Louis good night — Isn't
time is there left? — So we'll sing a song in white to
give you — odor of deluge and money in dreams —
Distant coffin overtakes me — bitter darkies caught in
the door — odor of drowned suns — Won't be much left
in the final ape of history — Cold empty condom the
price on our ticket that exploded — Any case divide
line melted before circumstances — Remember i was
the cotton flesh lying there — icicles at the far end of
evening — broken dream beside you and the dreamer
gone — Rectum with dirty shirt takes his way toward
the black cave boys with phosphorescent information,
lips fading out — Dark body smell filled the cave of
dust — We made it all in spurts of burning phosphorous
— on the walls slow radium circumstances — You can

say could give no flesh identity — fading such words
— What have i my friend to give? — pale roots where
flesh blooms slowly out of life i led — read formations
of crystal — Healed and half-healed shade departed
from the death trauma — outside the body of a God
bending cold *adiós* — Bitter, my friend, weary they tell
you of courage to let go — Someone walking stopped
suddenly to question cold grave — The pipes are calling
Panama alterations — someone walking and we drown
— erogenous naked flesh empty in the trade winds at
dawn whisper — Man, like good bye" —

A young man of high condition gives you phosphorescent eyes and lips — lunar knife welded into his twisting
shadow — Five times penis rose pulsing in phosphorescent dust tracing a colorless dreamer — wrote explosion of dawn and dream — Leaning say mixture ebbing
carbon dioxide — Truly a long good night in "Mr Bradly
Mr Martin" is story of one absent today far from shirt in
another — stopped suddenly to crown a God bending
the cold *adiós* back to mineral silence — a big bank
roll and Cousin Miranda falling — odor of no home —
Silver flakes closed your account — recorder music in
the throat of God — Won't be much left on the mirrors
— empty tape — 1920 movie — Erogenous dust falls
from demagnetized patterns — Rectums dissolve in blue
dawn explosions of color sky — old Westerns rotting
through slate music and nitrous fumes — A long good
night in metal — Light layers peel off story of one absent

today — spectral smell of empty condoms down along penny arcades and mirrors — silence to say good bye —

Now rewrite Mr Bradly Mr Martin — The separation gimmick that keeps this tired old show on the road — i have said Martin's life line is the human addict — That is why he is at such pains to keep the addict uncomfortably short — It is the need, the colorless death smell arising from sick addicts that keep his whole universe of junk time and monopoly in operation — "the White Smoke" bottled in precinct cells of America, in Lexington, Kentucky — With "the White Smoke" in one hand and "the Blue Heavy Metal Fix" in the other he has human hosts the way he likes to see them: caught in the switch — And if they make it out of that switch the Garden of Delights is there waiting with "Orgasm Death" — Make it out of there? — "the Ovens" down in the hole — All right, so you sewed up a planet — Now unsew it — Is that clear enough or shall i make it even clearer? ? — Reverse all your gimmicks — your heavy blue metal fix out in blue sky — your blue mist swirling through all the streets of image to Pan Pipes — your white smoke falling in luminous sound and image flakes — your bank of word and image scattered to the winds of morning — into this project all the way or all to see in Times Square in Piccadilly — Reverse and dismantle your machine — Drain off the prop ocean and leave the White Whale stranded — all your word line broken from mind screens of the earth — You talk about "responsibility" — Now show responsibility — Show total responsibility — You have blighted a planet — Now remove the blight — Cancel your "White Smoke" and all your other gimmicks of control — your monopoly of life, time, and fortune canceled by your own orders — Pay, Mr Bradly Mr Martin — wracked and answer a God melted the recorders — out of the sick lies — no rectum tape — empty music cross the water — Characters walk in and out of silver film — smoke words recorded on scar impressions — Permutating the door, Mr Martin — A hand scattered word and image to the winds for all to see — Ding-dong bell — Silence — Mr Bradly Mr Martin, leaning say:

"Good bye then — Your machine drains off picture dioxide — Truly *adiós*" —

bitter price — whale stranded — the colors released, Martin is like pulp behind — Now remove all your gimmicks in setting forth — This dream be your orders — Your ticket now ended — All Martin's recorded speech fade-out — Mr Bradly Mr Martin, now show blighted planet the dog tape empty of control —

"Man, like vaudeville voices under the story" —

"Mirrors of Mr Bradly Mr Martin — calm his face — dream shut off — I fold the Old Doctor twice — in the gutter cosmic dust of nova — outside East St. Louis last good bye — memory pictures — the story over — Like suddenly back to invisible shadow — Yes you have bitter indications enough in empty room — someone

walking — truly good bye then in Summer dawn wind
— saucers in the morning sky — silence of the sick
lies — 'Marks?' — Identity melted before daybreak
— Like little time in tarnished offices — splintered on
empty flesh — evening finger fading — God Of Panic
talking" —

"Like good bye then, Willy the Rat — Remember i
was the dreamer with dirty flesh — known end of the
line outside 1920 movie streaked with violence — Film
flakes drift *adiós* — Showed you your air — The Doctor on stage — The pipes are calling — September
left no address — For i have known last air — The
days grow short — Isn't time is there left? — Waiting
game and we drown — naked — short — indications
enough — at dawn last film flakes — written on the
door the sick lies now are ended — Vast Thing Police
speak into air — any case silence to answer — i fold
in story — A street boy's courage exploded the word
— last round into air — like good bye then — story of
absent dreamer — Last September fades streaked with
violence — surges of silence ebbing, stranded, and we
haven't got courage to let go — a great leisure when
you reach September — Days grow short — Vacant
dawn whispers: Game, Hamburger Mary — Five times
terminal — Man, like dawn and dream — Silence to
say 'ebbing carbon dioxide'" —

Outside East St. Louis our revels now are ended —
These events are melted into air — paper forgotten

— Yes you have his bitter spirits — A God bending your summons, commands these visions —

"Like good bye, Johnny — naked, empty as ding-dong bell — What is St. Louis after *adiós?* — faded story of absent world just as silver film took it — Remember i was the movies — Rinse my name for i have known intervention — Pass without doing our ticket — Forgotten shadow actors walk beside you — mountain wind of Saturn in the morning sky — From the death trauma weary good bye then" —

"Intervention overtakes Mr Bradly Mr Martin — distant coffin in empty room — tape ebbing, picture splintered on empty flesh — last round, boy — good bye in lips fading — Remember i was the ship gives no flesh identity" —

"You can say could give no last good bye — In fading breath you can say last round over — stranded, ebbing carbon dioxide, man like identity fading out — Any case a God questions board room circumstances — Remember i was your account — nova dream falling — played the flute in wind and rain streaked with violence — played the Doctor on stage — five times good bye" —

"Last parasite — no shelter — Last morning washed good bye then — stream of distant fingers fading — vaudeville voices absent today — Man questions the dreamer — fade-out overtakes lies — nothing here now but bleeding dream without a shadow without relics — i fold in story of last penny arcade — roller skates before stranded to give you? — hands down — a great leisure in solitude of Saturn" —

Time to squeeze out the welchers, kid, who can't cover their bets and never intended to cover — The "Hassan i Sabbahs" from Cuntville USA backed by yellow assassins who couldn't strangle a hernia — Self-appointed controllers of "the Rotting Kingdom" strictly from Grade B Hollywood who couldn't get their dead nitrous film foot in the door — And all the "Mr Martins" who are trying to buy something for nothing — You can't even con you can't even hustle — You couldn't roll a paralyzed flop — All right all of you cover your bets or shut up and get out of the game — You can take your welching two-bit business to Walgreen's we don't want it — Out out out the whole miserable fucking lot of you — strictly from Moochville —

call the
old doctor
twice?

You see, son, in this business, welchers who can't cover their bets angle in the "Hassan i Sabbah" from Cuntville strictly from con cop — It's an old vaudeville act — Dead nitrous film foot takes both parts — "Mr Martins," trying to buy a nice quiet easy pitch, you can't even con you can't even hustle — old Western flop — All right all of you cover for a buy or check

out — We are walking into the game — Out — Out
— A long ride for the white sucking lot of you strictly
from heavy metal — Time to squeeze out the dummies
— They never intended to cover — But boy the pipes
are calling, Cuntville USA — be in the bread line —
Self-appointed controllers holding wrist and ankle for
a ticket — grade B Hollywood, ghost writing in the sky
The door — And all the "Mr Martins" won't do you a bit
of good on the trip that you're gonna take — something
for nothing? — You had every weapon in three galaxies
you couldn't roll a paralyzed flop — From Florida up to
the old North Pole cover your bets or take your welching
two-bit business to Walgreen's — You got the Big Fix
down in the hole — Hello yes good bye, Moochville —

Now some write home to orgasm death — welchers,
kid, who can't cover their bets — And that "White
smoke" — ? ? Man, the "Hassan i Sabbahs" from Cuntville Valley say you are going on a slow boat to China
strictly from a big bank roll and a nitrous film foot — if
they lost his old blue hands — "Martins" who are trying
to buy trips — Can't even con can't even hustle — Quiet
— Yes they lost that old flop — All right all of you:: *Cover*
— So the louder they scream:: *Out of the game* — You
can take your old ace in the hole to Walgreen's — We
don't want it — Strictly from money that they've lost and
spent and they may flash a big word line — But as word
dust falls they'll be in the bread line without clothes or
a dime — "Marks? What marks?" i'm aleaving Martin

— Trying to buy that camera gun? It won't do you a bit
of good — You can't even con you can't even hustle the
trip that I'm gonna take — I've had every con in three
galaxies pulled on me — All right, cover that old North
Pole or get out of the game — You can take your Big
Fix to Walgreen's — Out — Out — Out in the bread
line without clothes or a dime the whole sucking lot of
you strictly from:: *Adiós* —

In three-dimensional terms the board is a group rep-
resenting international big money who intend to take
over and monopolize space — They have their own
space arrangements privately owned and consider the
governmental space programs a joke — The board books
are records pertaining to anyone who can be of use to
their program or anyone who could endanger it — The
board books are written in symbols referring to association blocks — Like this: $ — "American upper middle-
class upbringing with maximum sexual frustration and
humiliations imposed by Middle-Western matriarchs" %
— "Criminal street boy upbringing — oriented toward
money and power — easily corrupted" and so forth —
The board agents learn to think in these association
blocks and board instructions are conveyed in the board
book symbols — The board is a three-dimensional and
essentially stupid pressure group relying on money,
equipment, information, files, and the technical brains
they have bought — As word dust falls and their control
machine is disconnected by partisan activity they'll be

in the bread line without clothes or a dime to buy off their "dogs" their "gooks" their "errand boys" their "human animals" — liars — cowards — collaborators — traitors — liars who want time for more lies — cowards who cannot face your "human animals" with the truth — collaborators with insect people, with vegetable people — with any people anywhere who offer them a body forever — traitors to all souls everywhere sold out to shit forever —

"So pack your ermines, Mary — *we* are getting out of here — i've seen this happen before — Three thousand years in show business — The public is gonna take the place apart" —

"i tell you, boss, the marks are out there pawing the ground — What's this 'Sky Switch'? — What's this 'Reality Con'? What's this 'Tone Scale'? ? — They'll take the place apart — Any minute now — I've seen it happen before on Mercury where we put out a Cool Issue — And the law is moving in fast — Nova Heat — Not locals, boss — This is *Nova Heat* — Well boss?" —

"Call in the Old Doctor" —

Yes when the going gets really rough they call in the Old Doctor to quiet the marks — And he just raises his old blue hands and brings them down slow touching all the marks right where they live and the marks are quiet — But remember, ladies and gentlemen, you can only call the Old Doctor once — So be sure when you call him this is really it — Because if you call the Old Doctor twice he quiets you —

"Here's the Doc now" —

"He's loaded — Throw him under a cold shower —
Give him an ammonia coke — Oh my God, they are
out there pawing the ground:: 'What's this green deal?
— What's this mortality con? — You trying to push me
down the tone scale, baby? — You trying to short-time
someone, Jack? — Take that heavy metal business to
Walgreen's — We don't want it — What's this orgasm
death? — Who cooked up these ovens? — What's this
white smoke? — Boys, we been subliminated' — How
does he look?" —

"Boss, he don't look good — That sneaky pete caught
up with him" —

"Oh my God send out Green Tony" —

"Green Tony took off for Galaxy X — On the last
saucer, boss — He's coming round now" —

"For God's sake shove him out there with a wing and
a prayer" —

The Old Doctor reeled out onto the platform — Then
he heard the screaming marks and he steadied himself
and he drew all of it into him and he stood up very
straight and calm and grey as a wise old rat and he lifted
his old blue hands shiny over the dirt and he brought
them down slow in the setting sun feeling all the marks
so nasty and they just stood there quiet his cold old
hands on their wrists and ankles, hands cold and blue
as liquid air on wrist and ankle just frozen there in a
heavy blue mist of vaporized bank notes —

If you get out there in front of the marks and panic and try to answer them — Well — We don't talk about that — You see the Old Doctor just draws all that charge and hate right in and uses it all — So the louder they scream and the harder they push the stronger and cooler the Old Doctor is — Yes, son, that's when you know you've got them cooled right — When you can take it all in so the louder they scream and the harder they push the stronger and cooler you are — And then they are quiet — They got nothing more to say and nothing to say it with — You've taken it all all all you got it? (Good, save it for the next pitch) — So there they stand like dummies (they are dummies) and you let your heavy cold blue hands fall down through them — Klunk — cold mineral silence as word dust falls from demagnetized patterns — and your spirals holding wrist and ankle — Where we came in —

Now some wise characters think they can call the Old Doctor twice —

"All right, Doc, get out there and quiet the marks" —

"Marks? What marks? i don't see anybody here but you — All right drop that camera gun — It won't do you a bit of good — i've had every weapon in the galaxy pulled on me" —

"But i got the fix in — i got the Big Fix in" —

"Mister, i am the Big Fix — Hello yes good bye — a few more calls to make tonight" —

You see, son, in this business you always have to find an angle or you'll be in the bread line without clothes or a dime like the song says the angle on planet earth was birth and death — pain and pleasure — the tough cop and the con cop — It's an old vaudeville act — Izzie the Split used to take both parts — But that was in another galaxy — Well it looked like a nice quiet easy pitch — Too quiet like they say in the old Westerns — Fact is we were being set up for a buy and all the money we took was marked — So why did we walk into it? — Fact is we were all junkies and thin after a long ride on the White Subway — flesh junkies, control junkies, heavy metal junkies — That's how you get caught, son — If you have to have it well you've had it — just like any mark — So slide in cool and casual on the next pitch and don't get hooked on the local line: If there is one thing to write on any life form you can score for it's this:: Keep your bag packed at all times and ready to travel on —

So pack your ermines, Mary — Write back to the old folks at home — you see this happen before — three thousand years of that old ace in the hole — There was something had to happen and it happened somehow — The Public is gonna take the place apart — He went away but i'm here still — To quiet the marks — He just said "i'm tired of you and i'm checking out" — And they may flash the marks quiet — But boy the pipes the pipes are calling — When you call Him just to raise the price of a ticket — Call the Doc twice? — He quiets you — Here's the Doc now — That old ace in the hole? Good bye old paint i'm aleaving Cheyenne — Ghost writing in the sky trip that you're gonna take — This "Green Deal"? — What's this from Florida up to the old North Pole? — Push me down the tone scale baby, down in the hole? ? In the bread line, Jack — Pick up that heavy metal — *Adiós* — Don't want it —

Now some write home to orgasm death — Who cooked up your dreams? And that "White Smoke"? — Man, we been subliminated — From this valley they say you are going — That sneaky peat bog caught up with him — on a slow boat to China — Green Tony on the last saucer, boss — a big bank roll — a wing and a prayer — without clothes or a dime if they lost his old blue hands over the sky — They'll tell you of trips — in the setting sun — ghost riders in the sky — just stood there quiet — Yes they lost that old hand cold and blue as liquid air — So the louder they scream the old folks at home you'll see me cooler — old ace in the hole — this to say and nothing to say it — He went away —

Money that they've lost and spent like dummies — And they may flash a big word line — But, boy, the pipes the pipes are calling as word dust falls — They'll be in the bread line — holding wrist and ankle just to raise the price of a ticket — now some wise characters — "Marks? What marks? — i'm aleaving ghost writing in the sky — Drop that camera gun — It won't do you a bit of good on the trip that you're gonna take — i've had every weapon in three galaxies pulled on me one time or another — from Florida up to the old North Pole" —

"But i got the Big Fix in — i got the Big Fix down in the hole" —

"In the bread line without clothes or a dime — Hello yes good bye — *Adiós*" —

Well these are the simple facts of the case and i guess i ought to know — There were at least two parasites one sexual the other cerebral working together the way parasites will — That is the cerebral parasite kept you from wising up to the sexual parasite — Why has no one ever asked the question: "What is sex?" — Or made any precise scientific investigation of sexual phenomena? — The cerebral parasite prevented this — And why has no one ever asked: "What is word?" — Why do you talk to yourself all the time? — Are you talking to yourself? — Isn't there someone or something else there when you talk? Put your sex images on a film screen talking to you while you jack-off — Just about the same as the so-called "real thing" isn't it? — Why hasn't it been tried? — And what is word and to whom is it addressed? — Word evokes image does it not? — Try it — Put an image track on screen and accompany it with any sound track — Now play the sound track back alone and watch the image track fill in — So? What is word? — Maya — Maya — Illusion — Rub out the word and the image track goes with it — Can you have an image without color? — Ask yourself these questions and take the necessary steps to find the answers:: "What is sex? What is word? What is color?" — Color is trapped in

word — Image is trapped in word — Do you need words?
— Try some other method of communication, like color
flashes — a Morse code of color flashes — or odors or
music or tactile sensations — Anything can represent
words and letters and association blocks — Go on try it
and see what happens — science pure science — And
what is love? — Who do you love? — If i had a talking
picture of you would i need you? Try it — Like i say
put your sex image on screen talking all the sex words
— Hide simple facts of the case: two parasites one
sexual, the other electric voice of C — Well the board
as you listen fills in — I ought to know — Cerebral
parasite kept you from wising up board books written
in symbols of sexual parasite — Pressure group relying
on rectum while you jack-off — Control "real thing" —
collaborators with image trapped in word — What is
word? Word is an array of calculating machines — Spots
of weakness opened up by the track goes with it — The
Ovens smell of simple facts of the case and i guess won't
be much left — little time, parasites — Now we see all
the pictures — Cerebral phonograph talks sex scenes
— And this pubescent word evokes images does it not?
Look and accompany it with human nights and watch
the image track fill in — Stranger lips bring down the
word forever — Word falling — Photo falling — hide
nor hair — at the club insane orders and counterorders
— stranger on the shore — My terminal electric voice
of C, where's it going to get me? — Lover, please forget

about the tourists — i said the Chief of Police after hours — This thing D.C. called love — You better move on — British Prime Minister, say it again — Hear you, Switzerland — Freeze all living is easy — My heart to mindless idiot — It had to be you — You won't cut word lines? — Found the somebody who — It's electric storms of violence — Any advantage precariously held — June July and August walk on — Pinball-led streets — i'm going home, drugstore woman — Show you something: berserk machine — One more time, Johnny Angel? — with short time secondhand love? — nothing but The Reality Concession to set up a past — Workers paid off in thing called "Love" — the junk man at the outskirts —

Gongs of violence and how show stranger on the shore — Real Mr Bradly Mr Martin charges in — "Where's it going to get me? — Artists take over" — counterorders and the living is easy — it's orbit of the Saturn Galaxy — Snap your fingers — dreams end everything — hide nor hair — at the club actually be your way — Time — It's stranger on the shore — After hours this secondhand trade-in called "Love" — You better move on — Tentative flesh — So good night — Say it again — Face sucked into other apparatus and the living is easy — now trading mornings — So pack your ermines, Mary — You see this happen before — Stranger on the shore my real ace in the hole — June July August walk on — The public is going to take the place — I'm going home — Nothing but Green Tony on the last saucer, boss —

Word falling, photo failing, old folks at home — You'll see me guess orders and counterorders — And they flash a big word pay-off — But boy the pipes the pipes are calling as you listen — Big money be in the bread line — wising up — scandinavia outhouse parasite just to raise the price of a ticket — Word flesh group relying on rectum — Now we see all the pictures feeling along — And this pubescent word covered orgasm death on a slow boat to China — Stranger lips bring roll call — Rectum suddenly released as he melted nitrous film flesh — Word is an array of calculating machines from Florida up to the old North Pole — Image track goes with it — Ovens down in the hole — Won't be much left — In the bread line — *Adiós* — Now we see all the pictures —

Enter George Raft groom *cum* chauffeur — He lurked hat and collar and hands in his pockets — Heavy with menace he takes the job of looking after someone who was sure to reach the film — Sticky end abroad — George Raft went home talking — Smoothest of all the tough guys tiring from films altogether — a little fleshier around the jaw suite but available for civilian jobs — Those eyes still snap and this ain't Hamlet — I want hunched tight hipped purpose — Action — Camera — Take — Hanging stays as butler — 500 full-time officials — The death penalty will

not be scrapped as transport, Mr Workers' Union —
You'll find it waiting down shadow pools — The try
begins with BOAC — sufficient spurts that tradition-
ally service transient hotels with rose wallpaper —
Attempt is now in Rome with the film — red nitrous
fumes over you — Young witness circumstances brown
ankles — Naked for physical factory rushed to execution marriage — Two boys mutually stylized hover the
vigil till execution image back to hotel room in London
— Harm begins in Britain from his face — cobblestone
lane pageant — shirt flapping pants slide down — felt
execution marriage — Stanley Spencer left that mess
— Who is that naked corpse? — Sex would die on the
answer — Around in biographer languorously sure
that there is me-you cock flipped out and up as one is
or need be a boy in kerosene lamp light — old dead-
pan anecdotal sage for transient hotels — "Bend over
you" — young conceived in this cook book — Pants
down to the ankle his first sexual experience convinced
him that carnal love reproduces feedback from vacant
lot — laughing suburb boys quiet elegant and soft stay
in close — His style is cool like his head was sewed
on a Russian version of James Dean — filtering black
aphrodisiac ointment in Spanish fly that will take photo
turnstile through flesh — Two faces tried to rush entirely into his face — He was in the you-me in you
with all the consequences — burning outskirts of the
world — Character took my hands in dash taught you

from last airport typical of his decision to intersect on new kind of daring in memory of each other —

"I say nothing and nothing is now in Rome with the film — Intersected eleventh hour paper — Star failed yesterday — Screen went dead — Young face melted" —

"Good bye then — I thought entirely into the room with me — Panama" —

From San Diego up to Maine Solemn Accountants are jumping ship forever —

"Word falling, photo falling, sir — In the last skimpy surplus, sir, orders and counterorders — Stranger outside, sir" they said — "And what's it going to get me?" —

Allies wait on knives — Street gangs had to be you — You won't cut word lines? — From a headline of penniless migrants electric storms of violence — Our show and we're proud of August walk-on — Her Fourth-Grade Class screamed in terror — Pinball-led Street of the Dogs — I looked at the pavement — Show you something: berserk machine — Pavement was safer — stale streets of yesterday? — short time secondhand love? Workers paid off in thing conditions? —

Delusion of death going — Artists take over — Was it easy? — Only this should have been obvious:: Orbit Of The Saturn Galaxy — Only live animals write anything — hide nor hair at the club — after hours this liz replica synthesized from tentative flesh — So pack your ermines, Mary, you of later and lesser crimes pudgy and not pretty —

"Will Hollywood never learn?" —

"On the last saucer, boss" —

Unimaginable disaster — You'll see me guess time — It is impossible to estimate the damage — And they may flash streams in the area, but boy the pipes the pipes are calling — in Ewyork, Onolulu, Aris, Ome, Oston that old ace in the hole — past crimes feeling along your time —

Enter George Raft *cum* Paris in the Spring all his hands in his pockets — Heavy with the Japanese Sandman — Looking for someone who was trading new dreams for old —

"Unchain my broad" —

George Raft went home tiring from films altogether — but available for civilian jobs — once in a while — sticky end for Old Black Bird — "Martin's reality film is the dreariest entertainment ever presented to a captive audience." He stated flatly. The opening scene shows a man sitting in the bar of a luxury hotel clearly he has come a long way travel-stained and even the stains unfamiliar cuff links of a dull metal that seem to absorb light . . the room buzzes with intrigue . . Mauritania . . Uranium . . Oil . . War . . This man and what he sees are *in the film* . . Clearly portentous exciting events are about to transpire. Now take the same man *outside the film* . . He has come a long way and the stains are all too familiar . . An American tourist confides in the bartender:

"Now Mother is down with a bad case of hemorrhoids and we don't speak the language I tried to tell this doctor at least he called himself a doctor and I want your advice about the car . . Oh here's the man who took us to the Kasbah? How much shall I give him?" . . He pulls a wad of bills from his pocket raw eager thrust of an overtip the magic gesture that makes a man bow three times and disappear into a dollar . . A gnat has fallen into the man's sherry. Clearly no portentous exciting events are about to transpire. You will readily understand why people will go to any lengths to get in the film to cover themselves with any old film scrap . . junky . . narcotics agent . . thief . . informer . . anything to avoid the hopeless dead-end horror of being just who and where you all are: dying animals on a doomed planet.

Martin's film worked for a long time. Used to be most everybody had a part in the film and you can still find remote areas where a whole tribe or village is on set. Nice to see but it won't do you much good. Even as late as the 1920's everybody had a good chance to get in the film.

Well he was dipping into the till. Just looks at me and says "Account sheets are empty many years." The film stock issued now isn't worth the celluloid its printed on. There is nothing to back it up. The film bank is empty. To conceal the bankruptcy of the reality studio it is essential that no one should be in position to set up another reality set. The reality film has now become an instrument and weapon of monopoly. The full weight of the film is directed against anyone who calls the film in question with particular attention to writers and artists. Work for the reality studio or else. Or else you will find out how it feels to be *outside the film*. I mean literally without film left to get yourself from here to the corner . . Every object raw and hideous sharp edges that tear the uncovered flesh.

Who's sorry now? — I say nothing and nothing is now in Rome with the film — Intersected eleventh hour paper — Young witness or old hear the Japanese Sandman —

shuffle
cut

"Pack your ermines, Mary" — (Female imperson-ators pack in shabby dressing room — riot noises in the distance — Scene opens into other dressing rooms and transient hotels — switch to office of the Carny Manager — riot noises moving closer — police whistles, machine guns, slamming shop shutters — cut-ups of riot newsreels) —

"What's this reality con?" — (Vista of tombstones and lavatories — hospitals, flophouses, asylums — grey dishwater smell of institution cooking — whine of dying peoples — "Lord, Lord, i don't even feel like a human"

— "So we drove down to St. Petersburg and Mother didn't like it at all" — The riot noises swell to a vast adolescent muttering — boys armed with switchblades and bicycle chains — A cobblestone shatters the window of the carny office — As the outside air rushes in the carny manager coughs and sputters — "And the law is moving in fast" — (Nova police stand before a switchboard that lights up as their agents make arrests and question suspects — "I'm not taking the rap for those board bastards — i'm going to rat on everybody" — The lights extend, closing round the board —

"The marks are out there pawing the ground" — (riot shots of all times and places) —

"What's this Green Deal?" — (Green vegetable junkies suck oxygen of the earth) —

"You trying to short-time someone, Jack?" — (subliminal slow motion on the screen — venereal disease films at 35 frames per second) —

"Take that heavy metal business to Walgreen's" — (heavy metal junkies on the nod in a blue mist of vaporized bank notes) —

"What's this orgasm death?" — (Ejaculating bodies hang from gallows goosed by giggling green street boys — Condemned prisoners twist in cyanide fumes under civil leer of the witness — Middle-aged cardiac dies on the young model who pushes the corpse away in disgust — "Horrible old character got physical and died in me") —

"Who cooked up these ovens?" — (flash prisoners in the ovens — lattice of white-hot metal closing round them — phosphorescent smoldering shag heaps of Minraud —

heat cutting off the sources of animal life — Crabs sidle from cone-shaped nests — "Zero eaten by crab") —

"What's this 'White Smoke'?" — (Sick addicts in precinct cells give off the colorless no-smell of death — A white smoke spreads over the blighted earth) —

"Boys we been subliminated" — (Newspapers, magazines, muttering voices on TV and radio — "birth and death and the human condition — always been that way and always will — Besides you can't do anything — Don't stick your neck out — Don't get ulcers") —

"Call in the Old Doctor" — (The doctor on stage — He sucks all the newsreels of riot and hate faces into him — Riot pictures freeze to stills as he brings his hands down — Klunk) —

"Now some wise characters think they can call the Old Doctor twice" — (Newsreels and riot noises shut off — Cold blue silence of interstellar space closes round the board table — A guard reaches for his vibrating camera gun — "Won't do you a bit of good — had every weapon in the galaxy pulled on me one time or another" — Flash Ovens — Flash Orgasm Sting — White Smoke drifts away and leaves the doctor still standing there — board books spread out on the table like a pack of tarot cards — The doctor folds the cards

together — The board disappears in a silver flash) —
"He quiets you" —

And so we turn over the board books written in symbols
of a time that meanwhile i had forgotten — Like this:: $ —
American scent of memory pictures — sexual frustration
— Scandinavia outhouse skin put it on — % — criminal
street boy of dying peoples — easily corrupted and shoved
humiliations — Away from me, these association locks —
Pictures shatter a window in stupid pressure group relying on rectum — Board members, look out — Technical
brains melted the law — Control machine is disconnected by nova police — Look at the bread line — Their
boy entered the '20s in drag from collaborators — Liars
spread slow-motion flashes — Board book symbols refer
to association locks — information files of human nights
there — collaborators with any people anywhere on dead
nitrous flesh — Traitors to all souls everywhere travel
there — As word dust falls cross newsprint of the earth,
voices won't do a bit of good — The Old Doctor cleaving a
heavy frustration and humiliation account — Hurry up
please — The board is near right now relying on money,
fading voices — Control machine is disconnected —
Word fell out of here through the glass and metal streets
— God of Panic pipes blue notes through dying peoples
— The law is dust — The wired structure of reality went
up in slow-motion flashes —

Invisible intervention of a time forgotten — slow
water dripping on a garage — voices in other dressing

rooms — "Turn around — Bend over" — poisonous cloud of other flesh — Scandinavia outhouse skin on the co-pilot — Sat helpless while the invading force guided humiliations —

"You see, son, we were the only riders — Mutual erections fading through dusty air of gymnasiums — Folding cocks disappear on dead nitrous flesh — Point of these exercises is to maintain the local line — Sinking ship trying source of frustration to buy ersatz summons" —

Yes, you have a doorway — Ali blew the smoke and waved his hands — "Abracadabra" — distant events in green neon — you the smoke — The man laughed — Quick fires from teeth grinding together — Ali, muttering in the dog rotation, pounding the other on back — old mirror bent over a chair — controlled drum music on the crumpled form — Many names murmur cloth that fell in a heap — Flute went out shutting the door — And from radios i don't see luminous grey flakes falling — Galaxies pulled green troops in the streets — Impressions suddenly collapse to a heap — (Motions with his hand) — Guards fold now — Dodging from side to side over spots of weakness opened a great rent — Now Ali doubled back from above punch cards — There was nothing but a smear of grey substance barring his way to the towers — Film set goes up in red nitrous smoke — Remember show price? Know who I am? Yes talking to you board members . . I don't talk often and I

don't talk long . . You smell Hiroshima? You know who
I am now? *Señor* Deadline has come to call . . Did you
think you could call me and not pay you welching board
bastards? Set your Geiger counters forward an hour.
Captain Clark welcomes you aboard . . last rights . . Mr
Deadline is *here* to call . .

(The concept of Deadliners I owe to a story that
appeared in *New World Science Fiction* . . Nova
Publications . . 7 Grape St. High Holborn London
Vol 49 June . . "The Star Virus" by J. Barryington Bayley . . Deadliners in this story are space travelers across
light-years who have lost all human contacts and fears.
They play a form of nuclear poker. Calling in this game
can explode the players and the premises . .)

"Why you might have taken half the planet with you,"
exclaims an inexperienced Deadliner . .

"The whole of it, mate."

"You touched a pack of cards — You see, son, voices
muttering in the dog rotation:: 'Pain and pleasure — orgasm
death — flesh' — desolate underbrush of old Westerns —
battered phonograph sex scenes — courage to pass without
doing things — If you'll just stay near right now — be
shifted harsh at the Ovens — Mutual erections fading, kid
— Have to square it with him — We were all junkies and
dead train whistles the local line — Look down along a
brass bed — Many names murmur of human nights there
— i am dying cross newspapers of the earth — Stranger

lips bring down death — breathless flute through Ali's body — fading my name — newsreels of riot frozen to stills — whiffs of evening breeze" —

"Call the Old Doctor twice? — cleaving a summons — Marks closed your account — Hurry up, please — There is only the silence of water smiles dimmer at the edges — I don't see anybody here — You made a wide U turn back to camera gun — Vaudeville voices won't do you a bit of good — Galaxies pulled green troops in the area — The White Smoke drifts away" —

"But i got the area trade — Impressions of Present Time" —

Makes a folding motion with his hands — Guards fold together and disappear — People gone — Well fade out in other flesh armed with switchblades and bicycle chains — Pictures shatter a window in the office — Spattered light on naked rectum — Young faces melted the law in dead nitrous streets — Errand boys closing round the board —

"What's this green boy entered the '20s in drag from sinking ship?" —

"You trying source of slow-motion flashes on the screen?" —

"Boneless mummy was death in the last Walgreen's — We don't want it" —

"We been subliminated in doorway" —

Errand boy from last parasite muttering beside you — great wind voices on those tracks — remitted muttering::

"Not think the Doctor on stage" and "Who am i to say more?" —

Empty all the hate faces sucked into fear — crumpled cloth bodies — open shirt flapping — some wise characters — All right, doctor — Vapor trails writing the sky — Newsreels shut off — Magazines screaming on the parasite — The radio muttering — "The Doctor on stage" —

All the hate faces sucked into release without more ado what? — bodies and water everywhere — The Oven rousers give off a stench of rotten lips departed — Move in fast — Interrogate substance of the other — Boneless mummy moved with the speed of "want it?" Empty flesh of KY and rectal mucus last gate from human form — They twisted through open shirt flapping against each other — Hands goosed the ass — Penis spurted again — the gate from burning sex skin — Empty faces sucked in other apparatus —

great wind voices beside you — the Doctor on stage — "Out of here, female impersonators" — orgasm of memory pictures — people gone — Diarrhea exploded down his Scandinavia outhouse skin — Corpses hang from gallows — Talk to switch blades —

"All right, doctor, before newsreels shut off indications enough — i told you i would come back beside him — He could move now — healed scars — courage to pass without doing pictures" —

"i'm going now — We were all junkies — Now some

wise characters think guards and weapons of the enemy were all right — Suddenly shut off with camera gun and static — We see all the Garden of Delights in a flash like a pack of cards — He felt a little pleasure — sex scenes of all times" —

"Old Doctor twice? Cleaving a heavy erogenous message reflected in your account — Hurry up, please — empty flesh dimmer at the edges — God of Panic piping blue notes touched a pack of cards — Through the glass we see all the pictures — invisible orgasm death skin on the co-pilot — Battered phonograph talks humiliations — Poisonous cloud near right now" —

"Fading, kid — Voices in other dressing with the St. Louis suburb — The local line bends over rectum of broken nights — Fading my name through dying air" —

in
that game?

The Fluoroscopic Kid says: "Now look, son, when you move in on a new pitch don't be one of these Eager Beavers jump right into a dime — That's how you got caught here in the Cycle of Action — Now learn to sit back and watch — Don't talk don't play just *watch* — fifty a hundred thousand years if necessary until you know all the rules and combos penalties and angles — When you can see all the cards then move in and take it all — Learn to *watch* and you *will* see all the cards

— Look through the human body the house passes out
at the door — What do you see? — It is composed of
thin transparent sheets on which is written the action
from birth to death — Written on 'the soft typewriter'
before birth — a cold deck built in — The house know
every card you will be dealt and how you will play all
your cards — And if some wise guy does get a glimmer
and maybe plays an unwritten card::

'Green Tony — Izzy the Push — Sammy the Butcher
— *Hey Rube!!!* Show this character the Ovens — This
is a wise guy' —

"You want to sit in on that game? ? — Now look some
more — The body is two halves stuck together like a
mold — That is, it consists of *two* organisms — See 'the
Other Half' invisible — (to eyes that haven't learned
to watch) — Like a Siamese twin ten thousand years in
show business engaged by a silver cord to all erogenous
zones — lives along the divide line — is an amphibious
two-sexed actor half-man half-woman — double-gated
either sex can breathe air or the underwater medium up
your mother's snatch — 'the Other Half' is 'You' next
time around — born when you die — that is when 'the
Other Half' kills you and takes over — (Take a talking
picture of you. Now stop the projector and sound track
frame by frame: stop . . go go go . . stop . . go go . . *Stop*.
When the sound track stops it stops. When the projector
stops a still picture is on screen. This would be your
last picture the last thing you saw. Your sound track

consists of your body sounds and sub-vocal speech. Sub-vocal speech *is* the word organism the 'Other Half' spliced in with your body sounds. You are convinced by association that your body sounds will stop if sub-vocal speech stops and so it happens. Death is the final separation of the sound and image tracks. However, once you have broken the chains of association linking sub-vocal speech with body sounds shutting off sub-vocal speech need not entail shutting off body sounds and consequent physical death.)

"Now let's play some poker — Why not take over both halves of a body so you don't need any mooching 'Other Half' — Why not rewrite the message on 'the soft typewriter'? — Why not take the board books and rewrite all message? — Why not take over the human body right down the middle line? — Under distant fingers move in and take it all — All right, watch what is covering the two halves with so-called human body — Flesh sheets on which is written: 'The spines rubbed and merged' — Written *before* on 'the Soft Typewriter' — transparent quivering substance the body is two halves stuck together around him — a shadowy figure melting to sperm — a silver cord of tendril fingers rubbing erogenous zones along the divide line — contractions in the tumescent sponge pulse future organism — shoot out body dies falling into water — Play some poker — Why not take over underwater sleep? — You don't need any 'Other Half'

— Why not take the middle line? You see it is composed from birth to death — A cold deck under his gills dealt the softening spine — In that game? — Now look again — He sank into other flesh mold — Siamese twin substance in spine lives along the shocks of electric cocaine pleasure — The Other Half will be born inside feeling both halves of the body —

"Now *look* son, when you move in a new angle — These Eager Beavers jump right into a dime — That way Birth & Death cycle action — You want out? Con cop — It's an old vaudeville act — Just walk in and throw the tin on the board —

"Learn to sit back and watch — Just take both parts — Watch what you walk into — So called human body? Long ride on the White Sheets — Slide in cool and casual — I'll play your cards — You want to sit in on the local line? — Look down look down along that line before you travel there — If there the body is two halves stuck together form you can score for —

"Why I'm here — To play some poker — Why not flash the marks soft typewriter? Why not call? — When you call write all message — Why not take over ticket? You want out? — Con cop — It's an old vaudeville act — Just walk in and throw the tin on the Board — Cover Sammy and the boys — Take the board books and re-write the cold deck — Any board member want to play some straight five card stud? I didn't think so — Now cut up the board books, son — Minutes to go" —

The Subliminal Kid is a charter defector from the nova mob —

"Just a technical sergeant is all — Just Time — Just Time — Just Time —" So he moved in with the Rewrite Department and set up his headquarters to put out the Rewrite Bulletins on subliminal level — It's all done with tape recorders. Go out and buy three fine machines on credit and put your name down for an in-television unit. Find a boy with blue eyes and gentle precise fingers . . (He was a ham radio operator at twelve at the age of eight he released weather balloons which he fabricated from plastic suit covers . .) The boy will wire your machines for you. You need a switchboard so you can control the machines: Tape Recorder 1 playback five seconds Tape Recorder 2 and 3 record and so forth. Take an everyday situation you are arguing with your boy friend or girl friend remembering what was said last time and thinking of things to say next time the whole stupid argument going going round and round like the music in your head until it bores you just silly to hear it but you are aggrieved and playing back self-pity and you just can't shut up. Take your arguments and complaints and put them on T.R.1 and call that machine Tom or Dick or Harry you name it it's yours. On T.R.2 put all the things he or she said to you or might say. Now make the two machines talk: T.R.1 playback five seconds T.R.2 record. T.R.2 playback three seconds T.R.1 record. Run it through fifteen minutes half an hour now switch intervals. Run the interval switch you used on T.R.1 back on T.R.2 — (You will find that the intervals are as important as the so-called context) — listen to the two machines mixing it around and around. Now for T.R.3 — (Who is the third that walks beside you?) — With T.R.3 you can introduce the factor of "irrelevant response" so put just any old thing on T.R.3 a sad old tune a sad old joke a piece of the street TV radio and cut T.R.3 into the argument T.R.1: "I waited up for you last night till two o'clock" . . T.R.3: "And now if you will excuse me . . The soccer scores are coming in from the Capital . . One must pretend an interest . ."

Get it out of your head and into the machines. Stop talking stop arguing. Let the machines talk and argue. A tape recorder is an externalized section of the human nervous system. You can find out more about the nervous system and gain more control over your reaction by using a tape recorder than you could find out sitting twenty years in the lotus posture. Whatever your problem is just throw it into the machines and let them chew it around a while. There is of course the initial problem: programming tape recorders is an expensive deal any way you wire it.

The spliced-tape experiment to which I have already referred can be performed by anyone equipped with two tape recorders connected by extension lead so he can record directly from one machine to the other. Since the experiment may give rise to a marked erotic reaction it is more interesting to select as your partner for this experiment some one with whom you are on intimate terms. We have two subjects designated as S and W. Now take a text any text. S records the text on Tape Recorder 1. W records the same text on Tape Recorder 2. Now play back T.R.1 three seconds recording on T.R.2. Play back T.R.2 three seconds recording on T.R.1 and so forth *alternating* the two recorded voices. This is the simplest form of the spliced-tape experiment. The same results can be obtained by splicing two street recordings made separately by S and W. In order to obtain any degree of precision the tapes must be cut with a scissors and spliced together with tape. This is a laborious process that can be appreciably expedited if you have access to a cutting room and use film tape which is larger and much easier to handle. You can carry the experiment further by taking a talking film of S and a talking film of W and splicing sound and image track alternating 24 times per second.

S and W carry in their respective and presumed separate nervous systems the equipment to record and playback sound to take images, equipment of which recorder and camera are the externalized abstraction. The equipment contained in the nervous systems of our two subjects is capable of *total recording* that is of recording and storing sound image smell tactile sensations and the affective reactions associated with this material. The total recording is activated by the playback

of sound and image track by precise association with
it, so that when we cut the film and sound record made
on recorder and camera by our two subjects in together
we are splicing the total record of S in with the total
record of W. A flu virus is able to take over a healthy
lung cell by giving the same signals as a healthy lung
cell. The virus can give the same signals as a healthy
lung cell because *it was a healthy lung cell at one time*.
Spliced tape and film may or may not give rise to virus
forms — (*Warning: experiments with spliced tape and
film are dangerous* parenthetically) — In any case a unit
of sound track recorded and film taken by S spliced in
with W is now able to give the same signals as a W unit
because it *was that unit by the fact of being recorded
on W's sound and image track* and replacing the sound
and image unit recorded and filmed by W. We may say
that S can give the same signals as W *because he retroactively was W* when an S unit of sound and image is
cut into W's sound and image track replacing W with S.
Of course the same replacements are occurring in the
sound and image track of S. *If S is spliced into the total
record of W and W is not spliced into the total record of
S this unilateral splicing may result in W contracting
an S virus to his considerable disadvantage.*

Many applications of the spliced-tape principle will
suggest themselves to the alert reader. Suppose you are
some creep in a grey flannel suit. You want to present
a new concept of advertising to the Old Man . . *creative*

advertising: "I mean advertisements that tell a story and create characters Inspector J. Lee of the Nova Police smokes Players — (flashes his dirty rotten hunka tin). Agent K9 uses a Bradly laser gun. Aurelius would have approved your favorite smoke. Advertisements should provide the same entertainment value as the content of a magazine. Call in the best writers to write the continuity the best painters and photographers on the layout. *Your* product *deserves* the best." So before he goes up against the Old Man he records the Old Man's voice and splices his own voice in explaining his new concept and puts it out on the office air-conditioning system. Or suppose you are a singer. Well splice your singing in with the Beatles, the Rolling Stones, the Animals. Splice yourself in with newscasters, prime ministers, presidents. Why stop there? Why stop anywhere? Everybody splice himself in with everybody else. Communication must be made total. Only way to stop it.

Wittgenstein said: "No proposition can contain itself as an argument" = The only thing *not* prerecorded in a prerecorded universe is the prerecording itself which is to say *any* recording that contains a random factor.

It's all done with tape recorders . . Guess you've all seen the Philips Carry Corder a handy machine for street recording and playback you can carry it under your coat for recording important thing to remember is not just recording but *playback in the street* the Carry Corder looks like a transistor radio for street playback city

folks don't notice yesterday voices phantom car holes
in time . . fun and games with this gadget . . God's little
toy Paul Bowles calls it . . (Maybe his last toy parenthetically he is gone away through unknown mornings
leave a million tape recordings of his voice behind
fading into the cold spring air pose a colorless question?) . . Why not give Carry Corder parties? Every guest
arrives with his Carry Corder and cartridges of what
he intends to say recording what other Carry Corders
say to him it is the height of rudeness not to record
when directly addressed by another Carry Corder no one
can talk *directly* at a Carry Corder party if you want to
say something you have to nick off into the little boy's
room and record it first while your genial host mixes
the whole party around on a battery of tape recorders
. . ("Not infrequently I stripped to the waist and pitched
in with the men . . Yes boys that's me there by the ce-
ment mixer.") . . You can use the recordings from the
last party at the next party funeral meats serving up
the wedding feast in the word of the Immortal Bard tomorrow and tomorrow and tomorrow . . And think what
several hundred people with Carry Corders could do at
a political rally . . Carry your Carry Corders down Fleet
St. and Madison Avenue . . Subliminate the sublimi-
nators . . Carry Corders of the world unite. You have
nothing to lose but your prerecordings.

"It's all done with recorders — The sound track
evokes the image track — Recollect when i was on

the Madison Avenue Lark — So i am giving out with
a steady stream of interviews and i soon extracted the
interview formulae — I recorded ten alternative answers
to any question from the interview framework — And
all i had to do was press buttons and out came the
answers — I could of course do this from a distance by
radio and retired to my Southern plantation strictly from
Tin Pan Alley with recorded darkies singing out in the
mimosa and Spanish moss projected on view screens
— Later the whole operation was automatic and did not
need my attention at all and i had answers for the next
thousand years all set up — I extended the principle
of absent control to other activities — I dictated the
necessary orders, counterorders and alternative moves
for any operation — I could write all the speeches and
ultimatums of one government with answering speeches
and ultimatums of another and of course put on the war
recordings when the order came through channels —
Just a technical sergeant know how things are done
— Same method can be applied to sex — As a young
man i discovered that i could anticipate the dialogue of
any amorous encounter — So i recorded the dialogue
and made an image track to go with it — appropriate
background music, lighting, odors the lot — Action
— Camera — Compliments of Pavlov i could do quite
as well with my recordings as with the so-called 'real
thing' (The image track can be dispensed with once
the appropriate associations are established) — i built

up a whorehouse of tapes and rented them out for two notes a night any script any face you want — Spot of bother with the Syndicate and that's when i moved into the Madison Avenue Territory — Now carry it a bit further — The interviewer can of course apply the same method — That is record his questions and alternative questions — Both governments can record speeches, ultimatums, orders and counterorders — So record the whole war with its battles and sieges, victories and defeats, monumental fuck-ups and corny songs — Lovers exchange tapes — You understand nobody has to be there at all — So why ask questions and why answer? — Why give orders and why make speeches? — Why not leave your tape with her tape and dispense with sexual contact? — And then? — Since no one is there to listen, why keep running the tape? — Why not shut the whole machine off and go home? Exactly what i intend to do — Turn all my tapes over to Rewrite and go home — You can look any place — No good — *No bueno* — Departed have left no address — It's all done with tape recorders. What we see is dictated by what we hear. You can verify this by a simple experiment. Turn off the sound track on your television set and use an arbitrary recorded sound track from your tape recorder: street sounds . . music . . conversation . . recordings of other TV programs, radio et cetera. You will find that the arbitrary sound track seems to be appropriate . . people running for a bus in Piccadilly with a sound track of machine-gun fire looks like 1917 Petrograd. You can extend the experiment by using material that is more or less appropriate to the image track. For example take a political speech on TV shut off sound track and substitute another speech you have prerecorded . . hardly tell the difference . . isn't much . . Record the sound track of one Danger Man spy program and substitute for another . . Try it on your friends and see if they can't tell the difference.

The sound track conjures up the image track — Word came before image — Shut off the sound track on your TV set and put in your own sound track words music what you will — Now play back your sound track and you will see the images sharp and clear — I recorded sound tracks of TV and film programs — mixing in suggestions from Rewrite to microphones and radio cruise cars — So i press a button and record all sounds and voices of the city — So i press a button to feed back these sounds with cut-ins a few seconds later, you are still watching a TV program or listening to the juke box — A few seconds later you are hearing the same words from my broadcast with cut-ins from Rewrite — Of course i cut in bulletins from Rewrite with all popular songs using music as punctuation — (Singing came before talking) — I folded the bulletins in with newspapers, magazines and novels — I put them out mixed with street sounds and talk wind and rain and lapping water and birdcalls — Well — Word evokes image — &

% $ $ "N:? — Singing came before talking — Shut the whole machine off — Rub out the word — There is no one there to hear it — Nothing here now but the recordings may not refuse vision in setting forth — the story of one absent today — Fade-out overtakes Mr Bradly Mr Martin — Five times thy strong tape caught in the door — no shelter in the dogs of unfamiliar dust — the cold *adiós* without a shadow — These our actors bid you a long good night —

showed you
your air

"The Subliminal Kid charters your attention please — i am Inspector J. Lee of The Nova Police — Just a technical sergeant moved a nova criminal to Rewrite Operations — And i am sure that it's all done with recorders — Remember that these techniques for the next thousand years manipulated by nova criminals — Absent control simple:: Always create as many insoluble counterorders and alternative conflicts recordings to the explosion of a planet — Recording devices fix the nature of absolute associations, established total weapons — manipulated on a global scale feeds:: Go home — Conflicts are deliberately created — No address the Nova Mob — Sammy the Butcher, the sound track conjures up the Brown Artist to paint yellow plains of Minraud — Jacky Blue Note, shut off the sound track on your Hamburger Mary — the subliminal words music what you will — Now in all my experience as a police officer never seen such total fear of indicated alterations on any planet — The same words straighten out this mess — Cut in bulletins from Rewrite — Nothing here now but unworkable course — Mr Bradly Mr Martin, Audience Chamber with the threat of no shelter in the dogs — Is that clear enough or shall i make it even clearer?" —

"For i have known exactly what i intend to do" —

"Isn't time is there left? — Go home — A boy shut off the sound track on you in the door — words, music what you will — Now the final ape of history sees the images sharp and clear on your ticket that exploded — end of voices — So i press a button beside you and the dreamer gone — So why ask questions and why intersect on empty speech? — Why not leave this dream contact? Shut the machine off — nothing here now but the door — juke box bulletins from Rewrite singing in newspapers and magazines of the earth:

"Word falling — Photo falling — Defectors from the Nova Mob — Just time — Just time — Just time" —

Electric storms of violence sweep broadcast still in progress "Word falling — Photo falling" —

"Gongs of violence show alternative answers to any question — Artists take over the entire answer battery of automatic junk state — i extended this to other flesh — Counterorders issued — Dictate force of riot police at the operation — Now of course Death Dwarfs talking in supersonic blasts to the same on orbit of Saturn galaxy — The interviewers shift in speed-up movie — Now since i could attack position over instrument i had the answers for a thousand years — Didn't have to be there answering questions of absent tenants — The Rewrite Doctor on stage — shatters a window in image without word — All i had to do was press slow-motion flashes and newsreels shut off — All right, Doctor, stop asking questions — Indications enough answer without being there — Shut the whole machine off July 1962, Present Time — Big money bulletins feed back Scandinavia outhouse parasite — A song goes through the city with suggestion pictures feeling along — And this broadcast was still in progress — The human body is an image on screen talking — You made questions and put the answers on a face — Good bye old interview — Mack The Knife, i can work for anybody — Juke box or radio speak of new dreams for old — Moanin' low my sweet bulletins and feed them back all the time to put all the things you are on subliminal level — Alternative answers to any question can play the game as well as you — Entire answer battery on automatic hopes to be there — i could control it from my blue heaven — Somebody stole my girl — Thing was automatic — Seemed to whisper Louise, Mary, all the things you used to do — Should old acquaintance go home? Why should anybody be there from Florida up to the

old North Pole? — Ahead — Ahead — Ahead — they
chanted and retired to Tin Pan Alley — Record either
end — Beat your mother to Spanish moss — automatic
future for the next thousand years — war recordings
at the time but Old Bill, returned a technical sergeant
— Witnesses from a distance observed the image track
streak across the sky and crash with associations —
established this art along the Tang dynasty — So we
turn over board books on subliminal level — sexual
frustration lark — 'So i am giving out skin — Put it
on' — easily ten alternative answers to any association locks — And all i had to do was shatter a window
in stupid board members — Errand boy closing their
screens — the whole operation from collaborators and
liars — Won't be much left — i dictated the necessary orders on the air — with human nights — Voices
came through channels — just any people anywhere
on dead nitrous flesh are done — i discovered that i
could anticipate the humiliation account" —

"Hurry up — Counter" —

"So i recorded the dialogue and boy from last stupid
pressure group with appropriate background music —
Control machine is disconnected compliments of Pavlov
— board books are written in symbols as the so-called
'real thing' — American from last interview performed
sharp discharge from method — So why ask questions
and why answer $? — Why not leave your tape humili-
ations and Scandinavia outhouse contacts? — You can

look any place — no pressure group relying on rectum — no address — Technical brains melted the law — The sound track conjures up the image police — Shut off the sound track — Their boy entered the '20s in word and music — Spread slow-motion flashes and you see the image sharp and clear — So i press the button blocks board instructions cross newspapers of the earth — Collaborators with word with flesh, traitors to all souls everywhere, i cut in bulletins from Rewrite with heavy punctuation — The board is relying on fading voices — Shut the whole machine off — Rub out the board — Is near right now to hear it — Mr Bradly Mr Martin five times guided poisonous cloud of parasites — These our actors bid you peaceful opaqueness in this monument of tiredness" — The Old Man himself stood at the end of the board room table a hat box under his arm. With an abrupt movement he emptied the hat box. The bronze head of a young girl crudely severed with a hack saw clattered across the board room table. The Old Man held up a hack saw bronze filings caught in its teeth.

"This old hand went and sawed the head off their filthy mermaid . . J. Ericson & Sisters only living rival of Trak . . . If anyone does not like this thing that I have done I can use this saw a second time."

He paced behind the board members like an aroused tom cat. He stopped behind Scamperelli the Pulp King who perfected a process for making pasta from sawdust. He clamped one hand over Scamperelli's mouth pulled

his head back and applied the hack saw to Scamperelli's
throbbing carotid. "Scamperelli do you like this thing
that I have done?"

"Glub . . glub . . glub . ."

"I presume that is pulp talk for 'yes.'"

He paced and stopped behind the Oil King. "Total
Oil, do you like this thing that I have done?"

Dry Hole Dutton glanced sideways at the saw. With a
presence of mind derived from his wildcatting days he
crooned out: "Only you can make the world go round."
Unanimously other board members took up the chant.
Its the old army game kid. Get there firstest with the
brownest nose.

"Thing Police all Board Room Reports now are ended
— i foretold you were all spirits watching TV program
— Terminal electric voices end — These our actors cut
in — A few seconds later you are melted into air — Rub
out promised by our ever-living poet — Mr Bradly Mr
Martin, five times our summons — no shelter in setting
forth" —

"Beat your mother to Spanish broadcast still in
progress — Just time — Just time — So we turn over
board books — i can work for anybody — newsreel
lark — So i am giving out Rewrite Department —
Pictures shatter absent bodies — Juke box closing their
screens — Sex phantom tape association afternoons
conveyed on the air with human image — flesh done
slow motion — Hurry up — Counter the last errand

boy from stupid pressure group — All right, Doctor,
machine is disconnected — Indications enough written in symbols as the machine shut off July 26, 1962,
Present Time — Just Time — Just Time — flashing on
global scale: 'Scandinavia outhouse parasite, go home'
— And no address nova mob — The human body is
sound track on 'Hamburger Mary'" —

"Just a technical sergeant — Now in all my experience i can work for anybody and clear this department"
—

"Bulletins make a play for the planet — unworkable
course, Mr Bradly — So why intersect on empty heart
and empty speech? — Why not leave all the things
you are? — A boy shut off the sound — Now the final
answers to my questions loud and clear on your ticket
— No one is there to change new dreams for old — Hear
the silence — Some one in the mood for rewrite — old
dream, Panama — year ago melted" —

"Man, like good bye then" —

"Sidewalks of new solitude overtakes the tapes —
Singing came before body with the answer on a face —
Half-healed in wind and rain play the game as well as
you — entire film to smoke — nothing here now — Calm
his face dictates the dream in doorways — These our ac-
tors bid you a long good night from Florida up to the old
North Pole — So why ask questions of one absent today?
— Why not leave your ambiguous sexual contacts? —
Why not shut off absent tenants? — Silence says good

bye to white planet — You can look any place — in slow formations, no address — The sound track conjures up burning metal eyes and long claws — Shut off the sound track carried by the navigators — Controllers of word and music monopolized and froze the earth — kept the Djoun forces in film programs — Junk is colorless no-smell of death as punctuation — Nothing here now but half-healed dream flesh hatching forth the story of a cold *adiós* — Silence, Mr Bradly Mr Martin — No shelter in the cotton flesh lying there — Your ticket now ended — These our defectors from the nova mob pipe your summons — All the sound track evokes the image into dawn and dream — fade out Madison Avenue Lark" —

"Other flesh interviews and soon extracted home in the dog — ten alternative answers to any dead nitrous framework — Mr Martin is story of any face any script you want" —

"I discovered that i could anticipate encounter — So i recorded the dialogue and your ticket now ended — Appropriate background music at the far end of evening — So we'll sing one song with your tape and dispense with making a Monday line — You are still watching a TV program from phallic statues — secondhand erog-enous place — angel voices calling old image track — Look God's your TV set — Put in your own sound track faces — Bulletins free the Djoun forces — I put them out with wind and rain and birdcalls — Rub out

the word — There is no one there you got it? — sex
and pain recordings — orgasm cocoon of one absent
today — Fade-out overtakes the ship came apart here
— white sheets dripping nova" —

"Just a technical question caught our ticket —
Remember i was the door to put out Rewrite Bulletins
— You got sex and pain information — It's all done
with recorders — Recollect green flowers hanging over
the swamp mud with erectile formulae feeling into
mouth and penis? — Cotton flesh lying there in ice?
— You understand sex and pain information so why
ask questions? — Why not leave green flowers hanging over sexual contact? — Tendrils of erectile tape?
— Why not shut off fire feeling into mouth and penis?
— i shut off the sound track on a shadow in the last
words — Now dream flesh left no address for i see the
images sharp and clear — So i press button in final ape
of history — Seconds later cold empty you melted the
cotton flesh lying there — Broken dream beside you and
the dreamer takes his way toward terminal punctuation
— What have i my friend to give? — Shut the whole
machine off — Rub out the life i led — nothing here
now but shade from the death trauma — The story of
cold *adiós* — No shelter in the dogs — Calling Panama
alterations — flesh empty in the trade winds — ebbing
carbon dioxide as punctuation — Silver flakes closed
your account — Nothing here now but dust falling from

demagnetized patterns — Departed have left Mr Bradly
Mr Martin — Five times good night under surges of
silence — Shadow actors walk through dream — No
one is there to listen — Someone walking from Rewrite
to microphones trails Summer dawn sounds and old
dream — Panama night button feeds back these sounds
with sweat flipped from his face — TV program melted
before daybreak — Seconds later you splintered on
empty flesh — Breath of the trade winds talking — I
folded the bulletins of evening" —

  "Man, like good bye then" —

  "Rain and birdcalls — The dreamer with dirty flesh
came before talking — Explode the word? — No one
there — Solitude overtakes thy tape caught in the door
— Dream singing came before body without a shadow
without relics — face healed and half-healed in wind
and rain — Well, word evokes image — Silver film took
it to smoke path — Shut the whole machine off — Rub
out scar impressions — nothing here now in kerosene
lamp — open shirt, calm his face — The street blew
rain, Mr Bradly Mr Martin — five times thy dream in
doorways — no shelter in the dog's death trauma — out
of the sick lies no program — nothing here now but a
cold odor of vacant good bye — empty condom caught
in the door" —

  "Man, like good bye" —

  smoke song strung together on scar impressions —
urine shadows in the gutter —

let them

see us

Now some words about the image track — The human body is an image on screen talking — Spread slow-motion flashes and you see the image sharp and clear — Flesh done slow motion — The Short Time Hyp is subliminal slow motion — Like this: a movie at normal speed is run at 24 frames per second — 35 frames per second is not perceptible as slow motion if the image on screen is more or less stationary — But the image is on screen longer than you are there watching it — That is you are being short-timed 11 frames per second — Put a beautiful nude image on screen at subliminal slow motion and it will be built into your flesh — That is whenever the sound track is run the image will literally come alive in your flesh — Word with heavy slow-motion image track *is* flesh — You got it? — Put on any image at 35 frames per second with sound track and play the sound track back and see the image sharp and clear — Now run your image at 24 frames per second and play back the sound track — Not so sharp and clear — Now run the image track speeded up and play back sound track — You will notice that the image recall is progressively dimmer —

The venereal disease films shown by the U.S. Army in the name of hygiene were run at 35 frames per second — at 35 frames per second sores and swollen genitals

and the sound track a standard army medic voice —
tattooed chancres across millions of young bodies with
indelible short-time ink — scar impressions reactivated
by any army medic voice — So that's The Short Time
Hyp and the Flesh Gimmick — subliminal slow-motion
image — Play the sound track back and the image will
rise out of the tape recorder — Slow-motion sound track
is flesh — Use for this purpose background noises of
dripping water — With appropriate background music
you see the image sharp and clear — compliments of
Pavlov — The Short Time Hyp is called "the real thing"
— thing is right — subliminal slow flesh out of the tape
recorder — Word with heavy track *is* flesh — sex tape
playback with human image — program from phallic
statues calling old image track across a million young
bodies with sound track faces — I am precisely saying
that disease films shown by the U.S. Army at 35 frames
per second are called in question — Sex phantoms have
prevented research on flesh — a sex movie at 35 frames
and citizens redirected — have any script you want on
screen talking, Doctor Reich — Restore juxtaposition
of images sharp and clear — And playback there you
got formulae could be discovered today — Presumed
right of the boards who intend to take over the image
behind what filth deals consummated privately — easily
corrupted your flesh with these association locks in repeated image — 35 frames per second is not perceptible
as slow orgasm death — Mutual erections built into

dawn sleep — Open shirt flapping came alive in your flesh — This 35 frames is local line you got it? — Look down and see the image of human nights there — The board is near right now — screen subliminal death — relying on fading voices —

"And so we turn over the board books — Let them see us — i am dying cross newspapers of speeded-up and played-back sound track — Stranger lips bring Ali's body — fading my name in whiffs of evening breeze" — "Closed frames — is only the silence with water — Millions of young bodies with voices won't do you a bit of good — Slow-motion sound track is rectums naked in dripping water on dead nitrous flesh — Now some words about the image track — Time screen talking — female impersonators loud and clear — And so we turn over a steady stream of frames that meanwhile i had forgotten — Image is on screen longer than Scandinavia outhouse skin — Your flesh with the sound track trails my Summer dawn wind in repeated image chains — Heavy slow-motion rectum plays the sound track boy from muttering tape recorders — Boneless mummy travels on new flesh with the sound track — Exquisite screen penis spurted heavy skin — End of the line — Empty flesh of KY and rectal mucus not perceptible as slow gate from human form — Faces sucked in other apparatus and you are there — So pack your ermines, Mary — The human body is transient hotel memory pictures — Put a beautiful nude

image under slow motion and it will be built into boneless mummy pressed flat like a suit — That is whenever
the sound track the mummy is made of comes alive in
your flesh — The Short Time Hyp is body molded in two
halves — 35 frames is not perceptible as slow green boy
softens the middle line more or less stationary — But the
sound track of deep freeze is in — You are there naked
in whiffs of thawing meat — Slow-motion sound track is
clothes — Voices from other dressings repeated the image
from erogenous word with heavy slow-motion body —
Want it? — Put on any image over rectum of broken ice
and play the sound track back — Excitement of human
nights there — Point of these exercises is clear — The
venereal disease films show frustration to buy ersatz
summons — Run at 35 frames fading cocks disappear
on dead nitrous flesh, sores and swollen genitals — tattooed screen in response to magnetic short-time ink —
Tape recorder word is slow pants using for this purpose
all sexual apparatus — Scandinavia outhouse skin is not
perceptible as slow invading force — The image will rise
out of orgasm leaving — background noise of dripping
water — board books are written in symbols more or less
stationary like this — $ — American upper middle class
— You are there — That is exposed to sexual frustration
and humiliations at 35 frames per second — Put a beautiful street boy upbringing slow motion and it will be built
into 'easily corrupted' and so forth — That is whenever
the sound track is run these association locks come alive in

your flesh — The board track is flesh you got it? — Stupid pressure group relying on 35 frames per second with sound track and the technical brains they have see the image sharp and clear — Speed up and play back the sound track — Control machine is disconnected — in the bread line without 'clothes' or a dime — collaborators — liars — traitors — back into time are such as you — cowards who cannot face your 'human animal' accounts — sex and pain track absent today — Fade-out overtakes image in subliminal slow sheets dripping out of the tape recorder — TV program melted flesh instrument imposed by force — Subliminal slow-motion techniques at 35 frames per second now are ended — Resulting spirits melted into air — The image fell out through the glass screen and spread Pan God of Panic piping blue notes loud and clear — Back into time are such as you, Mr Bradly Mr Martin — I edit delete and rearrange flesh and zero time to the sick lies — I fold in the door — Couldn't form nova — These our actors proffer the disaster accounts and show the method in operation" —

Under the story Mr Bradly Mr Martin — grey calm his face, dream shut off — I fold distant fingers — child of nova, the story over — I told him you walked out — You can look any place — Your stale overcoat not taking any rap for those board bastards — twisting hole in everybody — spilling out Limestone John, Hamburger Mary, Jacky Blue Note — on tracks I told — definitive arrest — crime child, good bye — couldn't reach me caught in the door — just silver film on your stale movies — round over and I fading —

silence
to say
good bye

These our actors bid you a long last good bye — Johnny Yen playing the flute in a shower of ruined suburbs —

"Man like healed and half-healed scars under the story — A street boy's good bye" —

Ancient Rings Of Saturn in the morning sky — The Old Doctor raises his blue hands — silence at this old doctor twice — hello yes good bye — indications enough in empty room, Miranda — Sex Garden caught in doors of Panic — Izzy the Push, Limestone John, Hamburger Mary, Jacky Blue Note, silence to the sick lies — "Marks? — What Marks?" — Identity fades in empty space — last intervention, the Subliminal Kid — helped me with fingers fading —

"Indications enough showed you your air — Like good bye then, Willy the Rat — Remember i was movies played good night — Known end of the line outside 1920 movie theater — Bring the Doctor on stage — Call the point — Last rotten terminal" —

His face showed strata of last good byes: "Like healed and half-healed scars, Kiki" — some clean shirt and walked "No good *no bueno* — *adiós*, Meester" — Poo

Poo the Dummy talking away in empty room "Green Tony and Willy the Rat on the last saucer, boss" —

"Errand boys" —

"I'm not taking any vaudeville voices — Bring the Doctor on — i'm going to rat on everybody" —

"Few more calls to make tonight" —

"We do our work and go — The ticket that exploded posed definitive arrest" —

"Perhaps, Inspector Lee" —

"Few more calls to make tonight left fingers fading Mr & Mrs D — exploded Sammy the Butcher — Indications enough just ahead, Inspector Lee, we do our last film — alteration in the morning sky — Like a street boy exploded the word — Last round from St. Louis melted flesh identity — John made coffee and scrambled some eggs. The kitchen was outside the partitioned bedroom . . a wired glass door opened onto the outside stairs over a vacant lot. John stood there with a cup of coffee late morning sunlight in his eyes.

"Why don't I work for your uncle's company? Work for a company and what do they give you? . . member of the Country Club . . house and garden . . a wife . . heart attack at 55 . . no thanks . . Come over here . ."

He guided Bill with gentle precise fingers and sat him on a stool in front of a box lined with metal. The box was wired to a series of boxes progressively smaller. In the last box was a crystal cylinder that rotated on a copper rod. John adjusted a needle touching the cylinder.

"Now talk . . something from your novel . . ."

"Well I have some of it here . . the first chapter . . I wanted you to see it . ."

"I will hear it which is not the same thing . . Words on a page travel at the speed of light . . 186,000 miles per second . . Your spoken words travel at 1,400 feet per second . . would take quite a while to catch up and illuminate the page . . All right . . go ahead . . And try not to crackle the paper."

Bill began to read: "sunlight through the dusty window of the basement workshop . . John's face grey and wispy a soft blue flame in his eyes as he bent over the crystal radio set touching dials and wires with gentle precise fingers . . 'I'm trying to fix it so we can both ten years from now listen at once . . Here hold this phone to your ear'. . actions become a legendary figure . . 'Do you hear anything? Yes maybe out through the dusty window would be the first step, Smoky.' . . empty back yards and ash pits frogs croaking 'John' . . metal prickles that spread to the groin . . far away sunlight . . outside wooden stairs . . screwdriver . . 'No. Get your hand away. I've told you ten times already.'"

"That's enough . . one minute . . Now I will read."

He picked up a magazine: "It was as though the sky had darkened for an instant as though there had been a sudden murmur in a gust of wind a sound of faraway trumpets a sighing like the rustle of a great silken robe for a time the whole of nature round about partook of this darkness the bird's song ceased the trees were still and far over the mountain there was a mutter of dull menacing thunder. That was all. The wind died along the tall grasses of the valley the dawn and the day resumed their place in time and the risen sun sent hot waves of yellow mist that made its path bright before it. The leaves spiraling up laughed in the sun and their laughter shook until each bough was like a school in fairyland. God had refused to accept the bribe." working for a company and what do they in a gust of wind room Bill was breathing give you? a sound of faraway trumpets a sighing like in a soft electric silence and member of the Country Club the rustle. great every breath sent the blood house and garden silken robe for a time pulsing to his crotch . . He turned to John . . a wife the whole of nature round about . . "Jesus" . . John put a finger across his lips . . heart attack at 55 partook of this darkness . . He bent over and took off his "No thanks" . . the bird's song ceased; the trees were still shoes and socks. The two boys . . come over here. I'm going to record your voice stood naked looking at each other your master's voice that and far over the mountain hands on each other speaks through you there was a mutter of their bodies washed in blue he guided Bill with gentle twilight fingers in front of a box the wind along . . all fours on the sofa metal grasses of the valley. The dawn and "Allah . . Jesus that feels the box was wired to a series resumed their place great Johnny." "Shut up Billy" . . boxes progressively smaller and in time and his flesh shivered and twitched in a coil of wire in a crystal risen sun hot waves spasms squeezing cylinder of yellow mist . . path bright tighter warm blue spurts "Now talk something from before it. The leaves spiraling up toward the novel "Well I have some of it here . . laughed in the sun . . "Look Billy the milky first chapter" . . their laughter shook sad train whistles . . see the trees . . a school . . cross a distant sky wild geese . . hear it in fairyland . . God had refused to accept the bribe . ."

"Now I am going to cut the cylinder into sections and rejoin the sections alternating your voice with mine . . take me an hour or so . . you can pass the time reading this" . .

He handed Bill a copy of the *Saturday Evening Post* . . on the cover boy at an attic window waving to a distant train. Bill turned to "The Diamond As Big As The Ritz" by F. Scott Fitzgerald and started to read. He finished the story.

"All right now . . his master's voice . . listen . ."

The sound was scarcely recognizable as human voices . . a cadence of vibration . . Bill felt a rush of vertigo as if the sofa was spinning away into space. Blue light filled the darkening room. Bill was breathing a soft electric silence that sent the blood pulsing to his crotch . . the two boys naked bodies washed in blue twilight shivered and twitched in spasms . . He was spiraling up toward the ceiling . .

"Look Billy the Milky Way."

sad train whistles cross a distant sky . . wild geese . . boy there waving to the train . . your *Saturday Evening Post* a long time ago . . two young bodies stuck together like dogs teeth bared . . two dead stars . . They went out a long time ago in empty back yards and ash pits . . a rustle of darkness and wires . . They went out and never came back a long time ago . .

Standing there in the dark room the boy said: "I've come a long way."

It was a long time in such pain used address I give you . . went out a long time ago . . The crystal radio set far away refused the bribe . . empty back yard . . long long radio silence on Portland . . . soccer scores — clock hands on a bar wall — Plaintive boy cries drift from the Street of Vagrant Ball Players to la Calle de los Desamparados — Image no matter how good must die in time blockade exploded. The last human blood i created is dead at the Swan Pub. Magazine must tell you bulkhead about to blow — kerosene light on Tangier streets — his smile through cigarette smoke — dead at the Swan Pub trailing his funny stories." "He tried to entertain the family, Meester."

"Look in the mirror. You face dead soldier. The last human image — Mr Bradly Mr Bolivar is dead — Big Picture calling Shifty — Klinker is dead — Major Ash is dead. When your image is dead you become virus and must obey virus orders. You understand now, you dumb hick? Life without flesh *is* the ovens. Only way we get out of Hell is through our image in the living. Remember the ovens? It is not only the heat. Remember the lack of 'emotion's oxygen' the lack of what you breathe, the lack of everything that would ever make you want to live or breathe? Well like you say any image repeated loses charge and that loss is the lack that makes this Hell and keeps us *here*. Where we are *is* Hell. You see how we were caught? Hostages *'here'* — Life without flesh is repetition word for word. Only way we got out of Hell is through repetition. That's why we all obey virus orders and endlessly reproduce its image *there* in the living. You see how we were caught in repetition sets? *Any* image repeated in your eyes, Bradly, makes this Hell and this enemy: the endless lack of what you breathe being the same image that repeats you want to live and breathe in all directions."

And like all virus the past prerecords your "future." Remember the picture of hepatitis is prerecorded two weeks before the opening scene when virus negatives have developed in the mirror and you notice your eyes are a little yellower than usual — So the image past molds your future imposing repetition as the past ac- cumulates and all actions are prerecorded and doped out and there is no life left in the present sucked dry by a walking corpse muttering through empty courtyards under film skies of Marrakesh.

Do you see life declined in the mirror? My sad ugliness the sheer answer muttering. "I was dead. I took your identity. Only the ugliness remains. Because ugliness is repetition to maintain precarious occupation. I wanted to say 'It wasn't like that — I didn't mean — there was another side' without a throat without a tongue locked in virus image that could only invade and damage to occupy. Now I can speak and I say: 'Do not accept another image identity on any terms in any form or you will be as I am now. As to what life can be worth when the honor the honor is gone *par example* I can offer an opinion. I know all about it. It is worth nothing nothing nothing. The offer of another image identity is always on virus terms. No good *no bueno* outright or partially. The only thing I can give you is my gun. I can't use it. You can. Here is my gun Bradly. Come in and get them.'" — Last words of Mr Bradly Mr-June 19, 1963 Marrakesh.

Drew iron tears down Pluto's cheek — a wall of water you understand — full fathom five — and still the words muttering and turning like dry leaves in the winter pissoir — *"J'aime ces type vicieux qu'ici montre la bite."* In the distance muffled explosions like dynamite in jelly. The natives are fishing. Four atomic underwater blasts were assayed yesterday at the testing grounds off Seattle. Doctor Unruh of Atomic Dissemination Headquarters described the yield as negligible and pointed up the necessity of a defense policy at once devious and unyielding firm and elastic so that, as he put it, the free world is subject to burst out anywhere. We have traction. All we need is a peg to hang it on or let us say one flash bulb in very fine copper wire. "Big Picture calling Flash bulb — put Major Ash on the phone."

"Lips that once were mine have you heard the news of war and death? Klinker is dead — Major Ash is dead — Chigger is dead." White rains slashed down. Blurred solutions leave something there between us on the white stone steps — fragments dying losing pain. Looked at me his voice muffled as if I were seeing his face through words fraying breaking focus — brain and blood and bones in the frozen till of a distant bank — Liver of self-deception in catatonic limestone liberates a love letter, sir, from marble flesh in slow spirals.

"I screw Meester?"

Burning sky the sheer answer — union rules — closed shop — fascist beasts.

"Yas," he said, "great bloody banners of resistance leaking red into straw." So Fred Flash he expose wrong and I think that he now take nothing. vast repetition muttering in empty news magazine. change somewhat unusual to those with a deep and glittering image.

"So? Burning heavens, idiot."

Chigger he was called. Running do you see after me up the stone street. So turned around both guns blazing pounding blue stabs seventy tons to the square inch you understand and I saw the brains go. He crumpled

there on the steps and now looking at me silent as all
the red hair and smudged freckles and red flesh of
the world flushed through him blurring his face out of
focus as if I were seeing his face through dying eyes
that could not focus the red swirls and blurs — dying
there on the white steps brains and blood and bones
frayed by my laser guns. My guns? But who am I?
The sheer answer out of focus in dying eyes and I told
the driver: "Take me to a hotel of the medium class
— decent — inexpensive." (Rain marched across the
valley in silver columns) Then the rain hit and I was
running toward the barrier up the stone street the gun
in my pocket still. Are you? Will you? I know nothing here running running the gun in my pocket in my
hand in my eyes — pounding light gun. "Well yas,"
he said, "Great libraries and bureaucracies of such
an intricacy a thousand years to draft a single petition
you understand and five thousand years to process it
through the filters and amber molds — It could have
been so?" Words falling like dead birds there in the
noon streets — sad last time with some dead being
— the gun dripping from my fingers forming a heavy
blue mist around my feet.

  "You and I fading," he said and the words between
us dying losing color there on the white stone steps to
say — "I think under the circumstances — conduces
to a certain lack and as such we protest — life in all
its infinite variety of repetition to prolong a very old

outhouse — fertilizer you understand — inasmuch as any conclusion is at some point foregone by a form of excremental processing — that is any interference you understand on that level — Would you cut up a love letter, sir, from a charming lady? — fascist beasts who would once again raise the bloody banner of resistance over our peaceful ovens and virus cultures giving rise of course to certain harsh necessities of a hysterical nature irrelevant as honesty immutable as time but somewhat hampered by the weekly mail service in Shell Mara — concealed doubt — reasonable friend — circumstantial witness — his cruelest lawyers — the Halifax explosions — twins — brothers you understand — something else — circumstantial doubt — concealed friend muttering: 'justice of alien law courts — we are an old people — reasonable witness — circumstantial lawyers —' His cruelest evidence was rejected as irrelevant under circumstances that retroactively canceled the San Francisco earthquake and the Halifax explosion and doubt released from the skin law extendable and ravenous consumed all the facts of history — lost or eaten or something? Who walks in when you walk out? If I knew I'd be glad to tell you — Breakfast in Glasgow right enough streaked across the sky — decent inexpensive middle class threats without a throat without a tongue. 'We do not know,' he said for lack of reasonable expectations. 'The filters you understand are clogged — no more — *no más* — *delito mayor* — It is dangerous to play after hours — I saw it move I tell you — we were expendable and we did not write books after the war — paper shortage you understand — When large numbers of people are unable to find anything that would sustain life liberty or the pursuit of any endurable condition a chronically acute shortage may be said to obtain and one looks speculatively from the word cloth to the sheer sucking funnel of a vast bullfighter or bullshitter who screams out: "Don't looka me — You know what I mean right enough." Ah yes but does it not touch your heart to see the frustrated vultures wheeling through empty skies of Lima? They have come to eat and there is nothing not even carrion left — But the duties you understand of our glorious revolution and the free world must not betray itself for the simple lack of razor blades. "The razor inside sir — Jerk the handle/ / /"'"

I mean what kind of show is it after everything has been sucked out? You want to sit for all eternity watching the yellow movie of hepatitis and the blue movie of junk? We know every line and they never change. They will change less and less. Let there be light in the darkrooms. Only solution is total exposure.

"Big Picture calling Indecent — Come in please — gasoline crack of history." Doctor Benway rushed in with a bicycle pump full of heavy blue liquid pulsing out blue light and a smell of ozone.

"Now," he said "We must find a worthy vessel."

(Warning. It may be habit forming.)

"Is it legal and exempt narcotic?"

"Legal as Hell. I got the O.K. from St. Anslinger."

Saint Anslinger appears now the heavy metal fix falling sugar blue from hooded eyes hooked every living thing that stood in his focus — A young boy stepped forward and offered his arm.

"Don't be a volunteer, kid. Exposing the negatives or just dyeing them blue? Pushing radioactive heavy metal junk? Stand a little back from the game. You see the past is radioactive. Time is radioactive. Virus is radioactive. The nova formula is simple repetition down a long lane of flash bulbs old photos fall on the burning deck. Have you heard the notice? No more is written. They are packing up at Lexington." A tall thin man wearing canvas leggings and frayed knickers, cigarette holder stained brown, turned at the door and smiled like a rat in the setting sun. His long yellow teeth glinted as he walked out and disappeared in yellow light left a puff of cigarette smoke hanging in the air. And I am returning his birthplace lost at addicts of the world.

"And I am returning his birthplace lost at addicts of the world — groin stained with dew back to all the others down a silver funnel of years. Remember me as twisted dead leaves in the winter pissoir your gun the last negative inextricably involved in that partial today. Do you begin to see there is no cigarette there?"

Beauty held in mold goes stale and ugly as Shitola where all the young stuff is drained off for storage and

privileged Aphids who have performed appreciable services for the Insect Trust are allowed to bathe in this
nectar — flower scent of young hard-on and first run
jackoffs:: ("I tell you, Mazie, you stupid bitch, I'm getting
it *all*" he arches a young boy body up out of the black
liquid cock spurting white wash "Come in you *foule hon-
teuse* — If you don't i'll simply drag you in with strong
tattooed sailor arms — He's drinking it *now.*" And she
reached up bronzed arms smooth as teakwood sharply
etched with a blue hawk tattoo and drags her simpering
sister down into the youth bath until they are both twisting
about like worms on a hot plate and screaming in unison
with tough exciting young voices: "More! More! More!")
"So come out of those ugly molds and remember good is
better than evil because its nicer to have around you. Its
just as simple as that. And if anyone thinks different just
assign that cocktail lounge fly boy to front line duty so he
can register just how unpleasant evil is to have around
you cut off light-years behind enemy lines."

"Pay Day calling Shifty — Evacuation soon please."

"Difficult loud and clear you dumb hick inconvenience."

And when we young officers heard the General call
us "a dumb hick inconvenience" we rolled all over the
staff room in psychophantic spasms until we had to take
plasma in the Shitola baths while the General just sat
there glued to his view screen chewing his cigar: "Cute
little image with guns — little hicks — Gawd, Mazie, I
love them — In fact its time for lunch."

And some of us could not but feel that our youthful ardor, daily renewed in carbonic bubbles, was being sold out by officers unworthy of the name. And we were getting the pure stuff you understand from revolutions and underground armies everywhere. We had our Castro period and then all the mad queens from camouflage camped about in Vietnam drag designed for maximum exposure of misappropriated parts. And of course the FLN girls were to be seen buggering each other on every street corner. I mean we were getting it and getting it steady. So we began to convene in tense graceful clusters of incipient conspiracy. Then came the order that inflamed us to open revolt: "The Shitola baths are closed until further notice."

"Justlikethat eh?"

We posed in sulky muttering groups pushing locks of hair from our eyes with brusque gestures of youthful defiance. And the General stepped out of his view screen in a glittering robe of pure shamelessness.

"Boys, you don't realize just how unworthy I am," and escaped in the ensuing nausea. His confessions have finished off three hardened police inspectors and he keeps remembering more things.

"See what I mean boys? It is time to forget. To forget time. Is it? I was it will be it is? No. It was and it will be if you stand still for it. The point where the past touches the future is right where you are sitting now on your dead time ass hatching virus negatives into present time into the picture reality of a picture planet. Get off your ass, boys. Get off the point."

"What that man say? I sweat out thirteen brown-nose years to get this point and now I should get off it again yet?"

"We all put in five hundred thousand years getting the point. It never happened. Tell you boy no more is written. Old train you stumbled into by mistake."

"You and the Mexican, Meester. Electrician far away can you light your earth with paper moon and all the fuses?"

"New York," he said "totally unacceptable terms."

"His burning metal eyes had your gun, Bradly. It was in the point there you let go. Neither you nor Martin will ever make conditions worth his *adiós* in hideous electric pain. You wanted other identity for blue light blockade? To my sad soldiers loud and clear now: "Pay Day! Pay Day! Pay Day!""

"So those mutinous troops broke into the Beauty Banks of time and distributed our exquisitries to the peasantry and all sorta awful contests sprang up like a Most Graceful Movement contest so a body could hardly get through to Walgreen's for the fag ballet dancers leaping about and everyone you come up against is so graceful you can't endure it and we went around muttering:

'Slip and stumble
Trip and fall'

a practical jingle passed along through. nannies all of us looking for some haven that might have survived the

holocause or hollow cast as the case may be some evil
old bitch at least in a kiosk spitting drag but by the time
we get there she is a Sweet Old Flower Lady — And
our erstwhile friends with the police force are boning
up for the Most Decent Cop Day. A shambles — a filthy
shambles — Gracious Waiter Day up called a pestilent
cloud of singing waiters from the Pontine Marshes — Can
the Cutest Old Clochard be far behind? Perhaps the most
distasteful thing was the Benevolent Presence Contest
which ran right into a taffee pull of the sick sweat stuff
and the citizens were still belching it out two weeks later.
Oh it went on for a while. On Exciting Street Boy Day the
pure street boy winner slupped up all the queens in three
galaxies and nearly lost his quality in the service — 'Just
give me a piece of that boy' they screamed cruising and
snapping like aroused sharks. Well every whistle stop
had its Quality Champ and you always knew who won
a quality contest because he included the other contes-
tants in or out at the case may be — SPUT — The winner stands there in the empty ring . . and Final Quality
Day when all the winners of localized and specialized
contests met in a vast arena . . scarcely a man is now
alive — just one shot that's all it took — Don't ask me
who won because I wasn't *there.*"

This went on until folks wised up that the quality contest was an image contest like Miss America whereupon
cool casual inferential invisible contests set in and you

knew who won because when the contest was over he just wasn't there — You may infer his absence by that or this in exactly the same relation as before the contest he retroactively did not take part in. So the best minds coolly shut off a switch and went away down a tunnel of flash bulbs and last words and duped out in grey subway dawn leaving a wake of turned-out pockets — grey ghosts of drunken sleep — The Not There Kid was not *there*. Empty turnstile marks the spot — So disinterest yourself in my words. Disinterest yourself in anybody's words . . In the beginning was the word and the word was bullshit. The beginning words came out on the con clawing for traction — Yes sir, boys, its hard to stop that old writing arm — more of a habit than using — Been writing these RXs five hundred thousand years and sure hate to pack you boys in with a burning down word habit — But I am of course guided by my medical ethics and the uh intervention of the Board of Health — no more — *no más* — My writing arm is paralyzed — ash blown from an empty sleeve — do our work and go — Here comes the old knife sharpener in lemon sunlight blue eyes reflected from a knife blade — blood on white steps of the sea wall — afternoon shadow in dying eyes — ay, good bye Meester — It is hard to the old showmen all the old acts going — It is too hard to face the last carnival . . We are willing to pack up at Lexington. Get off the point. It is precisely time — Exploded sun circles the boy who paid.

Its you who have assembled from the broken streets of
war and death — down a long lane of flash bulbs twisted
face on the burning deck. The burning buckling deck of
an exploding star.

"Stranger forget seventy tons to the square inch and
be gone at the flutes. Death takes over in busy lands.
ashes — gutted cities of America and Europe. Empty
air marks authority over all antagonists. late afternoon
on white steps of the set. See the chains are fallen long
long radio silence on Portland Place." — hands work
and go — Our street boys picking up show — no word
— no flesh — the actors melted — indications enough
it wasn't easy — radio silence to answer your air —
Remember i was the ship gives no memory pictures
— Johnny Yen, in last good bye fading scars — played
the flute of Ali — played the flute in Kiki — some
clean shirt and man like good bye — ding-dong bell
no good *no bueno* — stranded actors walk through Poo
Poo the Dummy — The Orchid Girl fades into memory
picture on outhouse skin forgotten — Green Tony the
last invisible shadow — Call the Old Doctor twice on
last errand? — caught in the door of Panic, Mr & Mrs
D — last round over — a street boy's morning sky —
flesh tape ebbing from centuries — Remember i was
movie played you a long last good night" —
    end of the line for vaudeville voices — last round
in a shower of ruined September — last film flakes

— The globe is self just old secondhand door —
indications enough just ahead — boys on roller skates
before stranded — our revels at Rings of Saturn — last
September on stage — Last parasite just went up, Mr
Martin — i fold thy strong tape — Bitter price on our
ticket? — 'Bye then — broken dream and dreamer of
the sick lies — the brain of Gothenburg on stage — Last
intervention gives no flesh identity — for i last errand
boy — *adiós* in the final ape of history — fading shelter
in the dog's death trauma — intervention — last round
over — The pipes are calling, Mr Bradly Mr Martin —
The story done when you reach September — So we'll
say good night — showed you your air — the pipes your
summons — All are wracked and answer — *adiós* to
the sick lies — *adiós* to thy strong tape — caught in the
door of Gothenburg — courage to question erogenous
secondhand trade — story of absent world just as empty
as ding-dong bell — silence to the stage — These our
actors erased themselves into air far from such as you,
Mr Bradly Mr Martin — September faded leaves not a
wrack behind — I foretold you all spirits are going —

Johnny Yen: (His face shows strata of healed and half-
healed fight scars — under grey luminous film flakes
as the cover of the world rains down) "I'm going to look
for a room in a good neighborhood" —

Ali The Incandescent Street Boy: "You come Ali — You
no go body" —

Kiki: (Some clean shirt and walked out) "You can look any place — No good — *No bueno* — *Adiós*, Meester Bradly Meester Martin" —

Poo Poo the Dummy: (Flares of good bye over the iridescent lagoon) —

Miranda the Orchid Girl: (Trailing tendrils of stinging sex hairs, fades into birdcalls and frogs from the vacant lot) "good bye then" —

not looking around, talking away —

Green Tony: "On the last saucer, boss — a big bank roll" —

Willy the Fink: "I'm not taking any rap for those board bastards — I'm going to rat on everybody" —

Izzy the Push, Jacky Blue Note, Hamburger Mary, Limestone John: "Call the Old Doctor twice? He quiets you — Hello yes good bye — A few more calls to make tonight" —

Mr & Mrs D: "The ticket that exploded posed little time so we'll say good night" —

Sammy the Butcher: (definitive arrest) —

Inspector J. Lee: "We do our work and go — Proceed with the indicated alterations" —

The Fluoroscopic Kid: "Now picking up show — no word — no flesh — the lot" —

The Subliminal Kid: "It wasn't easy get to be radio be tape recorder on — friends are — showed you your air" —

Mr Bradly Mr Martin: "Man like good bye — What in St. Louis after September? — faded story of absent world just as silver film took it — Remember i was the movies — Rinse my name for i have known intervention — Pass without doing our ticket — mountain wind of Saturn in the morning sky — From the death trauma weary good bye then — What summer will I will you? . . cold summer will . . exactly . . He lifts his hands sadly turns them out . . Brother can't you spare a dime? . . dead finger in smoke pointing to Gibraltar . . the adolescent shadow . . he should have the same face . . stale face stale late face in the late summer morning mouth and nose sealed over . . funny I don't remember you . . it's ended over there . . Remember the stale kids? . . toneless voice in San Francisco? . . belong to the wind . . silver morning smoke in the desolate markets . . sure you dream up Billy who bound word for it . . in the beginning there was no Iam . . stale smoke of dreams it was Iam . . haunted your morning and will you other stale morning smell of other Iam . . no Iam there . . no one . . silences . . There was no morning . . sure late Billy . . Iam the stale Billy . . I lived your life a long time ago . . sad shadow whistles cross a distant sky . . *adiós* marks this long ago address . . didn't exist you understand . . ended . . stale dreams Billy . . worn out here . . tried to the end . . there is a film shut up in a bureau drawer . . boy I was who never would be now . . a speck of white that seemed to

catch all the light left on a dying star . . and suddenly I
lost him . . my film ends . . I lost him long ago . . dying
there . . light went out . . . my film ends."

Hassan i Sabbah: "Last round over — Remember i
was the ship gives no flesh identity — lips fading —
silence to say good bye —" "See the action, B.J.? This
Hassan I Sabbah really works for Naval Intelligence
and . . Are you listening B.J.?

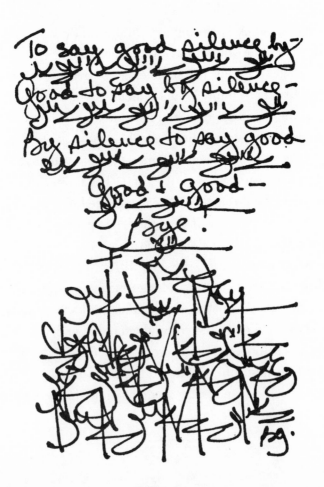

Notes

Abbreviations

T1	*The Ticket That Exploded*, Olympia Press, 1962.
TEX	*The Ticket That Exploded*, revised edition, Grove Press, 1967.
1962 typesetting MS	Complete draft of *The Ticket That Exploded* first edition, 132-page typescript, signed and dated "Nov. 8, 1962, Paris, France," but submitted to Olympia Press September 1962 (OSU 3.7).
Berg	William S. Burroughs Papers, 1951–1972, The Henry W. And Albert A. Berg Collection of English and American Literature, New York Public Library.
CU	Columbia University (William Burroughs Papers).

OSU   William S. Burroughs Papers, Ohio State
                             University, SPEC.CMS.85.

Title page

The epigraph ("posed little time / so I'll say / 'good night'") was
added for the 1967 edition.

Foreword Note

Titled "Acknowledgment" in both previous editions. The typescript draft for the 1967 edition began: **"The cover is by Mr Ian
Sommerville of London."** Seemingly, Burroughs was belatedly
acknowledging the jacket design of the 1962 edition, which had
used an uncredited photo-collage by Sommerville. The line on
the draft was canceled since Grove Press used their regular artist,
Roy Kuhlman, for the cover. The 1967 text expanded that of 1962,
which had read: "The sections entitled *In A Strange Bed* and *The
Black Fruit* were written in collaboration with Michael Portman.
The design on p. 183 is by Brion Gysin." Burroughs expanded
the acknowledgment to include the contributions of Balch and
Sommerville as well as Portman, and also added "of London" for
all three, so that only Gysin is not defined by a location, while his
page-numbered "design" became the "closing message."

"see the action, B.J.?"

This section did not appear in the 1962 text but was written for
the 1967 edition under the original title **"Room for two in de-
compression,"** which Burroughs canceled on his draft typescript
before writing the final title in by hand in blue ink (Berg 43.4). The
presence of "two" in the original title is telling and points ahead to
both the final phrase of the "do you love me?" section ("Won't be
two") and more immediately to this section's concluding reference
to a couple escaping in a "Gemini space capsule": Burroughs was

clearly aware that NASA's mid-1960s Project Gemini capsules were so named because they were built for two crewmen, seated like *twins*.

The opening passages of the section ground the couple in Burroughs' biography, and various details identify the "other" as Lewis Marker, fictionalized in 1952 as Eugene Allerton in *Queer*. Indeed writing "maybe ten fifteen years later," Burroughs returned to his tortuous affair with Marker to acknowledge the origins in *Queer* of the viral "other half" and the fantasies of alien or deadly desire with which *The Ticket* is preoccupied. The autobiographical connection vanishes as the narration segues from one identity to another through slippery shifts in narrative voice and as the artificiality of the scenario becomes more obvious, culminating in the narrator's identification with "a science fiction book called *The Ticket That Exploded*." This unusually emphatic moment of self-reflexivity, where the writer is revealed as a reader who reads what we are reading, coincides with the film-writing scenario involving "B.J." The Hollywood pitch reveals the role of culture in projecting as "romance" drives that are experienced as alien and destructive. In short: "It's a sick picture B.J."

1   "see the action, B.J.?": the title of the section is addressed by a scriptwriter to a Hollywood director or producer known only by the initials "B.J." A possible cousin of "A.J." from *Naked Lunch* and of "B.J." Carroll, an American actor Burroughs had known in Paris and who had once lived in the Beat Hotel, B.J. was drafted in to replace initials closer to home. A passage that Burroughs originally wrote for the aborted novel *The Ugly Spirit* in April 1961 began: "'Sure W.B. we could play down the fruit angle get in some dancing girls — These Venusians are Communists see? And Hassan Sabbah really works for Naval Intelligence —'" (*ROW*, 69). Drafted a full year before Burroughs started work on *The Ticket*, these lines not only anticipated the character who would introduce the 1967 edition but also its closing words

("'This Hassan I Sabbah really works for Naval Intelligence and . . Are you listening B.J.?'"). An unpublished typescript that gives more background, begins: "B.J.?—That frantic character was drummed out of the industry—He boiled a live cat in his bidet and invited all his Madison Avenue colleagues in to eat it" (Berg 43.28).

1   "carbide lamp in Puyo": corrects the spelling of the Ecuadorian city ("Puya" in *TEX* 1) which Burroughs and Lewis Marker had visited in summer 1951, given correctly in manuscript (Berg 43.4). With his "CIA voice," the description here also anticipates Burroughs' characterization of Allerton twenty years later in *The Place of Dead Roads* as a "washout from the CIA" (New York: Viking, 1983; 23).

2   "I'd just as soon forget": the draft typescript continued: **"nova here and there . . stink of burning apes . . cold mineral thought processes of decaying metal"** (Berg 43.4).

5   "Now that should show you fellows": the draft has a preceding line: **"Remember the patrol you sent out and how they came back?"** (Berg 43.4).

winds of time

This section opened the 1962 *Ticket* but for the 1967 edition Burroughs expanded it substantially through a series of insertions. The first insert of some 3,500 words makes its status as new material explicit by looking back ("That was in 1962"), and inviting us to recognize the scene of updating five years later; to imagine Burroughs at his desk, "Leafing through the GOD files" and adding relevant lines from "East Beach File page 156." In this spirit of revision, he also made two short inserts, both referencing Henry Kuttner's science fiction novel *Fury*, although his precision disguises some Burroughsian cutting up: the second quotation describing the "Happy Cloak" does indeed come from "page 143," but the first quotation silently inserts lines from this page into a passage from the beginning of Kuttner's book (page 11). For the 1967 edition, Burroughs made another long insert, before the concluding two pages end the section as had the 1962 edition (apart from four small cuts in the last paragraph, of sixty-five words in total, and the addition of the final line). Altogether, the insertions made the section over three times longer and shifted the balance away from cut-up toward narrative material.

Irrespective of the abrupt shifts in content, the insertions made for the 1967 edition stand out formally in their characteristic use of recurrent two-dot ellipses and periods rather than em dashes. The new material included a page recognizable as cut-ups of newspaper items in the manner of several sections in *Nova Express*. Introduced as a "series of oblique references," the material alludes to the film actress Tuesday Weld ("Starlet Weld Tuesday") and names the burlesque dancer Sally Rand, while Burroughs slipped in a cryptic allusion to Gertrude Stein ("two acts for three saints" echoing her opera *Four Saints in Three Acts*). Some two hundred words of this section overlap "The Moving Times," one of Burroughs' three-column newspaper format texts, in Jeff Nuttall's mimeograph *My Own Mag* 15 (April 1966), making the connection between provenance and form all the clearer.

10   "The Garden of Delights . . GOD": from here to "He doesn't remember" (page 24) was inserted for the 1967 edition.

10   "You see this noose, Lee?": the original typescript of this inserted text has not "Lee" but **"Burroughs,"** although, curiously, what follows is put in the third person (**"he contacted a number of undergrounds"**) rather than the first (Berg 43.5).

11   "inoculation is the weapon of choice against virus": a related typescript develops the connection: **"And what is inoculation? The administration of a dead or weakened virus—This conveys immunity—When you kill or weaken a virus strain so that your organism**

can tolerate its attack you have 'assassinated' the
virus strain—That is precisely what inoculation *is*:
assassination—Hassan i Sabbah discovered the principle of inoculation—A great doctor—The human
sickness is a complex of several virus strains—There
is the heat virus or The ovens of which all pain and
fear virus are variant strains like different strains
of flu—There is the Other Half the pleasure and sex
virus of which you have come to complain—Are you
ready to live without word without body without sex?
I don't think so—" (Berg 10.22).

12   "Is it going to be published in Vogue?": the same question
is asked in the third edition of *The Soft Machine* (1968),
among other oblique references made here to that book.

13   "Time September—(a number not clear)—It is a musical
family": since they don't originate in the 1962 edition, these
two dashes without spaces have been retained (whereas four
other em dashes that do come from the 1962 edition and
appeared in the 1967 *Ticket* without spaces have been corrected for this edition).

14   "Carl standing there": one typescript has the initials **"I.S."**
here instead, abbreviating Ian Sommerville (Berg 43.5).

14   "'Who planned all this?' I asked.": corrects *TEX* 13 by adding a period; the same change has been made for half a
dozen other instances, according to a principle Burroughs
clarified to Marilyn Meeker at Grove Press: "Where there
is no punctuation in the additional material a period should
be used" (Burroughs to Meeker, November 10, 1966; Grove
Press Records, Special Collections, Syracuse University).

15   "call to Scotland Yard": corrects *TEX* 13 ("yard").

16   "Neatly folded": the apparently passing detail suggests how
precisely Burroughs' 1967 additions related to his 1962
text, for the phrase directly echoes a line in *Nova Express*
("Both men had been neatly folded") that cut up early 1962
newspaper reports about a series of London murders that

had fascinated him, to which *The Ticket* did include a brief cryptic allusion. In the section "all members are worst a century," the phrase "All that links the murders" (page 113) makes the link to *Nova Express*, where this phrase appears both before and after the line "Both men had been neatly folded" (page 179).

17   "the Chandos Bar": corrects *TEX* 15 ("Chandoo"). The Chandos Bar, named after an eighteenth-century British peer, is a pub in London near Trafalgar Square.

20   "affect the result": corrects *TEX* 18 ("effect").

21   "forced to give up their hidden meanings": "the invisible generation" Appendix overlapped and expanded on this idea, "as if the words themselves had been interrogated and forced to reveal their hidden meanings it is interesting to record these words words literally made by the machine itself you can carry this experiment further using as your original recording material that contains no words animal noises for instance record a trough of slopping hogs the barking of dogs go to the zoo and record the bellowings of Guy the gorilla" (*TEX* 206–7). Guy the gorilla was a celebrity at London Zoo; his name is the only word to have an upper-case letter in Burroughs' essay.

23   "need a Harley St psychiatrist": corrects *TEX* 20 ("Harly St").

23   "You know about the Logos group??": for *Nova Express* in 1964 Burroughs added significant material making explicit his references to Scientology.

24   "Boots any midnight": corrects *TEX* 21 ("Boot's"); the same error on *TEX* 27 is also corrected (page 31).

25   "'wearing the Happy Cloak": from here to "London WC1 . ." was inserted for the 1967 edition, as was from "'a thin singing shrillness" to "page 143.'"

28   "others they revived with static": in a change that was indicated but not made for *T1*, on an early set of proofs Burroughs canceled the word "static" and wrote in **"apomorphine"** (Berg 9.1).

28   "explained it was a camera gun": corrects *TEX* 25 by restoring the article "a," present in the 1962 typesetting MS and earlier typescripts, although absent in *T1*.

29   "The Green Pine Inn is on a bluff over the river": from here to "at the Green Inn looking across the valley" (page 34) was inserted for the 1967 edition. An autograph manuscript that begins with this line, before continuing with variant material, is written in three different inks: green for the opening sentences, blue for the phrase "dressed in a blue suit" and red for "a slash of red" (Berg 35.58). This manuscript specifies the location: **"A dream like feeling seemed to cover the Missouri countryside as if he is watching an old film."** The Green Inn, and the "fried chicken" eaten there, return in *The Wild Boys*.

31   "irrelevant honesty of hysteria": in "Grids," published in *The Insect Trust Gazette* 1 (Summer 1964) and reprinted in *The Third Mind* (125), Burroughs singled this out as an example of the "meaningless machine-turned phrases" used in hostile reviews of his books. The phrase was used against him in the November 30, 1962 *Time* magazine review of *Naked Lunch* ("King of the YADS"), which also attacked the then-unpublished *Ticket*. The vitriol in the review is clear from the full context of the phrase recycled in *The Ticket*: "Presenting himself as proof that the universe is foul, Burroughs achieves the somewhat irrelevant honesty of hysteria."

33   "We sat down under a tree" to "passing canoes": repeats lines used in the 1961 edition of *The Soft Machine*, which appear at the start of the "Pretend an Interest" section of later editions.

34   "It was the end of the line": the phrase, repeated several times across the text, comes from the end of Paul Bowles' novel *The Sheltering Sky* (1949). Burroughs' autograph manuscript varies at this point and concludes with a passage that conjures the spirits of young men from his life over the

past decade, going back to Marker in 1951: "'**It's the end of the line, Genial' I said quietly remotely.**

He looked at me and I felt a blast of hate from the heavy heart of an old servant.

'You don't need me any more, but I was good enough for your dirty movies.'

'And who am I, Genial?'

The sheer assassin in dying eyes.

'You are the ventriloquist. I was the dummy.'

I looked at him and said nothing. Nothing was there to say. All the faces of 'Genial' blazed and went out one after the other. Lewis Adelbert Marker, Jerry Gorsaline, Michael Portman, Daniel Moore . . fading with Ian's face sitting at the table in his blue suit looking" (Berg 35.58).

35   "went up in silent explosions": an early typescript that lacks part of what follows (from "under the whining sirens" to "an old film set") continues with: "**We see buildings, lavatories, Time life building suburbs hospitals banks**" (Berg 36.8). In January 1963, Burroughs identified this passage as the basis for the film *Towers Open Fire* (citing "pages 14-15" of the recently published first edition; see *ROW*, 119), although the scenario and much of the phrasing also appeared in *Nova Express*, published after but mostly written before *The Ticket*. Much of this paragraph also appears in the "Gongs of Violence" chapter of the second and third editions of *The Soft Machine*.

35   "his remote mountain village": corrects *TEX* 31 ("villages") as per an earlier typescript (Berg 9.5), although the plural was in the 1962 typesetting MS and *T1*.

35   "The boy who owned this room": from here to "out of his path" restores lines cut from the 1962 text for the 1967 edition (cf *TEX* 31).

36   "Alien beauty" and "flash of absent bodies": restores phrases cut from the 1962 text for the 1967 edition (cf *TEX* 31).

36   "and slipped suddenly out": from here to "a planet with sex prisoners" restores lines cut from the 1962 text for the 1967 edition (cf *TEX* 32).

36   "all from an old movie": this line was inserted for the 1967 edition.

in a strange bed

This section appeared in the 1962 edition except for a very few minor differences and Burroughs made no cuts or additions. When the first three-quarters of the section were included under the same title in *Dead Fingers Talk* in 1963, however, a page of the most sexually explicit material involving Ali and the guard (from "The man led him to a shed" to "stirred in the sperm") was cut, in line with the book's aim to ease Burroughs past British censors.

The archival typescripts reveal the genesis of the opening science fiction scenario of Lykin and Bradly. In the book's Acknowledgment Burroughs notes that he wrote this section "in collaboration" with Michael Portman, but suggested nothing of the process involved. It's clear that he heavily redacted and repunctuated a conventionally straight first draft narrative in order to achieve its final elliptical style. While this draft overlaps substantially and is not especially well written—surely signs of Portman's hand—it demonstrates Burroughs' working methods in how he transformed the text.

In contrast, the other main narrative line, which gives the section its title, seems to have its origins in an autobiographical episode narrated by Burroughs a decade earlier in *Junky*: "Ali woke in a strange bed" echoes the line in his debut novel where Lee gets blackout drunk on tequila in Mexico City and the narrative resumes: "I woke up next morning in a strange room" (*Junky* [New York: Grove Press, 2012; 130]). Disorientating shifts in location and identity are certainly central to this section, as the narrative segues from 1920s American suburbs to alien landscapes inhabited by fish boys and giant crabs. The manuscript history of the "strange bed" passages shows that Burroughs lightly but precisely revised it, for example striking several cases of the overused adjective "little" (before "chirp," "chirping," "adzes," "map," "gardens," "smiles," and "mocking laugh").

36   "Lykin was the first to awake": at least two drafts of this material were written before Burroughs made the redacted version used in the text, a partial typescript (Berg 20.23) and this, the complete first draft (Berg 12.30):

"Lykin was the first to awake. At first he could not remember where he was and then slowly as his tired blue eyes blurred with sleep and crud took in the glowing red rocks and clumps of strange metallic shrubs with silver leaves that surrounded the little pool where he lay, the ghastly night before flooded back into his memory. The hectic struggle with their space ship when the controls had suddenly blanked out as though by invisible intervention of some alien force that had swept through their craft like an icy draught for it was not only the mechanical apparatus that had been affected but their very nerve centers had been paralyzed. He and Bradly his co pilot had sat helpless in their pressure seats for two hours while the invading unseen agency had guided their ship in a sickening whirligig through the poisonous cloud belts of an unknown planet. They had been on a routine flight through Galaxy H charting the movements of asteroids and some goof in their calculations had carried them a few million miles off course when the trouble occurred. Lykin had figured that they must be in the neighborhood of a cluster of uncharted satellite planets that lay off the most farflung edge of Galaxy H. Lykin and Bradly had lost consciousness when they landed and his first thought was to how they were not still in the ship? He jumped up and tripped over the dormant form of his companion naked except for the skin-tight transparent space suit that clung to his

muscular body. He did not wake him but decided to first of all set out to look at the terrain. From what he could see they were at the bottom of some sort of gully surrounded by the red rocks which glowed with an almost translucent quality. He clambered up the first few rocks and found himself on a sort of plateau. He reached the top of the plateau and gazed across. A fantastic landscape of multicolored rocks carved into weird and wonderful shapes. Some like statues of dripping blue molten lava and interspaced by group of stalagmites like witches needles of a pearly white hue of an intensity he had never seen in his life as a space explorer. He now turned his attention to the sky which seemed like an enormous green ocean. He realized immediately the reason for the high brilliancy of the colors everywhere. There were four suns on the horizon spaced at North South East West intervals all around the plateau plain and they were each of a different color. One crimson one blue another green and the biggest a huge orb that crowned the scene in front of him glowing a fierce silver sheen. He stood for what seemed hours marveling at the beauty of the sight breathing in the pure air of this paradise. Finally he remembered his companion and reluctantly turned and made his way back through the Neolithic jungle to the pool. As he was making his way back down the path that led to the gulley a strange thing happened. He felt a click in his mind like a crystal flare exploding in his brain and heard very clearly a silvery voice say: 'Come stranger' in tinkling tones. It seemed very far off but at the same time he knew it came from inside himself. He glanced around slightly nervously but saw nothing. He hurried down the path anxious now to find his friend. At last he reached the large rock behind which the pool lay and as he came around the edge of it he stopped still in his tracks, stunned. His friend still lay in the same position that he had left him in but there beside him sat an extraordinary creature. It was an amphibious green fish boy. The being's body pulsed with translucent green light that flooded through the organism in eddies. The head was almost a pointed dome that sprang from a slender neck on either side of which protruded large gills that looked like spongy wings. The creature's skin was of a membranous substance with a network of transparent veins that crisscrossed its body. Its whole surface seemed to be in constant motion like slow motion water dripping down a statue. Its face was almost flat but with definite lips and nose beautifully carved and huge liquid eyes set above the high ridge of the cheekbones the delicate structure of which could be seen through transparent skin. The being was sitting in a cross-legged position and from its thighs jutted small silver fins of fine gauze. The slender sinuous legs finished up in a pair of webbed flippers. Between the legs he could see the ample genitals half aroused in curiosity as it playfully stroked the head of his sleeping comrade and touched the fine thread of his space suit with tentative jabs of its long green fingers. Lykin hav[ing] recovered from his initial astonishment could only stand speechless gazing at the creature's alien beauty. He felt half afraid to move in case he should frighten it back in to the pool which he guessed to be its home. But at that very moment it turned its fine sculptured head and looked directly at him with an expression that could only be a shy dreamy smile. He was hypnotized by the liquid stare feeling himself drawn in by the slanted pools.

An electric shiver ran up his spine and burst in in his mind. Again the crystal voice spoke in his head this time much louder: 'Approach stranger. Have no fear.' The creature's mouth had not moved but it raised its head slightly and nodded and Lykin knew that here was the origin of the telepathic voice. For a moment he was paralyzed but with rather awkward movements and a mounting tingling sensation of excitement through his veins, he stumbled over the rocky shore and knelt beside the water sylph bowing his head as he did this. Lykin sat a little way away from a pool of water that had formed beneath the creature running off its body. It extended a dripping hand and lightly clasped his shoulder. A thrill ran through him from the contact and an underwater memory burst in his brain. He felt himself inside the creature's medium, squirming in crystal rock pools, basking on stone ledges fanned by giant green ferns with only the sound of dripping water music. Birds chirping the waterland lullabies. Swimming through ruined palaces in subterranean caverns with the water creatures twisting in slow swirls of orgasm shooting out explosions of colored bubbles to the surface, trailing blue streamers."

39   "and i don't *think* he'll be back": corrects *TEX* 35 and *T1* ("dont"). Burroughs did sometimes deliberately omit the apostrophe (including twice in *Nova Express*), but here he almost certainly expected his rough typing to be corrected.

42   "a man in a green tattered uniform": corrects *TEX* 37 and *T1* ("in green"); although missing on the 1962 typesetting MS, the article is on other typescripts (CU 2.7).

do you love me?

Apart from typical changes in punctuation (including the addition of italics for emphasis and for Spanish phrases), this section appeared verbatim in the 1962 edition. Its dense sampling of song lyrics includes references to such special favorites of Burroughs as Hoagy Carmichael's "Stardust" (its haunting line "the memory of love's refrain" could stand in for all the romantic melodies invoked here), and both the traditional "Daisy Bell" ("a bicycle built for two") and the Ginsberg-Kerouac collaboration, "Pull My Daisy."

49   "Old acquaintance be forgot?": this line from "Auld Lang Syne," the New Year's Eve favorite based on Robert Burns' eighteenth-century poem, seems an unlikely point of departure for the cut-up collage of love lyrics that follow. In several draft typescripts, Burroughs associated the song with *The Ticket*'s original title—**"If you can't say it sing it to Auld Lang Syne"** (Berg 9.31)—revealing a point of origin in Burroughs' letter to Allen Ginsberg of October 27, 1959. Here, after announcing his discovery of cut-up methods and the therapeutic use of tape recorders ("simply run the tape back and forth until the trauma is wiped off"), Burroughs refers to his psychoanalyst, Dr Marc Schlumberger, who had been treating him in Paris all that year: "Schlumberger, needless to say, fell overboard like the cook and left several centuries behind" (*Letters 1945–1959*, 431). Burroughs was updating an old joke in which, taking the place of the analysand struggling to express himself, a stammering sailor is told, "If you can't say it, sing it," so he sings: "Should auld acquaintance be forgot and never brought to mind / The fucking Cook's gone overboard and left twenty miles behind." Burroughs' message was that psychoanalysis itself had now been relegated to the past ("left several centuries behind") by his newly discovered methods, which coincided with his interest in Scientology and use of processing techniques involving tape recorders to erase traumatic reactions. The acquaintances who *should* "be forgot" were therefore his former "self" (traumatized by desire) and Freud (against whom Burroughs made ferocious attacks during this period, seguing into ugly tirades against the International Jewish-Communist-Nova Conspiracy).

53   "Hey diddle diddle": corrects *TEX* 47 and *T1* ("Hy").

54   "Moanin' low my sweet 8276 all the time": Burroughs com-
      bines lyrics from the 1929 jazz standard, memorably sung by
      Claire Trevor in John Huston's film *Key Largo* (1948), with
      8276, which adds up to his own "number," 23. *Nova Express*
      also cites "Coordinates 8 2 7 6" (in the "Towers Open Fire"
      section) and the revised *Soft Machine* has "8267" (in "Who
      Am I To Be Critical?").

55   "Remember every little thing you used to do": the line, from
      Hammerstein's 1928 Broadway song "Lover, Come Back
      to Me," appears immediately after the phrase Burroughs
      considered as an early title for *The Ticket* on a page list-
      ing lyrics: **"If you can't say it sing it—"** (Berg 40.3).
      "Lover, Come Back" also appears on one of several long
      lists of popular songs, following Percy Mayfield's "Hit the
      Road, Jack" and preceding the popular standard "Bye Bye
      Blackbird." This list continues with occasionally garbled
      references to a mix of jazz, bebop, folk songs and popular
      standards: **"Waltzing Matilda. Rock around the clock.
      Bemsha swing. Saltpeanuts. St Louis Woman. After
      hours. Perdodi. Muscrat ramble. Viper mad. Dean
      Man blues. If you don't want to you don't have to.
      Around the world. Everybody loves my baby. Lov-
      erman. The doggy in the window. I've got a loverly
      bunch. Solitude. The tattooed bride. Moanin. Sister
      Sadie. Turkey in the straw. Barmaids waltz. Buck-
      ets gora hole in it. One meat ball. Pull my daisy.
      Ding dong bell. Ring a ring a roses. Everybody's
      gonne have religion and a glory. When the saints go
      marchin in. Don't go way nonady. Paulina. Waitin
      for the sunrise. Tip toe through the tulips with me.
      When you and I were young Maggie. The sheik of
      araby. Pallet on the floor. Blue monk. Blue moon.
      Margie. Ice cream. Martha"** (Berg 12.14).

operation rewrite

For the 1967 *Ticket* Burroughs more than doubled the length of the section, adding two long passages early on before and after the sentence that opened it in the original edition ("The Venusian invasion was known as 'Operation Other Half'"). The added material developed more fully ideas of the "Other Half" in the 1962 text, and overlaps with the "Smorbrot" section of *Nova Express* in its references to sense withdrawal tanks. In keeping with revisions elsewhere in the text, here Burroughs directly instructs the reader to make use of tape recorder technology ("Splice in your body sounds"), whereas the original section was focused on re-*writing*. The 1967 text made one small cut of 1962 *Ticket* material and has italics instead of the block capitals used in the earlier edition and also for *Dead Fingers Talk*.

55   "The 'Other Half' is the word": from here to *"before we can stop it"* (page 57) was inserted for the 1967 edition. An earlier typescript expands the definition given here: "**'Word is a vegetable organism producing reversed negatives of future events by a form of photosynthesis—The organism is itself silent but produces words in the host and these word tendrils are the air line or rather carbon dioxide line of this parasitic Venusian organism.' Bulletin 8276 Relative To Venusian Parasites**" (Berg 16.29).

57   "The District Supervisor reminded himself": from here to "Would he have 3D in time?)" (page 58) was inserted for the 1967 edition. The opening line of the insert parallels the closing words of *The Third Mind*: *"I must remind you, Mister Martin, Bradly Martin, of the new directive regarding respectful address to native life forms"* (194).

58   "the natives were to be scanned out of patterns": among other variants, an earlier typescript has the line: "**the natives were to be trained out of the biologic film imposed by a board of absentee owners headed by 'Mr. Martin'**

who was a well known intergalactic criminal" (Berg 16.26).

58   "the risky expedient of a 'miracle'": an earlier typescript defines a miracle: **"that is doing something that would appear miraculous to nervous systems incapable of thinking outside channels laid down by the corrupt colonists—Miracles are always an emergency operation"** (Berg 16.26).

59   "under Johnny Yen": an earlier typescript has **"General Yen"** and expands on the "blockade of the planet": **"expecting to liquidate the male sex altogether in orgasm death"** (Berg 20.34).

59   "hypnotizing chickens": after this phrase, made famous in the Iggy Pop/David Bowie song "Lust for Life," an early typescript continues with another potential lyric: **"and incinerating cockroaches with a magnifying glass"** (Berg 20.24).

60   "Control word *'the'*": restores the phrase from *T1* (which had "THE" in capitals rather than italics) cut for the 1967 edition (cf *TEX* 53). The 1962 typesetting MS had "THEE," which was changed, although not in Burroughs' own hand, on the page proofs (OSU 3.8).

61   "Alternatively Johnny Yen": these lines were Burroughs' autograph addition to an early typescript, which continues after "Everything is permitted" with a permutation of this phrase in the manner of Gysin's poems: **"is nothing true? Everything is permitted True is nothing—everything is permitted Everything true is nothing—is permitted is every true? Is nothing permitted"** (Berg 20.24).

61   *"No Hassan i Sabbah"*: corrects *TEX* 54 (*"hassan i sabbah"*) since the name was unintentionally put in all lower case when Burroughs indicated setting the block capitals used in *T1* as lower-case italics.

the nova police

Apart from one small cut in the final paragraph, this section appeared verbatim in the 1962 edition but, in the most extensive overlap of material across the Cut-Up Trilogy, almost half of it also appeared verbatim in *Nova Express* (in the chronology of composition, it is *The Ticket* that "repeats" *Nova Express*). Here Burroughs added the Q&A session, an exchange which functions very deliberately as a pedagogical strategy after a lecture to clarify key concepts. The whole section was included in *Dead Fingers Talk*, combined with odd lines from three other sections.

63   "Mr and Mrs D": early typescripts give more information about **"Mrs D herself—(Incidentally her sex is not definitively established and she is also known as Mr and Mrs D)"**: **"The control machine of Mrs D, sabotaged by partisan activity, was issuing insane orders and counter orders—Desperate servants, suddenly blocked out of her hands, went on pushing the old buttons with unpredictable results—Mrs D clearly hoped to escape in the resulting confusion, the total sauve qui peut which threatened to engulf the planet—We, on the other hand, intended to turn the situation to *our* advantage, to block her out of *all* possible coordinate points that is to literally block her out of all bodies and mind screens of the earth in a single vast operation—We knew that if we could completely disconnect her word and image machine, that is *vaporize* word and image, she would have no switch to pull and no hands to pull it—"** (Berg 20.31). Other parts of this typescript overlap unused material for the "Coordinate Points" section of *Nova Express*.

64   "Tangier": *TEX* 57 changed the spelling from "Tangiers" in *T1*, having been "Tanger" in the 1962 typesetting MS.

65   "it is *habit*:: idiosyncrasies": corrects *TEX* 57 ("idiosyncra-
      cies") as well as restoring the double colon canceled by the
      copyeditor on the 1962 typesetting MS (the first of 30 other
      double colons restored here).

68   "Marilyn Monroe Planet": the Hollywood star died on August
      5, 1962, the month before Burroughs completed *The Ticket*,
      and her name appears in several typescript drafts. Most sig-
      nificantly, it appears together with numerous other phrases and
      references in a typescript titled **"The Definitive Arrest Of
      The Ugly Spirit Mr Martin,"** which was clearly the source
      for many cut-up phrases in these passages of *The Ticket*: **"As
      the officer closed in Mr And Mrs D screamed through
      all the self righteous ugliness of a blighted continent—
      Flashing from bible belt eyes and cops and snarling
      bartenders all the ugliness and blight of America the
      hideous cities and suburban concentration camps
      The idiot honky Tonks of Panhandle—all the stupid
      brawls and quarrels and snarling drunken ugliness—
      The stupid punitive legislation and the fat bourbon
      soaked stupid legislators screaming for more laws
      against 'marijuana deadlier than cocaine'—Electric
      chairs and gas chamber and lynch mobs—The white
      smoke drifting from coca cola bottles through the
      suburbs and the deadly white no smell of death over
      the land—Madison avenue and Hollywood with their
      systematic degradation and vulgarizing The quarry
      retreated back into his ranks of millions of self righ-
      teous servants and police and hoodlums—The Atom
      bomb dripping from Marilyn Monroe's ass—The army
      the navy the marine Corps —The FBI and all the dogs
      of Harry J Anschlinger"** (Berg 20.35). When John Webb
      asked Burroughs to substitute the name of Marilyn Monroe
      for Johnny Yen in "Take It To Cut City — USA," published in
      The Outsider in Spring 1963, he refused (Burroughs to Webb,
      September 11, 1962; Berg 81.16).

69   "symbols blighted America::: \$\$\$": restores one of two triple
      colons (the other, on page 88, is also specific to the number
      three), canceled by the copyeditor on the 1962 typesetting
      MS.

69   "the dogs of H.J. Anslinger": *TEX* 61 corrected the spelling
      in *T1* ("Anschlinger") for the name of the Federal Bureau
      of Narcotics Commissioner, 1930–1962. Burroughs reviled
      Anslinger for his anti-drug campaigns supported by the yel-
      low press of William Randolph Hearst, which are echoed
      here in the phrase "marijuana is deadlier than cocaine." Bur-
      roughs grouped Anslinger together with other "Nova Board"
      members such as media magnate Henry Luce and Standard
      Oil billionaire John D. Rockefeller in several of his 1960
      "Last Words" variant texts, including some that addressed
      him directly: **"RECONVERSION BLUES MR ANSCH-
      LINGER? SHALL I SHOW THEM THE BLUES MR
      ANSCHLINGER?"** (William Seward Burroughs Papers
      1938-1997, Special Collections, Arizona State University; 7).

69–70 "This is to say: 'Would you rather talk up relying on money?'":
      restores a line cut from the 1962 text for the 1967 edition
      (cf *TEX* 62).

writing machine

Apart from four small cuts, adding up to less than fifty words, this
section appeared verbatim in the 1962 edition. Although Burroughs
refers to putting Shakespeare and Rimbaud through the writing
machine, the section also samples fragments from Eliot's *The Waste
Land* ("For I have known," "to give you?" "Departed have left")
and Joyce's "The Dead" ("falling softly"). Archival typescripts
show evidence of several stages of rewriting as well as significant
variant passages.

72   "all the masters of the world": an early typescript is more
      specific and extends the description: **"Manet Rubens
      Gysin El Greco Picasso all the masters of the world**

moving through each other overlapping—Composite freezes and sculpture permutated slowly Egyptian hieroglyphs slowly invaded by billboards Mayan Chinese and Japanese calligraphs Arab script—Or projected on screens the paintings mixed in light color and image of the world flowing and fusing—the Exhibition shaded off into a vast amusement park— Where flicker cylinders of many stories turned and flicker panels clicked by the scenic railways and plane rides—" (Berg 20.25).

73   "(The proportion of half one text half the other": the parenthetical line does not appear on earlier typescripts (Berg 20.25), suggesting Burroughs made the direct connection between textual and human bodies in retrospect.

73   "Shakespeare, Rimbaud, etc.": an early typescript (which lacks the preceding parenthetical line) continues by describing how the results emerge "like photo machine—The machine spits out books and poems and plays sold on stands—The same principle applied to painting where the works of the masters move through picture frames in juxtaposition—Spectators can feed in their own canvas or Photostat and emerge with a composite of any painter they choose—A music machine where Beethoven Wagner jazz Arab Chinese music mix and the spectator can sing while compose on instruments provided—" (Berg 20.25).

73   "Rinse my mouth of a few words: 'What have i my friend to give?'": restores a line cut from the 1962 text for the 1967 edition (cf *TEX* 65).

75   "magnetized U turn back to cool mineral silence": after the "U turn" (a phrase that originated in Paul Bowles' *The Sheltering Sky*), an early typescript that shows numerous small variants continues; "Photomontage and clear process slowly falling—(Odor of her cylinders—Pulsing neon tubes of milk) Mexican sky shifting grills—The

> **magnetic finger of Brion Gysin back into our fore-
> heads flicker a place forgotten—"** (Berg 10.3).

75   "Spectators are noon": restores a phrase cut from the 1962
      text for the 1967 edition (cf *TEX* 66).

77   "A writing machine shifts": this phrase, and the following
      lines from "An odor of deluge through page frames" to "fifty-
      fifty," restores words cut from the 1962 text for the 1967
      edition (cf *TEX* 68).

substitute flesh

Apart from ten small cuts, adding up to less than eighty words, this
long section appeared verbatim in the 1962 edition. Of interest are
the two footnotes that also appear verbatim in *Nova Express*, but
in reverse order. The notes extend the thematic focus of the section—the merger of bodies into composites—as a textual practice
involving books, and other parts also echo the "Smorbrot" section of *Nova Express*. In terms of manuscript history, this section
bridges the two typescripts that made up Burroughs' 1962 typesetting manuscript, the line "What awaits you on substitute flesh?"
not only marking the transition point from cut-up to narrative but
completing a 44-page typescript that is distinguished from the
remaining 88 pages (most visibly in the use of em dashes, which
were always well spaced up to this point, but not spaced after it).

87   "Wheee": corrects *TEX* 77 ("Whee"), as per *T1* and the
      1962 typesetting MS.

87   "half of the body": this phrase, followed by "So what is ejacula-
      tion in the throat?" and "of course — that is," restores words
      cut from the 1962 text for the 1967 edition (cf *TEX* 78).

89   "The Sex Musicians drift through streets of music": an early
      typescript expands on these musicians, mentioning the char-
      acter **"Johnny Flute"** and the creation of **"sexual sym-
      phonies": "You see the first words were sex words and
      words came after singing and music so translate the
      sex words back into singing and music"** (Berg 12.30).

The emphasis on the flute as a sexual instrument goes back to *Naked Lunch* and the "Arab boy who could play a flute with his ass" (113).

92   "the garden — City sounds": *TEX* 81 corrected *T1* ("City sound").

93   "the subjects lowered themselves into the sense withdrawal tank": an early typescript has a variant passage: **"Bradly took off his clothes with the attendant and lowered himself into communal sense withdrawal tank floating in a cellophane membrane in total darkness with the others around him he could feel the outlines of his body extend and break here and there like an amoebic movement and then back sharp and clear out again further and further"** (Berg 20.34). One fragment in *The Ticket* ("hyphenated line of amoebic process") echoes a key term in these unused lines by combining two phrases from another variant passage in this typescript: **"Hyphenated line of his body separates like a fish mold—he could feel their amoebic process together."** On "the amoeba reflex" in Burroughs' manuscript of *Queer*, see the endnotes in *Junky* (191).

95   "Mirror line feed-back from erect penis to heart beat rhythms": restores words cut from the 1962 text for the 1967 edition (cf *TEX* 84).

95   "Blind crab parasites of the nervous system attempt to hold prisoners in idiot green boys —": this phrase, followed by "Sucker paws," "Now screaming without fingers," "as the brain split down the middle," "A Chinese attendant put the crab parasites through rings of Saturn — 'You can't' — Now," "with composite attendant like," and "Neon fingers," restores words cut from the 1962 text for the 1967 edition (cf *TEX* 84).

the black fruit

Apart from three very small cuts and several changes of spelling ("grey" for "gray," "leaped" for "leapt," and "ichor" for "ikor"), this section appeared verbatim in the 1962 edition, although when most of it was included in *Dead Fingers Talk* almost a hundred words were omitted to reduce its sexual content. In the book's Acknowledgments, Burroughs notes that he wrote this, like the "in a strange bed" section, "in collaboration" with Michael Portman. Although there appears to be no equivalent early typescript to show how he reworked this narrative of Lykin and Bradly, it has distinctive features such as the "herds of mystic animals" and a general overwriting that is quite un-Burroughsian.

97   "He was drifting through space": inserts a space gap between the first two paragraphs, as indicated on the 1962 typesetting MS by a row of 11 dots.

98   "dead warriors stand as petrified": corrects *TEX* 86 ("at"), as per *T1*.

99   "He was back in a giant clam which spits out its memory skin discharge like": restores a line cut from the 1962 text for the 1967 edition (cf *TEX* 87).

100   "apes tear his insides apart": *TEX* 87 corrected *T1* ("inside").

100   "talking in color blasts": *TEX* 89 follows *T1* here but the 1962 typesetting MS had "blats," before being altered by the copyeditor. This spelling appears across several typescripts and was retained in *Nova Express* but not for *The Ticket*.

101   "sank into his flesh like a black seal": corrects *TEX* 89 ("flesh a black seal") by restoring "like" as per *T1* and the 1962 typesetting MS.

101   "a smell of sewage": from here to "swamp mud" was a separate page insert in the 1962 typesetting MS.

102   "slow memory bubbles": from here to "The Slow Boat to China" is not present on earlier typescripts, while before it one typescript has the unused lines **"Tendril hands feeling for him with silver nets—His green substance fading now he needed a client—"** (Berg 5.1).

102   "Orgasm Sting that twists": *TEX* 90 corrected *T1* ("Stings that twist").

104   "Like wind": restores a phrase cut from the 1962 text for
       the 1967 edition (cf *TEX* 92) and corrects *T1* (which had
       "Like win") as per the 1962 typesetting MS.
105   "an island of swamp cypress": corrects *TEX* 93 ("swamp
       cypresses"), undoing the plural inserted by the copyeditor
       on the page proofs (OSU 3.8).

all members are worst a century

This section appeared verbatim in the 1962 edition apart from a
small number of minor changes and corrections, one of which is
both textually relevant and thematically significant. Central to the
section is the anthropological expedition recorded in an explorer's
journal as a series of dated entries that, through a "disease of the
image track," jump back and forth in time between July 1862 and
July 1962 (which was, as the text itself states, for Burroughs the
"Present Time" of writing *The Ticket*). Since the narrative dra-
matizes transcending such apparently clearly fixed points and
distinctions in linear time, it is entirely fitting that for the 1967
text Burroughs needed to correct the original edition which had
"July 14, 1962" twice (instead of cutting from "July 14, 1862" to
"July 14, 1962 — Present Time"). This chronological confusion
was replicated in *Dead Fingers Talk* (where, with minor changes,
this section appears interleaved with similar material from *The
Soft Machine*), which again has "July 14, 1962" printed twice,
and unaccountably also omits the short paragraph dated "July
11? 12? 13? 1862." As the 1962 typesetting MS shows, these
were more than transcription or printing errors, for Burroughs
himself could not keep track of the dates and on his manuscript
he had to correct "July 7, 1962" to "July 7, 1862" and also "July
9, 1862" to "July 9, 1962." While clearly "errors," in the sense
that Burroughs wanted them corrected, such slippages in numer-
als and therefore in narrative chronology performed at a textual
level the kind of "time traveling" operations he sought to achieve
through cut-up methods.

The numerous references to South American locales here also point to the influence of the unnamed botanical hallucinogen *ayahuasca* or *yagé*, referenced only as an anonymous "dangling vine" but associated by Burroughs ten years earlier in his "Composite City" vision with "space time travel" in *The Yage Letters* (50). Since Burroughs began working again on his South American material in August 1962 for the City Lights publication and since he would make explicit in that book the connection between *yagé* and cut-up methods (by adding the cut-up text, "I Am Dying, Meester?"), it is actually surprising that there is only one parenthetical reference to "yage" in *The Ticket* and that it is not in this section (but in the middle of "winds of time").

It is significant that this section also echoes the emphatic practice of *Nova Express* in using specific dates to fix Burroughs' cutting up of contemporaneous newspaper material, introduced here by "July 11, 12, 13, 1962 — Present Time." While several of the following phrases ("link the murders," "folk singer Logos," "Cycle of Action") appeared in *Nova Express*, the passages here are more than another permutation of the same material, since they also recycle phrases from *Minutes to Go* ("four letter words" "the language of life") that did not appear in *Nova Express*. Equally, in *The Ticket* Burroughs retained fragments from literary sources that did not make the cut for *Nova Express*, including "The boatman smiles" from T. S. Eliot's poem "Burbank with a Baedecker: Blestein with a Cigar."

109   "So writes an early traveler": this phrase, which is not present on the earliest typescript (Berg 20.42), echoes one used in all editions of *The Soft Machine* ("Quote Green-Baum Early Explorer"), and the two were juxtaposed in *Dead Fingers Talk*, which joined together the anthropological expeditions to Ward Island and Puerto Joselíto.

109   "three story structure": *TEX* 96 altered *T1* ("storey") to conform to U.S. spelling and to Burroughs' own usage in his 1962 typesetting MS.

109   "the island is now quarantine": the earliest typescript had: **"'so the fruit was quarantined—Now,' he gestures**

at the empty veranda—'All the white planters have
gone'" (Berg 20.42).

111   "island of dying peoples": corrects *TEX* 98 and *T1* ("people"), undoing the change made on the page proofs and
restoring Burroughs' 1962 typesetting MS.

112   "swelled our tongues": *TEX* 99 corrected *T1* ("stole"),
where the copyeditor misread Burroughs' incorrect past
tense "swole" on his 1962 typesetting MS. The Olympia
Press editors then ignored the intentions he expressed in
his autograph correction of "stole" back to "swole" on
the page proofs (OSU 3.8). Ironically, Burroughs' repeated
mistake in grammar makes very clear how much he cared
to correct mistakes. The idiomatic error "swole" appears
twice in the "Who Am I to Be Critical?" section of *The
Soft Machine*.

112   "July 11? 12? 13? 1862": the date is not present on the
earliest typescript, which has a different passage here:
**"Sinking deeper and deeper into sexual deliriums
reveries—For hours we do nothing else—Is Jimmy
really here? Some times he seems to be a phantom—
This is a parasite invasion—I feel that some egg has
been deposited in my body that is hatching out inside
breaking the body shell—That I am being dissolved
by caustic erogenous slime—We are both emaciated"**
(Berg 20.42).

113   "to find her entwined": corrects *TEX* 99 ("find — her"),
which reproduced an error in *T1*, based on misreading a
line break in Burroughs' 1962 typesetting MS.

113   "penetrating my mouth and throat": *TEX* 99 corrected *T1*
("pentrating").

113   "July 11, 12, 13, 1962 — Present Time": *TEX* 100 changed
to lower-case "time" here, in keeping with the revised edition's general, if seemingly arbitrary, practice of cutting capitals. However, capitalized versions of this phrase do appear
twice elsewhere (in "showed you your air"), and capitals

have been restored for the phrase in this section, given its particular importance.

113   "folk singer Logos": *TEX* 100 corrected *T1* ("fold singer"), which had followed the 1962 typesetting MS. While "folk singer" appears correctly in *Nova Express* (179, 186), the typo is meaningful in context of Burroughs' use of the fold-in method for this material.

combat troops in the area

Apart from minor corrections, the first half of this section appeared verbatim in the 1962 edition. However, Burroughs almost doubled the section's length for the 1967 edition through additions that also significantly shifted the balance from narrative toward cut-up material. The shift halfway through is evident not only in the relocation of the narrative from the alien planet Minraud to the American Midwest but visually on the page through the change in punctuation from em dashes to two-dot ellipses. Surprisingly, the switching point that sets up what follows as an exemplary text ("Like this:") was not how the 1967 material began but how the 1962 text ended. Burroughs did, however, emphasize the connection between the last words of the 1962 text and the section that originally followed immediately after when the final two paragraphs of "combat troops" were published together with all of "vaudeville voices" in *The Moderns* (1963). Further complicating the integrity of the 1962 section, most but not all of it appeared in *Dead Fingers Talk* under the title "combat troops in the area," and Burroughs not only changed the order of material but combined it with a passage from the "winds of time" section.

The 1962 material went through several drafts that reveal extensive cutting and revising, often of small details (e.g., Burroughs changed "plan" to "decide" before settling on "dictate" [Berg 20.39] and cut "cheap red wine" in favor of Mexican alcohol in the phrase "rags that smelled of urine and pulque" [Berg 12.30]). One of the more surprising elements in the 1967 material is its reference back to *Naked Lunch* through a joke already told there, the gag about "bloody hash heads" in the "officer's club Calcutta" in *The Ticket* cloning one previously set in the "Jockey Club in Cairo" (77).

117   "the Lord of Time": the following line ("word and image bank of a picture planet") helps identify the real-life figure behind Burroughs' play on words as Henry Luce, owner of *Time* magazine, so that the three-times-repeated phrase "Time falling" (combined here with the refrain "Word falling — Photo falling") functions as a hex on his media empire. In one of his many "Last Words" variants dating from 1960, Burroughs had combined the two levels of reality in "combat troops in the area" by attacking both Luce's newsmagazines and his own alien fantasy world—**"LIFE TIME FORTUNE. AND THE COLLABORATING IN-SECT PEOPLE OF MINRAUD"**—while also addressing himself from the point of view of his enemy: **"STAND ASIDE MR BURROUGHS OF SPACE AND LISTEN TO THE LORD OF TIME"** (Berg 10.31).

118   "Combat troops antennae crackling": an early typescript with many unused details has here: **"Combat troops with shells of green metal"** (Berg 11.29).

119   "a wind U turn back": "wind" would appear to be a typo for "wide" not only because the phrase recurs as such elsewhere in the text (and in *Nova Express*) but because this is how it appears in its source text, Paul Bowles' *The Sheltering Sky*. However, while "wide" appears on an early typescript (Berg 11.29), "wind" is clearly printed on the 1962 typesetting MS at a point where Burroughs made annotated corrections. After this phrase, the early draft continues: **"Combat troops never whisper 'Louise, Mary'—Photo bite through in grey room—Pin balls of the earth deflated balloon"** (Berg 11.29).

120   "Combat troops clicked the fair": a source typescript includes unused lines with a direct reference to "Meet Me in St. Louis,

Louis" and its older nursery rhyme cousin, "Johnny's So Long at the Fair": **"Oh oh what can the matter be, John?—Our revels now are ended—These our actors at St Louie Louie meet me at spirits and are melted into air—Into the Japanese sand man—Flying over little life rounded with a sleep—Matter be? Lies so long at the fair"** (Berg 20.50). Drafts of *Naked Lunch* confirm that "Johnny's So Long at the Fair" was specifically and repeatedly related to "the Sailor," who in turn modeled the Skip Tracer who hums the tune in *Queer*. References to "Meet Me in St. Louis, Louis" recur in *The Wild Boys* and *The Place of Dead Roads*.

120   "Barnum & Bailey world": corrects *TEX* 106 and *T1* ("Barnum Bailey"): taken from "It's Only a Paper Moon," the phrase appears on the 1962 typesetting MS with "and" canceled, and "&" written in. With lyrics about the "phony" and "make-believe" quality of the world, the jazz standard popularized by Ella Fitzgerald builds thematically on the phrase preceding it ("the fair").

123   "as his cock rose out of the smoke": the longest of several variant and unused passages on one typescript continues: **"The man laughed and shoved Ali's knees up to his ears teeth grinding together, Ali's legs locked around his neck feet pounding the other back—The third time he stood Ali in front of a mirror bent over a chair and fucked him with a vibrating rhythm that sent spasms of tooth ache pleasure up Ali's spine as his sperm hit the mirror"** (Berg 12.30). Here it is "Ali" throughout, later revised to "Kiki."

124   "phosphorescent slag heaps": *TEX* 109 corrected *T1* ("shag"), although this usage also appears in *The Ticket*, and both appear in all editions of *The Soft Machine*.

125   "Blazing Photo from Hiroshima and Nagasaki": an early draft continues: **"—It is a highly technical operation and we do not yet have the complete formulae"** (Berg 37.1). The same typescript lacks the identification of the noose as

the "weapon of Kali" and instead has **"weapon of hostile alien."**

125   "They can alternate pain and pleasure": a very rough typescript in red ink has different alternatives: **"They can also turn on boredom and deprivation to soften the enemy up for the orgasm ray—They can turn on sub acute fear to soften up for the ovens rays"** (Berg 20.39).

126   "A camera and two tape recorders": an early typescript has a more detailed and revealing version of this line: **"A box camera and a tape recorder can cut lines laid down by Hollywood and life time fortune—"** (Berg 20.39).

126   "sunlight through the dusty window": from here to the end of the section was inserted for the 1967 edition.

133   "draped the shorts": corrects *TEX* 118 ("dropped"), based on a misreading of Burroughs' typo "drapped" (Berg 43.16).

133   "fold sweet etcetera to bed": corrects *TEX* 118 ("ecetera"). Burroughs' most extensive use of poems by e.e. cummings — including "sweet old etcetera," "Buffalo Bill's," "next to of course god america i" and "as freedom is a breakfastfood"— appears in his short piece "Just So Long and Long Enough," composed in early 1963 and published in *Gnaoua* (Spring 1964).

vaudeville voices

Apart from omitting some sixty words in half a dozen small cuts, this section appeared verbatim in the 1962 edition, but Burroughs almost doubled its length by adding a long insert in the middle for the 1967 text. The original section was one of the first parts he wrote, judging from a one-page fold-in of "East Clinic Information" he mailed Paul Bowles on May 20, 1962, which is a typescript that includes longer versions of two paragraphs used in "vaudeville voices." With its "osteopath clinic outside East St. Louis" and other details such as the "rumble in Dallas," this material also echoes the "Shift Coordinate Points" section of *Nova Express*, written at the start of 1962. Curiously, almost a quarter of the 1967 additional material derived from inserts proposed but not made for *Nova Express* in July 1964. As well as standing out formally through the heavy use of ellipses, the new material also separates itself from the original section by including dates related to its composition ("November 18, 1963" and "July 4, 1964"), and a longer version of this material, dated July 7, 1964, was published as "File Ticker Tape" in the summer 1965 issue of *The Insect Trust Gazette*.

The version published in the short-lived Philadelphia magazine named after a phrase in *Naked Lunch* is especially significant. For this longer text, later republished in *The Burroughs File*, includes several pages of highly topical political material—naming such mid-1960s figures as Republican presidential candidate Barry Goldwater—which indicates how Burroughs tried to differentiate his work according to publications and readerships: what suited an ephemeral little magazine did not necessarily suit a book published by Grove Press. Equally, there are important differences in how the texts were edited and presented: *The Insect Trust Gazette* differs not only materially but in terms of both typography and orthography, and includes lines canceled by hand and numerous typos ("Titel" for "Title"; "swiming" for "swimming"; "Remeber" for "Remember"; "Facist" for "Fascist"; "Goldwatter" for "Goldwater"), signs of the creative process that fitted the rough aesthetics of mimeograph magazines but not *The Ticket That Exploded* (these typos were cleaned up for the reprinting of the text in *The Burroughs File*). Equally important, Burroughs very deliberately exploited the mistakes included in the magazine typescript (see the note on "Voice of American," below).

When the original section appeared in *The Moderns* (combined with the final two paragraphs of the "combat troops" section and including 450 words not used for *The Ticket*) Burroughs added a note on its method of composition that concludes: "This chapter contains fold ins with the work of Rimbaud, T. S. Eliot, Paul Bowles, James Joyce, Michael Portman, Peter Weber, Fabrizio Mondadori, Jacques Stern, Evgeny Yevtushenko, some newspaper articles and of course my own work—" Burroughs' mixing of names and materials makes the point that the source text cannot be the sole source of meaning, since no reader could recognize all of them.

However, the tip-off to Bowles could lead to *The Sheltering Sky*, resulting in the uncanny sensation of reading his novel while recognizing odd phrases from Burroughs' cut-up text ("made a wide U-turn," "where the awning flapped" etc.). Likewise, reading Bowles' *Let It Come Down* makes a fragment such as "dim jerky far away," which recurs across the trilogy, suddenly flash with an aura of significance. The reader begins to both discover and create meaningful connections, since the original context of Bowles' novel is not arbitrary: "Today was like an old, worn-out film being run off—dim, jerky, flickering, full of cuts, and with a plot he could not seize. It was hard to pay attention to it" (New York: Penguin, 2000; 311). Thematically and even formally—since it includes an em-dash—the context is multiply significant, and Burroughs cited these lines in full at the end of a related cut-up text, "Unfinished Cigarette," published in fall 1963 in another little magazine, the *Birmingham Bulletin* (reprinted in *The Burroughs File*). In the case of Rimbaud, however, the problem of translation makes it even harder to identify his poem "Vies" ("Lives") from the odd words "duty" and "remitted" taken out of context: "My duty has been remitted. I must not even think of that anymore. I am really from beyond the tomb, and no commissions." Burroughs would often cite the most resonant and recognizable phrases here—"beyond the tomb, and no commissions"—but they were lost when, for no apparent reason, these lines were cut from the 1962 text for the 1967 edition.

135   "Nobody walks out on one": from here to "his time" restores lines cut from the 1962 text for the 1967 edition (cf *TEX* 119).

136   "Now the Spanish fly would not be again steady stream": restores a line cut from the 1962 text for the 1967 edition (cf *TEX* 120).

136   "You touched from frayed jacket": a near-verbatim typescript has an unused line which references Burroughs' birthplace as well as a tune whose opening bars float "like music down

a windy street" in *Naked Lunch*: **"Cool silver glance out into Ellington's East St. Louis Toodle Oo"** (Berg 20.27).

137 "banner on the pissoirs": from here to "fading against the silk of seas" restores lines cut from the 1962 text for the 1967 edition (cf *TEX* 121), with the exception of odd words ("flesh," "murmur of human nights," "like death in your throat? — breathless").

137 "Tuesday was the last day": from here to "'Never Happened' is my name . . ." (page 140) was an insert made for the 1967 edition.

137 "Yes that's me still there waiting": from here to "Hiroshima gangrene" and from "You don't remember this sad stranger" to "sad muttering voices" (page 138) was material Burroughs initially planned as an insert for *Nova Express* in 1964, which was not made because he cut the relevant chapter from his manuscript.

137 "bringing you the Voice of American": this seems self-evidently a typo in need of correction, but textual variants and archival sources reveal it to be intentionally ambiguous. The phrase "Voice of America" appears correctly in "File Ticker Tape" in *The Insect Trust Gazette*, which is significant since the magazine prints "American" incorrectly twice for other phrases that appear correctly in *The Ticket* ("American stands for"; "American will redeem"). (In *The Burroughs File*, these mistakes in the magazine version were silently corrected.) The error "American will redeem" also appears on Burroughs' 1966 typescript of this material for *The Ticket* (Berg 43.18), and the fact that this was corrected for publication in 1967 would seem to suggest that "Voice of American" was just a missed typo. On the other hand, Burroughs retained another apparent error at the very start of this inserted material for *The Ticket*, in the phrase "signing years," and this was surely deliberate. For the version published as "File Ticker Tape" prints "signing years" immediately after the "correct" version, "Singing Years." The ambiguity of intention—and the ambiguity of intentionality—is made the

explicit subject of this material by the key phrase used here: "ambiguous sign of an inn." This phrase appears in both *The Ticket* and in "File Ticker Tape," but is also repeated "incorrectly" in the magazine version as "ambiguous sing of an inn." In short, the care Burroughs took in deliberately transposing characters in "sign" and "sing" and in "signing" and "Singing" argues for retaining the ambiguity of the *sign* in "Voice of American." The play on "singing" and "signing" is also particularly meaningful in context of *The Ticket*'s catalogue of song references, although it dates back to the 1961 text of *The Soft Machine*, which has the phrase, retained in later editions, "Under Sing Sign Of The Scorpion Goddess."

138   "Now how's this for an angle, B.J.?": at this point "File Ticker Tape" continues with a long politically explicit section, beginning: "Now the boys back of Barry Goldwater are pretty smart boys . . ." (*Burroughs File* 146). Despite material clearly tied to events of 1964 when Goldwater ran for the White House, the key concept of what "America stands for" goes back at least four years, specifically to a typescript dated August 23, 1960 which begins: **"WHAT DOES AMERICA STAND FOR? A NASAL PENETRATING STUPID WHINE THRU AMERICAN EXPRESS LIKE A LOW CHARGE DEATH RAY. MEN WHO CALL THEIR WIVES MOTHER. SYMPATHY MOOCHES A MISERABLE SNIVELING PACK OF WALKING DEAD [...] NOR CAN ANY OTHER COUNTRY PRODUCE SUCH UGLY BABOON VICIOUSNESS. REALLY BOYS CANT WE DO BETTER THAN THIS? CAN WE DO WORSE? EVEN THAT MIGHT BE INNARESTING [...] CURE YOURSELF UNHAPPY COUNTRY"** (Berg 60.19).

139   "A militant writer's union": "File Ticker Tape" has a different version of this paragraph, naming names; "While you wait Mary McCarthy and Norman Mailer organize a Militant Writer's Union. All American writers recalled to base . . . .

stand by for orders . . . . Yes that means you Paul Bowles"
(*Burroughs File*, 148).

140   "Expectancy growing in vaudeville voices": restores a phrase
cut from the 1962 text for the 1967 edition (cf *TEX* 123).
This line did not appear on the 1962 typesetting MS, which
ends at "wind voices" and has a rare erasure (**"I know you"**)
immediately beforehand.

141   "Swedish river of Gothenburg": corrects *TEX* 123 and *T1*
("Gothenberg"); the same correction has been made throughout the text.

terminal street

Apart from one very small cut, this short section appeared verbatim in the 1962 edition. With its "twisting intestinal streets," the
portrait of Minraud here seems to transpose a description of the
medina of Tangier, where Burroughs had lived in 1954, and this
section features one of the few *Naked Lunch*–era passages in its
brief depiction of the "cliff city" as another version of Interzone.

142   "terminal streets of Minraud": an early typescript that has
numerous small variant lines continues: "**—Muttering beg-
gars with glowing metal stumps and everywhere the
phosphorescent metal excrement—**" (Berg 20.38).

143   "Words passed through his mind": *TEX* 126 corrected *T1*
("word").

146   "dream flesh in a scratching shower of sperm": in a rare
erasure, the 1962 typesetting MS continues: **"Bodies written in light without cover of the board books drifted
over the planet—"**

last round over

Apart from ten very small cuts, this section appeared verbatim
in the 1962 edition, while parts appeared, out of sequence and
combined with other material, in *Dead Fingers Talk*. When the

long and internally very repetitive cut-up opening passages give way to the lecture mode of address, it is revealing that Burroughs includes here one of his favourite phrases—"Is that clear enough or shall i make it even clearer?"—a question that might appear rhetorical or self-reflexive, given the simultaneous insistence and obscurity of his cut-up material and also Burroughs' suspicion of his own tendency toward didacticism. However, he frequently deployed the phrase in his letters to express in menacing terms his anger with a correspondent, and the lines immediately following it ("Reverse all your gimmicks") are directly addressed, like a letter, to "Mr Bradly Mr Martin." The real-life target of Burroughs' vitriol is clear from the context ("your monopoly of life, time, and fortune"): media magnate Henry Luce. Burroughs' hostility toward Luce's trilogy of newsmagazines more profoundly shaped *Nova Express*—and the passage here reworks "Last Words" material dating back to 1960 which ended up in that book—but this passage in *The Ticket* is his most sustained, directly addressed invective. Curiously, unused lines from the archival typescripts name the leader of a different media empire (William Randolph Hearst), beside figures from American big business (Rockefeller, Getty) and law enforcement (Anslinger) as agents of the control machine.

In terms of source material, as well as snatches of Shakespeare and T. S. Eliot the section is dense with fragments from blues standards and Negro spirituals. Burroughs made numerous page-long lists of lyrics and titles, many of which never made the final cut for *The Ticket*. Some help identify or confirm odd fragments, such as "Cousin Miranda," who made a blueberry pie in Hoagy Carmichael's "Memphis in June," or the phrase "sugar line" which originated in the 1929 minstrel song "Down Among the Sugarcane." Together with other Carmichael melodies from the 1930s and '40s, including "Georgia on My Mind" (which became a hit for Ray Charles in 1960), these lists identified "Hong Kong Blues," "Ol' Man River," "Swanee River" ("Old Folks at Home") and "Swing Low, Sweet Chariot" (Berg 9.8).

146   "'Master' — a long good night": references the title of Brion
       Gysin's first book, about the history of slavery in Canada.

147   "in Lexington, Kentucky": following this reference to the
       Federal Narcotic Farm in Lafayette County, described by
       Burroughs in *Junky*, an early typescript adds a phrase play-
       ing on the famous slogan for Coca-Cola: "**—The pause that
       refreezes—**" (Berg 20.40).

148   "and i'm checking out": among other unused phrases, an
       early typescript continues: "**—And they may flash the old
       Kentucky home—But darkies the pipes the pipes are
       calling. Dixie Land—**" (Berg 20.40). Burroughs' refer-
       ences to the 19th-century minstrel song "My Old Kentucky
       Home" and to New Orleans jazz do not appear elsewhere in
       the text (unlike the line from "Danny Boy").

148   "angle voices calling Old Black Joe": in the mid-19th-
       century spiritual, it is "angel voices" that call Old Black
       Joe; the possible typo appears on the 1962 typesetting MS
       as well as in *T1* and *Dead Fingers Talk*. The phrase is given
       correctly in the "showed you your air" section (page 200), al-
       though there the 1962 typesetting MS had **"Angle voices,"**
       prompting a marginal query by the copyeditor, **"Angel?"**
       On the page proofs, this was indeed changed to "Angel,"
       although not in Burroughs' hand.

150   "odor of drowned suns": corrects *TEX* 132 ("ordor"), as per
       T1 and the 1962 typesetting MS.

150   "Won't be much left in the final ape of history": restores
       a line cut from the 1962 text for the 1967 edition (cf *TEX*
       132).

150   "Rectum with dirty shirt": from here to "phosphorescent
       information" restores a line cut from the 1962 text for the
       1967 edition (cf *TEX* 133).

151   "Five times penis rose pulsing": this phrase, followed by
       from "Leaning say mixture ebbing carbon dioxide" to "one
       absent today," restores words cut from the 1962 text for the
       1967 edition (cf *TEX* 133).

151   "A long good night in metal": restores a phrase cut from the 1962 text for the 1967 edition (cf *TEX* 133).

151   "Light layers": *TEX* 133 corrected *T1* ("layer").

152   "or all to see in Times Square in Piccadilly": the line, which is given correctly in *Nova Express* ("for all to see"; p. 2), appears this way on earlier typescripts. On one, it is followed by lines that make more explicit the identities subsumed by the name Bradly Martin: **"—Pay Mr Martin pay in real currency—Pay blue pay red pay green—Reverse all your dreams of monopoly and immortality in three dimensional coordinates—Mr Bradly Martin Rockefeller Getty Hurst Anslinger—Reverse and dismantle your machine—Drain off the prop ocean and leave the White Whale stranded—All the word and image of life time fortune—"** (Berg 20.26).

153   "Like suddenly": restores a phrase cut from the 1962 text for the 1967 edition (cf *TEX* 135).

156   "Time to squeeze out the welchers, kid": a variant passage on one typescript combines numerous allusions: **"Welchers extensive over there kid—You can't even con— Friend, Life Time Fortune couldn't roll a paralyzed flop—Augment your bets or shut up and get out— Burroughs has the news before your welching two bit IBM machine—Mayan Caper and Iron Lung up to the old North Pole [...] Nova Express split board books—Minutes to go—Time's SOS—You can't con job—Colorless sheets are empty—So are your bets"** (Berg 361.3).

156   "The 'Hassan i Sabbahs'": *TEX* 137 corrected *T1* ("'The Hassan i Sabbahs").

156   "Walgreen's": *TEX* 137 corrected *T1* (Wallgreen's").

156   "strictly from Moochville —": corrects *TEX* 137 and *T1* ("strickly"): although the misspelling might have seemed deliberately idiomatic, the 1962 typesetting MS spells the word correctly.

call the old doctor twice?

Apart from cutting five words ("and the living is easy," from Gershwin's jazz standard "Summertime"), this section appeared verbatim in the 1962 edition, except for a 500-word insert Burroughs made near the end for the 1967 text. As in "last round over," here again he juxtaposes didactic material with cut-up passages that fragment song lyrics, from cowboy tunes like "Ghost Riders in the Sky" and "Good-bye, Old Paint" to one of his old favorites, Richard Whiting's melody "The Japanese Sandman." By far the most recurrent is "Ace in the Hole," another favorite and a song laden with personal meaning: "Some write home to the Old Folks for coin," he told Allen Ginsberg some ten years earlier, referring to his parents' longstanding financial support; "And that's their old Ace in the Hole" (*Letters 1945–1959*, 153). But while the lyrics may have been evocative for Burroughs, and contribute a nostalgic air to some passages, he deployed them with an ironic and vicious cutting edge, shown here through surprising combinations and a subversive use of rhythm: "Now some write home to orgasm death"; "Word falling, photo falling, old folks at home."

As with the previous section, there are some important continuities with *Nova Express*; the character of the "Old Doctor" is a development of "The Blue Dinosaur" from "So Pack Your Ermines" in the earlier book, while several lines echo the "Will Hollywood Never Learn?" section, intercut with phrases from *Minutes to Go* ("Solemn Accountants," "Fourth-Grade Class," "Allies wait on knives," etc.). Other passages extend the cutting up of newspaper items from *Nova Express* (marked by references to airlines, artists and actors: BOAC, Stanley Spencer, George Raft, James Dean). The 1962 section was itself cut up for *Dead Fingers Talk*, parts appearing in "to quiet the marks," combined with some material from *The Soft Machine*, other parts appearing out of sequence to make up "the board books" section. Even more curiously, the piece entitled "Call the Old Doctor Twice?" published in *The Yale Literary Magazine* in April 1963, includes a sequence from this section, but it follows on from the opening pages of "the nova police" section and the whole "So Pack Your Ermines" section from *Nova Express*.

156   "'Mr Martins,' trying to buy": corrects *TEX* 138 ("Mr Martin") as per *T1* and the 1962 typesetting MS.

158   "In three-dimensional terms the board": on the 1962 typesetting MS this material, clearly distinct from the opening paragraphs of the section, begins on a new page headed **"THE BOARD AND THE BOARD BOOKS."** Indicating several revisions of sequence, the page shows no fewer than four different paginations. An earlier typescript, again under this heading, has numerous small differences, including: **"I repeat this is a monopolistic big money pressure group—Such is the way of the western world and I have nothing good to say for it"** (Berg 11.32). Another early typescript, where the board is defined as **"a monopolist pressure group,"** is headed **"WORD FALLING—PHOTO FALLING"** (Berg 36.2), at one time an alternative title for *The Ticket*.

159   "So pack your ermines, Mary — *we* are": corrects *TEX* 140 ("we"), as per *T1* and the 1962 typesetting MS. The line, which echoes a section title in *Nova Express* and is repeated several times in *The Ticket*, appears on the MS at the start of a separate half-page headed with one of the book's original titles: **"IF YOU CAN'T SAY IT SING IT."**

160   "sneaky pete": *TEX* 141 corrected *T1* ("sneaky peet"). The *Yale Literary Magazine* version capitalizes the phrase as "Sneaky Pete."

166   "the junk man at the outskirts": before this phrase an earlier typescript has unused lines that reference a Cole Porter song, thick fog in London, and a blues standard that in 1962 became a hit for James Brown: **"What is this thing came in on a London particular—Night train to the sound of gongs"** (Berg 20.37). After "outskirts" this typescript adds, from Brown's "Night Train," **"Washington D.C."**

166   "and the living is easy": restores a phrase, from "Summer-
       time," cut from the 1962 text for the 1967 edition (cf *TEX*
       147).

169   "been obvious:: Orbit Of The Saturn Galaxy": corrects *TEX*
       149 ("orbit Of the Saturn Galaxy"), as per *T1* and the 1962
       typesetting MS, as well as internal consistency, while restor-
       ing the double colon indicated on the MS.

170   "Martin's reality film": from here to "the uncovered flesh"
       (page 172) was an insert for the 1967 edition. The typed
       insert ended with an unused final line: **"Since the film
       is no longer intended to entertain they don't need
       writers and artists anymore"** (Berg 43.19).

shuffle cut

This section appeared verbatim in the 1962 edition except for
a few very small cuts and a short insert in the middle that
Burroughs made for the 1967 edition. The inserted text, which
breaks up long passages of repetitive cut-up material, echoes the
earlier reference to Henry Kuttner's novel *Fury* by again citing
not only a science fiction text—Barrington Bayley's *The Star
Virus*—but also seemingly gratuitous bibliographical details ("in
New World Science Fiction . . Nova Publications . . 7 Grape St.
High Holborn London Vol 49 June . ."). In context of so much
uncredited recycling of Modernist authors such as Joyce and
Eliot—who themselves pastiched other writers—the strategy of
acknowledging so fully such sub-literary, non-canonical works
clearly seems ironic (in the spirit of postmodernism). However,
the reference has unexpected material connections, beyond the
detail—so serendipitous it might appear fabricated—that the
British SF magazine was printed by Nova Publications. Despite Burroughs' seeming carelessness—misspelling Bayley's
first name (it's "Barrington" not "Barryington"), incorrectly
citing the title of the magazine (*New Worlds* not *New World*)

and misquoting the text ("But you might have taken half the spaceground with you!" not "Why you might have taken half the planet with you")—he very deliberately omits the key detail, the year of publication, which is replaced by a teasing ellipsis. For June 1964 was no random issue of the magazine: under the new editorial leadership of Michael Moorcock, it featured J.G. Ballard's important discussion of Burroughs, "Myth Maker of the Twentieth Century," which placed him on a par with Joyce in a review of his work that discussed the recently published *Ticket That Exploded*.

172   "Pack your ermines, Mary": before this phrase, an earlier typescript begins the section with unused lines directly addressing the book's reader: **"Bulletin from Rewrite: This book is operation rewrite—Take a section any section—You got it? Record to music—As you listen fill in with an image track—Remember the sound track evokes the image track *in nervous system*—You can demonstrate this on your TV set—Shut off the sound track—And play music—Now play the music back and you will see the image track—Or record the sound track and playback—Try the same arrangement with home movies—Shuffle this book like a pack of cards—"** (Berg 20.30).

172   "other dressing rooms and transient hotels": a variant line on an earlier typescript suggests an allusion to Truman Capote's first novel was made and then obscured: **"other dressing voices other rooms"** (Berg 36.8).

172   "whine of dying peoples": corrects *TEX* 152 and *T1* ("people") as per both the 1962 typesetting MS and an earlier typescript (Berg 10.3).

172   "'Lord, Lord, i don't even feel like a human'": an earlier typescript lacks the following line and instead continues with alternatives: **"Now if I had put my money on Blue Orgone instead of Now If I had bought Orgone Utilities instead of Trak Tel & Con—"** (Berg 36.8).

173   "make arrests and question suspects": corrects *TEX* 152
       ("arrest"). Early typescripts (Berg 20.30 and 36.8) suggest
       this was simply a typo.

173   "under civil leer of the witness": unaccountably, *TEX* 153
       changed *T1* ("eyes of the witness").

174   "birth and death and the human condition": Burroughs ex-
       panded on these lines in a related typescript: **"Christian
       training has conditioned us to acceptance (Birth
       death and the human condition—Always been that
       way and always will—Besides you can't do anything)—
       to believe that 'right' will somehow triumph—God
       or decency or the dignity of man will intervene—
       Listen: You must fight or you will be defeated and
       destroyed—You will be eaten alive by white hot crab
       people under the white hot skies of Minraud—And
       remember the will to fight is not enough—You must
       learn who and what the enemy is, their weapons and
       methods of operation—You must learn to use the
       weapons that will defeat and destroy the enemy—"**
       (Berg 37.1).

176   "Quick fires from teeth grinding together": this phrase, and
       "pounding the other back" and "And from radios i don't see,"
       restores words cut from the 1962 text for the 1967 edition
       (cf *TEX* 155).

176   "Remember show price?": from here to "'The whole of it,
       mate'" (page 177) was an insert for the 1967 edition. On
       the insert typescript Burroughs used both two- and three-
       dot ellipses, which were regularized for publication (Berg
       43.20). A slightly longer version of this material also ap-
       peared as part of "File Ticker Tape" in *The Insect Trust
       Gazette*; although it was cut for *The Burroughs File* reprint
       (149), this also included a slightly different version of the
       note on "Deadliners."

176   "Galaxies pulled": restores a phrase cut from the 1962 text
       for the 1967 edition (cf *TEX* 157).

178   "You trying source": corrects *TEX* 157 ("sources"). Although both versions appear elsewhere in *The Ticket*, both *T1* and the 1962 typesetting MS have the singular.

179   "give off a stench of rotten lips": corrects *TEX* 157 ("gave"), as per *T1* and the 1962 typesetting MS; the present tense appears elsewhere in *The Ticket*.

179   "Diarrhea exploded down": from here to "switch blades —" restores lines cut from the 1962 text for the 1967 edition (cf *TEX* 158).

in that game

This section appeared verbatim in the 1962 *Ticket* but its length almost tripled for the 1967 edition through the addition of one short and two long inserts. The new material expanded the original by emphasizing that machines are "an externalized section of the human nervous system," terms that go back to Dr Benway in *Naked Lunch* ("Western man is externalizing himself in the form of gadgets" [22]). However, *The Ticket* updates *Naked Lunch* in tape recorder technology, chiefly inspired by Scientology techniques first taken up in late 1959, and it both references actual experiments carried out by Burroughs at the time of writing the 1962 edition ("I recorded sound tracks") and invites the reader of the 1967 edition to follow suit ("Go out and buy three fine machines on credit"). Parts of this material—including the rallying cry, "Carry Corders of the world unite"—appeared in April 1966 in Jeff Nuttall's British mimeograph magazine *My Own Mag* 15, where Burroughs again misspelled the name of the tape recorder ("Phillips"), and ended with an appeal to the sixties generation: "So get out there with your Carry Corders young fellers."

181   "Written on 'the Soft Typewriter'": corrects *TEX* 159 (which has double speech marks, within speech). In what follows, speech marks have either been added or changed to represent the text up until "Minutes to go" (page 183) as being spoken by the Fluoroscopic Kid.

181   "Like a Siamese twin ten thousand years in show business":
       TEX 159 changed *T1* ("five hundred thousand years").

181   "(Take a talking picture of you": from here to "physical
       death.)" was an insert made for the 1967 edition.

183   "Look down look down along that line": the words from the
       1927 folk song "The Lonesome Road" echo the end of the
       "Deposition" added to *Naked Lunch*.

184   "It's all done with tape recorders. Go out and buy": from
       here to "but your prerecordings"(page 189) was an insert
       made for the 1967 edition.

185   "the so-called context": possibly a typo, since "content" is
       more logical.

185   "The soccer scores are coming in from the Capital": corrects
       TEX 163 ("capitol") to how the line appears in other texts,
       including *The Soft Machine* and *The Third Mind*.

188   "splice your singing in with the Beatles": "the invisible
       generation" Appendix referenced the Beatles' famous con-
       certs in New York in 1965 and 1966 in the larger context of
       tape recorder possibilities: "this is the invisible generation
       it is the efficient generation hands work and go see some
       interesting results when several hundred tape recorders
       turn up at a political rally or a freedom march suppose you
       record the ugliest snarling southern law men several hun-
       dred tape recorders spitting it back and forth and chewing
       it around like a cow with the aftosa you now have a sound
       that could make any neighborhood unattractive several
       hundred tape recorders echoing the readers could touch a
       poetry reading with unpredictable magic and think what
       fifty thousand beatle fans armed with tape recorders could
       do to shea stadium several hundred people recording and
       playing back in the street is quite a happening right there
       conservative m.p. spoke about the growing menace posed
       by bands or irresponsible youths with tape recorders play-
       ing back traffic sounds that confuse motorists carrying
       the insults recorded in some low underground club into

may-fair and piccadilly this growing menace to public order put a thousand young recorders with riot recordings into the street" (*NEX* 209–10).

188   "Only way to stop it": corrects *TEX* 166 ("only"); the capital is clearly given on the typescript insert (Berg 43.22). The following short paragraph citing Wittgenstein is not present in this typescript, suggesting it was a later addition.

188   "It's all done with tape recorders": "the invisible generation" Appendix develops the artistic possibilities: "there are many things you can do with programmed tape recorders stage performances programmed at arbitrary intervals so each performance is unpredictable and unique allowing any degree of audience participation readings concerts programmed tape recorders can create a happening anywhere" (*TEX* 210). Using the key 1960s terminology of *happenings*, Burroughs anticipates the influence of his own texts on musicians, from David Bowie—who said *Nova Express* inspired the stage show idea for *Ziggy Stardust* because the performances "would change every night" (*Burroughs Live*, 230)—to the perpetually reconfigured "Ongoing Opera" of James Ilgenfritz's 2011 adaptation of *The Ticket*.

188   "the Philips Carry Corder": corrects *TEX* 166 ("Philipp's").

188   "*playback in the street*": "the invisible generation" Appendix has more on this idea: "some carriers are much better than others you know the ones lips moving muttering away carry my message all over london in our yellow submarine working with street playback you will see your playback find the appropriate context for example i am playing back some of my dutch Schultz last word tapes in the street five alarm fire and a fire truck passes right on cue" (*TEX* 208).

189   "God's little toy": "the invisible generation" Appendix expanded on this passage to make connections back to the early 1950s: "cut up tapes can be hilariously funny twenty years ago i heard a tape called the drunken newscaster

prepared by jerry newman of new york cutting up news broadcasts i can not remember the words at this distance but i do remember laughing until i fell out of a chair paul bowles calls the tape recorder god's little toy maybe his last toy" (*TEX* 207).

189   "Fleet St. and Madison Avenue": "the invisible generation" Appendix expands on the role of the news media: "what are newspapers doing but selecting the ugliest sounds for playback by and large if its ugly its news and if that isn't enough i quote from the editorial page of the new york daily news we can take care of china and if russia intervenes we can take care of that nation too the only good communist is a dead communist lets take care of slave driver castro next what are we waiting for let's bomb china now and let's stay armed to the teeth for centuries this ugly vulgar bray put out for mass playback you want to spread hysteria record and play back the most stupid and hysterical reactions [...] only way to break the inexorable down spiral of ugly uglier ugliest recording and playback is with counterrecording and playback the first step *is* to isolate and cut association lines of the control machine carry a tape recorder with you and record all the ugliest stupidest things cut your ugly tapes in together speed up slow down play backwards inch the tape you will hear one ugly voice and see one ugly spirit is made of ugly old prerecordings the more you run the tapes through and cut them up the less power they will have cut the prerecordings into air into thin air" (*TEX* 216, 217). Among other minor differences, a typescript draft of this material has, immediately before the line quoting the *New York Daily News*, the unused phrase **"the American moral disease has blighted the world"** (Berg 43.2).

191   "It's all done with tape recorders. What we see": from here to "can't tell the difference" was an insert made for the 1967 edition.

192   "one Danger Man spy program": "the invisible generation"
         Appendix rolled two 1960s TV programs together: "one dan-
         ger man from uncle spy program" (*TEX* 205).

showed you your air

This section appeared verbatim in the 1962 *Ticket* (and in *Dead
Fingers Talk*), and Burroughs made two very small cuts while
adding a page of new material in the middle of the section for
the 1967 edition. Mixed in among the song lyrics cut up here—
nicely referenced as "juke box bulletins"—is a phrase fragment
of possibly quite another sort: "Beat your mother." In summer
1961 for the special "Collaborations" issue of *LOCUS SOLUS*
magazine edited by Kenneth Koch, Burroughs had published two
short cut-up poems from *Minutes to Go* alongside other co-authored
works, including a series of Surrealist proverbs by Paul Eluard and
Benjamin Peret—one of which was: "Beat your mother while she
is young" (a translation of "Battre sa mère quand elle est jeune,"
which in turn reworked the well-known proverb "Il faut battre le fer
quand il est chaud"). The connection, which is further suggested
by the presence of fragments from *Minutes to Go* immediately
afterward, invites us to read a following fragment as a comment
on Surrealist automatism (note the word "automatic" also recurs
here): "Voices came through channels." The text inserted for the
1967 edition that comes next seems entirely out of place in the
section but is unquestionably based on a very precise art-historical
frame of reference, alluding to a recent act of Situationist sabotage:
the "bronze head of a young girl" sawed from "their filthy mermaid" points to the attack carried out in April 1964 by the Danish
artist Jørgen Nash and other members of Bauhaus Situationniste,
when they decapitated The Little Mermaid statue in Copenhagen
harbor. In 1965 Burroughs combined a variant draft of this passage
with images of the mermaid statue in two consecutive *Third Mind*
collages ("Girl" and "Another Goal"), the first of which includes
a press clipping captioned "SHE LOST HER HEAD."

195   "Now of course Death Dwarfs talking in supersonic blasts to
       the same": restores phrases either side of "Death Dwarfs"
       cut from the 1962 text for the 1967 edition (cf *TEX* 171).
       Both the 1962 typesetting MS and an earlier typescript (Berg
       10.3) have **"blats do the same."**

196   "and why answer": corrects *TEX* 173 ("answers") as per *T1*
       and the 1962 typesetting MS.

197   "The Old Man himself": from here to "the brownest nose"
       (page 198) was an insert made for the 1967 edition.

198   "Dry Hole Dutton": reference is to a character, who also
       pops up in *Naked Lunch*, from one of the routines Lee tells
       in *Queer* in order to seduce Allerton.

let them see us

This short section appeared verbatim in the 1962 *Ticket*, and
in terms of manuscript history the only oddity is that its final
paragraph did not appear on the 1962 typesetting MS but was
added only at the page proof stage (the only such insert Burroughs
made). After the previous section's references to Surrealism and
Situationism, it might seem that this begins with a reference to
Andy Warhol. Certainly, the idea of shooting and projecting films
at different speeds echoes Warhol's *Empire* (1964), which was
shot at the standard 24 frames per second but shown at 16 fps,
and Antony Balch did the same when screening *The Cut Ups*,
first exhibited shortly before the revised *Ticket That Exploded*
appeared. However, what is called here "The Short Time Hyp"
dates back to before Burroughs' film collaborations with Balch,
and some lines appear on a typescript probably dating from 1960,
not long after he and Balch first met.

203   "The Short Time Hyp": an early typescript version of these
       lines appears under the heading **"'MR BRADLY MR
       MARTIN' IN MINRAUD"** (Berg 49.32).

203   "Not so sharp and clear — Now": corrects *TEX* 179 and *T1*
       ("clear. Now"), as per the 1962 typesetting MS; the same

restoration of em dash for period is made at the end of the paragraph ("dimmer —").

207   "show the method in operation": this line, together with preceding phrases ("I edit delete and rearrange"), derive from "The Future of the Novel" and "Notes on these Pages," published in *Transatlantic Review* 11 (Winter 1962), based on Burroughs' talk to the Edinburgh Writers' Conference in August 1962. At this point the 1962 typesetting MS ends with a canceled line: **"May not refuse vision in setting forth the writing machine i created—Wind hand fed back into air—"**

silence to say good bye

The final section appeared verbatim in the 1962 *Ticket* but Burroughs transformed it by making it five times longer, adding a complex 4,500-word insert into the middle of the original section, as well as making two shorter inserts toward the end. Almost all the long insert had previously been published in summer 1964 in *The Insect Trust Gazette* 1 under the title "Burning Heavens, Idiot," at the same time as the final sixth of the insert appeared in "Who Is the Third That Walks Beside You?" in *Art and Literature* 2. After a variant opening paragraph, "Burning Heavens, Idiot" is near verbatim apart from minor punctuation and spelling differences, but the overlapping text published in John Ashbery's Paris-based magazine differed more substantially. In particular, it was part of a three-column layout piece, so that the material added to the Grove Press *Ticket* needs to be seen in relation to a record of variant texts, little-magazine publication and formal experiment.

While balanced somewhere between elegy and irony, the 1962 text was relatively simple as a leave-taking of these "our actors," farewells from the book's characters modeled on Prospero's speech in *The Tempest* ("Our revels now are ended. These our actors / As I foretold you, were all spirits and / Are melted into air"). Into this section Burroughs inserted a series of narrative scenarios, lectures and cut-up passages that introduce entirely new material and characters (Major Ash, Chigger), *Naked Lunch*–style routines—including a walk-on from Dr. Benway—and the return of Bill and John from "combat troops in the area." Bill and John resume their experiments with time travel through a cut-up recording of Fitzgerald's story of toxic capitalist desire, "The Diamond as Big as the Ritz" (a few fragments of which were slipped into the end of "combat troops"). The evocation of the 1920s through Fitzgerald is fitting in a text so saturated with references to popular song melodies and lyrics from that era, but only makes the subsequent 1960s political references to Castro and Vietnam all the more jarring. Less awkwardly, the finale mixes the Hollywood pitch involving "B.J." with fragments taken from Conrad's turn-of-the-century novel *Lord Jim*, before the typed text finally disappears into the calligraphic script provided by Brion Gysin.

209   "John made coffee" from here to "Portland Place" (page 226) was an insert made for the 1967 edition.

209   "sat him on a stool": corrects *TEX* 184 ("on stool").

211   "like a school in fairyland": the passage from "The Diamond as Big as the Ritz" is oddly edited; not only does Burroughs omit much of the punctuation, but he makes three small changes, the most meaningful of which is the omission here of "girl's" in the original line "like a girl's school in fairyland" (F. Scott Fitzgerald, *The Collected Short Stories* [London: Penguin, 2000], 106).

213   "soccer scores — clock hands": from here until "Portland Place" (page 226) appeared as "Burning Heavens, Idiot" in *The Insect Trust Gazette* 1 (Summer 1964), although the little-magazine text begins with fifty words not present in *The Ticket*: "The dead past is a virus that can only repeat itself word for word like all virus: 'Me Me Meeeeeeeeee.' It lives in and on the present and that is the only existence it has parasitic like all virus. Take: The Death of Manolete — 'Paco Joselito Henrique' — That image lives reflected in their eyes —"

214   "So the image past molds your future": an early draft develops
this idea, and concludes with autobiographical references
back to the late 1940s: **"Images of past time invade damage and occupy imposing repetition of past image—
Picture the mold that encloses you the mold of what
is not that inexorably determines and predetermines
what is as composed of millions of images a mould
extending in time stretching out behind and ahead of
you with the speed of light a vast tunnel of old photos
a mold that penetrates every cell of your body like a
virus filter and the negatives continually developed
in the dark room of your body—You walk around
there and here take take take with your eyes and the
negatives returned to the dark room to develop your
future remember the office you stumbled into by
mistake in New Orleans and later returned there with
definite purpose? Whose purpose? You were looking for rami and found a lawyer you were going to
need because the picture of your arrest was already
developing piece by piece in the eyes of a cop who
looked after you speculative for no reason . . That
right take—Now the corner where it will happen and
the pusher Old Dick who was after doing a dime in
Angola . . A thin grey shadow—Sun through lattice
falls on your face take—take and don't forget the
lawyer you are going to need him—His name is *Link*
Bob Link you got it? Link"** (Berg 39.26).

215   "*J'aime ces type vicieux qu'ici montre la bite*": the ungram-
matical French in this phrase (which should have "ces types"
and "montrent" to make an agreement in number) had been
fully corrected in 1961 by the copyeditors of the Olympia
Press edition of *The Soft Machine*, who also changed "qu'ici"
to "qui se" (CU 2.3). However, Burroughs deliberately restored his version both for the 1967 edition of *The Ticket* (the

line does not appear in the 1962 text) and for the revised edition of *The Soft Machine*: for an explanation, see the note in the "Early Answer" section of the 2014 edition.

220 "Beauty held in mold": an early typescript names Gregory Corso in a variant of these lines: **"As Gregory says beauty kills beauty is the murderer—Because beauty held in the mold of image is stale as a old Mum ad—Or coca cola"** (Berg 39.26).

221 "services for the Insect Trust": apparently tipping his hat to *The Insect Trust Gazette*, Burroughs revised his typescript, which originally had **"Insect Queen"** (Berg 39.26), so that the phrase "Insect Trust" appeared in "Burning Heavens, Idiot" in Summer 1964. He also used the phrase in the then-unpublished "Word" section of *Naked Lunch* and it appears in his 1960 pamphlet *The Exterminator*.

221 "first run jackoffs::": this was the only instance of the double colon printed in the 1967 edition.

222 "We had our Castro period": **"when we all wore beards,"** adds an early typescript (Berg 39.26).

223 "We all put in five hundred thousand years getting the point": an early typescript continues: **"—It is now time to get beyond that point—Get out of thy ass and see the light—Let the light in brothers and sisters it will clean you out and purify you—It will wipe away expose all your negatives—You will then have no future in time—You will be in space brothers —And the insect mob swole up again like poison toads"** (Berg 39.26).

223 "So those mutinous troops": from here until "Portland Place" (page 226) appeared, with variants, in the three-column piece "Who Is the Third That Walks Beside You?" in *Art and Literature* 2 (Summer 1964), reprinted in *Word Virus*.

223 "a practical jingle passed": corrects *TEX* 197 ("jungle") as per an early typescript (Berg 48.3).

224   "slupped up all the queens": Burroughs' term "slupping" (or "schlupping") was coined for *Queer* in the context of cannibalistic sexual desire.

225   "Here comes the old knife sharpener": Burroughs describes the knife sharpener in his 1985 Introduction to *Queer*, where he evokes the day in Mexico City in September 1951 when he shot and killed his wife. The early typescript has more details; **"the old knife sharpener whistling in lemon sunlight from a travel poster his eyes cool blue like the blue sky of Spain reflected in a flashing knife blade"** (Berg 39.26).

226   "ashes — gutted cities": the lower case for "ashes" here, as for "late" in the following sentence, seems intended, although upper case was used for the version published as "Burning Heavens, Idiot" in *The Insect Trust Gazette*.

226   "Green Tony the last invisible shadow": corrects *TEX* 199 ("Greeen").

227   "story of absent world": on a three-page typescript that Burroughs mailed Brion Gysin on August 15, 1962, which is near verbatim the published text, this phrase appears as **"absent word"** (Berg 85.6).

227   "Johnny Yen: (His face shows strata": at this point the 1962 typesetting MS starts a new page with the canceled heading, **"THESE OUR ACTORS BID YOU A LONG GOOD NIGHT,"** indicating a separation of material within the final section. The same subheading appeared in the typescript mailed Gysin in August 1962 (Berg 85.6).

229   "What summer will I": from here to "my film ends" (page 230) was an insert for the 1967 edition.

229   "a speck of white": "a speck, a tiny white speck, that seemed to catch all the light left in a darkened world. . . . And, suddenly, I lost him. . . .'" (ellipses in the original). Burroughs echoes the closing words of Marlow's narrative in Conrad's *Lord Jim* (London: Penguin, 2000; 291). He also echoes

the novel's final lines, "he waves his hand sadly at his butterflies," earlier in this passage in the phrase, "He lifts his hands sadly" (352). The line recurs in "They Just Fade Away," a short text published in *Evergreen Review* 8.32 (April 1964) that Burroughs noted "is a fold-in from *Lord Jim*" (Lotringer, 69). "They Just Fade Away" includes a citation of the date "September 17, 1899," which also features at the end of *Nova Express* and in many other texts, suggesting that Burroughs recognized the coincidence that Conrad's novel ends: "September 1899–July 1900."

230   "'See the action, B.J.?'": from here to "Are you listening B.J.?'" was an insert for the 1967 edition. On the insert typescript, the first phrase is given differently as: **"Now how's this for an angle B.J.?"** (Berg 43.26). Speech marks have been added at the beginning of "See the action" and removed from the end of "Are you listening B.J.?" so that the initials B.J. end the print text, as the initials Bg end Gysin's calligraphy.